GRUNT LIFE

First published 2014 by Solaris
an imprint of Rebellion Publishing Ltd,
Riverside House, Osney Mead,
Oxford, OX2 0ES, UK

www.solarisbooks.com

ISBN: 978 1 78108 200 3

10 9 8 7 6 5 4 3 2 1

A CIP catalogue record for this book is available
from the British Library.

Designed & typeset by Rebellion Publishing

Printed in Denmark

WESTON OCHSE

GRUNT LIFE

A TASK FORCE OMBRA NOVEL

SOLARIS

"This isn't a war," said the artilleryman. "It never was a war, any more than there's war between man and ants."

H.G. Wells,
The War of the Worlds

PART ONE

PART ONE

People sleep peaceably in their beds at night only because rough men stand ready to do violence on their behalf.

George Orwell

CHAPTER ONE

IT WAS MY love of movies that made me choose the Vincent Thomas Bridge to kill myself. The bridge had gained a certain notoriety over the years. That it had been a shooting location for the films *Gone in Sixty Seconds, Lethal Weapon 2, To Live and Die in LA, Heat* and *The Island* was a bonus. But the chief reason I'd chosen to jump from it was because of my adoration of film director Tony Scott, and the fact that he'd jumped from this very same bridge back in 2012. The director of *Top Gun, The Last Boy Scout, True Romance* and the incomparable *Man on Fire* had parked his car beside where I now stood, climbed over the rail, and leaped. Some people said that Tony hadn't meant to kill himself, that a bad combination of drugs had affected his thinking, but I knew better. The truth was that sometimes life was just shit and there was nothing else to be done about it.

I fought against the fear of dying and concentrated on the lights of the harbor. A cruise ship was pulling in. Beyond it, giant cranes glowed with warning lights. To my right, the San Pedro hill was dotted with a thousand lights, each one a home, someone watching television, eating dinner, fucking, or simply staring off into space. To my left was the great plain of Long Beach, where another million souls did the same, unaware that a man who'd been awarded two silver and three bronze stars was about to take a swan dive, just to be rid of all the irrevocable memories of what he'd done, what he'd seen, and what he hadn't done as a soldier in far-flung countries.

Life was so far behind me, I don't know when I'd lost it. My current mission was death, and I'd come prepared. I wore black fatigues, boots and gloves. A black skull cap covered my head and I'd painted my face with black camouflage. I wasn't there to draw attention. I wasn't there to make a statement. I was there for one final selfish moment, to do something for myself, if only I had the courage of Tony Scott.

I remember laughing at the idea of suicide back before my life happened. I remember talking to my soldiers and scolding them, even ridiculing them, to dissuade them from committing such a final act. I knew it was the wrong thing to do. I knew a person should never give up. I absolutely understood that by killing myself I was dishonoring all of those who had laid their own lives on the line to preserve mine. I'd counseled these very same things on numerous occasions.

So then why couldn't I follow my own counsel?

I'd stepped over the rail and had backed into the shadow of a beam ten minutes ago. Cars sped past behind me, windows open to catch the sea air, leaving me with a random montage of music by which to die. Grasping the beam, I leaned forward and stared down at the stygian black water. I let my mind wander back to Iraq, to Afghanistan, to Mali, to Kosovo—a badly edited film filled with variations on deathly themes. The deaths of children lying like discarded dolls in the middle of an Iraqi street; at the bottom of a Serbian burial pit; atop a mountain near Tora Bora. The deaths of women, raped and left in a position so much like prayer. The deaths of men, body parts raining like confetti at an end of the world party. Death. Death. More fucking death.

Somewhere along the line I'd ceased to be a hero and had become a death merchant. The very term *hero* had become a laughable idea. "*Who do you think you are, a hero?*" my platoon sergeant had once asked. I'd wanted to respond that I did, that I was, but I knew that he'd already turned that corner where he no longer cared about the mission, but just wanted to survive. Heroism was so far beyond him he might as well have been back on his couch, getting fat and watching other people play sports. It was then that I'd realized that there would come a time when I'd be just like him. If I ever got to the point where I didn't know the difference between a hero or a zero and lost my grip on what's right and wrong, I promised myself that I'd end it.

So here I was.

Opened in 1963, the Vincent Thomas Bridge had a clearance of one hundred eighty-five feet, which was like jumping from an eighteen story building. It used to be lit by only a few random bulbs, but in 2005 that had been changed to a hundred and sixty solar powered LED lights. It looked like I was about to leap from the side of an alien spacecraft.

If only.

I tensed my body and prepared myself. I'd decided not to swan dive. That worked in the movies, but it was the sort of stupid gesture that would make me tumble and flail in my final moments. The last thing I wanted at the end was to be out of control. My design was to jump straight out and allow gravity to bring me to grace.

"This could be a beginning instead of an end, you know?"

The voice startled me so much that I almost slipped and fell right then. I saw a figure climbing over the rail. Dressed in a black suit with a white shirt and a black tie, he had a drawn, pallid complexion. Like that actor from *Reservoir Dogs*; what was his name?

"Get out of here," I snarled.

"It's a free country," he said.

Was he being serious? "What the fuck are you doing here?"

"Trying to see if we can convince you to stick around for a while." The man seemed at ease and spoke with the authority of an officer. Closer now, I saw the pockmarks on his thin face. That was it: I was thinking of Steve Buscemi.

"Do I know you?" I asked.

"No, but we know you. Benjamin Carter Mason, assigned to 173rd Airborne Brigade Combat Team in Logar Province, Eastern Afghanistan and on leave in Los Angeles, until your untimely death in a house fire."

Wait a minute. Was I already dead? Was this the synaptic backwards flip of a brain that had already become lifeless?

"I assure you that you're not crazy." Mr. Pink grinned and held up a finger. "At least not to the degree to which you think."

"I didn't die in a fire," I said with as much authority I could muster under the circumstances.

"*Au contraire*," Mr. Pink said, pointing towards San Pedro. A point of light expanded, becoming a raging orange blob. "Seems there was a gas leak. They'll find a body inside matching your general height and weight. During the autopsy when they check your DNA and fingerprints, they'll find that they match the deceased. They were lucky the fire didn't spread to the rest of the apartment complex. Your next door neighbor, Ms. O'Brien, is passed out in her chair, sleeping through a rerun of *Survivor*."

After a few moments of staring at the fire, I managed to stammer, "Why are you doing this?"

"It seemed to us you were determined to end your life. We hastened to help so that you can start a new one."

"Who are you?"

"No one you've ever heard of."

I couldn't help but laugh. I'd seen some version of this in several bad made-for-cable movies. Then again, I'd also seen movies about how insane people believe in conspiracy theories or that everyone is out to get them. A line of dialogue from a Woody Allen film came to mind. '*There's a word for someone who believes that everyone is conspiring against them—perceptive.*' I also remembered my favorite radio talk show host, The Night Stalker. '*Conspiracies are what smart people call the truth, and what stupid people call too complicated to be real.*'

Conspiracy or no conspiracy, whether they substituted my body or not, whether they wanted me to work for them or not, didn't change the fact that there were people, places and events I could never remove from my mind... things I'd done and hadn't done, which could only be obliterated by an eternity of nothing.

"You shouldn't have gone to all the trouble," I finally said.

Then I jumped.

I was in free fall for three glorious seconds before I hit the net. I bounced once, twice, three times, then got my legs entangled. By the time they lowered me to the ship below, I was calling their mothers things that would shock even a jail house whore.

SETI was the search for extraterrestrial intelligent life. It was our outreach program to the stars. In 1995 it lost federal government funding. Was that because we couldn't afford it? Did we decide we didn't need a welcome wagon for future alien friends? Or did we no longer need it for a specific reason? Had we already made contact? There are those who would laugh at us and call us conspiracy nut jobs. There are those who would lump us with people who speak in tongues, believe in Bigfoot, and worship the Abominable Snowman. Not that anything is wrong with these things, but they are indicative of a willingness to believe in something that is largely not provable. But let me ask you this, my night time listeners, how come a private company took over the program almost immediately, pumping more money into it than the federal government ever did? Why is a private corporation pouring billions of dollars into a program the U.S. government shut down because they believed it was a ridiculous idea? Come on, America. Answer the question, if you dare. What do you believe?

Conspiracy Theory Talk Radio,
Night Stalker Monologue #899

I offer neither pay, nor quarters, nor food; I offer only hunger, thirst, forced marches, battles and death. Let him who loves his country with his heart, and not merely his lips, follow me.

Giuseppe Garibaldi

CHAPTER TWO

THEY DROVE ME to LAX in the back of a white van with blacked-out windows. Mr. Pink, who called himself my 'recruiter,' sat beside me in the first row of bench seats. The two rows behind me were empty.

After the boat, they'd taken me to a room near the San Pedro Detention Facility—a place where those trying to illegally immigrate were usually taken until Customs and Border Patrol could come and get them. When they'd first pulled me from the net, I was as mad as a cat in a tub full of water. I must have hit and kicked five or six of them before they managed to subdue me by tossing a bucket of water on me. The shockingly cold water of the bay stiffened me, and they pulled me roughly but calmly to the deck. I managed to elbow one full in the chin, rocking his head back. For a second, he looked as if he was going to haul back and dust me. By his size, in retrospect, it wouldn't have taken much. He had arms the size of water pipes and a nose that looked like he'd modeled as the 'before' picture for a Beverly Hills plastic surgeon. Another man with his head shaven on the sides, leaving only a short bit of fuzz on top—what we called a high-and-tight—held my right leg and gave him a look that stopped him in his place. Evidently I wasn't to be touched, which pissed me off all over again. I tried to kick at high-and-tight, but he held on, his smile straight-lining as he gripped tighter, isolating my knee so it wouldn't bend.

The boat docked shortly afterward and they carried me into a lighted complex surrounded by razor wire and patrolled by guards. In the receiving area, they placed ankle chains around my legs and cuffs on my hands. Then they attached a chain from the cuffs to the bonds around my ankles, which made me hunch over a little. Finally, they tossed me into a room with only a mattress and a metal chair. The chair was bolted to the floor in the middle of the room. The mattress, on the other hand, could be moved around. If there'd been a window, I might have done so, shifting the filthy striped thing so I could get a better view of the bay. But since they'd chosen to house me in their special Prisoner of Zenda suite, I threw myself down and huddled as best I could in my wet clothes, occasionally shuddering and thinking about how I'd almost made it, how my nightmares had almost been banished forever.

I'm not sure how long I slept, but when they next came for me, I felt the acrid taste of dust in my mouth and my clothes had almost dried. My shoulders ached and my wrists were chafed from the cuffs. The same two men who'd subdued me came in and lifted me up. They were gentler than they had been before. Which was good—I didn't feel like putting up much of a fight. I was tired and hungry, and had to pee.

They removed my bonds, escorted me to the bathroom and closed the door. It was a regular institutional bathroom with several urinals and stalls, much like you find in elementary schools, prisons, and libraries. On the counter next to one of the sinks was a pile of clothes. I relieved myself, then picked through them. They were all my size. I ditched my clothes and slid into these. Soon I was standing in front of a mirror wearing jeans, a fashion-faded Captain America T-shirt, a light jacket, and Converse athletic shoes. I ran my hand through my light brown hair. It was still too short to comb, but the sidewalls from my own high-and-tight were starting to grow back. I'd have to get them shaved.

My hand stopped in mid-stroke. I was thinking about the future. I couldn't remember the last time I'd done that. Everything had been on the here-and-now since I'd decided to kill myself, months ago. Yet here I was, thinking about a haircut, as if that was so damned important.

Someone banged on the door, making me jump.

"Okay, already," I called.

I took a moment longer to wash my face, removing the last vestiges of the camouflage I'd put on the night before.

I looked at the pile of clothes I'd left on the ground. What to do with them? I'd already transferred my wallet and my St. George medallion. Mr. Pink had something in mind for me and I doubted my old clothes would be necessary, so I left them on the floor of the bathroom.

I was curious about Mr. Pink's claim that a Fortune 500 Company wanted a used-up sergeant with too many deployments. When I exited the bathroom, Mr. Pink was waiting for me. He wore a black suit with a white shirt, just as I'd remembered from last night. All that was missing were the sunglasses. I wondered if he knew I called him Mr. Pink. And I wondered if it would piss him off.

Despite myself, I smiled when I saw him.

"Hungry?" he asked.

I nodded. "Famished."

"This way."

I followed him down an institutional hall lit with fluorescent lighting. His two men fell in behind.

"Get a good night's sleep?" Mr. Pink asked.

"If you can call it that. Not exactly the best accommodation."

Mr. Pink stopped, as did his men. He turned to me. "Sorry about the cuffs. We were worried you might hurt yourself."

"Is that what it was?"

He turned and resumed walking, and we followed. "Early in the process, we had some accidents. So if there was any treatment that appeared to be rough, realize I did that for your own good."

For my own good. How many times had I heard that one before?

"Nevertheless," he continued, "we have provided some sustenance for you. We weren't sure what you wanted, and it is going on noon, so I decided to give you some choices for lunch."

As he finished, we entered what looked like an executive dining room. There were three tables, two of which were covered with food—plates of steak, fried chicken, French fries, cheeseburgers, and several salads. Several cardboard containers of Chinese food were open and steaming, as were several pizzas. One half of a table contained various pasta dishes. Another half had fruit, yogurt and healthy alternatives. But what made me laugh were the immense martini glasses filled with shrimp and the three-pound Maine lobster resting as a centerpiece on a plate in the center of the nearest table.

"I take it you have enough to choose from," he said.

My mouth was already watering. I wanted it all, but if I even tried to taste everything, I'd make myself sick. But it was hard not to imagine myself hunched over and filling my face. We used to talk for hours about food in Afghanistan. Beside movies, sex and cars, it was our favorite topic of conversation. And here, in front of me, was everything me and my friends had ever wanted and then some.

"So what'll it be?" he asked.

I stepped forward and grabbed an empty plate. I could treat this as a buffet and have a little of all worlds, but somehow I felt

I needed to be more specific. If this was my last meal, what would it be? Looking at the table, I realized it was no choice at all.

I grabbed a half-pounder cheeseburger and I added mayo, lettuce, onions, bacon, and ketchup. I filled the other half of the plate with fries, adding a nice pool of ketchup to dip into. Then I took my plate to an empty table and sat down.

"Want something to drink? Beer? Wine?"

I did want a beer. But this wasn't about wanting. This was about remembering. So I said, "Milkshake, please," wondering if I might have just asked for the one thing they didn't have.

"Vanilla or chocolate?"

"Vanilla."

I placed a napkin in my lap and watched as one of the men went to a cooler and pulled out a vanilla shake. When he brought it over, I sipped it, a cold velvet dream of winter. Then I ate, and as I did, I thought about Trujillo, who lived in Gilroy, California and who always talked about cheeseburgers, fries and shakes at the local drive-in. I thought about how he'd smiled wistfully when he'd talked about the way he'd bite into the burger and the juices would mix with the ketchup. I thought of the detail he'd go into when he talked about his favorite food. And I thought about the roadside bomb that ate him from the inside out the week after I left Iraq.

WE PULLED TO the curb at LAX's Terminal Three, and the two thugs stayed with the vehicle while Mr. Pink escorted me inside. We bypassed all the counters and went straight to security. Instead of getting checked like all the other customers, Mr. Pink knocked on a windowless door beside the security setup. When it opened, he flashed a badge. The heavyset black woman took one look at it, backed up, and decided she didn't want any part of it. She motioned us through, then locked the door behind us. We walked down a warren of halls, passing ground crew, TSA agents coming back from break, and stewardesses, eventually coming out by a gate that was already boarding. The sign read Flight 1445 to Cheyenne. Looks like I was going to Wyoming.

As he slid me into an aisle seat in first class, he said, "You'll be met at the other end. Enjoy the flight."

I thought about saying something to him. *Thank you* didn't seem appropriate, but I felt I had to say something. The problem was I wasn't sufficiently in charge of my thoughts to even begin to know what. He made it simple, though, and left before I had to try.

They closed the door to the aircraft and a flight attendant handed me a fluted glass.

"Don't want to leave you out, soldier," she said with a twinkle and a smile. I could get used to looking at her.

I took a sip and realized there was alcohol in the drink. I took another sip and stared at it.

"It's called a Mimosa," said the woman sitting next to me.

I glanced at her. She looked to be about fifty, wore a flowered suit and pants, and had more diamonds on her hands than a store in the mall.

"Mimosa, huh?"

She nodded.

I leaned back and took another sip. I liked that word—*mimosa*.

The flight attendant took my glass when I was finished and the plane prepared for takeoff. I leaned back in the seat and closed my eyes, thinking about Mr. Pink and what he'd said to make me decide to give his Task Force OMBRA a chance.

"GIVE ME YOUR best pitch," I said, finishing the lunch, the taste of meat and cheese dissolving with the memory of the roadside bombs exploding.

Mr. Pink smiled like an uncle who had something he wanted to tell you about the family. He'd been standing patiently throughout the meal, but now he pulled out a chair and sat on it cowboy style. He placed his elbows on the table, but didn't turn towards me. "If you want to kill yourself, why don't you let us do it for you?"

I confess I'd expected a little more effort.

"That's your pitch? That's the best you can do?"

Mr. Pink shrugged, minutely. "I didn't think I had to say any more than that. You want to kill yourself. If you come work for us, you'll probably die, but at least you'll die for something other than your own sense of guilt."

I felt the blood begin to boil beneath my skin.

"At least your death will mean something."

My hands clenched until my knuckles burned white.

"At least you'll be able to ameliorate your own broken pride."

A thousand epithets begged to be spoken, but I didn't trust my mouth to work around the ball of anger lodged in it. I barely managed to ask, "What the hell are you talking about?"

"You know."

I closed my eyes and flexed as every muscle in my body came alive, screaming to be set free, well aware that the goons in the room could see me and would most likely try and stop me. I almost didn't care; my anger needed a release. I said as evenly as I could, "There's nothing I could have done that I didn't try to do to save those who died."

"Except die with them," Mr. Pink said simply. Then he stood and straightened the front of his suit coat. He began walking away. "I'll be outside when you're ready," he said over his shoulder. "Please note, Mr. Mason, that we have a flight in two hours."

I stared at his departing back, twin death rays scorching him. If only. What did he know, anyway? I'd been to the requisite counseling sessions. I'd learned about survivor's guilt. I'd spoken with chaplains and social consultants and my chain of command. I'd checked all the boxes and was deemed no danger to myself or others. Was it such a bad thing if I'd reconsidered and decided to just fucking end it all?

What's so wrong about a little bit of suicide as long as I keep it to myself?

What's so bad about me dying with a little peace and privacy in the dark of a Los Angeles night?

But Mr. Pink had known what he was doing. He'd struck a chord, which once heard, I wanted to hear again. I wanted to know more.

"Get him back," I said to one of the men.

When Mr. Pink eventually returned, he sat and we talked and he told me about OMBRA Enterprises LLC. When I asked what they wanted me to do, he told me *help save the world*. When I asked him from what, he said that it was on a need-to-know basis. Now I was back in recognizable territory. After all, I was just a grunt. They'd tell me what I needed to know when I needed to know it. In the meantime, I was in it for as long as it held my interest.

Which was good enough for Mr. Pink.

"I'm not insane, sir. I have a finely calibrated sense
of acceptable risk."

John Scalzi, *Old Man's War*

CHAPTER THREE

CHEYENNE AIRPORT WASN'T exactly in the middle of nowhere, but
it was in the same zip code. Flat land surrounded us on three
sides. The Rockies rose into the clouds to the West. I could see
where the city of Cheyenne started, but not where it ended. The
city was so flat that there wasn't enough terrain to see it all.

A cowboy wearing a denim shirt, pants, and weathered silver-
tipped boots met me at baggage claim, with a cardboard sign
that read simply *TF OMBRA*, in an uneven scrawl. His face
wore the seasons like an almanac. Somewhere between forty
and seventy, he had a stare that promised he'd seen it all, and
if he hadn't, what was left to be seen wasn't important enough
to matter.

I approached him. "That's me," I said, pointing to the sign.

"Waiting on one more," he said.

I raised my eyebrows. Another? On my flight? I turned around
and stood beside him, watching the passengers come down the
gangway. Eventually, a slim muscular girl stopped and looked
around. Her long hair hung in a waterfall of black. Her eyes
were almond-shaped. Her nose held the memory of Spanish
conquistadors. Her skin was the color of leaves just starting to
turn. And beneath her dark eyes were full lips that looked as if
they'd never smiled.

Her eyes finally rested on the sign. She came over, gave me a *who are you staring at* look, then stuck out her hand to the cowboy.

He took it.

"Michelle Aquinas," she said. As she shook his hand, her shirt sleeve pulled back, revealing white gauze wrapping her wrist. I glanced at the other wrist, but she saw me and shoved her hand in the back pocket of her jeans.

"Follow me," the man said. He folded up the sign and slid it into the back of his pants. He walked straight as a fencepost. We followed him out the door into the dry, hot air of the plains.

He took us to an old pickup truck parked at the curb in clear violation of the law. A police officer glanced at us, but gave us no further attention. The cowboy got in and motioned us to do likewise. There was only the long bench seat. Aquinas and I appraised it.

I saw immediate relief on her face when I said, "I'll get in back."

The cowboy shook his head. "We're going on the highway. Don't want to get pulled over."

I looked at her to let her decide. She frowned, but then shrugged and got in the middle. I climbed in beside her. As I did, I brushed against her and she flinched. Jesus. We were already packed in so tight. How could I keep from making her uncomfortable? I strapped on the old-fashioned lap belt, and scooted all the way to the door, allowing her about four inches of space. I caught her looking at it. When she looked up at me, I smiled. She turned away. Yep. This was going to be a long ride.

"Where we going?" I asked.

"Middle of the state," said the Cowboy.

I wasn't up-to-date on my U. S. geography, but I thought I remembered that Cheyenne was in the southeastern corner.

I attempted to get him talking. "Pretty far, isn't it?"

It took a moment as he stared out the window to consider the philosophical implications of my question. Finally he said, "It's a piece." Then he put the truck in gear and headed out. Within minutes, we were cruising north on I-25. If I'd expected a briefing about who he was, where we were going, and when we'd get there, I was disappointed; we found ourselves listening to farm futures reports on the AM dial. I never knew you could say so much about corn.

Two and a half hours later we reached Casper. By then I knew all about the price of beef on the hoof and barley futures. I'd tried to open a conversation with Michelle, but she feigned sleep both times. So I passed the trip in silence, watching antelope and prairie dogs scamper about the plains, wondering what they'd think about a few roadside explosions in their neighborhood as images of similar drives in Iraq and Afghanistan superimposed themselves on reality.

We drove through Casper and up a dirt road, then eventually stopped in a field about three miles west of the city.

"Get out," the cowboy said, looking straight ahead.

"Here?" I asked, looking around.

He nodded. "They'll be along shortly."

I glanced at Michelle. The doubt in her eyes mirrored my own, but she nodded in grudging acceptance of the order. She was right. No use arguing with the old man.

We got out and the truck sped away.

We stood there for a few minutes, observing the terrain.

"Looks a lot like Afghanistan," I finally said.

She looked at me sharply.

"Have you been?"

She nodded.

"Two tours. One in Helmand and one in Logar," I offered. "You?"

"Nangarhar," she said, looking away.

I stared at her. Nangarhar was in the middle of the shit. It was right in the teeth of the fighters pouring across the border during the fighting season. I'd seen more than my share in Helmand and Logar, but Nangarhar was the place we threatened to send people if they began acting up.

I was about to ask her more when we heard the sound of a helicopter. It came in low over the hill to our west, a Black Hawk. It sat down fifty yards away, whipping up dirt and sand. We shielded our faces with our arms and joined the beckoning soldier in the helicopter.

We lifted off and turned west.

Above the sounds of the helicopter I heard the crewman who'd let us in say into his microphone, "Two more for TF OMBRA."

We spent the rest of the ride listening to the rumble of the engine.

It is human nature to start taking things for granted
again when danger isn't banging loudly on the door.
Col David Hackworth

CHAPTER FOUR

I AM FIVE years old and King of the Universe, or at least Count of
the Cul-de-sac. I race my red, yellow and blue Big Wheel machine
around and around in circles, the sound of the road against my
plastic wheels a white static I leave in my wake to confuse the
zombies. Ever since I saw *Army of Darkness* when my babysitter
let me stay up instead of making me go to bed, I've had them
following me when I'm on my Big Wheel. And I'm fast. They
can't catch me. They can't even come close to me, trailing me
like the tin cans we tied on my cousin Ronnie's car when he got
married to that ugly girl, Susan.

Ernie and Ben come out with their bikes, all shiny and new.
Ben still has trainers on his, but Ernie has barely a wobble as he
pedals hard. He looks good and part of me wishes I could have
the same thing, but I know my parents can't 'ford it, so I love my
Big Wheel even more.

They wave.

I wave.

Then an explosion makes Ben evaporate, pieces of him and
his bike and his trainers firing off in all directions at a billion
miles an hour, becoming part of the land and sky. It rains Ben
parts, the sound like M&Ms hitting the pavement. I raise
my head and open my mouth and Ben tastes like raisins and

bacon. I kind of knew he would taste like that. Everyone tastes like bacon eventually.

My mom comes out and high fives the zombies as they rush by. She carries a basket, and begins to pick up Ben's M&M body pieces. I know she's going to stuff it into the chicken. I love it when she does that.

Suddenly, Ernie races up to my mom. He turns to wave at me, then they both explode. But instead of pieces, I'm showered with blood. Cold and wet and hot at the same time, it covers me and the Big Wheel completely. I have a vision of Carrie, covered in blood onstage before she kills everyone, except I have no special power except to pedal, but I can't pedal fast enough with the slickness of the blood making my feet slip and slide. The zombies catch up and grab me, and throw me down on the ground in a pool of my mother's and Ernie's blood, and they begin to eat me.

They begin to eat me.

I JERKED AWAKE as we began to descend, my hands scrabbling frantically at my sides. I'd twisted my shirt into knots. I glanced over at Michelle, who was watching me from the other side of the helicopter, cool and collected, as if she were an expert at extracting herself from her own nightmares and mine was nothing special. I let my gaze drift to her wrists and she crossed her arms and stared outside the window. We were coming up on a single story building in a wide parking lot with a smaller building next to it.

If I'd thought Cheyenne was the middle of nowhere, I was terribly mistaken. Cheyenne was definitely a *somewhere* compared to this place. No roads led to it. No cars were parked in the spaces. Surrounding it, for as far as the eye could see in any direction, there was no sign of humans or human habitation, just lonely plains, antelope, and the occasional curious prairie dog.

"Jesus," I said.

We landed with a jolt. The crew chief slid the door open and gestured us out. Michelle slid to the ground first. She grabbed her bag and started walking, then looked back for me. I grinned. Not exactly love at first sight, but at least she'd thought of me. A voice inside me explained it was probably because she was scared shitless and wanted me to be there in case she needed to kick me in the shin and run, leaving me victim to whatever monsters were going to run out of the small building. Still, when I stepped onto the tarmac with my own bag, I was smiling.

She turned and shook her head.

The door slammed behind us and the helicopter began to rise.

We watched it leave, shielding our eyes with our hands. When it was about three hundred feet up, it turned a one-eighty and roared back the way we'd come, as if there was much to do in Casper and they didn't want to miss it. More likely that they just didn't want to hang around this place any longer.

We looked at each other, then at the building.

"I don't think zombies are going to come out of there and get us," I said. "If that's what you're worrying about."

She grinned for the first time. It brightened her Filipina features, transforming her face into someone who didn't slash her wrists and end up signing up for TF OMBRA, which was quickly becoming the clearing house for the poor, downtrodden, and those unable to kill themselves. I reminded myself I was one of them.

"Shall we?" I lifted my chin towards the building.

As she began to walk, I fell in beside her, careful of her space.

As we approached, there was a simple sign on the door that read *ENTER* in computer block type. I lifted the lever and the door opened outwards. We went into a spartan room covered in fake wood paneling. A single desk sat directly in front of us. An Air Force airman sat behind it, a laptop in front of him.

"Wallets and IDs, please." He held out a tray.

"Excuse me?" I said. "You want my wallet?"

"TF OMBRA will be caring for your needs from now on."

I shook my head. "I might want to buy a gift or something. Maybe for my mother."

"Your mother is dead. As is your father. Wallets and IDs," he said, giving the basket a jiggle.

I didn't like him. His chin was too small, his eyes were too narrow. And where did he get off talking about my dead parents like that? Still, I jerked out my ID, handed it to him, then tossed my wallet in the basket. For a moment, I lamented the loss of the condom, the picture of a Scottish girl named Wren I fucked six ways to Sunday during R&R in Dubai, and a photo of my family when I was thirteen and we were at the lake. Then I wiped them from my mind. If I was willing to forget about them when I jumped off a bridge, it should be easy now.

Michelle followed suit, not seeming to care one way or the other.

"Against the wall, please," he said, pointing to our left.

I watched as he upended the basket into a large box behind him, already filled with wallets and purses, then I joined Michelle on the wall.

"What now?" I asked.

The airman grinned and pressed a remote.

The wall opened behind us, and we turned and saw an elevator. I entered. Michelle did too. We stood facing the airman, who seemed to be enjoying our discomfort. Probably the only excitement he got except for pulling at his own pud.

He pressed the remote one more time.

The doors closed in front of us.

There were no buttons, but I could feel us descending. I glanced at Michelle, who had her eyes closed. I did the same. A short time later we stopped.

As I opened my eyes, the doors parted, revealing a painted red concrete floor, shined to a glossy finish. In front of us was a lean black man in black fatigues. On his head was a red beret, with a red flash with the black letters OMBRA stitched to the inside of a triangle.

"Aquinas and Mason, I presume."

We nodded and stepped off the elevator. I felt humidity. The air smelled of old socks and food.

"I'm Proctor Todd. You're the last of them. We only have a few minutes until lights out, and the initiation of Phase I. We held the kitchen open for you."

"You do know that it's only late afternoon and that it's light outside, right?" I asked, trying not to sound too smart-assed.

Proctor Todd smiled patiently. "We are no longer concerned with the rise and fall of the sun. It has nothing to do with our cycles here in the Complex. What happens up there is for the people up there."

"Okay," I said, sorry I'd mentioned it.

Proctor Todd turned and began to walk down a hall to our right, and we fell in behind him.

Twice we came to intersections, and twice we continued through. A pair of blast doors slid open and, beyond, the hallway opened into an immense room, easily the size of a football field. We were immediately assaulted by the roar of conversation from hundreds of people. But when we entered, most of the talking ceased. Men and women sat or stood at tables, on chairs, in corners, in knots or alone. All shapes, sizes and ethnicities, I could feel their gaze like an itch against my skin. Most wore street clothes, although some had on pink or blue surgical scrubs, worn by both men and women without reference to gender. I caught several of their gazes and offered a friendly nod. Some smiled back; others merely stared. All of them, at least all the ones I saw, had the same stare as everyone in my platoon, whether it be Iraq or Afghanistan, and in those gazes I could see the far horizon where death and life didn't matter.

The ceiling was at least fifty feet above and was a glistening white. Doorways gaped every few feet around the edges of the immense room. I could barely see into the narrow rooms presented by those near me.

Proctor Todd escorted us to a table where several men were making way for our arrival. A remote controlled cart approached. With rubber tracks instead of wheels, it was almost completely silent. Its sides held a myriad of openings, and it was topped with runner strips to keep things from sliding.

"We have ten of these machines, and they're all named Rodney," Proctor Todd said. "They'll take care of you for the next phase of your indoctrination. Rodney, meet the new folks."

A panel slid back on its side and a tray came out. Hot tomato soup, two grilled cheese sandwiches and a carton of milk. A plastic spoon and a paper napkin also sat on the tray. I took what was offered and placed it on the table.

"Better eat," Proctor Todd said. "It's almost time."

I took a taste of the soup. It was great. I hadn't realized I was so hungry. I took a bite of a grilled cheese and chased it with more soup. Soon Michelle was sitting at the table too, albeit with a large space between us. I resumed eating, but watched out of the corner of my eye as a Hispanic man with knife-sharp features and a scar beneath his left eye sauntered up to Michelle and sat down. He folded his hands on the table. A tattoo of a diamond with a dot in the middle stood out on the soft part of his left hand, between his thumb and forefinger. He grinned at me, then turned his attention on Michelle.

"Hey, *flaca*." He touched her with his tattooed hand. It was a mistake. He screamed as Michelle tossed her soup on him.

"Don't fucking touch me!" She stood, her fists balled.

I leaped to my feet.

"You bitch!" He held his shirt away from his body and glared at her. He made a disgusted sound and, for a moment, it looked like he was going to lunge at her.

I stepped between them.

"You want her, you've got to go through me, *cabron*."

"Olivares, get to your quarters," Proctor Todd said from a few feet behind me.

The lights began to flash slowly. A voice echoed down from the ceiling. "*Commencing lockdown for Phase I. Everyone to your quarters, please.*"

Olivares pointed at me. "This isn't over, *puto!*"

"Oh, I think it is," I said, grinning out of sheer bravado. "I really think it is." I didn't really care if I won or lost. I just wanted to fight someone.

"Yeah." He nodded. "We'll see. We'll just fucking see."

I saw my opportunity to fight getting away. I surged forward, but Proctor Todd caught me in a head lock. I swung at the air for a moment, then stopped moving.

Olivares sneered, then turned on his heel, holding up a middle finger by way of goodbye. Classy.

"Okay. Okay," I said, and Proctor Todd let me go. I watched the departing back of my brand new enemy and congratulated myself. It usually took me at least a day in a new place to establish lifelong enemies. I think I'd broken the record.

Only the dead have seen the end of war.

Plato

CHAPTER FIVE

TEN MINUTES LATER we were all inside our own little rooms. Evidently, Proctor Todd had been waiting for us. Now that we were here, they could begin. On the command of *stand back*, bars slammed into place from the ceiling and the floor. Each bar was as thick as the grip of a baseball bat and more solid than the stone beneath us. We weren't going anywhere soon. In fact, it looked like we were locked up like uncommon criminals.

I could see the cells across the room from me, but not those to my left or right. Still, I could hear grumblings at the locking of the cells. Evidently they hadn't been locked until now. I had to wonder what they had thought would happen. It seemed an obvious conclusion.

Five minutes later the big voice returned.

"*Please review your tablets. Follow the guidelines for your release schedule.*"

In a fabric pocket at the base of my single bed was a tablet computer. I touched the screen and it indicated, with the outline of a hand, that it wanted my palm print. I pressed my palm to it and the screen went blank for a moment, then switched to a command screen.

WELCOME PVT BENJAMIN CARTER MASON.
ARE YOU READY TO BEGIN?

Suddenly a voice erupted from my left. "Fuck this shit, *puta*!" I heard a crash and saw a tablet hit the floor and shatter.

Olivares—had to be. I shook my head. I wasn't so sure he didn't have the right idea. Still, I was willing to try.

Movement caught my eye and I saw a Rodney heading towards Olivares's cell. I watched as the side of the robot opened up and a new tablet was proffered on an extender arm. Olivares took it. No sooner had Rodney turned away than the tablet was arching through the air, crashing and shattering, skidding to a stop near the first one.

The robot seemed to assess the situation for a moment, then disappeared into a niche in the wall where he had entered the room.

I resumed looking at my tablet.

I didn't know how long the others had been here, but I had to figure for some of them it had been quite a long time.

WELCOME PVT BENJAMIN CARTER MASON.
ARE YOU READY TO BEGIN?

So I was a private, now, huh? I'd been a staff sergeant when I left Afghanistan two weeks ago. Quite a demotion. Still, I was no longer in the U.S. Army. I was now in TF OMBRA and I guess I had to prove myself. For a moment I wondered if the Army would put me down as AWOL. After thirty days, they'd convert that to Desertion, which was a serious and jailable offense during war.

Then I pictured Mr. Pink's curious mug addressing my commander and I felt better. Somehow, someway, I imagined that it would be handled.

I pressed the screen, but nothing happened. I spoke to the tablet. "Yes. Begin. Start. Go. Commence. Fuck." Still with no response.

I checked the sleeve I'd found the tablet in and pulled free a thin Bluetooth earpiece. I found the power switch and placed it in my ear. A circle appeared in the top right corner of the tablet. When it stopped pulsing, I figured it was ready.

"I am ready," I said.

The screen switched to the logo of TF OMBRA—a triangle like I'd seen on Proctor Todd's beret, but with the addition of the letters TF at the base of the triangle. The voice began to speak.

"Welcome to Task Force OMBRA. You have been chosen to be a member of a special brigade tasked with saving your planet. We call the threat to Earth the Cray. During the next several weeks you will learn about this creature and our interactions with it. We will also assess you for positions within the brigade we will be forming during Phase II. You will be expected to work, read and listen during these weeks and to conform to the schedule provided by your tablet.

"While we understand that many of you have been through more than your fair share of combat, we ask you to give just a little more. Each and every one of you has been diagnosed with Post Traumatic Stress Syndrome. Many of you were eager to commit suicide. Still more of you had mentally checked out, reliving what had gone on before, until reality had no meaning. We offer you a new choice. We offer you new memories, a reality that has meaning, and for those of you still eager to kill yourself, a chance to do it for the greater good of humankind.

"But that's the worst-case scenario. We at Task Force OMBRA are working every day to learn more about the Cray, what they want with Earth, and how we can best defeat them. While the nations of our planet will fight them, you will be the world's special brigade. Task Force OMBRA. Saviors of Earth."

The voice faded and the words *WOULD YOU LIKE TO REPLAY OR CONTINUE?* flashed on the screen.

I stared at the screen for a moment. It was right out of a science fiction novel. We were being attacked and a rag tag group of men and women were Earth's only hope. Only this wasn't a novel, this was reality; and I was starring as a Star Trek redshirt at the end of humanity's existence.

I became aware of cursing and yelling from the neighbouring cells. I listened for a moment, then tried my best to tune them out. While there were dozens of voices of protest, most of us—me included—were too curious about why we'd been brought here and how we were supposed to help Earth.

I contemplated how we were to be trained to use the top secret advanced weaponry necessary to help us defeat the aliens, then I paused. What led me to believe that an alien species might have military superiority just because it had interstellar travel? In *Starship Troopers*, the aliens were crude creatures who could hurl organic bombs from deep space. The romance of *Star Wars* had pre-loaded the idea that most space enemies would be humanoid in nature. For all I knew, the Cray were the shapes of dandelion cotton balls and could disintegrate anything they came in contact with.

I looked at the bars separating me from the great room on the other side and shuddered. Jesus on a pogo stick. That was about the scariest fucking thing I'd ever thought of in my life—a scene of children playing in a field only to be blown apart when the wind picked up.

I shook the image from my head and returned to the tablet. I'd been sitting on the edge of the bed. Now, I arranged the pillow and leaned against the wall, balancing the tablet on my knees. I was once again faced with the screen which read *WOULD YOU LIKE TO REPLAY OR CONTINUE?*

"Continue."

It switched to a list of links. At the top of the page, it read *WHAT WE THOUGHT WE KNEW* with a subheading which read *PRE-CRAY HYPOTHESES*. Under these were several links. I tried them. Each had pages and pages of information, but I stayed only long enough to get the gist of each one. I'd never been terrific at science. My majors in high school had been football and track, so I soon found my head hurting with the presentation of advanced equations and ideas.

There were the *ZOO HYPOTHESES* which posed the idea that an interstellar species would wait until a planet had discovered space travel for first contact.

Also present was the *FERMI PARADOX*, which basically argued that if a space-faring species had the superior technology to cross great distances, Earth would have already been colonized.

I read with interest the *PALEOCONTACT HYPOTHESIS*, also known as the *ANCIENT ASTRONAUT HYPOTHESIS*, which purported that Earth had been visited by intelligent beings in the past, pointing at ancient religious reliefs and such wonders as the Nazca Plains as evidence of earlier visitations.

The *DRAKE EQUATION* baffled me as it put forth a mathematical concept to show when and how Earth would be visited. But even I understood that with so many unknown variables, it was an equation which could only be used in hindsight to prove itself.

Then there was the *NEANDERTHAL POSTULATE*, which identified the idea that once an intelligent species reaches a certain point, it destroys those who might compete for the same resources. I wondered if this was what the Cray were doing. Perhaps they saw us as a threat to their existence and had decided to remove us prior to us attaining a similar level of technology.

I skipped over several others and ended up on *HOSTILE TERRAFORMING*, which presented the idea that our planet could be rendered uninhabitable for us, and inhabitable for the invading species. Several quotes from *War of the Worlds* were present, including one I remembered from my middle school reading: "*No one would have believed in the last years of the nineteenth century that this world was being watched keenly and closely by intelligences greater than man's and yet as mortal as his own; that as men busied themselves about their various concerns they were scrutinized and studied, perhaps almost as narrowly as a man with a microscope might scrutinize the transient creatures that swarm and multiply in a drop of water.*"

There were arguments noting that the Earth was becoming hotter, more arid, and that the ice caps were melting, and extrapolating that we were already being terraformed. The conspiracy theories continued. I tried to pay attention to them, but my gaze kept returning to the Wells quote. The idea that we were being watched by some intergalactic Peeping Tom was terrifying.

> We find that the Romans owed the conquest of the
> world to no other cause than continual military
> training, exact observance of discipline in their
> camps, and unwearied cultivation of the other arts
> of war.
>
> Publius Flavius Vegetius Renatus

CHAPTER SIX

I WOKE UP the next morning—or at least it felt like morning, even though I had no possible way of knowing—and returned to my tablet. *COMPLETION OF YOUR PROGRAM OF INSTRUCTION WILL RESULT IN RELEASE FROM PHASE I TO PHASE II* were the words I read with excitement, until I saw what was expected of us. The sheer number of books and papers I was supposed to read seemed impossible. I counted ninety-six manuscripts, forty-seven movies, and seven biographies which we were expected to read well enough to provide *interactive input* to the tablet upon completion. It was a genius strategy. With no bars, it might take some of us forever to complete this list. Hell, let's face it, most of us wouldn't even try and finish, if we weren't locked inside the cells. By limiting our freedom, then offering it back to us if we completed, they were giving a huge incentive. Even the laziest of us would be inspired to get this done.

The biographies included Julius Caesar, Chesty Puller, David Hackworth, and several other soldiers.

Of the movies, I'd seen around half of them. They were the usual suspects: *Kelly's Heroes, A Bridge Too Far, Guns of Navarone,*

Hamburger Hill, They Were Expendable, We Were Soldiers, The Dirty Dozen, Where Eagles Dare, Saving Private Ryan, and *Platoon.* But there were also some foreign films I had never heard of, like *Ivan's Childhood, Kanał,* and *Gallipoli.* There were also some science fiction movies, such as *Starship Troopers,* the modern version of *War of the Worlds, Battleship, Battle: Los Angeles, Invasion of the Body Snatchers, The Puppet Masters, They Live,* and *Independence Day;* I'd seen all of them except *They Live* and *The Puppet Masters.* I wanted to look forward to watching them, but I had all those books to read as well. I had a choice. I could either let the tablet read them to me, or I could read them myself.

Although I wasn't the fastest reader in the universe, I wasn't bad. I'd preferred Mack Bolan and Casca books, growing up, and enjoyed immersing myself in anything with guns. Plus, there were some books which were passed around the military that I'd already read. These included *Armor, Starship Troopers, The Forever War, Old Man's War, Ender's Game, The Mote in God's Eye, Legion of the Damned, Hammers Slammers* and *Bolo.* But there were a lot I had never read, books by C. J. Cherryh, David Gerrold, Jerry Pournelle, and Robert Buettner, to name a few.

Still, when I saw the list, it didn't seem too bad. I'd read enough of them that I thought I could get a head start by answering questions about those I already knew. I must have read John Steakley's *Armor* a dozen times. When I'd been working mechanized infantry, it had been all the rage. I remembered it being filled with violent combat scenes, something me and the other guys loved. But I also remembered it having a certain sensibility, as the main character developed almost a reluctance to continue killing an enemy who wouldn't stop. Was this perhaps why they wanted us to read it? Because they were concerned for our humanity?

I selected *Armor* on the tablet, then skipped right to the test. The first question glowed on the screen: *DESCRIBE HOW YOU WOULD OVERCOME YOUR LOVE FOR A COMRADE*

MUCH LIKE FOREST DID FOR KENT IN ORDER TO SERVE THE GREATER GOOD?

I stared at the question for several minutes. Perhaps I'd exaggerated the number of times I'd read the book. I might have only read it once. In fact, I might not have finished it at all. The idea that I'd actually read it once, much less a dozen times, might have been overly-optimistic. For the life of me I couldn't remember any character named Kent. I know there was a pirate. And I knew there was a guy in a mech suit doing a lot of cool shit, but that's all I remembered.

I tried to select the next question, but I couldn't get to it without answering the first. I was going to have to read the book. Damn them.

I chose *The Forever War* instead. I was sure I'd read that at least twice, once in basic training, and once at a FOB in Iraq. I'd read that the author, Joe Haldeman, had been in Vietnam. There weren't too many books written by people who'd actually been in war. This was one of them, and I remembered staring into the night and wondering what was out there beyond our position, and if Mr. Haldeman had done the same when he was in Vietnam. Had he had the same thoughts? A menagerie of fast food sandwiches, television shows, songs I used to dance to with a certain girl, and the recent memories of the death of one of my platoon mates, all squished and smashed like a human-sized pizza, but with too much red sauce. Or had he been thinking about writing *The Forever War?* When a girl I'd been dating for several months between deployments once asked me what my favorite book was, this was the book that came to mind. Whether it was my favorite was up for debate, but it was as good a contender as any of the others. I told her that it perfectly described the inability of a soldier to ever return to civilian life. She looked at me in stunned silence for a moment, then turned and left. It took me a long time to realize that I'd just said that I'd never be able to be with her, never really give my heart and mind to her. I'd basically told her I was broken.

Which I was.

The same as I was now.

I reminded myself that the only reason I wasn't going bat-shit crazy right now was because of the mystery of it all. The newness of my predicament, the shared predicaments of all of us in the underground bunker, and the idea that even as broken as I was, I might be worth something, someday, if I ever had time to read all the books, watch all the movies, and pass all the tests.

I found myself looking around my tiny room. I didn't pretend that I didn't know why. I knew exactly why. I was looking for something I could use to take my life. Not that I was going to take it right this minute, but if I wanted to, and I knew I would, I wanted to be ready when the feeling arose.

I cursed. The problem with an institution creating cells for men and women who might try to commit suicide was that they generally knew all the things one could use to accomplish the job.

No sharp objects.

No access to electrical.

No way to tie something from the ceiling.

No way to slam your head against an outcropping.

The bed was an ergonomically curved frame, and the only part that extended was the mattress. A shelf along one wall was recessed. The shelf I pulled the tablet from was made of fabric. The mirror above the recessed sink was made out of stainless steel and was part of the wall. Even the toilet, which moved in and out of the room at the touch of a button, was made of a rubbery substance that made me not want to sit on it for any longer than was necessary.

Someone cried out, followed by a chorus of *shut up!*

Nothing like a bunch of soldiers with whom to commiserate.

No state has an inherent right to survive through conscript troops and in the long run no state ever has. Roman matrons used to say to their sons: 'Come back with your shield or on it.' Later on, this custom declined. So did Rome.

Robert Heinlein,
Time Enough For Love

CHAPTER SEVEN

SIX WEEKS PASSED as I worked through the list. Days were punctuated by three meals and a midnight snack, provided by our trusty remote servants. Sometimes I read right through the night, interested in the battles and relationships with the characters, other nights I paced back and forth, staggering sometimes, as I tried desperately to stay awake so I could complete the task sooner. Twice I took tests which I failed, meaning I had to go back and read those sections of the books I'd failed to understand the first time. I should have known better. Whenever I thought something wouldn't be on the test, it was, as if the test controllers had chosen the densest parts of the book to use to quiz me.

My strategy was to read all the books first and leave the movies for last. What at first had seemed daunting had become a succession of hills to take, military objectives. Once I conquered one, it was time to run down and conquer the next. My reading was getting faster too. Not that I'd learned how to scan, like PFC Paulsen back in Iraq, who seemed capable of reading a book a day, but I was no slacker.

We hadn't seen anything of the officials running the complex, except when they came to remove all the tables and chairs, and when they came to remove the bodies. Two of our members had been determined enough to find a way to kill themselves. I watched as their bodies were carried away. I was detached. Other than Michelle and the asshole Olivares, I didn't know anybody else. Unlike in a military unit, we didn't share anything except our nightmares of war and the agreement we'd made with TF OMBRA to try and save the planet. Once we made it to Phase II, we'd have plenty of time to bond. Now was the time for concentration.

It took me a while to work out how they'd killed themselves. Whoever had constructed the rooms had done a magnificent job eliminating corners and sharp edges. Even the light fixtures were immovable. The silverware was made from Teflon rubber. The plates were made from indestructible plastic. Really, other than slamming one's head against the walls, bars, or floor, there was little someone could do to hurt themselves.

Except for the underside of the bed. Doing sit ups my third day I saw it. The metal loops of the springs ran from one side of the frame to the other in a continuous interlocking web, both holding the mattress up and adding spring tension so it was less like sleeping on a rock and more like sleeping on a board. All of the metal pieces had been spot welded, probably to make certain we couldn't use one of the ends. But the last spot weld at the foot of the bed on both sides was loose. I pried free one end, revealing a nasty-edged piece of wire, which once freed, I could bend with only a little amount of force.

It would take very little effort to rake my arm from wrist to elbow, dragging the metal through tissue and vessels to end it once and for all. At least once a day I found myself on the ground, staring at it. The metal represented a release, a way out. It was an alternative I could choose to take, or not.

Yet the more time passed, the less I looked at it. The more I immersed myself into the lives of fictional soldiers and contemplated the reality that there were real aliens out to get us, the more I wanted to live. It was extraordinary that the threat of an alien invasion could do what all the counseling and consulting had failed to do.

That is, of course, if I believed lock, stock, and barrel what TF OMBRA was telling me.

My thoughts slipped to my Aunt Nancy, who was as fond of conspiracy theories as she was of her gin. I could still see her, sitting at the Formica table in her tiny kitchen in Hackettstown, New Jersey, drinking gin and juice and smoking cigarettes like she was a major stockholder in a tobacco company. She'd wave her hand around, making miniature tornadoes as she turned the news of the day into something conspiratorial.

If a plane crashed, it was the government trying to cover something up. Her favorite theory was that every single plane that crashed was the result of a UFO encounter and it was our government's secret treaty with the aliens that made them kill their own people. If there was a train wreck, it was to cover up some release of energy/noxious gas/alien technology/fill in the blank from whatever Top Secret government facility was nearest the crash site.

Then, of course, there was the weather. Major disasters were the result of the government's weaponized weather machine spinning out of control. She'd theorized that the machine was located somewhere in the Midwest, which was the reason states like Kansas, Oklahoma and Texas were always hit the hardest.

When once asked about hurricanes, she'd laughed, explaining how the Soviet Union had put their own weaponized weather device into the hands of Fidel Castro. All one had to do was look at a map and see that all the hurricanes came from around Cuba as proof.

I'd developed my love for listening to the Night Stalker on late night radio from her. No matter how extraordinary her theories, the Night Stalker's conspiracies were even crazier. Except that listening to his cold, velvet voice on the late night airwaves, I couldn't help but believe in what he had to say.

My Aunt Nancy loved him. Often three sheets to the wind, she'd listen and provide a constant commentary about whatever the topic of the evening was.

Even into her sixties she'd dressed like a *House and Garden* housewife from the early nineteen-sixties. She always wore old fashioned party dresses and high heels. She was never seen without pearls. She wore her hair high on her head, the curls under tight control, until the day wore on and the New Jersey humidity took its toll. About the time the gin started to make her wobble, her curls would fall loose over her eyes. Sometimes she'd pause in mid-sentence to toss her head and get them out of her way, but more often than not she'd use the same hand she used to hold her ever-present cigarette, its red hot tip coming within millimeters of igniting the layers of hairspray.

As a kid, me and my cousins would watch her talk and wait for the inevitable. It was funny and we couldn't wait, sometimes running into the yard and twisting as if we were in flames, burning, burning, burning. I used to find it funny, those memories of my Aunt Nancy. But when I saw D'Ambrosio do his own burning dance on a road in Iraq one fine evening, I lost all appreciation for those kid games. He bounced twice off the Bradley after being sprayed with the contents of an exploding Corolla's fuel tank, as if the twenty-seven tons of metal could put him out. I remember raising my M4 and tracking him through my ACOG, thinking I might shoot him to save him, but chickening out at the last moment, not wanting to play God. Last I heard, he'd made it out of Walter Reed Burn Center, gone home to his family's house, and drank a bottle of Drano.

Would have been simpler if I'd have just shot him.

And I bet knowing what he knew as he raised the blue liquid to his lips, he'd have begged me to do it.

The problem had been that I was already responsible for so many deaths. Could I be responsible for one more? Could my sanity take it?

All this seemed like so long ago.

The six weeks did a miracle at resetting my morale clock. Still, that last night before we got comms, I found myself lying on the floor, staring at that piece of broken spring and wondering how fast I'd be gone if I ripped into my arms, and how much it might hurt.

War is the ultimate reality-based horror show.

Col David Hackworth

CHAPTER EIGHT

I AWOKE TO voices.

"Marines are another thing altogether. If a Marine wants to kill himself, he locks the doors, bars the way with heavy furniture, keeps the windows shut with a long stick, and has three or four things at hand to do it. I once knew a Marine who was found with a rope around his neck, his wrists bled out, a knife through his chest, and later they found he'd taken twenty-five Ambien. He was one determined man."

"So what happened to you?"

"What do you mean?"

"You were a Marine. Why didn't you succeed in killing yourself?"

"Maybe I had second thoughts."

"Did you?"

"No. The rope broke and before I could re-tie it to the overhead pipe, my Gunny Sergeant had me in lock down."

"How does that stack up to being a Marine?"

"Pretty badly. I couldn't even do that right."

"Makes you want to kill yourself, doesn't it?"

"Yes, it does. All over again. This time I'd do it right."

I'd fallen asleep on the floor. My back felt stiff. My left leg had a cramp from where I'd had it crossed over my right. The Bluetooth earpiece was still in my ear and the tablet was lying flat against my chest. I lifted it up. Instead of the usual black screen which appeared when it was resting, the words *COMMUNICATIONS TREE* were displayed across the screen.

As I stared at it, other people began to speak.

"I saw my best friend get shot through the face."

I closed my eyes as I listened.

"She was standing next to me behind the sandbags," came a female voice, raw with emotion. "She was telling me about her prom dress and how her stepmother had helped her get it, but she was too embarrassed to let her mother know. She turned to me and smiled, then a round came from nowhere and made her dead. There wasn't even any fighting. We didn't even know to be careful—I mean, we were always careful, but on that day we didn't think about it. It was almost like we were regular people again. Is anyone even listening?"

I opened my eyes.

"I don't know what good this damn thing is if no one listens."

"I'm listening," I said hesitantly. My voice was still rough with sleep. I cleared my throat and repeated myself.

"Oh," came the voice, a little softer, a little less raw. "Sorry, I think it was my turn. I listened for a long time to get up my nerve."

"What's your name?" I asked.

"No names. Didn't you read the rules?"

I lifted the tablet and saw the link for the Community Rules FAQ. I'd need to review them at some point.

"I just woke up," I said.

"Well, it's your turn if you want to."

I thought about it. "I think I'll just listen for awhile."

She hesitated, then said, "I'll listen for awhile, too, just to see if you want to talk about what it was that made you want to—"

"Kill myself?"

"Yeah." She said in a breathy whisper. "That."

I thought of a dozen things to say, but none of them held the appropriate gravitas. I'd always deflected seriousness with humor, and death was no different. In fact, I'd pushed death even farther away with jokes that everyone used, making fun of the termination of life like it was the turning of the page in a book.

As I thought about this, someone else spoke up.

I glanced at the screen. I noticed the text beneath COMMUNICATIONS TREE read SUICIDE 101. Beside this was another branch of the tree which read DEPRESSION 101 for those who were so locked in their own holes they hadn't thought to commit suicide.

"I ran into traffic," began the voice of a somber man. "I thought I'd timed it just right. It was a big delivery truck. But when the asshole saw me, he swerved." It was a moment before the voice continued. "I learned later it was a mother and her two children he crashed into. Their names were Mary and Brett Sykes and they were in sixth and seventh grade." A longer pause. "How do you live knowing that even when you tried to kill yourself you killed other people?"

The silence on the line was resounding. No one dared answer the unanswerable question. Finally, the voice said, "Thank you," and was gone.

It was soon replaced by what sounded like a young black man. "The sound of someone screaming with their legs missing is something I go to sleep with every night. Even when I listen to music, it's there, in the background, some sort of instrument torturing the notes into the same fucking sound."

I stood and tossed my Bluetooth onto the bed. I wasn't ready for a notional Kumbaya group hug. Mention of the deaths everyone else was responsible for brought mine front-and-center. It didn't matter what barriers I'd constructed. The memories slid past and confronted me.

Brian, Jim, Frank, Steve, Lashonne, Mike, Mike 2, Isaiah, Jesus, Todd, and Nathan all pushed and prodded for attention. Eleven friends, eleven comrades, eleven soldiers with whom I'd served and fought and laughed and cried and cursed the universe. The relationships in war are like none other. When you're scared and the world is shooting at you, your love for the soldier next to you is so transfigured that only those who've been there can really understand. I once tried to explain that to a psychologist at Walter Reed Army Medical Center. He strung together a dozen or so ten-dollar words to express the simple fact that warriors on the battlefield love their friends more than their own lives. We do this without knowing it or acknowledging it. We'd rather we died so that they might live.

So the idea that I'd survived eleven instances of friends dying, eleven separate times where someone I'd loved more than myself passed forcibly from this life into another, felt like a God-wielded ball-peen hammer to the soul.

And they wanted me to fucking talk about it?

Might as well give me a knife and let me stab myself over and over. That would hurt less than having to relive the violent deaths of eleven men who were, each and every one, better than me. I sat on the edge of my bed and stared at the ear bud for several minutes. Then I took it and placed it on one of the recessed shelves. I went back to the bed and picked up the tablet, and scrolled until I found the rules for *Suicide 101*. A strain of unwanted music filled my head as Blue Öyster Cult sang about forty thousand men and women everyday who killed themselves. What was so bad? I mean if the pain got to the point where it was unbearable, why not deliver yourself from it? I found what I was looking for, and as I read, my chin sank deeper into my chest. I had to *bear witness* before I could move onto the next step.

Fucking mindjacked!

I dropped the tablet on the bed as explosions shook the surface of my mind, rounds whizzed past my head, a helicopter swooped in from somewhere and crashed. I staggered to the other side of the room, put my back against the wall, and sank to the floor. I let my arms dangle over my knees as I stared across the room with slitted eyes, barely able to see the Bluetooth over the horizon of my many dead.

Rodney came and went.

Whichever meal it was, I skipped it. It wasn't the first time. The robot waited a moment, beeped a few times, then moved on.

And I continued staring.

During the entire time I was trying not to relive anything. I was trying to make my mind a blank. But like that old trick where you tell someone not to think of a white horse, all I could think of was what I was trying not to remember. But my mind was getting it wrong. Frank died from a sniper, but in my mind he was run over by a tank. Lashonne was hit with an RPG, but in my head he was shot by a platoon of five-year-olds with Kalashnikovs. The more I tried not to think about them, the more my mind rebelled. It was that damned, overwhelming sense of responsibility I had for them.

Mike 2 knew it better than all of them. He'd been a Baptist preacher, married with three kids in some podunkity place in Arkansas when he'd figured out one day that he was gay and couldn't continue to live the life he lived. He divorced his wife, gave her everything, resigned from the church, and joined the Army. He could have come in as a chaplain's assistant, but he became a grunt like me. When I asked him why, he said, "I was once a foot soldier for Christ, now I'm a foot soldier for the American people. I think both them and Christ are pretty much oblivious to my dedication, but that doesn't really matter. What matters is in here," he'd said pointing at his heart.

That same heart gave out during a skirmish in Karbala. Mike 2 was thirty-four when he joined. He'd lost sixty pounds and was in perfect condition. But his heart had been the victim of years' investment in pastries and wine and didn't reflect his current state.

I held him as he died. He joked about the movie *Heathers*, where the burly father says to a church filled with people, *I love my dead gay son*.

When he saw I was crying, he cupped my face and I looked at him and in that moment, I loved him more than anyone else in the world.

"This isn't your fault. None of it is your fault. People die. Shit happens. Don't be that fucker who survives and feels guilty. If you survive, you should live. In Corinthians, it says, *Be sorrowful, but always rejoice. Rejoice in the idea that we died with you by our side. We died with your friendship*."

And then he passed.

I realized I'd been blubbering for some time. I wasn't sure how long, but a pool of tears had gathered on the floor between my feet. I rubbed my nose with the back of an arm and got up and walked across the room. I grabbed the ear bud and put it in. I waited silently for the person who was speaking to stop.

When they did, I began. And I told them about my friends. And I told them how much I loved them. And then I told them about the bridge and what I'd tried to do.

And then it was someone else's turn.

The alien culture in C.J. Cherryh's *Faded Sun* trilogy is very similar to the Muslim culture. Do you believe that if every soldier had read this before combat in Iraq and Afghanistan, their reactions to those countries' peoples and customs would be different?

TF OMBRA Study Question

CHAPTER NINE

CATHARSIS.

An Army chaplain explained it as going through an event which transforms you. My platoon sergeant said it was like being eaten whole by a lion and coming out the other end more or less intact. Regardless of how one described the word, it meant pain, pain, pain, then an acceptance of pain, then spending your entire life attempting to live with a journey you never asked for but finally understood.

I'd stood with my head leaning against my cell for hours, staring at the great expanse of floor. I stood there long enough for the cold to creep into my brain, numbing it. I stood there long enough for Rodney to come again and see if I was hungry, then leave with a few somber beeps. I stood there long enough to see another of our merry troop of world saviors be dragged across the floor, his hair sliding behind him and leaving a trail of blood as our all-purpose robot pulled him indelicately by his heels across the wide, empty floor and through the door in the far wall, before returning to clean away the evidence.

I went back to my bunk and lay on the ground so that I could see the wire. Catharsis. Eaten by the war, shit out the other side, and left to stink by the side of the road. Lion shit. That was me all over. What was clearer than any other feeling was the hatred I felt for myself.

I gripped the underside of the bed. My hands slipped off the mattress at first and I had to find just the right hand holds. Finally, I was able to pull myself up in a reverse pushup so that the end of the bent wire was a mere inch from my eyeball. I was strong and fit, so holding myself wasn't an issue. All it would take was a solid jerk and I could put the piece of wire through my eye. If I hesitated, or if I didn't commit, I'd just blind myself. I had to pull hard. A solid jerk, like a pull up, would do it; as long as I could jam the wire deep enough into my brain it would free me from my friends. I said goodbye to Mike, Mike 2, Jesus, Todd, Isaiah, Nathan, Steve, Frank, Lashonne, Jim and Brian. I said goodbye to their memories, to their stories of home and their favorite movies and books, to their favorite foods, their tales of sexual conquest and pretences at prowess, to their fears and loneliness, their family photos, their service to their country, to their friendship and their death.

Then I jerked upwards.

Or I wanted to.

Death has many faces and I've seen hundreds of them. Some people believe in angels, some believe in devils, but as far as I knew, no one believed in a robot named Rodney. As I lay wracked with emotion, barely able to breathe, Rodney stood silent at the bars of my cage, my anthropomorphic needs creating a nurturing and tender being in the place of the logic-brained metal and silicon construct who was as much our jailer as he was our feeder. He didn't beep. He didn't buzz. He just stared.

Catharis.

Lion food.

Lion shit.

When the edge of self-pity stole into my grief, I found my way to my feet. It was hard at first, but I finally made it, like a drunken sailor getting his balance on the high seas.

And Rodney was still there.

Realization crept into my thoughts. Rodney wasn't there to help me. It was a machine. It was there to remove me, like a piece of trash.

"What?" I shouted.

Nary a beep.

"What the fuck do you want, you fucking R2D2-wannabe? What are you waiting for, you mechanical vulture? You want to drag another one of us out? You want to witness us at our very fucking worst?"

I ran at the bars. I slammed into them before I could grab him, of course. My nose exploded with blood. Instead of covering it with my hands, I gripped the bars with the power invested in me from three wars, eleven deaths and a lifetime of suicidal thoughts.

"You know!" I craned back my head and laughed. As it rang through our prison, it slid towards a cackle. But I couldn't help it. The realization was too much. "You know about the wire! What is it? Did Mr. Pink and the rest of you have a pool? Was I next? Were you waiting for me to kill myself so you could pass each other money and laugh about how fucked up we are?"

"Shut the fuck up," someone yelled.

"Fuck you! You shut the fuck up, you fucking fuck!" I glared at Rodney, now fully anthropomorphized into everyone I ever hated. "You think a few sad tales of woe from the rest of these suicidal rejects is going to make me end it all? Do you really think I'd be so weak that I'll kill myself just to pleasure your sadistic ideas of saving the world? Hey, I have an idea. Let's pick the most fucked-up soldiers from every corner of the planet right at the moment they're about to kill themselves, then tell them they can save the world, only to lock them up in some godforsaken prison beneath the most godforsaken state anyone's never been from. And hey! Just to make sure, let's have each of our sorry asses weep into a magic tablet that can cure all of our wounds if only we believe that we deserve to live, that our friends deserved to die, and that God didn't make some immense fucking mistake, you know, like he did when he invented cyanide, midget bowling, internet porn and starving people in Africa."

"Dude, we can hear you," a man's voice shouted.

"Will you please shut up?" someone else said, the words barely intelligible amidst her sobbing.

I backed away from the bars. My hands and arms were shaking. I felt something wet on my face. I reached up and wiped away blood from my nose.

Rodney turned around on its tracks and headed out of the room by its usual route.

I guess they'd seen what they wanted to see.

I guess they'd had enough.

I staggered back to my bunk and curled up, my hands between my thighs, facing the wall. I let my nose bleed, the cold wetness the only thing that reminded me I was alive, a dull ache in the very center of my soul.

I have nothing to offer but blood, toil, tears, and sweat.

Sir Winston Churchill

CHAPTER TEN

"BETWEEN FEELING SORRY for oneself and pure hatred is a chasm of responsibility few cross. Feeling sorry is the easiest of emotions, allowing a person to believe that it was the enemy, the victims, and the universe that had conspired to cause an action, rather than something they did. To get through to the purity of self-loathing, however, one must tread the treacherous path through realization and truth, reliving and recounting what it was they'd done that had caused the actions to be true. And it is only through this journey that a man or woman can truly find themselves. Although they'll face self-hatred, it is a mirror which can be broken, and once shattered, provides a path through self-realization, allowing the person to live free of the action with an understanding of their own limitations."

I awoke and sat up, wondering who'd been speaking. Then the voice came again.

"Between feeling sorry for oneself and pure hatred..."

I reached up and grabbed at my ear, only to find that the earpiece had been replaced. I snatched it away and stared at it, wondering how I'd come to be wearing it. My eyes darted to the shelf where I'd left it. Of course it wasn't there. I checked the bed and saw that it was perfectly made. Then I remembered my bloody nose. There should have been a stain on the sheet.

I felt at my face, but there was no blood. I got up, ignoring the stiff complaints from my legs, and padded to the mirror. My face was clean. In fact, it had been shaved. I felt at my nose. It still felt tender, which gave me some relief. At least I wasn't imagining the whole event. But I knew someone had been in my cell without me knowing. To clean me up meant they'd have to have used drugs. I rubbed my hand across my face and stared at the eyes in my metal reflection. They looked clear. I felt good, actually.

Then the full memory of what I'd almost done came back to me. I closed my mouth and gritted my teeth. I ran the water, putting my hands under it just as they began to shake. I held them beneath the flow as I stared into the mirror and met my own gaze, the words coming back to me.

"Although they'll face self-hatred, it is a mirror which can be broken, and once shattered, provides a path through self-realization, allowing the person to live free of the action with an understanding of their own limitations."

I realized I could recount the entire passage. It was part of me now. How many times had it played while I was unconscious? What other things had they fed me—fed us—unconsciously?

"Mr. Mason. I'd like you to come with me, please."

My gaze shifted to where Mr. Pink stood outside my cell. As I watched, the bars disappeared into the floor and ceiling. He regarded me for a moment, then turned and walked away. I hurriedly dried my hands and followed him. Instead of turning to my right, which would have been the way I came in, we turned to the left, heading for a door at the far end of the great room. Mr. Pink moved at a fast clip, his wingtips ticking quickly across the floor. I tried to keep up as best I could, but my mind was still trying to come to terms with the sudden change. My universe had grown from the size of a cell, to the size of this big room, and would soon explode to the size of total freedom.

Check that. While I might be allowed out in the world, I was pretty certain my leash would be on, perhaps tightly wrapped around Mr. Pink's fist.

I glanced at my neighbors, seeing them for the first time. They were all asleep on their beds. Some on their backs, with an arm thrown across their foreheads, some on their stomachs, some on their sides, curled like they were children. The rooms were identical, the only difference the occupants.

I paused when I saw Michelle. With her arms no longer covered, I saw the complete topography of her agony. The cuts at her wrists were only the latest she'd inflicted upon herself. I could hear my own breathing as I counted the scars, arrayed like tick marks from her elbows to just below where a watch would go. Each cut had been made with such precision that once healed, they were geometrically perfect representations of her pain? Why were some people cutters and some not?

It was as if Mr. Pink could read my thoughts.

"Some are unable to put into words the emotions they are feeling. The responsibility you feel for eleven of your fellow soldiers dying is something you can grasp. Not everyone can understand so clearly why they want to kill themselves, or why they're so depressed."

I glanced at him sharply, but his attention was solely on the sleeping form of Michelle. I drew my gaze up her arms and let it caress the curve of her jaw. She appeared to be so peaceful in her sleep.

"You're able to compartmentalize your pain and anguish and bring it out when you need to. It's more common with male soldiers than it is females. Female soldiers often feel the need to redeem themselves for what they view as their faults. Most often that comes in the form of pain. Whether it be as simple as a rubber band they continually snap against their wrist, or something more dedicated, like young Private Aquinas.

"The physical pain also provides a brief respite from their self-loathing. With the pain comes momentary forgetfulness, and also, interestingly enough, endorphins, which can become quite addictive." Mr. Pink turned to me. "Good thing you decided to jump off a bridge. Imagine deciding to jump off the bridge a hundred times and actually doing it." He turned back to Michelle. "That's what she felt every time she hurt herself."

He looked at me, his face implacable with his dead, expressionless eyes. "Cut, cut, cut," he said, miming slicing his forearm with a razor blade. "All the pain in her little overwhelming universe lined up in a row."

He turned and continued toward the door.

I hastened to follow, noting that I passed two cells with no one in them.

The successes.

Or failures.

I guess it depended on one's point of view.

In the second-to-last cell, two men dressed in yellow jumpsuits had a young man sitting on the bed, clearly unconscious. One of the men helped him upright, while the other used an electric shaver to remove beard growth.

I felt my own face and remembered realizing that I'd been shaved before I'd awoke. How had they done this to me? To all of us?

Then it hit me.

I followed Mr. Pink through the door.

"You're gassing us," I said to his back.

"Makes it easier for the therapy to work. Don't feel so worried. We're not exactly making this up as we go along, you know."

This stopped me. "Really? So you have *another* underground bunker with a thousand messed-up soldiers to fuck around with?"

This made him pause. He turned and pointed to a door to his right. "Go through there. Get changed. We're airborne in twenty mikes."

"Where we going?"

"Dothan, Alabama."

"What for?"

"A young man who scrubbed floors on the night shift at a local supermarket decided to take all of his weapons into an elementary school and kill twenty-three children and five teachers before turning his guns on himself."

Oh, Jesus. "And what does it have to do with us?"

"The invasion has already begun. I want to show you. I want you to understand."

"Why me? Why spend this time on me?"

He turned and walked down the hall. "We'll be airborne in eighteen mikes. You need to hurry."

Live for something rather than die for nothing.

General George S. Patton

CHAPTER ELEVEN

IF THERE'S ANYTHING worse than the site of a school massacre I'm not aware of it, and I'd seen man-created misery at its very finest. We'd landed in Fort Rucker in a TF OMBRA jet. Two dark green Suburbans were waiting for us. I got into the second one with Mr. Pink. The first carried three men who looked like they spent their lives playing video games. The glance I got of their hi-tech equipment made me wonder if that was what they were doing even now, as their SUV made concentric circles around the event site.

I did as I was told. I stood tall, silent and still, wearing army boots, 5.11 tactical camouflage pants, a black TF OMBRA polo shirt, a P229 on my right hip, and dark glasses. They'd given me a comms unit that fit into the back of my belt and had a wire to my ear, much like a Secret Service agent. And everyone left me alone. I stood a few feet back from Mr. Pink, following him as he processed through the authorities, his TF OMBRA badge as effective as anyone else's.

Miss Anne Cloverfield Elementary School was founded in 1928 as an all-black school for the children of field laborers. Named after the suffragist who turned her fight to help the plight of poor children everywhere, it was through guilt, guile, and manipulation that she convinced the plantation owners to pony up enough money for what had been in the day the best school for black children in the county. Fast forward past Governor Wallace and Selma and America's decision to have a black president and Miss Anne's, as the community came to know it, had become a magnet school, bringing the best and brightest of all races through its doors.

Which is why the entire world watched, stunned, not understanding the capriciousness of a universe that would allow a lone gunman to walk into the school and kill so many innocent children. That this same crime had been replicated in different states over the years made it beyond tragic. It should have been stopped. Some wanted to arm the teachers. Some wanted to post guards at every school. Some wanted to pull their children out and home school them. The only thing everyone could agree on was that they were sure it wouldn't happen to *their* children.

Although the shooting was past and the families had been notified, news reporters and concerned citizens still filled the school's parking lot.

"What exactly are we doing here?" I asked, leaning forward to engage Mr. Pink before I remembered I wore comm gear.

"Waiting, actually," he said, just loud enough for me to hear.

"For what?"

"You'll know when it happens." He turned to me. "Can you feel anything?"

"Feel? I feel sad to fucking be here."

"No. Like a buzz or a vibration."

I shook my head. "I don't feel anything except for a lot of anger at how fucked up all this is."

Mr. Pink looked disappointed, but he quickly recovered. It was the first show of emotion he'd let slip.

"What are we waiting on?" I remembered him mentioning that the *invasion had already begun*. I might be able to buy that, but what did it have to do with this?

I watched as a policeman, standing with his arms crossed on the other side of the police line, said something to one of the reporters. I was too far away to hear it, but I didn't need to. It was all variations on a tragedy. I closed my eyes and listened to the sound of the breeze and the coming and going of cars.

"You called me Mr. Pink." Mr. Pink had turned and was facing me, blocking my view.

"What?"

"Back at Phase I, when you almost killed yourself. You called me Mr. Pink."

"What of it? It's not like I know your real name."

He nodded slowly. I was aware of a Warrant Officer and his wife on the ground behind him, arm in arm, sobbing together. I refocused on him.

"I've never been called that before. Out of curiosity, why Mr. Pink?"

I explained about his likeness to the actor Steve Buscemi, and about the character in the Quentin Tarantino movie.

"I liked that movie. Who was the one who cut off the man's ear?"

"That was Michael Madsen. He was Mr. Blonde."

"Oh. Any chance you could switch to Mr. Blonde?"

We were interrupted by a voice in our earpieces. "We have positive vector."

Mr. Pink moved and I was right behind him. "Report locus," he said, as he strode past a dozen vehicles to our own.

"Two blocks west. Yellow house. Picket fence."

We got in our SUV. Our driver took us around the long way to bypass the local media. Mr. Pink pulled out a tablet, much like the one I'd left back in my cell, and had the other team relay a satellite image of the area. I watched as his tablet synced with theirs, then zoomed in. The street looked normal except for a red flashing box around one house.

"How far away is it from the perp's?" Mr. Pink asked.

"Less than fifty meters. Next street over and down. Light green house."

Mr. Pink placed his finger on the red blinking house, then traced a route through backyards. He tapped the image of the house with the tip of his nail. "Do we have dragonflies on station?"

"Roger."

"Show me a view through the windows of the subject house."

The screen went blank and was replaced by a whirling, sickening view from something that seemed to be flying through the air. I watched the view change as it came up to the house, then hovered first by the living room window, then a bedroom window, then the dining room window. It paused there as we took in the scene. It looked like a family of four was sitting at the table, but no one was moving.

"Switch to IR," Mr. Pink said.

The image switched to grays and greens. Each of the bodies had an orange core, with yellow trailing down and through the floor. *Strange*.

"Team two, secure the perimeter. Team three enter and locate, but do not engage. Team four, wait for me." To the driver. "Faster."

The driver stepped on it as we carved through the streets towards the home.

"We discovered them accidentally," Mr. Pink told me. "A local cop in Coeur d'Alene, Idaho was canvassing homes after a similar incident six years ago and found a family in their living room. The Huyck family was alive, but no longer human." He paused, as if expecting me to ask what he meant by *no longer human*, but he continued before I could ask the obvious. "You'll see when we get in there. Don't touch anything and let me know immediately if you feel your thoughts are no longer your own." This time he did look at me.

I nodded.

We pulled to a stop in front of the home. It looked normal, like a place a family might be happy in. Flowers grew in pots on the patio. A bicycle had been left by the front steps, as if dropped by a kid dashing to dinner. Several newspapers had been tossed onto the porch.

The driver got out and stood by the vehicle. A team of four shooters stood ready on the porch, wearing Kevlar vests and arm pads. Their heads were covered with helmets I'd never seen before, with no openings to see and hear. They must have been using HUDs, about as high-tech as I'd seen short of a science fiction movie.

As we moved towards them, I saw signs I'd missed. The pile of newspapers. Leaves covered the back wheel of the bicycle and a spider had made its web between two spokes. The flowers, once bright orange pansies, were now brown, water-starved, and sagging against the sides of the clay pots.

The team was stacked at the door, one behind the other. I'd been in their place a hundred times before, clearing buildings in other shithole countries. Each doorway represented the possibility of life or death or something in between. No one knew who—or in this case, what—was on the other side. Bad guys could be pressed against the wall, just waiting for someone to pass, to show a vulnerability. Sometimes all they wanted to do was kill one of us, their own lives already forfeit. Sometimes, they waited with bombs strapped around their bodies

One Hajji—we never knew where he was from, because there wasn't anything left of him—had welcomed me and my three soldiers when we stacked onto a landing on the second floor veranda of an old German hotel in Baghdad. His smile had been the same one I'd seen on the face of every smartass I'd ever known, ever wanted to punch, ever wanted to shut up. Only this one held a remote control in his right hand. His hand was raised beside his face, so we wouldn't miss it, along with his cock-and-balls smile.

My M4 was already against my cheek, and I raised it an inch, sighted, and removed his smile, his face, and his right hand in a blistering peel of rounds that emptied my magazine. I'd been ready for him to explode, ready to die even as I killed him. What I wasn't willing to do was stand there and take what he was about to give. If I was going to go, he was coming with me, and on my terms. We stood, eyes slitted behind our goggles in anticipation of the explosion, but nothing happened. The dust settled, as did pieces of his hand and face. A slop of something that could have been a cheek hit the floor, and we were left watching the body, still standing. His handless arm had fallen forward, blood sliding down his pant leg. His face was a cartouche of my violence. But he was upright.

Then we saw it. The suicide bomber had been leaning back against the railing at the edge of the veranda. I stared at his bulging, compartmented vest, at the daisy chain of wires going from one bundle to the other. Anywhere near that sort of power meant instantaneous death, bodies pummeled by enough force to render each of us to our separate molecules.

Then Williams took a step forward, spun and kicked him in the sternum, sending the Hajji up and over the rail.

I remember flinching, but nothing happened.

Williams turned and grinned. "Welcome to the war, motherfucker," he said.

Then the bomber hit the stairs three stories below and his vest blew.

Williams was flung forward, his Kevlar ripped away by the force of the blast, his back and legs a flat mass of red muscle and meat. We caught him as we were forced back into the wall. Protected from the blast by space and distance, we held Williams in the last moments of his life, long enough to love him, long enough to see his smile fall into something less victorious.

The team at the door of the house in Dothan were my brothers. I knew their each and every mission. One high, one low, one left, one right, sweep, change, move. Close Quarters Battle drill, or CQB for short, was both an art and a science whose only metric for success or failure was to come out alive.

Their rifles were different from any I'd ever seen. Between the wires and LED readouts, I couldn't figure out how they worked, until I saw the lead running from inside a jacket into a socket just forward of the magazine well. Electrical. Which must have meant that beneath their Kevlar vests were rigs of batteries—looking, perversely, similar to the explosive vest of a suicide bomber.

"Status," Mr. Pink whispered into his cell phone.

"Everyone's in place. Family is still at the table."

Mr. Pink glanced at me once, then tapped the last man on the shoulder.

The first man placed a device into the lock and pressed a trigger, and within five seconds the door was open. The team stacked inside, connected and close. Mr. Pink and I allowed them room to maneuver, aware that if there was any firing coming from inside the house, the closer to the action we were, the more liable we were to get hit.

They cleared the living room, then moved into the dining room, where they fanned out.

Mr. Pink and I followed them. A stench hit me, causing me to bring my hand to my face. Rot and feces and something else. I'd pulled out my pistol and held it ready. As I walked through the living room with pictures of a family vacation to Yosemite prominently displayed on a wall, I felt like I was trespassing.

As we turned into the dining room I saw what had happened. How this all-American family had been chosen or how they'd become what they'd become was something I might never learn. But for now I was transfixed, my jaw fallen open, the pistol dipping dangerously as I observed father, mother, son, daughter, held in place with pink and white filaments.

The father was bald, had a tattoo of the Tasmanian Devil on his right arm, and had creases around his mouth and the corners of his eyes as if he liked to smile.

The mother wore blonde hair in a bun, although judging by her tan lines she usually wore it down. Ample breasts pressed against a bright orange-and-yellow paisley tank top.

The girl was a miniature version of her mother, including the way she wore her hair, although hers seemed more an affectation than utilitarian necessity. Probably trying desperately to grow up and be like her mother, even while wearing a sparkly *My Little Pony* T-shirt.

I could barely look at the boy. While the others seemed to have been caught unawares, he'd known what was going on. His face was twisted in horror. His vacant milky eyes twisted towards his father, as if to warn him, or beg for help, or merely so he could watch him succumb to the same raw beast that had them all breathing and shitting and pissing themselves on what had once passed as high-end dining furniture.

Plates of rotting food sat in front of each of them. Worms crawled through something that had once been a casserole. Flies swirled above the family's last meal.

"Look but don't touch, Mason," Mr. Pink said. He eyed my pistol. "You're not going to need that."

"It makes me feel comfortable," I whispered, unable to take my eyes off the scene.

The filaments held the family in place, affixing their wrists, arms, legs and ankles to the chairs, and disappeared into the floor. I bent to see a circular orange growth pulsing with light beneath the table, several thick orange trunks running right into each of their abdomens. The surfaces of the trunks held millions of fine white cilia.

Then I saw it. As the growth pulsed, the family breathed, in unison, their chests rising and falling in a mockery of life.

I found myself taking aim at the orange growth. I didn't know what sort of damage my bullets would do. They might not do anything. But firing at the damn thing would surely make me feel better.

"Not here. Let's go downstairs," Mr. Pink said.

"What about them?" I asked.

I'll give the man credit. He could have said any number of one-liners, but instead he told me the truth. "It's too late for them. We don't know what they're doing or what's been done to them. Best guess from the experts is their brains are being used to transmit data on a frequency we don't normally use."

"Are you talking telepathy?" I asked.

"One man's radio is another man's telepathy. There's too much of the brain we don't understand."

"The aliens sure seem to have figured the shit out."

Mr. Pink grudgingly nodded. "If we could communicate with them, maybe we could ask them."

"How many have you found like this?"

"With aliens in residence like this one?"

I nodded.

"Sixteen."

No shit. "And how many others?"

"We were too late twenty-three times."

"So on thirty-nine separate occasions, you've never figured out what they're doing?"

"Not exactly, but it doesn't take a genius to figure out that they're prepping for an invasion."

"How can you even know that?"

Mr. Pink pointed at the four family members. "We don't know *what* they're broadcasting, but NSA satellites have picked up their outbound transmissions. Attempts to decode them have fallen flat, but that the aliens are landing and setting up transmissions out of the ionosphere is enough to convince me that they're doing *something*, and invasion's the top candidate."

"How do they get here? Is there a spaceship on the roof?"

Mr. Pink gave me a sharp appraising look.

"What?"

"You asked the right question almost right away. Then again, military men always do. It never occurred to the early scientists studying this event to wonder how they got here."

"You've been detected," came the voice of the tech team through the comms.

"Shit."

One of the orange trunks had released the young girl, who was now slumped onto her rotting meal. It waved in the air, millions of white cilia twitching.

Mr. Pink began moving across the room. "Downstairs, and fast."

The team found the stairs and stacked down them.

Mr. Pink followed. I ran to catch up.

The stack was already moving down into the basement when I arrived at the door. The uncarpeted wooden stairs creaked with their weight. The walls were lined on one side with canned vegetables and on the other with old license plates. A bare light bulb dangled from a length of cord at the bottom of the stairs, low enough for the second man in line to brush it with his head.

As bad as the air had been in the dining room, it was far fouler in the basement.

"We have positive contact," said one of the men.

Mr. Pink put his hand on my shoulder. "I want you to see this." Then he descended the rest of the way and walked out of sight.

I crept down a few stairs and leaned out. I could see something moving on the other side of the picket of men, a flesh-colored mass about three feet high, from which a thick trunk rose through the broken ceiling above.

"Is it like the others?" Mr. Pink asked.

"Yes."

The word had been said quickly, but held a finality to it that I couldn't understand. That is, until the men stepped aside to let Mr. Pink see what was in front of them. And in that moment, I saw the babies, at least a dozen of them, rising and falling in a sea of alien flesh, like they were bobbing, or maybe sinking, in and out of the substance. Their eyes were closed, but their mouths were open, emitting a chorus of low-pitched hums.

Mr. Pink fell back, his hands over his ears.

I watched him, wondering what was happening. Then I saw him for what he was. He was an intruder. He was causing the babies pain. They'd done nothing to harm him, yet here he stood, ready to kill them. I looked down at the pistol in my hand, then brought it up, and aimed at Mr. Pink. He was so close I didn't even need to align the sights. The humming grew and embraced me, and I could hear screams hidden inside the sound. The screams of babies. Mr. Pink was killing babies. I had to—I pulled the trigger as fast as my finger would move. Never once did my aim waver. Never once did I hesitate. But the sound continued unabated.

I watched in stunned amazement as Mr. Pink turned to me, raised his own pistol, and pressed it against his head. He squeezed the trigger over and over, his mouth open in a silent scream.

The sound of the alien children was cut off as the four men fired their Taser rifles. Four, eight, twelve lines of electricity sunk deep into the alien flesh. Suddenly the babies were gone, replaced by a frozen sea of spikes.

I realized I'd been screaming, and I shut my mouth. I made eye contact with Mr. Pink, just as he lowered his pistol, and just as I stopped firing my own weapon at him. Except neither of us had loosed a shot. I didn't check, but I was sure that my rounds were dummies, as were his. I put my pistol away with a shaky hand. Probably the reason the team wore their sensory-deprivation helmets.

Mr. Pink passed by me, pulling me along as he went.

We moved back through the dining room and living room and out of the home. I didn't even glance at the family this time. My mind was on what I'd almost done. What I'd done. What would have happened had there been real rounds in our weapons.

Back at the SUV, Mr Pink lit a cigarette. I hadn't known he smoked. His hand shook slightly, but I made no comment. He inhaled half of the cigarette before he spoke.

"The first teams killed themselves. We didn't know why, until we were able to film the second team." He shook his head, making the smoke swirl. "They know what scares us. They know how to get to us. Most importantly, and something we have yet to crack, is they can make us do things to each other, to ourselves."

"Is it always like this?" I asked, not knowing how to voice the thousand other questions I had.

"Pretty much. I don't normally carry, nor do I participate in the clean-up, but you had to see it. I knew this was going to happen." His hand shook as he dropped the cigarette and stepped on it. "It's fucking terrible."

I wasn't sure if I liked the idea that this whole thing had been a lesson. Nor did I like the fact that I'd essentially killed Mr. Pink. Had there been rounds in my Sig, he would never have made it out of the basement.

"Don't look so pissed. Some lessons you can't learn by tablet. You have to see them for yourself."

Finally I managed to say, "I had no control over what I was doing."

"They know so much more about us than we do them. We're going to bring this one back for study, but it's really just a show-and-tell. We've learned all we can about the Cray. We just don't have the technology to learn more."

An ice cream truck rounded the corner and drove slowly down the street, musical chimes echoing from the clown-shaped speaker on the roof, returning me for a moment to my childhood. Down the block, two kids ran out of a house waving dollars in the air. Their mother came onto the porch and watched them, her arms crossed, a smile on her tired face. It took a moment for the transaction, then the kids ran back to the house, each carrying a red, white and blue Bomb Pop. They were oblivious of the alien in their midst, and that was the core of the problem. No one knew. And if they did, what would they do? Mr. Pink had said it: *we've learned all we can.*

"You called them Cray. How do you know what they're called?" I asked.

"You'll get this on your tablet, but I might as well tell you now. We don't know *what* they're called. As you saw, we have yet to discover a way to communicate with them. They're named after Joshua McCray from Glasgow. He was the first to discover them."

"They're in Scotland too?"

"As far as we know, they're all over the world. In every country, in every city, doing whatever an alien species does before it invades."

I thought about it for a moment, and said the only answer I could come up with: "Reconnaissance."

"Good a term as any. Although I don't know how much they care about our way of life. Xenobiologists from Freie Universität Berlin posited that these creatures were determining the chemical composition of our planet."

"Like tasting the soup," I said.

"As apt a metaphor as any, I suppose."

I'd read about xenobiologists in an Orson Scott Card book, one of our required readings. At the time I read it, I'd romanticized the occupation, thinking of them as part Airborne Ranger, part

Indiana Jones, part scientist, going to other planets to test flora and fauna and ascertain their base makeup. I hadn't really imagined someone in Middle America checking out a house in the suburbs to try and ascertain why something was eating a family of four from the inside out.

"Is it always like this?"

"Do you mean is the family always beyond hope? Is the creature little more than a sentient puddle of muck? Or is there always a school shooting nearby?"

"Yes, yes, and yes."

"So far, I'd say yes to the first two questions, although we have a woman who survived for sixteen hours after we pulled her free. You'll see her video once you reach Phase III. As far as the third question, the answer is no."

He climbed into the back seat of the SUV. I went around the other side and slid inside. He asked for my pistol and I passed it to him, along with the belt clip and the two spare magazines.

"Everyone isn't built the same way. There are some whose brains are capable of aligning to the frequency the Cray use to broadcast. These people can hear, or rather feel, the broadcast, but they don't understand it. We don't know whether it's a biological reaction or a psychological reaction, but we've noticed a graphic increase in violence surrounding the Cray sites. School shootings, mall shootings, and murder-suicides have become an indicator of possible Cray presence. It's only accurate about forty percent of the time."

"And the other times?"

"They're either not connected, or we can't find the connection."

"So instead of it being a crazy person committing these vile acts, it's someone under the influence of an alien broadcast?"

"Oh, no. These people *are* crazy. In every instance there's been a history of mental illness in one shape or form. Perhaps that's what makes them susceptible. Scientists are working on that right now. Maybe the broadcasts push them over the edge. Maybe they just hasten what was going to happen anyway. There's no evidence that the alien broadcasts *create* violence in people."

"We do a good enough job with that on our own," I said, as much to myself as I did to Mr. Pink.

We pulled away from the curb and passed a fire truck barreling down the street past us. I turned around and watched as it pulled to stop at the house. Smoke and flames were already pouring out of the dining room window. I envisioned the family, shriveling and twisting in the fire. Like D'Ambrosio. Like a bus filled with Pakistanis hit by a VBIED motorcycle bomb, the bus tipped on its side, everyone trying to get free from the flames but unable to break through the wire mesh on the windows.

I closed my eyes and let my head soak in the coolness of the breeze until we reached the airport. When we pulled to a stop, it was clear I was the only one getting out.

He handed me my identification and a plane ticket.

"Why did you bring me here?"

He didn't look at me, but stared at his hands resting comfortably in his lap. "You've felt responsible for more deaths than almost anyone we have in TF OMBRA. There's nothing we can do, or at least want to do, to remove those images from your mind that wouldn't leave permanent scarring and loss of cognitive function. We want you to learn. We want you to understand. We want you to be able, when the time comes, to help the world defend against the coming attack."

"But why me?"

Mr. Pink sighed. "You sit there like a petulant child, the universe revolving around you. Have you learned nothing from all the books you've read? Haven't the world's best authors taught you that the world doesn't revolve around you, but rather you revolve around the universe, and if you want to continue do to so, you have to protect it?" He looked at me for the first time, and I could see the anger behind the act. "You need to get over yourself. Yes, bad shit happened, and it happened to you. Yes. We know. Now get over it. You want to kill yourself, then fucking do it, but don't fucking draw it out and cry about it. This is our world and it's about to be attacked. We don't know how, we don't know why, and we don't know when. All we know is we have to be ready. And if we have to use a brigade of lost souls to do it, then we'll do just that. Figure out if you want to be a part of the future or a part of the past. The future you can help. The past has already happened. Now get out. You have a plane to catch."

I got out and watched the SUV race away. When it was out of sight, I turned and went inside. I checked in, made it through security, and sat in a bar, sipping a beer and watching the aftermath on television. When the time came for my plane to leave, I paid my bill and shuffled into line. I was flying first class again. I could get used to it.

But as I was checking my seat, I saw the date. That couldn't be right. I looked and saw the same date on the board near the gate. But that was impossible. We couldn't have been in the facility for longer than six weeks, but according to this, we'd been gone for eight months.

But how?

Then I remembered.

The gas.

There are no secrets to success. It is the result of preparation, hard work, learning from failure.

General Colin Powell

CHAPTER TWELVE

MY ARRIVAL AT the Wyoming facility went unheralded. Everyone was still in a state of forced sleep when I returned. As far as I knew, they'd been that way the entire time I'd been gone. I don't know what gas they were using, but they succeeded in hydrating us and keeping us from tracking the passage of time. A niggling worry in the back of my mind questioned why we had to be asleep so long. If the threat of attack was so imminent, shouldn't we be making the most of our time? But my mind was too fogged with all I'd just learned for me to do anything other than shove the question aside for later scrutiny.

I soon found myself lying on the mattress with the same feeling I used to have after returning from a mission. It was a matter of extremes: one moment I was driving down a road in an up-armored vehicle, my butt clenched as I wondered if I might get blown up at any moment, then moving from one point to the other on foot, taking fire, returning fire, killing, dodging, running, bleeding, cursing, crying, screaming... and the next moment I'd lie back on my bunk and stare at the ceiling, listening to whatever new song was hitting the charts on my iPod and reading articles about which pop star had an eating disorder and which actor was fucking who. No matter what innocuous, meaningless thoughts I tried to sprinkle through my haggard mind, it kept attempting to relive the events of the recent past over and over and over again.

Like it was doing now, visions of the rotting family at the dinner table juxtaposed with the sweet ass of the flight attendant in first class, juxtaposed with the undulating mass of babies in the basement, juxtaposed with me shooting Mr. Pink as he'd had his own pistol pressed against his temple, juxtaposed with a first-class-cabin plate of poached salmon on rice and a glass of chardonnay, juxtaposed with the kids eating Bomb Pops, juxtaposed with fucking D'Ambrosio dancing in the fire. The images dueled with themselves, dueled with me, begged me to bring one front and center, to let it represent me. But I refused. As soon as one surfaced, I'd flick it off, the good, the bad, the happy, the sad, I didn't want anything in my mind. I just wanted to be blank for awhile. I just wanted to think about nothing.

During my first tour in the Army I'd been deployed to Bosnia. My rack was in an old Quonset hut built by the Russians back when they'd been stationed there to keep the peace. Above me on the ceiling someone had stenciled the word *antidisestablishmentarianism*. I'd lie in my rack and stare at the almost unpronounceable word, wondering what it meant. I'd eventually come to understand it was an ideology that believed in the combination of church and state, but the meaning never really mattered. It was the word. It was a puzzle. It was an alphabetical Escher that drew me in and wouldn't let me out. I'd stare at it for hours, always wondering why someone would take the time to place the word there. It couldn't have been easy. They must have wanted it there badly. And why in English and not Russian? Did I have a Russian soul mate, one who was drawn to the word such as myself, or was it written later, by some bored Ivy League graduate American?

Then came Cerska, where I saw my first mass grave. Up on the side of a hill, hidden from the road by a copse of trees, we smelled its sickly sweet stench half a mile down the road. At first we thought it was a barbecue. Private Adams made a remark, joking that the sergeant was taking us to a party.

Ain't no parties in a graveyard, he'd said, as solemn as a tombstone.

That had shut us up. The ten of us and the sergeant were in the back of an open-backed deuce-and-a-half, swaying from side to side in the deep backwoods ruts. All of our eyes were aimed ahead, wondering what it was we were getting into, wondering what the U. S. Army had volunteered us for.

When we crested the hill, we saw two United Nations vans and a bunch of men in light blue helmets and suits standing around. They watched us for a moment, then returned to staring into a pit the size of a football field, excavated by dozens of local workers dressed in old rags.

Everyone else couldn't wait to discover what was in the pit, but I already knew. I'd seen it in the faces of the men with shovels. They couldn't meet my gaze. They didn't want to. They had a misery to carry. Maybe they'd known about the bodies. Maybe they'd helped bury them in the first place. No one lived in a place without knowing what went into the ground, especially Muslim men and boys, each one shot in the back of the head and pushed into a pit. So the men just stared at the earth, saying nothing, smoking as much to alleviate their nerves as to hide the smell of decay.

They gave us white hazmat suits with filtered masks. At first the filters worked, but soon they became clogged with dust and debris and we couldn't breathe. We were forced to remove them as we moved each body, one by one, the dead laid side by side except at one end where it seemed as if their killers had been in a hurry, maybe to get back to the bar or the family dinner.

They chose us because they couldn't trust the locals not to accidentally desecrate the bodies. So we were given the honor of packing each and every one of the one hundred and fifty corpses into body bags. Many had been shot with their hands tied behind their backs. Others had died twisted, as if the shot had turned their bodies as they fell.

But the one that stayed with me was the child with his hands over his eyes. About seven years old, he lay face down in the muck of the grave. I turned him over as gently as I could, aware that in this state of decomposition, even the most careful movement could separate bones from a body. But I still couldn't see his face. I tried to move his hands, but they wouldn't come free. I didn't dare try again for fear I'd break them, but I spent the rest of the day wondering how terrified the boy had to have been, and how he probably thought if he couldn't see what atrocity was about to be levied on him, if he wasn't able to witness the terror, it wouldn't affect him. He'd probably been right: by the size of the hole in the back of his head, he never felt a thing.

We were allowed to drink that night and I came back wasted, blitzed out of my fucking mind. We'd drowned our outrage in as much local hooch as we could pour down our throats, puked, then drank some more. I couldn't remember anything, much less my name, which is probably the sole reason I was able to sleep. Because after, when I awoke and my mind was clear of the confusing effects of alcohol, I remembered what I saw and it wouldn't go away.

But then my eyes drifted to the word on the ceiling— *antidisestablishmentarianism*. I stared at it. I pronounced it. I found myself breaking the word into its composite parts. I noticed how it could be several different words. I noted how a simple addition of a prefix could change the entire meaning. I began to make smaller words out of the larger one, words like *British* and *animal* and *shiniest* and *heal* and *shit* and *mist* and *sin*. My entire universe became that word, and in the understanding of the letters I could be safe from the images of the dead little Muslim boy with the immovable arms, just as I would the dead little boy at the dining room table, the one who'd turned to his father as if to ask why the alien had shoved something in their stomachs and taken over their bodies.

Once we have a war there is only one thing to do.
It must be won. For defeat brings worse things than
any that can ever happen in war.

Ernest Hemingway

CHAPTER THIRTEEN

EVENTUALLY IT HAD to happen. One of us finished Phase I training.
I'd later find out her name was Ohirra. When the sound of the
bars retracting echoed through the facility late one night—at
least I thought of it as night, because it was in the middle of a
sleep cycle—all of us rose and ran to our own immovable bars.

Her cell was about ten down on the left. I craned my head and
watched as she took her first few tentative steps. After a few feet,
she stopped and stared at the place where Rodney entered and
exited the room, as if she were waiting for someone to realize
they'd made a mistake.

We all looked as well. I hoped she would be okay. I also knew
that there'd be those who wished her the opposite. I bet Olivares
was one of them.

After enough time had passed for even the most doubtful of
us to come to the conclusion that nothing was going to happen
to her, she straightened and began to do a combination of dance
moves, propelling her to the center of the room. There she did
a jig, then raised her face to the ceiling and screamed. Those of
us who hadn't been paying attention sure were now. She spun
several times in a circle with her arms held out, then sat, her
hands folded gently in her lap.

Five minutes went by. Then Rodney came, followed by two men in red jumpsuits. One handed her a set of clothes, and the other began setting up a small table and chair in the center of the room. She ran back to her cell with her clothes, while the men set the table with things provided by Rodney. Soon, the white tablecloth carried plates of fried chicken, steak, French fries, and sushi, along with a tall bottle of Sapporo and a glass.

Ohirra returned wearing her new gear. Urban camouflage with white boots. A strip of white T-shirt could be seen from the V of her camouflage top. I found the color combination odd, especially the boots and T-shirt. We didn't wear white when we went to war... unless it was meant to blend into wherever we were going.

She sat and began eating. I watched for a moment, then couldn't take it any longer. With a watering mouth I returned to my tablet and reviewed the curriculum I had yet to finish. It seemed like so much. As it turned out, I finished in about three more weeks. I wasn't near the front or the back, but in the middle of the pack. Michelle finished right after Ohirra. Olivares, the same man who destroyed two of his tablets, finished a day before me. Soon we were all complete, released from Phase I, and squarely into Phase II: small unit training.

After each of us had our own graduation meal—mine was a double cheeseburger with jalapenos and cucumbers, fries and a tall Belgian white beer—we began an exercise regimen designed to capitalize on cardio. I'd kept in shape in my cell, but my cardio had suffered. They turned the center of the room into an exercise area with a hundred different pieces of equipment. Rubber matting was included for martial arts and yoga. A track was laid around the circumference of the room, allowing for serious running.

So we exercised and learned small group tactics from our tablets, many of which I'd learned already, but wasn't aware of their origin. We broke into six person groups and got to know each other. I was partnered with Frakess, Thompson, Ohirra, and Aquinas. We'd originally had a Frenchman named Mateusz, but he'd had words with Olivares, who seemed determined to be around Michelle, no matter how much she ignored him. So Olivares forced his way into our group as well.

I thought about trying to change the course of events, but there was always one in every group.

"Grew up in Michigan," Frakess said. He was tall, with a wide Scandinavian face and piercing blue eyes above cheeks pocked from acne. "My folks were against me joining the military, but I wanted to be in the Navy so bad. Maybe it was all the movies, but it looked like one hell of a life."

"My father was in the Navy," Aquinas said. "He was a Navy mess chief. It was how he became a citizen. I would have grown up in Subic Bay instead of Seattle if it hadn't been for that."

The rest of us had our sleeves rolled up, but Aquinas and a few others, most of them women, had theirs rolled down. No one commented about them. We all sort of understood.

"501st APR," Olivares said. "82nd Airborne Division. *If you ain't airborne then you ain't shit*, and all that crap they used to make us sing during cadence." His face was pure hate as he said the words. "They drilled it into us that we could only count on each other. Taught us to hate everyone else. I could live with that. It was how I grew up."

"My name's Tim Thompson," said the quietest of us. Barely five feet four inches, he had elfin features. His normal speaking level was just above a whisper. "I was a drummer in the Marine Corps Band. All I ever wanted to do was play music. I never once thought it would be in Afghanistan."

I remembered reading in the *Stars and Stripes* about the suicide bomber who took out most of the band. Looking at the scarring on Thompson's face and hands, it was no mystery where he'd been on that day.

"I'm a Marine, too," Ohirra said proudly. I'd gotten to know the slender Japanese girl. She wasn't cocky, but she was confident, and so far she'd been able to back everything up, including being the master of the mat. Her father was a small circle jujitsu master. "I was never in combat, so I don't have the same stories as the rest of you."

She said more in that sentence than the rest of us had all day. What was it that had made her try and kill herself? What was in her past? What had she seen or done that made her hate herself enough to want to end it all?

I tried to get out of it, but it was Olivares who cornered me. "And what about you, Mr. Gringo? What's your story?"

I couldn't help but raise an eyebrow at his choice of name. It was stupid, really. How could he expect me to be angry with something so stupid? "U. S. Army. I'm a grunt through and through. Infantry. Until recently, assigned to the 173rd Airborne Brigade Combat Team in Logar Province. Spent time in Iraq and Bosnia as well."

Thankfully, that was enough. It might have been that they remembered me from our confessionals. It took awhile, but once I was able to hear Ohirra's voice again, I realized I'd recognized it. She'd never been in combat, but she'd killed a family of five one night drinking and driving. It'd been her twenty-first birthday. She never really drank alcohol, other than a taste here or there. But some friends had met her at a restaurant and proceeded to get her plastered. Ohirra had stayed in her car in the parking lot for hours afterward, trying to sober up. But when it began getting close to time for morning formation, she decided she absolutely had to leave. She'd never once been late to a formation and 'couldn't imagine living with the embarrassment of being late.' That's how she said it: *the embarrassment of being late.* Thanks to her size, her blood alcohol was still well above the legal limit when she took to the road. Plus, she'd hardly slept, nervous and jittery with terror at merely being in such a condition. Fate being what she was, Ohirra took to the road, and halfway back to base she crossed the center line. She caught herself at the last second and swerved back into her lane, but the damage was done. Bob Willis had decided to miss the traffic by driving at night. Taking his family back to New Jersey from their annual trip to Virginia Beach, he saw the oncoming car and swerved violently. The reaction caused his minivan to flip, and by the time the vehicle came to rest in the front yard of a retired Marine Gunnery Sergeant, the van was half the size it'd been just a few seconds before. The family never had a chance.

And after that, neither did Ohirra.

We couldn't be more different.

We couldn't be more the same.

A single event had changed her entire life, reforming her into something she'd never thought she'd ever become. Mine was the culmination of years, each event chipping away, reforming me into a hateful being. And here we were, me, Ohirra, and the rest of us, destroyers of lives.

After introductions, we were given a list of exercises and events we were supposed to do. We started with sparring.

No pads. No rules. We fought until someone gave.

It became very evident that Ohirra was the most talented on the ground. But standing up was another matter. While she had the edge, Olivares and Frakess had the bulk. They also had the strength. Frakess hit her twice in the face, hard enough she was rocked back on her heels. Olivares feinted to her face, then sunk a fist deep into her stomach.

I almost launched myself off the mat, but Aquinas grabbed me and shook her head. "Let her get out of this," she insisted. I glanced at her hand on my arm, just as she hurriedly pulled it away.

It was clear that both Frakess and Olivares had thought getting her on the ground was to their advantage. Twice they almost managed to tap her out by lying on her. Each time she was able to circumvent what had seemed a sure thing by locking their arms into chimeras and forcing them to tap.

We urged Ohirra to take a break, but she wouldn't have it. Aquinas was next. She kept her sleeves down and stood awkwardly. Three times Ohirra tried for a takedown, but all three times Aquinas slipped free, looking off-balance and scared. When Ohirra came in next, feinting a takedown and rising to grapple, Aquinas was ready. Her left leg shot out and caught Ohirra on the side of the head, sending her tripping sideways. When she recovered, the small Japanese-American girl gave the lithe Filipina-American a look halfway between surprise and suspicion. But Aquinas gave nothing away. She backed awkwardly, and moved clockwise around the mat. Ohirra held her hands out, ready to grab and attack. This time she feinted to the head and dove for Aquinas's legs, only to meet a knee dead centre in her face. Ohirra fell hard to the mat, her nose gushing blood.

Aquinas barely reacted. She walked calmly over to a table, grabbed a towel from a stack, and returned.

By the time she was back to the mat, Ohirra was sitting up, one hand cupping her nose. She accepted the towel as I helped her to her feet. I began escorting her off the mat, when Olivares stepped in front of me.

"Not so fast, Mr. Gringo. Let's see what you got."

I tried to ignore him and push past, but he shoved me hard enough to knock me back several feet. I felt the steam rise. I knew my face had turned beet red. I could never hide my anger. When I got pissed, it was like a neon sign was flashing over my head, which was one reason I'd gotten picked on as a kid.

Olivares grinned at me and unleashed a string of Spanglish that succeeded in putting my mother and the family pet in an awkwardly symbiotic relationship. Then he began to dance on his feet. I watched the way he carried his hands as his feet moved across the floor. He'd been trained as a boxer. I immediately knew I had no chance with my hands, but I stuck them up nonetheless. In fact, I wanted to see exactly what he could do.

He lunged in and snapped a lead left into my face.

My head rocked back. I felt my lips begin to swell.

He came in again, but this time I covered up. He switched to try and hit me with a kidney punch, I brought my elbows in and let his fist land on the edge of the bone.

He shook his hand. "So you've been hit before. Good, Mr. Gringo," he said happily. "But you haven't been hit by me. Not really. Not yet."

All the while he spoke, he danced around me. I stood in one place, light on my feet, turning to meet any attack he might launch.

He had me in weight, but I had him in height. His arms seemed about the same length as mine, the way his shoulders sloped down. But my legs were longer than his. It was all a matter of timing.

He came in again, his cockiness increasing. I ducked a right cross and let him hit me with his slower, weaker left. He caught me in the side of the head and I feigned hurt. Seeing weakness, he came in, first swinging for an uppercut. When that missed, he tried for several left hooks. I leaned into his range and grabbed him around the neck. While he began to punch me in the stomach, I raked my right foot down his shin and slammed it into his instep.

His reaction was immediate. He gave a little squeak and raised his foot. Which is when I did the same to his other foot. He backed away, hopping from one foot to the other.

"That's right. Dance, motherfucker, dance."

The Nunez brothers had taught me well. Born to surf and fight, each of them stood just over five foot two. They'd been in daily fights right up until the point their father had put them in martial arts. Six months later, there wasn't a fight they couldn't win. Their swift savagery destroyed any opponent's will to fight.

I stood a little taller as Olivares began to circle counterclockwise. Gone was his smirk, replaced by a grimace. He was tender on his feet. Exactly how I wanted him. He feinted twice with his left hand and I just smiled at him.

He came in quick. I brought my right leg up, but instead of kicking him high, I brought it down on the side of his knee, following through with a yell.

He dropped to the ground as his knee collapsed.

I stepped in to catch him with a right cross, but he blocked his face and head with his arms. Instead of hitting him where he expected, I brought a knife hand down on his carotid artery. He fell to the mat, his eyes rolled up into his head.

I'll give Aquinas credit. She'd shown professionalism; I didn't have any right now. I walked back to where I'd been, grabbed a towel, and sat down cross-legged. Everyone stared at me. I didn't even shrug. I just watched Olivares as the blood once again began to flow to his brain. His legs twitched. His arms spasmed. Then he snapped back to consciousness. Throughout it all, I had a smile on my face.

It was only when I registered the *WTF* look from the rest of my team that I realized that I'd done something wrong. And then it came to me, as my blood settled and my breathing relaxed: I'd let him get into my head. I'd made it personal. And although he was an asshole, there he was laying on the ground.

Now who was the asshole?

My face began to turn red again, but this time my anger was directed at myself. What the hell had I been thinking?

One minute can decide the outcome of the battle, one hour the outcome of the campaign, and one day the fate of the country.

Russian Field Marshal Prince Aleksandr
Vasilyevich Suvorov

CHAPTER FOURTEEN

"LISTEN UP, BOYS and girls. I'm going to show you how to kill someone eighteen different ways, using only your hands."

"And a bottle opener," someone added, from behind me.

Everyone who heard laughed. The muscle-bound behemoth standing in front of us looked like he drank a gallon of steroids for breakfast. He stood about five foot five and seemed to have shoulders as wide as he was tall. His arms were as large as my thighs. Even so, he was so fastidiously serious with himself that we could hardly stand it.

"Who said that?" he said, squeezing his hands into fists that could crush pool balls.

I'd seen his type before. An expert at fitness who parlayed his good health into the idea that he knew how to fight. Not fight on a mat in a studio, but fight during the piss and shit of war. These pretenders were all cut from the same cloth. The first time he was forced to run from one point to another with full battle rattle, a rifle and a helmet, he'd pull up with a strained muscle, screaming like it was the end of the world and never get to the point where he'd get to use any of his eighteen ways to kill someone, much less call 1-800-GETMEOUTTAHERE.

When no one spoke up, he continued. "You all might be experts at one or two things, but I'm certified in seventeen forms of martial combat, including..."

As the Giant Pretender rattled off a list of martial arts like he was a walking Wikipedia, I let my mind wander. This was the fourth expert to come into our facility to give us *instruction*. Now that we were in Phase II, they'd taken away our tablets. I never realized how much I'd come to appreciate that thing. I wished I had it now. My tablet was a lot less stupid than this shit, but then every military in the world had its own form of professional development where good-intentioned leaders brought in experts who ended up being ill-prepared for the reality of a roomful of soldiers.

Mr. Pink and several of the senior facilitators, now dressed in black slacks, shoes and Polo shirts with the red, stylized TF OMBRA logo on their left breasts, had been interacting with each of the groups. They'd been stressing the need for team building, which was ironic, since my team pretty much hated me. I'd beaten down Olivares three weeks ago and hadn't been able to get much traction since. We'd fought every day. As it turned out, the first day was to test our control. It looked like I failed. The next day they issued padded kicks, gloves and helmets.

"You," I heard from somewhere far away.

I unglazed my eyes and realized that the steroid monster was looking at me.

Pretending like I wasn't sure, I put on a patented *who me* look and pointed at my own chest.

He nodded. "Yes. You. Why don't you come up here and let me demonstrate?"

I glanced at my team beside me, but their eyes were everywhere but on me. No one wanted to help. Why should they? Every group had an asshole, and it looked as if I was that guy. I stared for a moment at Olivares, hoping he'd give me one of his snide smirks, but he was playing his part perfectly.

I shook my head.

"You want me to come up there, sir?"

"Yes, Sleeping Beauty. I want you to come up here so I can give you a kiss and wake you up."

I blinked as everyone laughed. I could feel my face turning red. "Seriously?"

Steroid Monster rocked his head back and laughed; it was surprisingly high pitched. "Of course not, genius. I need you to help me demonstrate moves. I need you to attack me." At this, he turned to the audience and grinned, all teeth and confidence.

My blood had begun to rise and I fought to keep it down. I excused myself to leave my row, then walked to the front of the room. I was dressed in the same urban cammies as before, but now, like everyone else, I wore white running shoes. The number 19 over my left breast showed which team I was on.

At the front of the room, I glanced back at the thousand-odd people staring back at me and turned to Steroid Monster. Although he was several inches shorter, he was as wide as a minivan.

"What's your name, son?"

I hated being called *son*. "Mason."

"Well, Mason, where are you from?"

"Los Angeles."

"Do much fighting there?"

"Some."

He smiled again. Teeth and confidence. "Good. I didn't want to get an 'expert,'" he said, his fingers making air quotes around his last word.

I sighed on the inside. Why was the world filled with so many asshats? I was so busy rolling my eyes on the inside that I missed what he said next.

"What?"

"I said, attack me."

"Any particular way?" I asked, wondering what he was up to.

"Surprise me." He flashed the crowd a smile again, and the first few rows laughed.

"Aren't you going to get into a stance?" I asked. He was just standing there, his right leg in front of him as he put his weight on his left leg, his hands resting imperiously on his hips.

"I'm good. Ready whenever you are."

He gave me a look that said *you can't do nothing to me, you sniveling little excuse for a man*. I'd never been one to be intimidated. I glanced once at the crowd, scanning the rows until I found the rest of Nineteen. They were all watching except for Olivares and Aquinas, who were deep in conversation. I saw a smile on her face, then a smile on his.

"Come on, son. We haven't got all day."

I shouted a loud *Keeya*, turned and in one swift move brought my right elbow down on his left thigh, just above his knee. I felt the point of my elbow dig through muscle until it tapped his femur. Then I stood and stepped back.

He crumpled to the ground, screaming.

I looked at the shocked crowd and gave them a smile. All teeth and confidence. Then I shrugged, and walked back to my seat. My team, as I suspected, didn't give me the time of day, which was fine. I didn't need them. After all, I was the designated asshole.

Mr. Pink and three others went to the front of the room. He directed that they help the man writhing on the floor, while he turned to the crowd.

"Looks like our 'expert'"—he aped the man's air quotes—"wasn't prepared for your expertise." He shook his head and shoved his hands in his pockets. He looked at home in front of a big crowd.

He pointed to me. "Sorry to do this to you again, Mason, but would you come up here?"

A low murmur went through the crowd, the collective sound of people who thought I was in big trouble. I felt the same way. I got up, excused myself yet again, and walked to the front, thinking of the dozen walks to the principal's office I made when I was a kid.

"It's okay. Mason isn't in trouble," Mr. Pink said. "On the contrary. He's demonstrated two very important things to you. Can anyone tell me what they are?"

I found myself looking at the ground. Being talked about in third person always made me uncomfortable.

"That he's a jerk?" someone offered.

It seemed as if everyone was laughing.

I stared at a space a thousand feet past my toes, nodding and smiling, as if I was part of the joke.

"No, no. I was talking about what he did up here," Mr. Pink said.

"We were, too," someone else said, to another round of titters.

Mr. Pink glanced at me. I caught his gaze. I could tell he wasn't happy. Then he turned his gaze on the audience. They soon shut up.

"What we've learned here is not to be reckless. Underestimating your enemy is reckless. You saw what happened to your instructor, right? He expected Mason to throw a punch or a kick; that Mason would demonstrate a move the instructor had practiced defending against a thousand times." He began to pace, but kept his head towards the audience. "You'll note, however, that I said *practice*. Which means he probably has never used it in real life."

"You been in combat, Mason?" he asked me.

"You could say that," I murmured.

"What? Speak up so the rest can hear you."

"You can say that. Yes, sir."

"You do any of those moves in combat?"

I envisioned the Hajji inside the second floor door of a house we were clearing in Baghdad who'd lost his knee the same way, right before the guy behind me double-tapped him in the head. "Yes, sir."

"Practical experience beats practiced experience every day of the week. Mason has used what he knows in combat. He's used it to survive. Laugh all you want. Call him a jerk all you want. But Mason is a survivor.

"Another thing we have to learn from this is expectations. It's a cliché and you've heard it a million times, but you must expect the unexpected."

He turned and pointed at me.

"Your instructor expected Mason to know one of the popular martial arts that deal with kicks, punches and joint locks. This is not what he knows. What did you train in, Mason?"

"Kapu Kuai Lua, sir."

"Kapa Kuai Lua, or Lua, is a Hawaiian martial art pre-dating King Kamehameha. It involves bone breaking, muscle bruising and pressure point manipulation. There are no high kicks. While they learn elements of joint locking, it's more to defeat the locks than to apply them. Is this right, son?"

I glanced at Mr. Pink, who was smiling.

"Yes, sir."

"And I can guarantee that your instructor had never experienced Lua before. I mean, who else but Mason in this room would have thought to dig an elbow into his thigh and bruise his femur?"

Not a single hand raised.

Mr. Pink nodded.

"I said I had two things. There are actually three. One of the reasons none of you would have thought of bruising the man's bone, aside from not knowing how, is that he's a fellow human." Mr. Pink rounded on me with a full-on glare. "Maybe when we recruited you all to this endeavor, you didn't understand what we said." He put his hands to his mouth and shouted. "We are about to be attacked by aliens, and the human race is under threat of extinction."

He paced to the other end of the front.

"Did everyone hear that?"

The crowd gave a resounding *yes*.

He turned to me. "Did you hear that, Private Mason?"

"Yes, sir."

"Then why do you keep hurting your fellow human beings instead of protecting them?"

I stared at him, at a loss for words.

"I asked you a question, son."

I shook my head. "I don't know."

"Bullshit. Why'd you do it?"

I shook my head again, then said, "Because he pissed me off." I didn't have to repeat myself. You could have heard a pin drop in the great room.

"You hurt a fellow human because he pissed you off." Mr. Pink moved straight at me. I backed up a few feet, but he only put his hand on my shoulder. "Listen, and listen close, everyone. This shit is real. The aliens are coming. They're going to invade and kill most everyone on the planet. There's literally nothing we can do right now. We're struggling to figure out a way to defeat them, but the amount of information we know about the enemy is pathetic. We can't fight ourselves before they even attack. We surely can't fight each other once they attack. We have to stick together. This isn't a matter of black, white, brown, red; this is about being human. We have this club, you see, and you are all members. To be a member, you have to be human. To be a member, you have to fight to save the human race. Nowhere in the club's charter is there room to fight each other and to hurt each other."

He let go of my shoulder, but I could still feel the weight of his hand.

"So fucking *stop* it. Get over it. This is not the world you knew. This is a new world, where the loss of even one of you could mean all of our doom. Do we understand each other?"

The crowd and I gave a resounding *YES, SIR*!

"Good. Then get this room changed around. We have more training to conduct. We need to be strong. We need to be ready. We need to be able save the planet, even if that means every one of us, me included, will die doing it. Because believe it or not, me and those like me were recruited for the same reasons you were recruited. To give us a second chance to make a difference."

Then he walked out.

I stood there, mind reeling. Until this very moment, I hadn't known what I'd felt for these people. They weren't part of my unit. My unit was back in Afghanistan. They weren't my friends. My friends were littered on the bomb-laden road of my past, scattered like ashes across all the good and bad things I'd ever done. They'd really been nobody to me. They'd meant nothing. I'd grown fond of Michelle only because she seemed worse than myself. In my hubris, I'd believed I had the power to save her, even when I couldn't save myself.

Each and every man and woman sitting in their chairs believed a variation on this theme. It wasn't something we'd done intentionally. But it was the result of committing oneself so entirely to undoing one's very being. We'd tried to not only kill ourselves, but the ideas of ourselves we'd created by becoming warriors. Somewhere along the way each one of us had made a decision, took a turn, or done something which we felt was incontestably the worst thing anyone has ever done. And to punish ourselves, we'd tried to pay the ultimate price.

But were we really that horrible?

Had we become so irredeemable that we had no way to overcome the events that had brought us to this point?

Could we not save ourselves, and in doing so, save everyone

else as well?

I realized that this was what Mr. Pink had been trying to say all along. It was the unifying force that tied each of us together. We no longer had our original units to return to. We'd denied ourselves any affiliation to them when we'd taken our own hands and tried to invoke destiny. Now we were part of a different unit. We were Task Force OMBRA. The unit had no regional or national identity. It was beyond red, white and blue. Instead, we had an idea—an idea which encompassed everyone in the great room beneath this broad Wyoming plain and imbued us with a sovereign responsibility, to be the absolute force to come together and fight for the survival of our species.

I stared at the assembled men and women who until recently had designed to kill themselves. But as I watched them, an interesting thing happened. The features of their faces, which had appeared forcibly subdued, took on a different life, as if each was just now realizing the combined force they represented. We'd joined in a single moment of catharsis when we'd all just figured it out. The culmination of all the books, all the movies, the osmosis, and the forced self-recriminations seemed to make sense at this moment. Alone we couldn't save anyone, much less ourselves, but together—*together*—we had the power to change the destiny of a planet, if only we could overcome our own ideas of guilt, innocence, responsibility and complicity.

Then it was as if they were looking at me for guidance.

I cleared my throat and stood a little taller. "You heard him," I said, my voice gathering power as I found the words. "Let's get this stuff moved and get back to training."

During the first two hours of the invasion no one knew what was happening. Everyone suddenly lost power. They had no way to call. They had no way to report or receive information. Even when we established generator power, there was no way to communicate without satellites. We had to send messages by *horse*. *We went from the Computer Age to the Dark Ages in a matter of minutes.*

Conspiracy Theory Talk Radio,
Night Stalker Monologue #967

CHAPTER FIFTEEN

WE LOST POWER for three days. We had generator power, but it left us in ridiculously low light. We were fed cold food and left to our own designs. For the most part, teams stayed together, and Nineteen was no different. I'd come to terms with my own behavior. I still didn't like Olivares—I thought he was a slimy dirt bag—but there was no denying his abilities. He was a crack shot in the simulators. He was a better than average fighter, especially now that he knew not to take other fighters for granted, thanks to my energetic lesson. He could also work well in a team, both as a leader and a team member. The days without power were spent conducting small unit leader's training, which involved problem solving and delegation, such as how to get everyone on the team from Point A to Point B without touching the floor and with minimal materials. The answers were always there, but they sometimes required counterintuitive deduction and teamwork to figure out. The sign of a good leader was one who listened to the recommendations of his or her team, processed them, then after analysis, developed a plan. The sign of a poor leader was one who listened and did what they wanted anyway. Olivares had proven himself to be a good leader, getting us through more obstacles than any one of us. In fact he did so well that everyone began deferring to him. Even me.

Thankfully, the team didn't give me an intervention. I was afraid they'd sit me down and embarrass the hell out of me. I knew I'd lost focus, that I'd messed up. I wanted to get over it, not talk about it. The speech by Mr. Pink did more to help me put things in perspective than anything else. After that I saw things differently.

Thompson was the one who really broke the ice. During workouts and sparring, I was included, but it was clear I was a sixth wheel. About two days after Mr. Pink's speech, we were stretching on the mat and Thompson, who was stretching beside me, asked if I'd show him some moves.

"Why is it you use your elbows so much?" he asked. He was the smallest of us and small boned. I had a sudden image of him lying dead on a dusty plain, his face upturned towards the sky with the same questioning look.

"When you think of a hammer, each part of it is hard, right?"

He nodded.

"But when you swing the hammer, it's the culmination of all the force into the head of the hammer that does the damage."

"Doesn't it hurt?"

"Only if I don't do the move right. Half an inch to the left or the right and I could shatter my elbow. It's a dangerous maneuver, but done right, it can be devastating."

"My father was a wrestler in high school and college. He was All State. He wanted me to follow in his footsteps."

"So why didn't you?"

Thompson turned his head slightly and smiled. "I liked music. After homework and church, there was only so much time in the day. I didn't want to spend all of my time doing exercises and trying to maintain weight like the other guys in my school."

"You don't like fighting very much, do you?"

"How'd you guess? The only reason I joined the military was to be in the band."

"And the Marine Corps, of all services. Did they have a special basic training for band members?"

Thompson shook his head. "No, unfortunately. Marine basic is the same for everyone. We all have to survive the Crucible."

"I heard it's the toughest. If you survived that, you must be tough. Sparring can't be more difficult than that."

"I survived," Thompson said. His gaze was fixed to the floor. It was clear he had more to say.

I offered a bit of my story. "I'm not sure about the Crucible, but our final field problem in basic training was terrible. We were beyond exhausted. We were cold. I've rarely felt anything worse."

"But you made it through," Thompson said.

"Just as you did."

Thompson brought his head to both knees, stretching his hamstring, grabbing the soles of his feet to pull himself completely down. When he spoke, his eyes were closed as his forehead touched his knees. "I cried, you know."

"We've all cried. I think I might have cried too."

"But you don't understand."

"Sure I understand. Crying is human nature. It's usually psychological rather than physical. We cry because our bodies are exhausted. We cry because of stress."

"I cried because I wanted to die."

I paused for a moment, reliving the worst moments of my own basic training. All said, they weren't as bad as I was letting on. I'd been in terrific shape and had understood the game and thought the training was fairly easy. The hardest part had been playing the game—allowing myself to be cut down so the drill sergeants could *remold* me.

"We've all felt that way, Tim. Don't be so hard on yourself."

"My father used to call me Sissy. He wouldn't call me Tim. He'd call me Sissy when I'd cry. *Hey, Sissy, stop crying. Oh, look, the Sissy is crying.* Or, *Hey, Sissy, get me another beer.* Then he'd take me into the basement and make me wrestle. He thought if he taught me I could try out and make the team. Be All State like he was. But he always ended up hurting me."

"Fathers can be assholes. Some people say that kids are lucky to survive childhood. It's not like our parents had to take a class or something. Hell, an adult requires more education to drive a car than to raise a child."

"A car can do more damage," Tim said, barely audible.

"Tell that to the parents of the kids killed by Eric Harris and Daren Klebold. Or the parents of the children in Sandy Hook murdered by Adam Lanza. Their parents should have had a license for certain." Even as I said it, I thought of the family in Alabama, the thing in the basement, and the teenager who'd walked into the school and killed the kids. *Tell that to the victims of Miss Anne's School.*

"My dad could have used a license," Tim said, after a moment.

"Then again, he might not have passed the test. And if he didn't, you might never have been born."

Tim was silent as if he was imagining what a parental test would entail. Then he laughed hollowly. "Maybe that would have been for the best."

"Then we'd be at a loss without you."

Tim smiled weakly.

"No. I'm serious. Your asshole father notwithstanding, the military has had a great tradition of drummer boys, going back to the revolutionary war. They couldn't march or move or communicate without drummer boys. I'm actually pretty thankful you're on the team."

"You're just saying that."

"Not at all. Mark my words. Sometime soon we're going to be in the shit. We're going to be fighting and you're going to come and save us. Your drums are going to make the difference."

"I'm not going to be able to take my drums into battle."

"There are all sorts of ways to communicate."

Suddenly the lights came back on and there was a cacophony of raised voices from across the room. Tim and I stood. I noticed Aquinas off to the side, staring at us, but now her attention was on the disturbance.

Ohirra and Frakess came up beside us.

"What's going on?" Ohirra asked.

"Yeah, what's all the excitement? It's just a little light," Frakess added.

A klaxon began to sound. We couldn't help but put our hands over our ears. The white lights dimmed and red safety lights began to flash. I looked around. Everyone was like me, bewildered and almost deafened.

I turned back to the crowd at the other end of the room. I picked out Mr. Pink in his black slacks and polo, shouting something to a similarly dressed man, who took off running past the row of open cells towards the intake point.

The men and women around Mr. Pink began to disperse. Some wore heavy frowns, while others grinned with hideous glee. Whatever the news, it was tremendous. I spied Olivares coming towards us. A tight smile cut across his face. It was then I knew. Glancing at some of the other teams closer to where Mr. Pink had met with the group leaders, I saw the reactions of those who were being told. Several just sat on the ground, their eyes staring towards a vision of something the rest of us couldn't see. Others stood, bodies crackling with energy.

"Gather around, Nineteen," he shouted over the klaxon, waving us towards him.

We formed a half circle in front of him, close enough to hear. Ohirra knew and I think Frakess knew, but the others showed no indication. When I looked up, Olivares was staring at me.

"Want to tell them?" he asked.

"Me?" I brought my hand to my chest. "I don't know anything. All I can do is guess."

"What's your guess?"

I don't know why he wouldn't just come out and tell us. I couldn't figure out why he insisted on dragging out the announcement. Fine. If he wanted me to tell everyone and steal his thunder, then I'd do it.

"The Cray have attacked," I said with solemn certainty. "How bad is it?"

Olivares nodded as everyone looked at him. "That's right, Sherlock. We've lost L.A, New York and Denver," he said.

I let *Sherlock* go. The news was just too devastating.

"Any news about Seattle?" Ohirra asked.

Olivares shook his head.

Ohirra sucked in air through her teeth. Aquinas put a hand on her shoulder and looked at Olivares for more information.

Thompson sat on the ground. "Oh, my God," he began repeating over and over.

"What about the rest of the world?" I asked.

"All satellite communication is gone."

"Gone?" Aquinas repeated the word.

"Like it was never there. But before it went, we heard from Paris, London, Rome and Tokyo. They've been destroyed."

"What?" I tried to imagine an Earth without London or Paris. Not that I'd ever been to either, but they seemed so old, so permanent. "But how?"

"We don't know. TF OMBRA is grabbing all the information it can—"

The klaxon ceased and the silence was filled with raised voices. The red lights stopped flashing and normal illumination resumed. We all turned towards the front of the room. Mr. Pink was moving towards us, listening to communications through a Bluetooth. When he got to the center of the room, he stopped.

"Come on, gather around. Find a seat," he said.

He sat on the seat of a Nautilus machine.

"By now you know the Cray have launched their attack. That they've been successful is no surprise. We all knew that in the first days of the invasion they'd have the upper hand. After all, they were able to learn about us for years. They were prepared."

Murmurs of speculation and outrage began to build, but he held up his hand for silence.

"There's nothing we could do about it. There's nothing we could have done to better prepare. We didn't know what we didn't know." He let the words sink in for a moment, then continued. "But now here we are. We have enough information to begin formulating a plan of action."

"What is it?" someone shouted.

"Yeah, what's the plan?" came another voice.

"How'd they do it?" someone else shouted.

Mr. Pink turned towards the last voice. "They seem to be completely biological in origin. Even their ships are biological. They also evidently have the ability to project EMP pulses. Although our satellites were shielded, the continual assault of EMPs knocked them out, along with most everything the militaries brought against them. Our planes literally fell from the sky as they came in for attack. Basically, the entire grid has been blacked out. The only reason we know anything is because of our remaining ground-based communication systems and that won't last for long."

That silenced everyone. It took a moment to digest the idea of a world without electricity. I tried to remember what I knew about electromagnetic pulses. We were once concerned with them as a side-effect of nuclear explosions; the blast and radiation would decimate a target, while the EMP would render all electronic equipment unusable. Is that what happened? Was everything now broken? If so, then how could we hope to win?

The murmur of conversation had risen again and Mr. Pink, waved it back down. "I see you all working through the problem. That's good. Also know that we have TF OMBRA's R&D Department working on it as well. In fact, we'll meet with them shortly."

This got my attention. What was he talking about?

"We're going to evacuate this facility in two hours. We're too close to Denver and don't want to lose you to whatever happened there, or whatever may be coming.

"Your team leads have their orders. You need to pack your own things, and we need to prepare food stores for the trip. Look to your leads and be ready. We may have to leave sooner."

"Where are we going?" someone asked, but Mr. Pink was already up and moving. Then voices crashed into each other as everyone began asking questions at once.

We all turned to Olivares. He grinned, but now, up close, I could see it wasn't a grin. It was a grimace, or a snarl, or halfway between both. He gestured for us to follow him, moving through the crowd like an ice breaker until he came to his room. We entered and gathered around as he sat on his bed. It was immediately much quieter.

"Where we going?" Frakess and Ohirra asked at the same time.

"Alaska. Make sure you get enough blankets, because it's going to be cold as hell. Now listen up. Here's the plan."

We need to invent new words to describe our fear. *Scared* and *terrified* can't aptly describe how we felt when our Earth was taken away from us. We used to fear the power of the government taking away money from taxes. We were truly a pathetic species.

Conspiracy Theory Talk Radio,
Night Stalker Monologue #1023

CHAPTER SIXTEEN

FEAR SMELLS LIKE vinegar, vomit, and body odor, or at least it did inside the Amtrak train we were on, heading north in the middle of the Wyoming night. We'd packed in such a hurry, I didn't really even know what was in the bag I was carrying. We were each given surplus duffel bags, which we stuffed with our few clothes and blankets, adding whatever food Rodney delivered, much of it wrapped in foil.

Then we ran down a tunnel we'd never been down before, lugging our duffels like we were first-time privates being screamed at by drill sergeants. But it was worse than that. Denver had been destroyed. A Cray craft of some sort had landed in the middle of the city and had taken root there like a living skyscraper. Casper was less than three hundred miles north of the once-great Rocky Mountain capital, and there was no telling if or when Cray foot soldiers would arrive. Already there were reports of power losses in Cheyenne. Casper would be next. And if Casper, then—

The tunnel took us to a light rail that ran seventeen miles and dead-ended at a blank wall. Stairs ran more than a hundred feet to the surface. We hustled upward, arriving up top huffing and puffing. We'd been working out, but the stresses of combat and fear were completely different on the human body. As we exited the stairs, we stopped and gasped, gripping our knees and our sides, clustered around the entrance.

Mr. Pink and his crew were already there, yelling at us to keep moving. A real train awaited us this time and most of us stumbled towards it. But I couldn't breathe. I stopped. Thompson was beside me. As I fought for air, leaning my head back, it felt as if I was on the surface of another planet. I didn't recognize the stars or the moon. Devils Tower loomed in the distance across a flat black plain. Humans had been here for millions of years; whether we stayed here beyond the next few months was up to us.

Thompson and I boarded, eventually finding the other members of Nineteen. We were crowded into our own coach room, sitting on two cloth benches facing each other. It didn't take long for the train to get underway. I'd never been on a train before, unless you counted the New York City subway system.

It smelled of vinegar. Ohirra claimed it had been wiped down with it. However the smell had gotten there, the inside of the train reeked of it. We opened the windows, but soon found the air getting too cold. Except for the moonlight shining through, the cabin was dark. Whether by design or not, the electricity had been shut off.

We sat in silence for the first hour until another recruit came down the hall, calling for all leaders to meet in the dining car, which was back near the caboose. Olivares got up and left without a word, leaving us to speculate on what was happening.

"Smells like vomit underneath the vinegar," Frakess said, his nose wrinkling as he pulled a blanket to his chin.

I sat between Thompson and Ohirra, who was next to the window.

Olivares had been sitting beside Aquinas. Frakess was on the other side, also by the window.

"Wonder what it was used for," Thompson mused in a barely audible voice. "Wonder how TF OMBRA got its own train."

"Same way it got its own underground facility," I said. "They probably bought it. My guess is it was probably a party train, traveling to Atlantic City or Vegas. I had an uncle who used to go on those. The casinos would pay their way and give them free booze, just so they'd come spend money."

"They liked all the money your uncle lost?"

"Hell, no. Listen to him tell it, he won every time."

"Then why?"

"Word of mouth. Everyone wanted to get his treatment."

"Will you stop it!" Ohirra spun towards me. "Don't you get it? Atlantic City, Las Vegas, San Francisco, they're probably all gone!"

I blinked at her, unable to respond.

"Did you think that all of the reading they made us do and all of the movies they made us watch was just for fun? Is all of this a joke to you?"

I didn't think I'd ever seen her this angry. "I never said or thought it was a joke, Ohirra. Take it easy. We were just talking."

"He didn't mean anything," Thompson said, coming to my aid.

Ohirra slammed back into her seat, pulled her blanket up and crossed her arms over it.

"We'll know what's going on when Olivares gets back." Frakess smiled, trying to defuse the tension.

"If he tells us," I heard myself saying. I didn't know it was going to come out, but since it did, I stood by it.

"Oh, knock it off," Aquinas said, each word a dagger.

"Wait a minute," I said. "I thought you didn't like him when we first met him."

"I didn't like you, either. I didn't much like myself. I didn't like anyone." Her eyes flicked to me, then back to the floor. "But you have got to get over yourself."

"What?" I didn't get it. I hadn't done anything to her. There was no mystery that I had my differences with Olivares. I'd been stationed with men like him before and knew their kind. I just didn't like them.

"Maybe she's talking about the way you look at him," Ohirra said.

I turned to her. When had this become a *let's fuck with Mason* intervention? "The way I look at him?"

"Like he did something to you." Thompson said.

"You too, Thompson?"

He couldn't meet my gaze and instead stared at the window.

"I need to get some air," I said, getting up and exiting the cabin.

The corridor outside the room was barely as wide as a man's shoulders. For some reason there was traffic, and I immediately had to press my back against the wall to let someone pass. I moved to the rear of the car and found a little breathing room by the door to the next car.

The door opened and shut as someone moved past. I smoldered as the draft stole through my thin garments. I was aware that we needed winter gear to go with our cammies, but I had more serious problems than creature comforts to deal with. Somehow, in my effort to be the good guy, I'd become the bad guy. How the hell had that happened? And how had Olivares become the good guy?

I breathed deeply, trying to bleed the stress from my system.

In Iraq, I'd had friendly rivalries with the other squad leaders, but I'd never hated any of them. So what was it about Olivares that set me off? I thought back to that moment when I first saw him, remembering the leering smile, and the predatory gaze when he'd looked at Aquinas.

I remember getting immediately angry, which in retrospect, seemed crazy. Why had I reacted that way? It wasn't as if me and Aquinas were together. She'd just said she hadn't even liked me—which demonstrated how skewed my point of view had become. I hadn't detected that vibe at all from her.

No. The more I thought about it, the more it seemed as if I'd taken on a responsibility I never should have. Olivares's predatory look had switched my protective instincts to DEFCON 1. Not that Aquinas needed protection. She was as messed up as the rest of us. At that time, what had made me think I had the capacity to protect her anyway? Just because I was a man? Just because I was a sergeant? I'd abrogated that role when I'd bailed on my unit.

Ultimately, Olivares was okay. Now I needed to figure out if I should say something. I could handle this one of two ways—either find a moment to pull him aside or do nothing at—

"Aren't you cold, Mason?"

I blinked into the cold wind flowing through the open door. Olivares stood there, a tablet in one hand, holding the door open with the other.

"Freezing," I said, after a few too many seconds. "You get us any coats?"

"Won't be any until we get to our destination."

"All the way to Alaska?"

"We're hoping we can turn on the electricity once we get into Canada, but that's seven hours away."

"We could freeze by then," I said.

"Not if we get friendly." He let the door close and clapped me on the back. "Come on. Let's brief the rest of the team."

He moved down the corridor ahead of me. I hesitated for a moment, then hustled after him.

Back in the cabin, everyone wanted to know what was going on. He told them what he'd told me and got the same reaction.

"Fact is," he began, "I think TF OMBRA, for all of its fancy training and techniques, was surprised. They didn't know where or when the attacks were going to be. They didn't know much of anything."

"I thought they had recon information," Frakess said.

Olivares shrugged. "They did, but what they saw weren't the warriors." He took a moment to let this set in.

"Not warriors?" Thompson repeated.

"Like ants," Ohirra said suddenly. "Or bees."

Olivares nodded. "The insect kingdom is all they have for an analogy. The brains of TF OMBRA—who we haven't met yet, mind you—are thinking along the same lines. They call it task-organized hierarchy."

"So there's a queen?" I asked.

"No. Yes. Maybe." Olivares shrugged. "We don't know. I doubt it's anything like we think it is." He turned to me. "Did you tell them what you saw in Alabama?"

I stared at him. Mr. Pink must have told him. Why wouldn't he have, after all? Olivares was the team leader.

"Mr. Pink took me to Alabama during Phase I," I said.

"You left?" Aquinas shot me a look.

"Mr. Pink wanted me to come with him. We went to Dothan, Alabama. There was a mass shooting and—"

"Wait." Frakess's face was a mask of rage. I'd never seen him angry before. "You mean you went on a field trip while we were locked up in the cells?"

"As I said, Mr. Pink took me."

"His name is Wilson," Olivares corrected me, as if it mattered.

"Fine." I fought my own anger. "Whatever." I wasn't about to tell them how close I'd been to killing myself. "He woke me up and took me." Everyone was quiet as I related what I'd seen. I could see the anger and confusion in their eyes, but they let me talk. I described the chaos of the scene at the school where the children had been killed. I told them about the house and the family of four at the dinner table. I even described the expression on the boy's face as he stared through dead eyes at his father, both of them turned into some sort of alien antenna by the monster one floor below them. Then I told them about the basement. I left out the reaction to the sounds and how I had tried to kill Mr. Pink and he'd tried to kill himself. But I described the polymorphic mass as best I could, to the point where everyone except for Olivares and me had looks of extreme disgust on their faces.

"Then he brought me back."

Everyone was silent as they let it sink in.

Olivares made eye contact with me and smiled slightly.

"What were we doing when you left?" Aquinas asked.

"Sleeping. All of you were sleeping and there were people taking care of you." I glanced at Olivares, who was now staring at our reflections in the window.

"What do you mean, taking care of us?"

Olivares turned and raised a hand. "We'll talk about this later. Right now, we're on the subject of the Cray." He glanced at me. "Before you all begin getting pissy with Mason, let me tell you that I was taken out of here during Phase I as well."

This got my interest. I'd been staring at my hands, trying to deflect everyone's attention, but when Olivares said this, my head snapped around. Was he telling the truth? Had he really been taken out?

"I went to Bemidji, Minnesota. A disabled war vet with a plate in his head stormed into a Wal-Mart and shot seventeen people before he was taken out. Mr. Pink, as you call him, went with me. We found the vet's home. His wife and adult daughter were sitting in chairs in front of the television, much like Mason described the family at the dinner table. It was like roots had grown through the floor and skewered them to the chairs."

Olivares paused to lick his lips. All eyes were on him.

"Downstairs we found some sort of reconnaissance alien. I don't know what it was. I'm not even sure it was the same species as the Cray."

Our assigned readings had been filled with the ideas that one species could conquer another and make it do its bidding. But where did it end? It was easy for humans to anthropomorphize aliens in their own image, with their own thoughts and ideas, but that was a road to nowhere. This wasn't an Edgar Rice Burroughs novel, where a soldier could find people to agree with on Mars. Humans had trouble agreeing with their own kind across a body of water, much less across an ocean of space. This was real life. In fact, it was much less about *why* and more about how to stop them. For whatever reason, aliens from across the galaxy had decided to raid our little piece of heaven and remove us from it. In order to save ourselves, we'd have to be able to understand the threat and figure out a way to counteract it.

"Why'd he pick you two?" Frakess glared at us.

Both Olivares and I shrugged, but Olivares was the first to speak. "Have no idea. I wish he hadn't."

But Frakess wasn't happy. It was clear he felt left out. He scooted into the corner and stared out the window.

"If he took two from each team," Thompson said thoughtfully, "and if each time there was a mass murder of some sort, then how many aliens are there doing reconnaissance?"

"And how many mass murders did that make?" Aquinas asked. Then she added, "Not that it matters in the face of an all-out invasion."

We found ourselves contemplating our own version of darkness. I began to try and imagine what the invasion looked like. Was it massive spaceships? Was it like in the movies? I wondered which author had come closest to the truth.

But Olivares brought us around. "All right, you nervous Nellies. Stop being so damned cheerful. We got a long, cold ride ahead of us. You want to talk about something, let's start talking about how we're going to survive this thing. I don't know about you, but I got a date with a senorita and a cerveza when this is all done."

A small smile pushed past my frown. He'd said what I'd expect most any sergeant to say, distracting us from thoughts of our mortality. Sex, alcohol and freedom were big sellers. Maybe Olivares really was okay after all.

Whoever said the pen is mightier than the sword obviously never encountered automatic weapons.

Douglas MacArthur

CHAPTER SEVENTEEN

WE ALMOST FROZE on the last seven hours of the trip. If we weren't close before, we were close now. Huddled together, rotating one person to exercise in the hall to heat his or her body, then welcoming them back within our flesh-on-flesh huddle. There was no place for shyness during the cold, and we kept ourselves warm as best we could.

I'd say we arrived in the middle of the night, but I wasn't sure if this was real night or the middle of the Alaskan winter. I just didn't know. Whatever the time, it was dark and frigid as we rushed single file down a street from the railhead to a large concrete bunker. Crossing the door felt like passing through the threshold between Heaven and Hell. My knees almost buckled as I entered, a blast of warm moist heat engulfing me from several blowers at waist and head level. I might have fallen, but we were packed so close together going down the metal stairs that I was held upright by the others. We'd left everything on the train by order, so it was just us, gripping the metal rail as we descended eleven flights, putting us more than two hundred feet beneath the surface.

The stairwell opened into a room that dwarfed our previous space, a huge natural cavern that may have been carved out of the rock by a subterranean lake. The ceiling was more than a hundred feet above the floor, which was itself at least a mile long. The walls were roughhewn in places, showing the marks where man-made tools had perfected what nature had already created.

A team of TF OMBRA officials in black military fatigues awaited us at a set of tables labeled with the initials of our last names. I got into the *M* line with several hundred other people. It reminded me of the cattle call when I'd first signed up at Fort Jackson, South Carolina—the shouting, the orders, the fumbling, and the carefully choreographed confusion.

Soon I found myself at the front of the line. A well-built woman with red hair in a buzz cut asked my name and I gave it to her. After a moment consulting her laptop, she shouted out a string of letters and numbers. A young man with acne scars and a flattened nose, his chest straining at his black T-shirt, began shoving things into a duffel bag. I watched as two pairs of tan boots, four pairs of desert-colored multicams, brown underwear, socks and t-shirts, and two wrapped packages were stuffed into the bag. Then he selected an already prepared rucksack and passed both to me.

"Report to Tin 22," the woman said, pointing off to the right, where I saw a line of men and women snaking towards the far wall.

I put my arms through the duffel so that I carried it on my chest, then shrugged into the rucksack. That done, I joined the line of folks with their gear. The procession moved slowly, but eventually we got close enough for me to see the cargo containers stacked from floor to ceiling and from wall to wall. There must have been hundreds of them, stacked twelve high. Ladders provided access to the higher levels and I could see men and women climbing up and down them. Here and there members of TF OMBRA were standing and changing into their new uniforms in full view of everyone. Nakedness didn't mean the same as it had before the invasion.

I arrived at the base of the stacks and looked around for Tin 22. I spied Ohirra first, already dressed in her new uniform and waving at me from six containers up and over to my left. I shuffled my feet past several men trying to find their own tins. One stopped me.

"Know where Tin 24 is?" he asked.

I was prepared to tell him no, then I realized the numbering convention. His was two to the right of ours. The numbers were painted in black paint on the underside of the ceilings just inside each container's open end. In the shadows of the entrances, they were easy to miss.

"There," I said, pointing.

His grimace of frustration changed to a relieved smile. He hurried to his ladder as I headed to mine.

Climbing with packs on the back and front was a precarious gamble. With my arms completely outstretched, they could only bend a few inches. I had to make sure I got a good grip, because the ground was dropping farther away with each rung I ascended.

Ohirra reached down the last few feet, grabbed my duffel and hauled it up, and I came with it. I stumbled into the container.

Olivares stood inside, already in uniform. Of course he was. He nodded in my direction, then turned back to folding his remaining kit and placing it in his rucksack in something more orderly than a shoved-in pile.

The container was wide enough for us to lay our sleeping bags perpendicular to one wall with a walking space at our feet. The rear was taken up by a table and chairs, as well as a couch and built-in closet. A door in the far right corner marked the water closet.

Ohirra had taken the space nearest the door. I looked inside, wondering if I wanted closer to the bathroom or closer to the exit. With no ventilation, the container, or our *tin* as they called it, would begin stinking in no time. I decided to unload my gear next to Ohirra.

I fished my fatigues out of my bag, and was soon wearing the new gear. I struggled into the boots, not willing to sit, then I found the rank. I held it and stared at it. Twin chevrons. Corporal. The back was covered with Velcro. I took the rank and applied it to the square on the front of my fatigues.

Ohirra had a rocker and a chevron. Private first class.

Olivares had three chevrons and a rocker. Staff sergeant.

I'd most recently been a staff sergeant. I'd been a corporal twice before, and could be one again. I just wished I'd gone back to being a staff sergeant.

Thompson and Aquinas made their way up the ladders next. Thompson found a place next to me. Aquinas took the spot on the other side of him, which left a space for Frakess between her and Olivares.

"Oy! Is this 22?" came a voice with a distinct Scottish accent.

We all turned to see a wide-shouldered middle-aged man with a shock of blonde hair and 1970s sideburns standing on the lip of our tin.

"I'm PFC Ohirra," said our welcoming committee. "And yeah, this is Tin 22."

"Then I have the right place. Where's the sergeant?"

Olivares stepped forward and the new guy dropped his gear.

"Staff sergeant, Lance Corporal James V. MacKenzie, British Royal Marines, reporting for duty, sir." The Scotsman saluted, palm out, and brought his heels together.

"Lance corporal. We call that private first class here." Olivares shot me a glance.

"If you will, please, I'd prefer to be called lance corporal," MacKenzie said, eyeing everyone nervously.

"Fine, if you're going to be so fucking polite about it." Olivares pointed next to his bag. "Put your stuff there."

MacKenzie shouldered his way gently through us, excusing himself each time.

"Wait, where's Frakess?" Ohirra asked Olivares.

"He's been reassigned," Olivares said. "By his request."

"You can do that?" Thompson asked. "You can just ask to be reassigned? Really?"

"Thinking of a change, drummer boy?" I asked.

"No. I was just wondering why he'd want to leave us."

I gave Olivares a look and he nodded. "Must have been something we said," I commented. It had been clear the man was pissed at not having been chosen to leave the base during Phase I. Had I been given the choice, he could have taken my trip. Getting angry about something like that, something over which we'd had no control, was idiotic. Good riddance.

Thompson made his way to MacKenzie's area and watched as the newcomer inventoried his things.

I thought it was awkward the way he stood there, but I didn't want to say anything that might hurt the boy's pride.

But Aquinas didn't have that concern. "This isn't a zoo, Thompson. Stop staring at him."

Thompson turned. "Huh? Oh. I was just looking."

"*Look at the Scotsman in his native habitat,*" said MacKenzie in the voice of a TV announcer. "*Dangerous when not fed, the Scotsman can be seen rooting in bogs for whiskey seeds and chicken fingers.*" He turned and grinned.

Thompson laughed. "He's funny."

"He's also right there," Ohirra said. "You don't have to talk about him in the third person."

Thompson nodded but didn't say anything. Finally he asked MacKenzie, "What's the V for?"

"Victory," MacKenzie announced proudly.

I shook my head. "No, it's not."

"You think you know better? It's my name after all, mate."

"Might be your name, but we know you aren't being truthful. Shame on you," I said, shaking my head. "The V is your scarlet letter you have to wear, so we know where you've been, what you got, and why you have to scratch so often."

Thompson gave me a questioning look, then his eyes shot wide. "Oh, shit! Is it true?" Thompson made a face and turned to MacKenzie.

I grinned from ear to ear. My work here was done. MacKenzie gave me a dirty look, but there was a smile behind it.

How much time did we spend fighting amongst ourselves instead of preparing to fight an alien invasion? Sophists would argue that we didn't know we were going to be invaded, so it really wasn't our fault. To this I drop the bullshit flag. The very idea that we are alone in the universe is like a child closing his eyes and thinking he's alone in *his* universe.

Conspiracy Theory Talk Radio,
Night Stalker Monologue #921

CHAPTER EIGHTEEN

As IT TURNED out, Lance Corporal Jim MacKenzie of the Royal Marines might have been the best thing to happen to us during this end-of-the-world alien invasion. Ohirra clearly had a thing for him. Thompson treated him like a new puppy. Both Olivares and I found ourselves cracking up at his war stories. Even Aquinas smiled every now and then. Not that there'd been anything wrong with Frakess, but MacKenzie seemed to be the piece that had been missing from Team 19, or Tin 22, or whatever they were calling us today.

There was a lot of conversation about what was going to happen next. What kind of unit would we form? Would we be some elite special operations element, sneaking behind enemy lines? Did enemy lines even exist? We didn't know anything about what was going to happen, and damned little more about the aliens.

Luckily, word was sent around that there was going to be a briefing. We prepared our uniforms until they were STRAC, then queued with everyone else as they made their way to the main area.

A raised stage was set against a section of cavern wall painted white. We'd been stood waiting for about half an hour when a video image appeared on the white wall. First it was of a family visiting the Empire State Building. A woman and a little girl smiled into the video and waved, then the camera panned Central Park.

Then the image went black.

There wasn't a sound in the entire place.

The image came back on, shakily. We watched as a half-mile long spike, pointy end towards the sky, thick end alive with thrusters that seemed to be controlling its descent, landed in the middle of Central Park. The ground shook, causing the camera operator to lose his balance for a moment. When the view was once again still, we saw the entire length of the creature. Now it looked less like a spike and more like a slender mountain, or a galactic-sized termite mound, like I'd seen on television shows about Africa. I could make out shadowy depressions along its entire length, but I couldn't imagine what they could be used for.

Then creatures began to soar from them, whirling into an angry cloud near the pinnacle of the spike. From the camera's viewpoint, each of the creatures seemed tiny, no larger than an insect. But their size was skewed by distance.

The whirling mass increased in size until there were tens of thousands of the creatures, intertwining in a cloud that itself began to twist and turn like a tornado.

The tornado spun towards the camera. Before the person holding the camera could turn and run, a flash of light burst from the onrushing creatures. The image pixelated, then went black.

The lights came back on. Everyone was still staring at the wall. This was what we had to fight? Those things? Us? I couldn't see it. I couldn't imagine how. I felt hollow inside; my heart filled with despair. I began to drift towards the version of myself who'd wanted to end it all, to find a place where this wasn't reality.

But Mr. Pink had something else in mind. He waved at a guy, who pushed forward something draped under a tarp. When it was in front of the crowd, he motioned for everyone to be silent. Then he grabbed one edge of the tarp and jerked the cover free.

The collective intake of breath was so loud it seemed to fill the cavern. I couldn't stop staring at the legs and arms and wings, each joint knobbed with a spike, arms ending in claws several feet long. It was seven feet tall, but looked as if it could stand much taller. Three pairs of wings arched behind its back, ready to send it skyward. Its head, triangular like that of a praying mantis, was tilted at an angle as if it was appraising the assembled mass of TF OMBRA. Its eyes were clustered in the centre of its head, like a spider's.

"Those creatures you saw exiting the mound in the video are this," Mr. Pink said.

He flipped the image back on and rewound it until it showed the twisting cloud made up of thousands of these things.

"For now we're calling these things drones."

"Fucking bad *ass*," a guy standing next to me said.

Mr. Pink brightened. "My sentiments exactly." He walked up to the drone and knocked on its head. "This, of course is not a real one. As far as I know we haven't killed any. This is a three-dimensional representation based on the footage we've been able to gather. I want everyone to study this. I want you to make yourselves very familiar with it. If you get close enough to see one in the flesh, it might be the last thing you see."

Then he nodded at the assembled mass and walked away.

A hulking man in TF OMBRA fatigues and a red beret strode to the center of the stage. His tanned skin looked like a hundred miles of bad road. His nose lay against his face above a handlebar mustache.

"All right, you grunts. I'm your regimental sergeant major for the next however the fuck long it takes you to figure out how to work together so we can save this sorry globe. Everyone gets a speech, even at the end of the world, and you sad lot are no different. You all come from all corners of the world, from countries I can't pronounce, and places I'd never want to go. Some of you were born rich, others poor. We have men and women and everything in between. We have people who were once soldiers, sailors, airmen, Marines. We have active military and reserves. We have paramilitary police, paramilitary snipers and parachutists. We have men who've lived aboard submarines, women who've flown jets, and some who played in the can-you-believe-it marching band. We have people from all races, creeds, religions, nationalities, and social affectations. All of you were different when you stumbled your pathetic frozen selves into this place at the asshole end of the world. But that difference stops now. As of this moment, you all are the same. You are no longer any of those things you were before. All of those labels cease to exist. From now on you'll be one thing—*grunts*. This is what you call yourself, this is what you will be called, and this is what you do. Do you understand me, grunts? Do you understand your new role in life?" His voice rose to a bellow. "*Do you understand me, grunts?*"

After a moment of stunned silence, the pride that had been welling up within us escaped into thunderous applause. The RSM grinned before striding towards the drone and stared at it with all the drama of Dr. Charles Darwin seeing the Galapagos for the first time, hands on hips, eyes wide, mouth twisted into a sneer.

"Pretty big fucker, isn't it? Looks like it could mow down half of you before you were able to get your dicks out of your hands and around the stock of a rifle."

In one smooth move, he jerked a knife from his web belt and sunk it to the hilt in the center of the beast's head.

"He ain't so tough. I think I can take him. But then again, I'm the RSM in charge of a brigade filled with grunts, so I know how badass I am."

He glowered at us. From this distance it looked almost like a smile, if you missed his feral lean and predatory look.

"Now get your asses in gear and head to your teams. I want every team sergeant to give me an inventory of all equipment and a list of what's missing by 0400. Breakfast is at 0430. Training begins at 0515 sharp."

Everyone looked at each other. Like me, they didn't even know what time it was.

"I said MOVE!" he shouted, and his bellow set our feet in motion.

Before a war military science seems a real science, like astronomy; but after a war it seems more like astrology.

Rebecca West

CHAPTER NINETEEN

TIME WASN'T ON our side. It never was. Local time was 0430 and since we were finished with our inventory, it was chow time. We bumped and elbowed each other as we prepared ourselves, then scrambled down our ladders to powdered eggs, powdered potatoes, and reconstituted sausage patties. We drank coffee like it was a drug before making our way to the main hall.

TF OMBRA was going to be used to form the infantry portion of an infantry brigade combat team, or BCT OMBRA. A BCT was a recent phenomenon for the U.S. Army, which had been organized around the brigade structure since World War II. After spending decades with a constant need for a task-organized, quickly deployable force, the U.S. Army had finally created one. Replacing the brigade element is the brigade combat team, which had been streamlined to provide more combat forces and less administration and logistics. A regular BCT numbers between thirty-three and thirty-four hundred soldiers and is meant to be moved from one place to another within seventy-two hours.

BCT OMBRA was to be comprised of two infantry battalions, a reconnaissance squadron, fires battalion, a special troops battalion and a brigade support battalion.

Each infantry battalion had a headquarters company, three rifle companies, and a heavy weapons company. The headquarters company was assigned a medical platoon, reconnaissance platoon, fire support platoon, anti-aircraft defense platoon, signal section, sniper section, and staff section. The rifle companies had three rifle platoons and an anti-aircraft defense section. The heavy weapons company had four weapons platoons assigned.

The special troops battalion had the signal and military intelligence companies I expected. But they also had an electrical engineer section, a mass propulsion section, and a xenobiological section. These new sections were clearly to address the Cray.

The fires battalion had two batteries of 8-inch Howitzers, equipment which hadn't been used in the U. S. inventory for more than two decades, and a fires acquisition battery. Two Howitzers had been brought into the training area and were to be used to retrain the artillery men and women how to use the older, slower, but much more powerful artillery pieces.

The reconnaissance battalion had a headquarters company, two reconnaissance companies, and a special reconnaissance company. The SRC was comprised of twelve infantry squads, a sniper section and a communications section. No longer Team 19 or Tin 22, we were now known as 3rd Recon Squad, Special Reconnaissance Battalion, Brigade Combat Team OMBRA.

Once the unit organization was laid out, we separated into our battalions, then our units. One problem I saw right away was that we didn't have any weapons or body armor. And it wasn't just recon. The infantry units didn't have any weapons either. But after a hurried conversation with the RSM, our non-commissioned officers returned and told us not to worry about it. The equipment was on the way.

We immediately began to go over basic infantry maneuvers by squad. We'd practice later, but for now our instructors, more black-fatigued TF OMBRA men and women, wanted us to be able to learn and regurgitate basic infantry maneuvers such as traveling, bounding, overwatch and combinations therein. Olivares and I knew them, but neither Ohirra, Aquino nor Thompson had ever practiced them. MacKenzie knew them, but he called them by different names. Once he grasped the concepts, he was able to spit it all back to the instructors, and soon we were all speaking the same grunt language.

But something was missing. Not only didn't we have the right equipment, but we didn't have a target. These maneuvers were meant to attack something on land. Moving from one piece of cover to another didn't mean a thing with a hundred thousand Cray flying overhead who could see your every move.

"Do you ever wonder how many species there might be?" Thompson asked one day after training.

"All the time." We all wondered, usually pushing the overwhelming ideas into the farthest, darkest corners of our minds, back to where the creatures in our closets flourished and the beasts under our beds lived.

Thompson stared at the palm of his hand. "What if there are some we can't see?"

"You mean like invisible?"

"No. Not really invisible. But what if there are aliens so small we don't even recognize them?"

I stared at the smallest member of 3rd Recon. The idea of something so small never crossed my mind, but now that it was there, I felt the impossibility of combating it.

"I remember when I was a kid living in Iowa," Thompson began, his forefinger of his right hand brushing away something invisible in the palm of his left. "I used to chase the white cotton that flew from dying dandelions. I'd capture it and stare until the ball disintegrated, and I wondered if I was seeing a universe in microcosm. I always thought, what if this is a colony and they were suddenly removed from life as they knew it, carried by winds they had no control over?"

He glanced quickly in my direction, but I merely smiled. I was entranced by what he was saying. I wanted to hear more.

"Remember that movie awhile back where the plants on Earth turned against us? They let off some sort of pheromone that set us to killing each other, sort of a way for our planet to weed us out." He turned back to his hand. "Remember that, Mason?"

"Yeah. I remember."

"What if the aliens were like that? What if they were so small you couldn't see them? What if even now I'm like the finger of some retarded god poking into a universe I didn't even know existed?"

"Where would these microscopic aliens live?" I asked after a few moments.

"Everywhere. Anywhere. In here," he said, pointing at his head. "We already know that there's a species of Cray that can invade our bodies and control us, or make us kill ourselves, or just make us die. What would we do?"

Thinking about videos we'd seen, from Japan, of people ripping into each other, I wondered. Was it as simple as that? Were the Cray making us kill ourselves? If they were capable of that, then why send drones? Why not just send in their microscopic army to make us fight each other?

"Maybe it doesn't work on every species," I said. "They'd have to have an expectation of certain brain activity. They probably knew how our brains were constructed through their reconnaissance. They could have even tailored the other species to attack us more successfully." I remembered seeing footage of one man holding his daughter, right before another woman came and bashed his head in. "But it doesn't work on everyone."

Thompson smiled broadly. "No, it doesn't." He smacked his hands together so loud I jumped. "It works on most, but not everyone. I wonder if TF OMBRA knew something about that. I wonder if they chose us exactly for that reason. You know there are some scientists who believe that suicides have different brain chemistry."

I regarded him. I'd been humoring him at first, but the drummer boy might be onto something. "That would suggest they know more than they've let on."

"They've been sharing knowledge as we need to know it."

"Are you saying they're working *with* the aliens?"

"No, not at all," Thompson said. "Although I wouldn't put it past them. What I'm saying is that they've known for some time. They knew enough to choose us because they know that our brains are the only ones that can't be affected by the Cray."

I laughed. "This is supposition, wrapped in conspiracies, stuffed with a suicidal filling. You don't really believe this, do you? Don't forget, that thing in the basement in Alabama was all over the inside of my mind."

"That might be something only the Sirens can do." Thompson shrugged and resumed picking at an invisible universe in the palm of his hand. Then he looked up. "Why not a conspiracy? I have a lot of time to think. I spend my life trying to figure out the *what-ifs*. This is no less logical than that TF OMBRA just figured they'd go to all this trouble just because it's a no-return mission. I mean, heck, it'd be a lot simpler just emptying the prisons or asking random soldiers from around the world if they wanted to either save the universe or be killed by an alien invasion."

And then he was silent.

I wanted to laugh at him. I wanted to scoff at his theory, but like most good theories, it had enough logic to make me wonder if he didn't really have a better idea about what was going on than the rest of us.

I got up and headed back to our tin with a new respect for our little drummer boy. He might be crazy, but he was *our* crazy, and who knew, he might just hold the secret to beating these damned aliens between the beats of the drum in his mind.

You, you, and you... panic. The rest of you, come
with me.

Anonymous U.S. Marine Corps
Gunnery Sgt.

CHAPTER TWENTY

THREE MONTHS PASSED.

We gathered for briefings at regular intervals as footage
of the world's decimation was shown to us from cameras
found outside of Cray-occupied areas. With all aboveground
communications arrays compromised, only subsurface and
subsea communications methods were working. Project Unity,
which was completed in 2008, had created a ten-thousand-
kilometer undersea fiber optic cable system linking North
America with Asia. Multiple cables tapped into this network,
creating an electronic pipeline capable of transmitting almost
eight terabytes of data per second. At the time of its creation,
Project Unity had added twenty percent to the world's data
capability, but after the invasion, it became a hundred percent.
Without it, BCT OMBRA would be living in the black, surviving
on supposition, rumor, and conspiracies.

By day we saw the destruction of Los Angeles, Moscow,
Beijing, London, Prague and a hundred other cities. When Tokyo
went down, we all began shouting for Godzilla, half-joking and
half-wishing.

By night, we talked about it all. With no booze, no drugs
no music and no movies, we had nothing but stories acros

proverbial camp fire. But what do you talk about when the most terrifying thing has already happened? You talk about what could be worse, such as the possible nefarious purposes behind the formation of OMBRA.

We talked about Thompson's idea about our brain chemistry, and the more we spoke about it, the more it seemed to be a possibility. Our conversations sparked a wildfire within the tins. Our little drummer boy, honoring his profession in the best of ways, had laid down a beat to which everyone had begun marching.

Then one day Mr. Pink met with us. We expected bullshit. We expected to be lied to. The last thing we expected was the truth.

"I've heard the rumors," he told us. "I understand your frustration. First let me say that we have a delivery being made right after my speech. This delivery will change our way of fighting the Cray. It will make all the difference in the world. It will give you a chance to kill them, and it's better than anything we had before. It's a prototype. More are being made, but this is what we have thus far."

A rumble of conversation soon drowned him out. But then the RSM came on stage and ordered us all to silence. It took him several tries, but eventually, grudgingly, we stopped talking.

"So I've heard that you all think you were chosen because your brain chemistry is different from 'normal' people's, that having suicidal thoughts rewires your brain." Mr Pink said. "I've been told that this is the most ridiculous theory anyone has ever wasted the time to create. I've also been warned that I shouldn't tell you the truth. Let me dispense with all of this

face you like a leader.

ight."

it was.

rily forgot about the promised salvation and

listened to him as he began to talk to the geography of my mind.

"We knew early on about the Cray's ability to use the human brain as a transmitter. We have forty-four members of BCT OMBRA who we allowed to witness the vile subjugation of the human consciousness. These men and women, whom I shall refer to as the Forty-Four, will be made available to speak to each and every one of you, to carry the word, the truth, to the darkest corners of this cavern. It's important that all of you know. That all of you see."

He swallowed and sought me out from amongst the thousands, as if he knew exactly where I was standing. "Until then," he said, "let me share with you the results of one afternoon in Dothan, Alabama.

"Lights!"

The lights went out and a scene I knew very well began to play out on the screen, from the POV of one of the assault team.

We saw the team break through the door and rush into the dining room.

A collective gasp seemed to shake the room.

The view shifted first to Mr. Pink, then to me, and I saw for the first time how terrified and sickened I was at the sight of that family. My fellow soldiers began to glance at me and I ignored them, my gaze riveted to the screen.

Then the stairs, then the basement, and then the—

Cries of shock and disgust filled the cavern as we saw the polymorphic mass. I clamped my hands over my ears as those baby heads began screaming. Even with the electronic filtering, I could see the effects of the alien siren song on those around me. Their eyes glazed over. Their hands became claws which opened and closed, finally resolving into fists. Their faces sagged as the weight of the universe and everything they'd ever done and left undone settled on their consciences.

M*A*S*H had it all wrong. Suicide isn't painless. It's the end of pain, and there's nothing worse than the pain one's own mind can exert upon one's soul.

The sound snapped off.

The lights switched on.

But the image of Mr. Pink and myself and our weapons remained frozen on the screen—Mr. Pink's gun to his own head and my gun pointing at him.

Thank God the guns had been empty.

"We're just now learning how the aliens manipulate the chemistry of the human brain to their advantage. For the most part, you all are immune to the Cray. They can't use you like they can the rest of humanity. Your minds are shadowed to them. The only way they seem to be able to affect us is with this polymorphic mass we're calling a Siren.

"Our scientists compare our immunity to our own serotonin deficiency. One of the metabolic products is a chemical called 5-hydroxyindoleacetic acid, abbreviated as 5-HIAA. Through autopsies and drawing spinal fluid from the living, our scientists have found decreased levels of 5-HIAA, as well as amino acid tryptophans. The bottom line is that what made you the way you are is what's going to allow you to be able to get close enough to kill the Cray.

"The Forty-Four were there. They can testify. They've seen the power the Siren can exert on the mind. Listen to them when they speak to you. Ask them questions. Don't let them leave with anything unasked or unsaid.

"We've also been able to ascertain that using the human brain, the Sirens pulse their information in bursts of layered code. So far we've been able to find three distinct layers. The top layer was a distress signal, intended to provide proximity data. The second layer was geological and meteorological information, to include the water and salt content in the atmosphere. The third, and perhaps the most interesting, was the schematics of all electrical infrastructure grids on the planet."

He let that sink in.

Then he stepped forward.

"Now for my surprise."

Modern American war is as easy to script as a B movie.

Colonel David Hackworth

CHAPTER TWENTY-ONE

THERE WILL ALWAYS be those who think that science fiction authors copy the best ideas and discard the worst, pillaging effortlessly from the body of work that has come before. The fact is, modern realities and an author's own insistence on following the physical laws of the universe limits possible choices, especially when trying to construct something that can protect the wearer while enabling him or her to cause as much damage as possible. So when the Faraday Suit was revealed, none of us were really surprised. We'd read Scalzi and Steakley and knew how they'd portrayed power armor and powered exoskeletons. Did they copy from Heinlein's *Starship Troopers?* Had he copied from E. E. Doc Smith's *Lensman* novels? Was Ridley Scott a big old cheat for letting Sigourney Weaver use one to defeat an alien? Or was it a simple reality that the limitations of our imaginations reflected the physical certainties of our universe, that there were only so many things we could actually do to stay alive in a hostile environment or against a hostile force with greater physical attributes?

Whatever the truth of it, the entirety of CBT OMBRA gasped, then cheered as a man in a powered exoskeleton walked noiselessly from the shadows to stand beside Mr. Pink, half again taller than the slim gentleman in the black fatigues. Like a used car salesman at the end of the world, Mr. Pink ran down the important elements of the suit for us, including the thirty anti-aircraft missiles resting in a left shoulder array which he called a Mini-Hydra. This was complemented by an XM214 rotating-barreled machine gun and what we'd come to learn was a harmonic blade. These, he said, were the *martial trinity of the Electromagnetic Faraday Xeno-combat Suit (EXO)*. The suit was designed specifically to keep the wearer alive against the mass attacks of the Cray drones. Inside, an intentionally rudimentary electronics package was protected by an electrified micromesh that completely covered the outside skin of the suit, itself creating a miniature Faraday cage which would protect it from the electromagnetic pulses generated by the Cray.

Half an hour of marching back and forth on the stage, and every one of us wanted to get into an EXO. Like an infantryman with a new rifle, a teenager with a new car, or a child with a new toy, each of us imagined the joy we'd feel once we strapped in, switched on and locked out. My entire body itched with the need to wear the suit.

Then came the news that they only had twenty ready.

We'd have to share.

We broke into our groups and waited for orders to filter down from the RSM. As it turned out, Recon was given six of them, probably because when we finally made it out of our underground lair and into the war, we'd be the first to wear them, the first to lay our asses on the line. All grunts might be equal, but some grunts were a little more equal than others. Recon was among them.

I'll give you this. Olivares could have decided to take a turn in the suit first, but instead, he let us draw straws. MacKenzie got it first and we laughed our asses off as he struggled to wear it. There wasn't even an instruction pamphlet. This was all trial and error.

"Hope I don't set off these missiles trying to find out how to close this *focking* thing," he cursed.

And then we watched as he trundled around the cavern like a storm giant come to Earth.

And then it was my turn.

And then it was everyone else's.

And eventually, we figured out how to use them just in time to take a slow boat to East Africa, where we'd find a way to beat the Cray or let the world die as punishment for our mistake.

Another shooting. Another apparently perfect neighbor walked into a public school and blasted seventeen kids and five teachers. Now the experts are telling us that the person was disturbed, that he'd been under treatment. Do you own a weapon? Have you ever sought counseling from a mental health professional? You know, like a priest or a rabbi or a psychologist? What would they say about your past if you went into a school and began shooting people? What is that? You say you'd never do that? Maybe that's the point of all of this. Maybe the guilty would never do this either. Maybe it wasn't them. Maybe they were made to do it. I've asked a lot of questions today. Answer the question if you dare. What do you believe?

Conspiracy Theory Talk Radio,
Night Stalker Monologue #466

PART TWO

Africa has no future.

V. S. Naipaul

CHAPTER TWENTY-TWO

ACCORDING TO HEMINGWAY, Kilimanjaro means 'House of God'—
as fitting a place as any for humanity to make its last stand. Both
the story *Snows of Kilimanjaro* and the movie with Gregory Peck
were on our tablets in Phase I. I have to admit, I liked the story
better. There was a sense of something impending and momentous
in the story, whereas the movie was only concerned with death
and regret. The battle between those ideas—of predetermination
and redemption—had become the fuel for our trip across the
Pacific to this remote African mountain in the heart of Tanzania.
After all, we were going to save humanity, redeem ourselves from
who we'd become, and transform ourselves from meager grunts
to great heroes. We might die doing it, but if we did, we'd do so
knowing it was in the service of mankind, with no regrets and no
complaints.

Whatever the truth was, I think Jimmy MacKenzie called it
right when he decreed it to be the *big focking mountain at the
end of the world.*

And as we stood there on the flat African plain, staring up at
it, the only thing that seemed larger than the mass of Kilimanjaro
was the Cray Mound.

The journey from Alaska to Africa had taken thirteen weeks.
Wrapped in the putrid bowels of an old oil tanker, we cruised
south through the Pacific, cutting between the Antarctic flow and

the southern coast of Australia. We tried to stay away from land. Drones seemed to be unwilling to brave either the water or the cold.

Especially the cold.

Somewhere south of Fiji a drone found us and gave chase, only to run out of energy. With nowhere to land other than the tanker we'd named the *USS Liberator*, it crashed to the deck and pulled itself into a ball to protect itself.

MacKenzie and a member of 1st Recon engaged it with their EXOs and we managed to subdue it. We kept it chained to the deck and studied it. Then, when the temperature dipped below forty degrees, it died. We wondered if the alien invasion was limited to warmer climates, but Mr. Pink and the rest of the original TF OMBRA staff had left us.

We passed into the Indian Ocean, then were forced to wait for twelve days off the coast of Madagascar while a storm built around us. When the hurricane finally struck the east coast of Tanzania like a giant hammer, we landed with it, using the winds and rain to hide our entrance. Staying well north of Dar es Salaam and Zanzibar, we paralleled the Kenyan border, following old mining roads as we trudged in our EXOs past mudslides, through flooded areas, and around what had once been a refugee camp but had turned into a bloody harvest. We strode through the driving rain past a forest created by the broken and twisted limbs of those who'd only wanted to be somewhere free, whether it be from a warlord or from an alien visitor.

We'd seen destruction on the footage we'd been shown, but we'd never been face to face with the actual devastation brought by the Cray upon our species. I felt somber and angry, much like I had the day terrorists flew planes into the World Trade Centre. But these were terrorists of a different sort. The Cray were terrorists on a galactic scale. The combined murders of every man, woman and child who'd ever been unlucky enough to cross a terrorist in our history was nothing in the face of the desires of the Cray to own, not only our land, but the air we breathed.

Musing as I stomped through the mud and scrub, my servos making the trek no more effort than a walk across a field, I wondered if there was even now a planet where the Cray waited and relished our demise, celebrating our misery with frescoes and sculptures.

When we finally made the plain in front of the mound, it was near dawn. The Cray, who mainly flew during the day, were grounded by the remnants of the hurricane's driving wind and rain. We were led through a succession of trenches into an abandoned mine, an old vestige of the dormant volcanic system of Kilimanjaro. We parked our EXOs and were led to our bunk areas.

When I finally fell into a troubled sleep, it was to dreams of the dead refugees, their limbs moving in the wind, hearing all the while the words of our crucified drone, chittering in a voice wracked by sorrow that we were being punished for our sins and that we should stop whining about it and take it like men.

> The soldier above all others prays for peace, for it is the soldier who must suffer and bear the deepest wounds and scars of war.
>
> Douglas MacArthur

CHAPTER TWENTY-THREE

SOMEWHERE I'D READ about the Battle of the Somme between British and German forces during World War I. Over the course of the battle, more than one million soldiers were killed or wounded. It was trench warfare at its very worst. The soldiers cowered in their trenches, keeping their heads down, praying to their God, and hoping that when the next whistle blew and they were told to climb the ladders and rush over the top they wouldn't be mowed down by a fusillade of bullets.

Trench warfare had become synonymous with the futility of war. On July 1, 1916, the British Army had more than fifty-seven thousand casualties in one day, marking the darkest day in Britain's military history. That is, until three alien ships landed in London and killed more than seven million. And now, as we stared out across the flat plain between our positions near the village of Boma Ng'ombe and the mound that was dead center in Kilimanjaro Airport, I wished we had those fifty-seven thousand with us; it would be better than the three thousand we had now.

It would take a miracle of modern warfare for us to win. I'd never been one to believe in miracles, but like those British soldiers in the Battle of the Somme, I prayed, promising God, the universe and everything that if only I'd come out of this alive, I'd do whatever they wanted of me, because from my vantage point there was absolutely no hope of winning.

Kilimanjaro has three volcanic cones: Kibo, Mawenzi, and Shira. The latter two are extinct, but Kibo is merely dormant, inspiring several geological agencies to come together in the 1980s to build lava diversion zones. Using the southwestern slope of Kilimanjaro as their test bed, they created a series of concrete and steel-reinforced furrows to re-direct the lava flow past the population zones and into a huge cavern beneath the flanks of the mountain.

This, of course, had never been tested, but what it had done was leave a network of serviceable battlements for BCT OMBRA. The trench systems were arrayed downslope from the mountain, and after the application of removable metal roofs, they created a staging area of which our First-World-War ancestors would be envious.

In the no-man's-land between us and the mound was what used to be the village of Boma Ng'ombe. Continually inhabited for three thousand years, the place's name meant *Village of Cows,* but it was now a graveyard of bones, seven destroyed mud huts, a concrete building with its roof and walls staved in, and a 1958 Chevrolet Bel Air. Missing tires and windows, the auto's red paint still glistened in the morning sun, as if it had just been washed. The only thing more out of place at the foot of a twenty-thousand foot free-standing mountain in Tanzania was the Cray mound itself... which was starting to show a little activity.

As I watched, a black speck climbed free from one if its protrusions. It began to circle, ranging higher and higher. The low hum alerted everyone. Men came and pulled the metal roofs across the trenches. One nudged me aside and shot me a withering look, treating the *noob* with contempt. I grinned, but he moved on, rushing down the line.

He was a member of the Brigade Support Battalion, or BSB. They'd been here for two months, dragging gear into place, and preparing for our arrival. They'd also managed to preposition the rest of the EXOs and the eight-inch Howitzers. Now that we were here, they could finally get their war on. They'd been attacked for sixty straight days, but hadn't been allowed to fight back. Now that we'd arrived, they would finally get a chance to see what sort of damage we could do.

I left the battlements and headed back inside. I passed dozens of men and women dressed in the same desert multi-cam fatigues, moving more steel into place to hide the day away. The fatigues, which had seemed so out of place back in Alaska, were the same color as the Tanzanian plain.

Watching the men and women of the BSB, I couldn't help but imagine how impossible their task must have seemed their first day upon arrival in the shadow of the alien mound. A few creases in the earth and an underground cavern was what they had to work with, and with that they were required to build a fortification strong enough to keep us from being killed while we fought. There was a lesson there for our own mission: the BSB had got on with the job, putting one foot in front of the other, and we would do the same.

I headed out of the trench area towards the main cavern. I stepped aside to allow an eight-inch Howitzer to trundle by on ancient tracks, moving into line with the others in the last trench. I covered my mouth and nose with one hand as it passed, throwing up dust.

I kept heading downhill, passing men and woman rushing to their duties. The cavern was lit with electric lights. Although the facilities were too far beneath the surface for the drones' EMP to affect them, the generators were still hardened, as were the computers. Techs from the BSB had created Tempest-level Faraday-caged rooms in the event the worst happened and a pod of the damned creatures got inside.

I made it back to our squad just in time for our mission brief. We were to back up 10th Recon Platoon, which was going to make a nighttime reconnaissance on the mound. They were to rendezvous at Boma Ng'ombe, then wait to determine how the drones would react to their presence. The Cray were largely inactive at night and we wanted to see if they'd remain so. While we were standing by, the eight-inchers would lay down a barrage. The artillerymen had also mounted Vulcan cannons on the Howitzers' flanks, to provide anti-aircraft defense if needed.

We were all tense. This would mark the first use of the EXOs in combat. We'd practiced with them, we knew their flaws and their strengths. In order to protect against EMP bursts, each suit required grounding, much like a lightning rod. Conductive studs on the soles of the EXO's feet allowed the damaging surges to dissipate into the ground. This of course limited an EXO to ground-based maneuvers, but provided constant protection for the wearer and the EXO's internal electronics.

This was all well and good, but we soon learned that the EMP hardening caused immense problems with communications. Fortunately, TF OMBRA came up with a method using Extremely Low Frequencies (ELF) with a ground dipole antenna established through the soles of the EXO's feet. Since the majority of EMP energy is seen in the microwave frequencies, the system was capable of operating on a battlefield in which EMPs had been brought into play. Then advanced digital modulation techniques allowed them to compress data on the signal, allowing real-time feeds between team members and back to base. A backup, transmit-only communications system resided in an armored blister atop the helmet. Called the Rotating Burst Transmission Module (RBTM), it was comprised of a one-inch rotating sphere inside of the blister with its own battery power. One side of the sphere was able to pick up a packet of data when rotated 'inside' the Faraday cage of the EXO, then rotated 'outside' this protection to transmit the packet as a burst.

The EXO itself was an armored and EMP-hardened powered exoskeleton suit that stood about nine feet tall and had about double the bulk of a strong human. The outer covering alternated layers of Kevlar and titanium, bonded together to protect both the wearer and the grounding web. Internally the suit had hardened electronics for video feeds, voice communication, targeting, night vision, sound amplification/dampening and vital sign monitoring, along with heating, cooling and an air re-breather system with CO_2 scrubbers, all powered by extremely light, high-energy rechargeable batteries. All systems were controlled by eye movements, through an internal HUD system with Gaze technology, or remotely from base as a backup.

Each Recon EXO had three primary weapon systems.

The integral rocket launcher (IRL) was mounted over the left shoulder on rails, so as to rotate it back out of the way and bring it forward to firing position when needed. Standard payload was thirty Hydra rockets with air-burst warheads set to detonate at a range determined before launch by the suit's internal targeting system. Missiles were free-flight after launch, with a hardened internal timer for detonation. This system was designed to engage alien drones at maximum to medium targeting range.

Pulled out of mothballs at Aberdeen Proving Ground before the invasion, the XM214 was the EXO's primary attack armament, comprised of a six-barrelled rotating minigun fed from a backpack ammo supply through an ammo feed arm. TF OMBRA modified the original 1970s General Electric design, giving the system three backpack-mounted 500-round ammo boxes linked together, for a total of 1500 rounds. The original 1970s electronic controls, which could modify the rate of fire on the fly, were micronized, hardened against EMP and incorporated into the ammo boxes, giving the system triple redundancy and protecting the electronics. The servo that spun the barrels only engaged when the automatic harness system that pulled the weapon back out of the way was released.

When all else failed, a grunt needed a blade. Nearly a meter long and sixteen centimeters wide, TF OMBRA's harmonic blade vibrated at ultrasonic frequencies, making it thousands of times more effective at slicing through armored opponents than a normal blade. The weapon was made from Stellite to help resist the deleterious vibrational forces as well as any environmental extremes an OMBRA grunt might encounter, and the vibration was generated in the hilt by an electrically isolated system powered by a high energy battery and grounded through either the suit glove holding it or the sheath it rested in.

When the time came, we climbed into our suits. They'd been cleaned and recharged by the BSB techs. I checked my HUD. Front and rear feeds worked. Ammunition inventory was a check. Power was at ninety-nine percent. I tested the servos in the legs, hips, shoulders and elbows, as well as the automatic harness for the minigun. All were functioning properly. I conducted a radio check with Olivares, then came up on the Team Net and communicated back to base. Check. Check. Check.

Once everyone was ready, we moved out. Six of us, each half again taller than a man, moving fluidly up the incline to our trail position behind 10th Recon, who were already in place inside Trench One.

This was it. All the learning, all the hours, all the exercise, all the speeches came down to these few minutes. We'd prepared for months and were as ready as we could possibly be.

We heard the Net Call.

"All Stations, this is Net, standby on radio silence. Operation in progress."

The occasional chatter died to nothing.

"Romeo One-Zero, this is Base. Prepare to move on my mark."

All the recon elements had become Romeo elements for ease of communication. 10th Recon had been redesignated Romeo One-Zero. We were Romeo Three.

"All Romeos, engage sound deafening."

Using Gaze technology, I keyed down external sound to five percent. Then I began counting. When I reached thirty, the eights fired in unison. The ground shook. Dust fell from the surface into the trench. A low rumble made my teeth ache.

"First volley away. Fire two."

Five seconds later, a second volley shook me. Then the BSB techs moved the steel plates to the rear. Romeo One-Zero pulled themselves up and out, and began running across the plain.

We moved forward and climbed so we could see over the edge. We had a ground-level view and watched where the first and second volleys impacted. Great plumes of smoke lifted into the air as the Armor-piercing Depleted Uranium (APDU) shells hit the mound.

The drones were in chaos. They flew at odd angles, often colliding in mid-air.

"Fire three."

The third volley left the eights. We could track them through the air using our telemetry system, moving in ballistic arcs, slamming into the mound.

We cheered. And as we cheered, so did the rest of the Brigade Combat Team, who were watching the fight through helmet feeds and on plasma TVs arrayed throughout the complex.

I couldn't help but smile.

Any minute now, I expected the mound to fall. The combined might of thirty eight-inch Howitzer rounds was impossible to defend against... or so we thought. When the smoke cleared, we saw that there'd been no damage. Not even a dent in the surface of the mound's exterior.

"Base, this is Romeo Three Alpha. No evident damage. I say again, no damage."

I felt Olivares's words like punches to the gut.

The drones were no longer in chaos. Now that they knew what was happening, and that their mound was undamaged, they reformed into a spiral.

Romeo One-Zero, meanwhile, was almost to Boma Ng'ombe.

But soon the tornado of drones descended upon the recon squad and EMP flashes burst from them as explosions from shoulder-fired missiles flared and blossomed. Before any of the members of Romeo One-Zero could make it to cover, the drones fell upon them, ripping and slashing. For a brief moment, I could make out the EXOs holding their own. Miniguns opened fire; blades sliced through alien bodies. I heard screamed commands through the net. For one brief moment, I keyed into the feed from Romeo One-Zero Alpha. He was blind except for the constant moving of drone limbs, hammering, ripping, and twisting past the front and rear camera feeds. Then there was light as his feed gained distance from the fight. Only it was moving higher and higher.

I switched back to my own visual and watched as a drone dropped the head of Romeo One-Zero Alpha back to the Tanzanian dirt. Then as one, the drones reformed and spiraled upwards. Two EXOs still stood, and then as one they fell, dust pluming around them.

The drones moved above their mound and spiraled angrily.

We stood there for an hour watching.

Five times, Romeo Three Alpha asked to bring back the bodies.

All five times his request was denied.

For one brief moment we'd felt as if we could win.

Then had come the reality.

A small part of me, a piece that had broken off from my previous hopes, told me it was all over. That we should give up now. I might have followed the advice. The only problem was that there was no one to give up to.

It was either live or die.

There was no in-between.

Fucking aliens.

When world traveler Johann Rebman reported that he'd seen at the latitude of the equator a vast mountain capped with snow, the British Geographical Society laughed. Rebman had the last laugh though, when the world came to know the magnificent Kilimanjaro. Come laugh with him, as you travel the old trail up the side of this magnificent mountain. Complete packages available for $3999.99.

Tanzanian Travel and Tourism Bureau

CHAPTER TWENTY-FOUR

EVENTUALLY THE TOC ordered us to stand down. We returned to our squad bay, powered down our EXOs and disengaged. I kept replaying the decimation of Romeo One-Zero in my mind and couldn't hit on a way the outcome could have been any different. They'd conformed to the mission parameters and had reacted appropriately, even though the mound had remained impervious to our weaponry. The problem was that there were too many drones and, following mission protocols, they had not engaged the swarm until too late. I went through all possible scenarios. Better armor and faster reaction time might make the EXOs last longer, but with so many drones, it was only a matter of time before they were torn apart like Romeo One-Zero. Either there was absolutely no hope of defeating the Cray, or our tactics were woefully mismatched.

Cleaned up and back in our fatigues, we sat on the benches in our bay, elbows on knees, staring at the polished stone floor.

Olivares excused himself and left, but none of us moved. After a time, he returned.

"Okay. We need to go over what happened," he said, straining to keep his voice level.

"Romeo One-Zero got *focking aten*," MacKenzie said without looking up.

I thought of a dozen things to say, but none of them would have been much help right now.

"There were so many of them," Aquinas said, distress shaping her features. "How can we hope to defeat so many?"

"We don't really have a choice," I said, although I almost used the word *chance* instead. When I noticed everyone was looking at me, I sat up a little straighter. "This is it. We have to make our stand here."

Thompson gave me a look, but didn't say anything.

Ohirra did the same.

Olivares stepped forward. "What happened to Romeo One-Zero won't happen again. OMBRA techs were able to monitor the events and are prepared to make improvements to our suits."

MacKenzie looked up. "They selling you that? I wouldn't buy it."

Olivares shrugged. "We have no choice but to buy it. Mason is right, no matter how hard it is to believe. It's not like we can go back and wait somewhere. It's not like there's someone else standing in the wings to back us up. We are it."

"Period," I added.

Ohirra sighed and stood. "So what are we supposed to do?"

"Techs are going to be working on our suits in an hour. I want everyone to get some chow, then be back here when they start."

Thompson stood with the last of them. He seemed so frail standing next to MacKenzie. "What are they going to do to the suits?" he asked.

Olivares shrugged. "I don't know. We'll have to see what they have planned. Now get moving. I'll be along right after you."

I decided to stay behind, not having the stomach to eat at that moment. Olivares waited until the others had disappeared around a corner, then sat heavily on a bench. He pulled a rag from his back pocket and wiped his face.

"Okay?" I asked.

"They don't know what they're doing," he said, his usual sneer returning. "They're going to get us killed before we can even show the Cray what we're made of."

"That bad?"

Olivares looked around before replying. "Want to know how bad it is? Check this out. We need a win. We need one real bad. The morale of the entire brigade is at a stake. Romeo One-Zero was literally fucking torn apart, and the eights haven't so much as made a dent in the mound."

"This can't be good," I said, as a sinking feeling enveloped me.

"It's not. In fact, it's a last ditch effort, which means if this fails, there's nothing else that *can* be done. Literally. This is going to be the final rabbit they pull out of their hat."

"What is it?"

"I'm not supposed to say."

"Are you serious? All that buildup and you can't tell me?"

"Okay. Fine. Check this out. They've been holding back a Boeing 727. It landed on a desert runway east of Darfur and has been kept under wraps the entire time. The pilots are from Egypt and have been communicating with OMBRA for the better part of a year."

"Don't say it."

Olivares nodded. "You guessed it. They want to fly their plane into the mound."

September 11, 2001 lit up my mind like the devil's own drive-in movie theater. Before the coming of the Cray, it was the worst I'd ever felt. It wasn't like they'd attacked a member of my platoon: they'd attacked *America*. Every man, woman and child had been attacked, and it had set America on the path to more than a decade of war. "What's command saying? What does the RSM say?" I asked.

"The command is for it. They think it'll reinvigorate the brigade, give them some momentum."

"And the RSM?"

"He thinks it's a bad move, but as long as command is for it, he's for it, with one exception."

"That being?"

"He thinks we should keep the identities of the pilots to ourselves."

I thought about it for a moment. "I don't know. Those pilots had nothing to do with 9/11. If they want to help us—help the world—who are we to deny them their sacrifice?" I shook my head. "That's not how grunts think."

Olivares grinned, turning the scar on his cheek white. The effect was a little scary. "Tell me how grunts think."

"Nationalities as we knew it are a thing of the past. Sure, we're going to have Americans and English and French and all that shit, but now we also have terms like *Earthlings* or *OMBRA* or *grunts*, all of which we belong to in some sort or fashion. Wanna know how grunts think? It's simple. It's us or them, and those pilots are *us*. So who the hell cares what nationality they *were* before all this started? They're us, now."

He laughed. "No shit. That's definitely how grunts think."

"So when's this going to happen?"

"Tomorrow, early evening." He pulled out the rag from his back pocket again and wiped the sweat off his forehead. "The plan is to wait for most of the drones to have returned to their mound. The plane's going to be at high altitude, then come sharply down, fully prepared for the EMP to take out its electronics."

"By then it will be a missile."

"Oh, yeah. And one more thing." He stood and pushed the rag back into his pocket. "There might be more."

"More than one plane?"

"We got the idea that there might be a lot of planes waiting for a reason to fly again. They know they can't carry any passengers—one EMP burst and everyone would be dead—but they could fly one last time and deliver some payback. There's a message going out on ELF." He shrugged. "We'll see."

"It's going to be one hell of a show."

"Let's hope it's more than a show. We need this to be a win. We need to give some hope." Olivares headed out of the bay. "Come on. Let's join the others."

I fell in step behind him. We hit the chow hall, then returned to our suits. I had to force myself to keep quiet about OMBRA's plans for the next day, especially when Aquinas approached me.

Where I'd originally felt a special connection with her, I'd completely misjudged what sort of woman she was. I thought she might be one of those delicate flowers who needed attention, but that wasn't her at all. She didn't need me or anyone.

"What was it that Olivares talked to you about?" she asked, pulling the missiles from her Hydra. She removed each carefully, one at a time, then placed them on the anti-static foil in the bottom of our weapons locker. Once she had all of them put away, she removed the harmonic blade assembly—battery pack, sheath and blade. She added them to the locker, then turned back to me when she was finished.

"You didn't answer my question," she said, hands on hips. She was no longer the woman she'd been when we'd shared the helicopter trip way back before we'd even heard of the Cray. She had a jut to her stance and a shine to her features.

"We talked about Romeo One-Zero."

"Oh, yeah? He say anything more than what he told the rest of us?"

I tried to think quick, but the look on my face must have given it away.

"Don't bullshit me, Mason. What did he say? What are our plans?"

"You heard him, we're to watch the improvements the techs make and—"

She laughed a little too loud, then turned around and began checking the connections on the inside of her suit. "I guess I can't have it both ways. I wanted you to stop acting like a child. I guess now that you have, I can't really complain."

I stared at her.

I'd just been insulted.

And complimented.

I wasn't sure how I felt. A big part of me wanted to tell her, but then it would invalidate her compliment. What was a man to do?

"Don't just stand there with your mouth open," she said without looking back. "Get over here and help me."

I stepped forward.

"Not mine, silly. We have to take care of yours."

I smiled. "Of course we do."

We repeated the process, stowing the missiles and removing my blade assembly. We didn't look at each other or communicate, but we worked in concert, each one filling in where the other left off.

When we were finished she hefted her blade and removed it from its sheath. "Oof. It's not really heavy, you know? Just longer than anything we've trained with."

I grinned for a moment as I watched her holding the blade like a sword. Then my gaze drifted to the rivers of scars along the inside of her forearms. She must have seen the expression on my face because she frowned.

"Do you think my plan was to wait until we arrived on this godforsaken African plain, then do myself in with this thing?"

She laughed sharply. "If I'd have wanted to end it, I would have done it with the bed springs back in Wyoming."

"The bed springs," I said, thinking back to what I'd been preparing to do.

Her angry smile softened. "It didn't take long to find it, did it?"

I shook my head. "No. It was right there."

"Although I bet regular people wouldn't expect to look there."

"Regular people don't go places and figure out how they might kill themselves. They normally look for a fire exit or something."

She shoved her blade back in its sheath and sat down on the bench. "Fire exits. Remember going to see movies? I bet I look like the type who loved to watch chick flicks, don't I?"

I didn't dare nod. Frankly, I had no idea.

"Would you believe I loved horror movies? The scarier the better. The ones that got me the most were the ones about possession. Can you imagine? Being taken over by another entity and not being able to control your own body?"

I laughed. "Possession is the last thing to be afraid of now." Then I remembered how I'd been possessed by the Siren in the basement of the home in Dothan.

"Why do you say that?"

My mind was still somewhere in that basement when she asked me again. I cleared away the memory with a hard blink of my eyes. "Look at where we are. The aliens attacked and took our planet. Do you think a God would allow that?"

"Do not presume to know the will of God. For all you know, this could be the next Great Flood. It happened once. Why not again?"

I was about to retort when I saw the expression on her face. She was dead serious. "How can you believe in God after all this?"

"How can you not?" she countered. "Just because you can't fathom why this happened, doesn't mean there isn't a God. It doesn't mean *He* doesn't have a plan."

I couldn't help but show my distaste, even if it meant losing all of her goodwill. "A plan. Fate. The idea that everything bad, everything good, everything *period* has been figured out ahead of time, is impossible to believe." I could see her getting angry, but I couldn't stop myself. "That the Inquisition, the Black Plague, 9/11, pedophiles and the Cray are part of God's plan is ludicrous."

"I didn't say they were part of His plan, smartass. I said just because we don't know what's going on doesn't mean *He* doesn't have a plan. Is it *all* part of His plan? I don't think so. Maybe events happen, then His plan goes into effect." She stood and put her blade away. "Here's what I've learned." She walked up to me, her face inches from mine. She was beautiful and angry at the same time. "Just because you don't believe in God, it doesn't mean He doesn't believe in you."

Then she stepped quickly away. "What does that even mean?" I called after her.

She flipped me off.

"Not very God-like," I shouted.

Her single finger salute changed into a double-finger salute. Then she was gone.

Thompson came around the corner after a well-timed three seconds. "I think that went well."

I turned back to the room, looking for something to do. Why is it I always like the complicated girls?

Thompson began fiddling with his EXO.

"Don't you have somewhere to be?" I asked.

"Yeah," he said. "Here... removing the weapons from my suit so they can work on it."

"I'll do it," I said. "I'll do them all."

"You sure?" he asked.

"Yes, I'm sure."

"Are you sure you should be even touching the missiles?" he asked, a grin beginning to form.

"Yes, I'm fucking sure! Now leave me alone!"

He stepped backwards out of the room, then paused. I saw him waiting out of the corner of my eye.

I felt bad for yelling at him. I was angry at too many things right now. I needed time to process it. But I was also aware that he was a friend and a team mate. I had to make time.

"What is it?"

"She was trying to explain that God has you as part of His plan even if you don't believe in Him."

"What if I don't believe in the plan?"

He shrugged. "It doesn't change her point."

I put my hands on my hips. "You too, Thompson?"

He cocked his head. "Don't get pissed at me. I'm just explaining her position. I don't necessarily agree with it, but it's what she believes."

I raised my hands. "Enough."

"If you're going to want to get to know her better, you're going to have to deal with her religion."

I spun towards him. "What do you mean by that—*her religion*?" He'd said it like it was a funerary cloth she carried.

"I've said enough." Thompson backpedaled, then spun around the corner.

What was it with people getting the last word and leaving me hanging? I stood there waiting to see if anyone else was going to chime in, but no one came. Finally it appeared as if I was alone. I began to take down Thompson's suit, all the while wondering about his final comment—*You're going to have to deal with her religion.*

> In the final choice a soldier's pack is not so heavy as a prisoner's chains.
>
> Dwight D. Eisenhower

CHAPTER TWENTY-FIVE

THAT EVENING SAW Romeo Six bringing back the few parts of Romeo One-Zero that still remained. When they returned, we stood solemnly, ingloriously glad it hadn't been us who'd gone out first and mourning the loss of our fellow grunts, especially Frakess. Of the men and women of Romeo One-Zero, what was returned wouldn't fill a wheelbarrow. But it was important that each part, no matter how small, was given a proper burial.

Afterwards, we got some shut eye. Instead of a foam pad on the steel floor of the container, like in Alaska, we were given cots, of a type I'd used on several occasions and which had probably been ordered and produced in bulk sometime between the Korean and Vietnam Wars. With metal bars, the nylon could be stretched to create some semblance of give. Not as good as what we'd had in our cells during Phase I, but the view here in Africa was so much better.

I tried to get Aquinas's attention, but she was studiously ignoring me.

MacKenzie was trying to get a game of Poof together, but none of us were up for it. We didn't even know how to play it. It was some sort of card-guessing-truth-or-dare thing which would invariably result in embarrassment on one side and hilarity on the other. He tried to explain it, but he had no takers. He grumbled a bit about us being spoiled Americans, then packed it in.

After breakfast the next morning, we were treated to an amazing sight. During the night, techs from the BSB and OMBRA had come together and tested one of the spare EXOs. They covered it completely in oil, set it on fire, then maneuvered it through the underground complex. It operated for seventeen minutes before one of the hip servos overheated. The oil attracted all of the dust stirred up by the feet, creating a tarry glue that wedged in the joint.

When the brainiacs were finished cleaning the suit, they were back to square one. If the problem was with the EXO, then it was a design flaw and no field expedience was going to help it survive the onslaught any better. But then they had an idea. Instead of making the suit stronger, why not reduce the number of drones attacking the wearer? With the Cray having almost total air superiority, anything on the ground was fair game. The trick would be to lure the drones into descending, while sending another recon squad along an alternate route.

Thus was born Project Vulcan Logic, named by a pair of *Trek*-loving BCT techs when they realized they'd had the answer in front of them all along. They'd been so locked into the idea of using the Vulcans to protect the artillery pieces that they'd failed to see the guns' usefulness to the quickly moving EXOs. Why not a mobile air defense system? Twin Vulcan cannons could be mounted on a wheeled sled, to be pulled and operated by members of the infantry companies. They'd move towards cover in the village, waiting until the drones were in line like fighters coming in for a bombing run. Once online, the Vulcans would open up with two 20mm cannons capable of slinging 6600 rounds per minute towards the drones. BCT OMBRA only had SAPHEI rounds—incendiary rounds with a delayed high explosive package and a follow-on zirconium pellet—but that was fine for the purposes. It was a wonder they hadn't thought of this in the first place.

They began preparing Project Vulcan Logic immediately, with the goal of having it ready to move by nightfall. Word had already gone out and rumors were abounding. Everyone had taken to calling it the *Big Show*, and it was reckoned that it would be the make it or break it moment.

BCT OMBRA had thirty Vulcans and several conexes filled with ammunition from which to draw for their new experiment. Until now they hadn't been used, but they had been prepared for air defense operations by the infantry companies. Each weapon system had been modified with mini-Faradays to protect them against EMPs.

Or at least we hoped they were protected. The lights, the repair equipment and the ventilation system were powered by an immense group of hydro fuel generators that leeched water from an underground river seventy-five feet below the surface. Not only were they necessities, but they were one of the last links we had to the civilization we once had.

MacKenzie had seen the generators and had commented on them. "These Task Force OMBRA lads seem to have a lot of science behind them. One of these days I need to ask why they been keeping it to themselves."

None of us had needed to ask what he meant. We'd all been thinking the same thing. The planning, the technology, the knowledge of the Cray, all pointed to a group with a major investment in the alien attack. Of course there wasn't any larger payoff than being responsible for the survival of your own species. I, for one, was thrilled to be a part of it. Why wouldn't I be? The alternative wasn't acceptable.

The next day was spent war-gaming and planning a variety of attacks. I kept checking the clocks, eager for night to fall. I couldn't wait to see what an entire airplane could do to the alien mound.

The RSM gave the official word just after sundown.

Most of the battalions were satisfied to stand and watch the events unfold on the battery of screens, but the Recon squads and several of the infantry platoons wanted to see it firsthand.

In fact, Olivares called everyone into the squad bay and had everyone don their EXOs. "You want to see it on a television, then use your HUD," he said. "This kamikaze mission might just work, you know? And if it does, the Cray are going to be pissed. Looks like we're the only humans within several hundred miles to take it out on, so you take a guess where they'll come when we piss them off."

"Hey, Thompson." Olivares turned to the former drummer boy. "What happens when you shake a hornet's nest?"

"You piss the hornets off, Sarge."

"What happens to a bee keeper who ain't ready?" Olivares asked no one in particular as he affixed the servos to his legs.

"He runs or he gets stung," Ohirra said, already in her suit and going through system checks.

"And what happens if he's ready?"

"They can't sting him through his suit," MacKenzie said.

"That's right. For a time in hell we're beekeepers. We're going to disturb their hive and see what happens."

"Damn big bees, or hornets, or aliens, or whatever you want to call them," I said as I slid my helmet into place.

After we suited up, we checked each other. Each of us had three status lights on the exterior of the left side. Green was good and red was dead. We could also check the status from our individual HUDs. Gaze tech, similar to what jet pilots had used, allowed us to select suit information on our own suits as well as every member of the team's, making each system accessible by the other.

"Incoming ten miles," came the voice through our comms.

"Romeo Three, positions."

We moved in file from the bay, up the gangway and to Trench One. The steel covers had been pulled partially aside, leaving just enough room for us to climb out. Olivares pulled himself up first, and soon we were all standing tall, side by side, and staring at the western sky. My minigun was swung forward and ready, my blade was charged, and my missiles were primed.

Activity around the mound was dying down. Less than a handful of Cray were circling lazily overhead. Far less than the usual hundred or so that blanketed the sky during the day.

"Five miles."

"They said that the pilot is Japanese," Ohirra said. "I used to hate Memorial Day, because they'd play all those old World War Two movies on television, making the Japanese look so stupid. So mean. So hopeless."

The pilots were Egyptian, but I kept my mouth shut.

"But now I feel different," she said.

"Three miles."

"I get it now. I understand why they flew their planes into ships. It was a last act of defiance."

"There it is." Thompson pointed towards the west at a pinpoint of black.

Our HUDs tracked the incoming Boeing 727 jet. We watched it grow larger until we saw it nose down as it headed for the mound. If it missed, we'd been warned that debris from the plane could pose a danger to anyone on the ground. We didn't care. We'd rather have front row seats.

The plane was from some African airline I didn't recognize. I could envision the inside with all empty seats, the brochures and puke bags in the back of the seat pockets, never to be used again.

"One mile."

The Cray finally noticed the inbound aircraft, dropping at a forty-five degree angle. We could hear the scream of the engines through the amplification systems inside our helmets. The drones in the air turned to meet the incoming plane. EMP flashes lit the sky as they flew towards it. More Cray shot from the launch ramps on either side until the air was swarming with activity.

The plane tore through a phalanx of drones like they were nothing.

A cheer went up from inside the caverns.

Ohirra raised a fist into the air, and the rest of us joined her.

More and more Cray attacked the plane. I couldn't figure out why they were even trying, until my telemetric showed that it was now off-course. The fuselage would miss the mound.

Five, four, three, two, one.

The plane struck the mound high on its upper third. A last minute correction by the pilot made the fuselage strike a glancing blow. The left wing shattered as it hit, then the plane broke apart. Pieces of it rained down on the plain between the mound and the village. The amplified sound was a terrible cacophony of carnage. The tail section landed just this side of the mound, burrowing into the African soil.

We stared at the Cray hive, waiting for the dramatic collapse.

But nothing happened.

Nothing.

"More incoming," comms declared.

"We weren't sure if they were going to follow through," Olivares said. "A consortium, of sorts: bush pilots, mercenaries, and contract pilots."

Our telemetry began tracking thirty-two additional aircraft. These were all small single- and twin-engine jobs, the kind used to puddle-jump and carry tourists and hunters back and forth across Kenya and Tanzania. We watched as they angled towards the mound. Our HUDs mapped their ballistic paths, showing the various locations they would strike the mound.

But where the drones had no effect on the larger plane, they obliterated the smaller ones. Pulses of EMP killed electronics, making the planes nothing more than bombs with wings. The drones attacked in midair, ripping away wings, tearing free engine housings and jerking pilots from shattered windscreens.

Not a single one of the planes made it to its target, each one crashing and littering the African floor with pieces of what could have been something special.

All except one.

A single plane still soared, out-maneuvering each of the drones. My HUD told me it was a P51 Mustang. World War Two vintage, it was used for long range bombing and reconnaissance against the Japanese. It had to be versatile to outmaneuver the Japanese Zeros, and now I watched as it dipped and twisted and somersaulted its way over and through the Cray. Here and there it opened fire, sending rounds scything through the drones.

The Mustang was unaffected by the EMP because it had no electronics. It was pure combustion engine, through and through. I wanted to cheer as I watched it, but I held my breath instead. It was getting closer and closer until finally, it hammered midway into the side of the mound.

The front of the plane crumpled as the propeller shattered. One of the wings snapped free. Then the plane tumbled unceremoniously to the ground.

The mound remained intact.

We stood there for several moments, staring at the terrible monolith, waiting for it to collapse, or break apart, or *something*. Anything to show that the lives of the men and women flying the planes hadn't gone to waste. But nothing happened. Nothing.

Then, instead of attacking, the Cray returned to their hive. Soon the air was free of them and the empty, unprotected night sky laughed at us. It was galling. The aliens didn't even have the courtesy to attack us back for what we'd just done, as if it had meant nothing. In fact, one could argue, that was exactly it.

Olivares was the first to leave the trench. We followed him in silence. No one said a word as we returned to our squad bay. We sat for a long time and said nothing.

A warrior is free to be a hero and pull off daring do
and the soldier is irresponsible if he does it.

C. J. Cherryh

CHAPTER TWENTY-SIX

ABOARD SHIP ON the way to Africa, OMBRA Techs provided lessons on electromagnetic pulses. The pulses created by the Cray were a result of high energy generation transmitted through biological mechanisms, characteristically similar to high energy radio frequency (HERF) weapons that had been researched but never successfully fielded on Earth. Because of the diminishing strength of the EMPs local to a mound, the techs projected that the power locus for the pulses was contained within the mound, and that the drones were capable of storing and transmitting the pulses much like a HERF weapon, but at a diminished capacity.

Our mission was to plant ground-penetrating sonar and radar detectors as close to the mound as possible. We needed to know what they were doing inside. How large was the interior? What sort of complex did they have? If the Cray didn't self-generate their EMPs, was there a central location within the interior that provided them access to power, like a charging station? Basically, we need to know anything and everything. Without the availability of human reconnaissance reporting, our only hope was the single-use machines, which would transmit data seconds after operation. We had little hope that they'd last past the first EMP pulse, but if they could give us an understanding of the internal layout, we'd at least have a target. Right now all we had to aim at was the impervious shell of the mound.

Four recon platoons, Romeos One, Three, Six, and Eleven, were partnered with two infantry platoons. While the infantry platoons' job was to provide covering support in the retrograde, ours was to plant the devices in a prescribed pattern around the mound. Each of us carried two devices. Their pre-designated locations were programmed into our HUDs.

First platoon was assigned to Romeo One and Eleven. They had the most difficult mission, depositing their devices on the far side of the mound. Second platoon was assigned to Romeo Three and Six and had the easiest of it. We were also fielding the sled-pulled Vulcan cannons, AKA Project Vulcan Logic. The techs had promised that they were shielded and would be fully functional in the middle of the attack, but like most everything promised by a tech, we wouldn't know whether it was good or bad until we were in the middle of the shit.

A lone Cray flyer circled the mound; a black silhouette against an even blacker sky. We poised on the edge of our trenches, now more than ever like our World War I predecessors. Except when our predecessors rushed their opponents, it was with throaty yells and fixed bayonets. Recon, on the other hand, had to keep silent, each gripping the handle of a gator box securing the device we had to implant.

We waited for the signal.

A *beep* filled my ears. I pulled myself up and began to run. My target was the half-wrecked concrete building in Boma Ng'ombe. My composite-shod feet tore across the desert scrabble, faster than I could move outside the suit. The distance was two miles; I covered it in eight minutes, breathing no harder than if I'd run a quarter of that distance. I pulled up against one of the remaining walls and put my back to it. I couldn't see what was going on from this vantage point, so I accessed Olivares's feed, as his position had been midway between the village and the trenches. The drone still circled lazily, as if it had all the time in the world.

The view shifted as Olivares turned to Thompson.

"Move out."

Thompson got up from where he was crouching beside Olivares and ran towards me. I switched to Thompson's feed. Watching me get closer from his aspect was unsettling; we'd practiced aboard ship, but I didn't know if I'd ever get used to it. When he was about ten meters away, I switched back to my own feed.

Systems check. Ninety-five percent power. All green.

In thirty seconds all members of Romeo Three were in place.

We were situated at the east end of the village. The main drag ran east to west before curving south, as if it knew it had to miss the mound. On the other side of the dusty road lay several collapsed huts, among the standing structures. One minute later, Romeo Six had leap-frogged us and was in place on the other side of the village.

The next rendezvous point was the wing of the 727, the largest piece of the aircraft still intact. But we were to stay in place in the meantime until after two things happened.

The first was Romeos One and Eleven getting into position. They were working their way to the far side and required far more time. Moving in traveling overwatch, their ETA was forty-one minutes.

The second was rendezvousing with the Vulcan sleds. Four sleds, each with two Vulcan cannons and operators, were to set up in the village. Their mission was to protect Romeo elements from air attack.

Although untested, we were counting on their firepower. Hell, I knew *I* was counting on it.

I tuned in and switched views from the Vulcan teams to different members of One and Eleven, then back to ourselves. I saw Olivares gazing at Aquinas and tried to check into his view, but was locked out.

Hey. Not cool. I wondered what the hell he was talking to her about.

I was about to say something, when Olivares contacted me.

"Move forward with Aquinas and put visual on the mound. I want full magnification."

I acknowledged, and Aquinas and I settled on the Chevy Bel Air. She'd take the front and I'd take the rear. We moved as silently as silk and were soon in place.

Telemetry said there was nothing else moving in the sky except for the single drone, but I didn't believe it. The idea that it had seen us and had done nothing was incomprehensible. Either the Cray were preparing for something, or they didn't care enough about us to do anything. I'm not sure which was worse.

I settled in and occasionally glanced over my shoulder. Although I couldn't see her face, I knew enough of what she looked like for my imagination to begin working. I keyed Aquinas on a private channel. "Old car like this would be good for a date."

She ignored me.

"Put the top down. Turn on some tunes. Watch the lights."

"Stay on mission."

"Maybe listen to a little end-of-the-world radio," I said. "You and me could get comfortable and—"

"You'd have a better chance with a drone," she said, shaking her head.

I laughed.

"What's so funny?"

"At least I have a chance," I said.

She sighed.

"Concentrate, you grunts." As squad leader, Olivares had the access to listen in on everyone if he so chose. Even though he had last word, as stern as it had sounded, I could have sworn that it was delivered with a smile.

I turned my attention to the mound and zoomed in. I had to fiddle with the sharpening tools to get any clarity, which wasn't as easy as it should have been. Flipping back and forth between vision modes, I decided that as the mound wasn't putting off any heat it would have to be the green and black universe of Starlight mode. It didn't take long to figure out that there was nothing going on. Just shadows and that lone flyer above the mound.

I was about to say as much when Aquinas's worried whisper made me start. "The shadows... they're moving."

I concentrated on the mound.

"They're crawling on the outside," I said.

"They're not taking to the air. They must have figured out we can track them," Aquinas said.

"Like they can sense the radar."

My mind was in a dozen different places. If they knew about the telemetry and they were moving stealthily, it meant that they weren't ignoring us. In fact, they were preparing for our attack.

The Cray clung to the outside of the mound, flattened against the surface as though trying to hide, their wings plastered against their backs.

"All Romeo elements, key in on my optic. Cray are outside the mound and waiting. They know we're coming. I say again, they know we are coming."

What followed was a barrage of orders and comments, from the members of Romeo Three and Six. One and Eleven remained silent, awaiting orders.

Finally, they were told to hold their position while a decision was made. I could imagine them, squatting out in the open, waiting in the shadow of the mound for a decision to be made. Would they be allowed to return to the trenches or would they be asked to Charlie Mike?

When the word came back, it didn't surprise me.

Charlie Mike.

Continue Mission.

There was going to be blood, and it wasn't just going to be between One and Eleven and the Cray. We'd get ours, too.

Aquinas turned and looked at me. I couldn't see her face, but I felt her fear. I felt it within myself. We were about to be in the shit, but there was nothing we could do about it except Charlie Mike.

"Romeo Three, stand by," Olivares ordered. "Check status."

Systems check. Ninety percent power. All green.

Romeos One and Eleven were about two hundred meters from the mound. They switched from traveling overwatch to bounding overwatch, moving carefully and covering each other, but also covering as much ground as they could. Problem was that if they were required to use their miniguns, they'd lose precious seconds dropping their sonar/radar packages in order to swing the weapons into place.

I accessed one of the rear-facing cameras. Where were the Vulcan sleds? They were too far back for me to see. Unable to increase another EXO's magnification, I could only guess they were still hundreds of meters to the rear.

"Romeo Three, prepare to move out."

But it looked like I might have the chance to find out.

I switched my view back to my own suit. I saved my dialed-in magnification of the mound feed in a small screen in the upper left of my HUD, and fixed the rest of my view on what was in front of me.

"On my command, bounding overwatch to your marks." Olivares's voice was tight. We all knew what was coming. BCT command had decided it was allowable for Romeo elements to be attacked. That was just how it went.

Thompson, Ohirra and Olivares moved forward as we remained in place, scanning the sky and ground.

When it was our turn, they remained in place, and Aquinas, MacKenzie, and I passed them and moved forward another twenty meters.

Bounding overwatch worked best when you had a place of cover and concealment from which to defend, but once we passed the village, there was nothing other than the remains of the 727. We'd planned on meeting Romeo Six there, but the plan had changed. Command didn't want us clumped together. They wanted us to form as wide a line as possible. I wasn't sure if I agreed. Together, we had a strength of fire we lacked individually. The alternative was to be alone, strung out along a picket line, which Six was doing.

We made it to the 727 without event.

Olivares ordered a systems check.

Systems check. Eighty-six percent power. All green.

We regained our breath and prepared to move forward when we heard the first of the screams.

Romeo One was under attack.

To the soldier, luck is merely another word for skill.

Patrick MacGill

CHAPTER TWENTY-SEVEN

I SWITCHED TO a view from Romeo One and watched the ground recede at an impossible rate. Then the image tumbled and I saw myself plummeting back to the earth. I pulled back to my own feed before I hit the ground, irrationally afraid of what would happen, like anyone who'd ever gone to sleep and dreamed of falling.

My vitals showed my heart rate at 140 beats per minute. My breathing had risen to match it. I was sweating in my suit. I tried not to panic while listening to the screams and missile detonations from my sister recon squad.

I missed a command from Olivares.

I tore myself away from the HUD, and watched as the rest of my squad moved forward. I was a second behind them and soon caught up. No overwatch. We were making a dash towards the mound. It looked like we were going to implant our devices and retreat.

A great clamor, like the sky being unzipped, erupted from the other side of the mound; I could hear the Vulcan cannons both from my feeds and through my suit. I wanted to switch back and watch them in action, maybe witness some of the Cray disemboweled by the blizzard of bullets, but I needed all my attention on my own space.

We'd made it halfway to our mark when Hydra missiles began to fly from behind us in a barrage, striking the outside of the mound. I made out dead and dying Cray in the explosions. They'd been lying in wait, but Romeo Six had provided us covering fire.

I ached to have my minigun in my hands instead of the two cases. Charging the mound like this made me feel so exposed.

"Six is coming up behind," Olivares shouted breathlessly. "Watch your weapons."

I checked my telemetry and saw a vicious battle on the other side of the mound. The Vulcans were still screaming. Although there were no missiles from the EXOs, I heard the steady chatter of miniguns as they added their rounds to the fray. Either the other squads had given up the mission or they'd completed, which meant we were next.

Suddenly the mound was upon us. We'd covered the distance faster than I'd believed possible. My entire horizon was covered with the shadow of the hive. I knelt and snapped open the gator boxes.

I set the sonar in place, and watched it run to green, then begin to transmit data. Then I removed the radar. Just as I put it in position and flicked the switch, it went black. I checked the sonar; dark as well.

EMP.

Killed them already.

I just hoped they'd been able to provide enough information during the short time they'd been functional. I'd hate to think that all this had been a waste, although it wouldn't have been the first time I was part of a mission that had felt like that.

I snapped my minigun in place, comforted by the weight and heft of it in my Kevlar-gloved hands, even though most of it was held by the support arm. I depressed the firing lever and let the barrels spin several cycles as I began to scan the mound and the sky above us.

A shadow moved and I opened fire. The flash from the exploding rounds illuminated the limbs and wings of the drones in a jerky, stop-motion sequence. The barrels of the XM214 minigun spun madly as they hurled shells into my targets.

I began to back away as I continued firing.

"Olivares, orders," I shouted.

After unleashing a volley of bullets beside me, he said, "Back away slowly and cover Six as they lay their devices. Aquinas, Thompson and Mason, to the left. All others to me on the right."

For a moment there was no firing. No Vulcans. No miniguns. No missiles. Which meant that either we'd beaten back the Cray, or they were just waiting for us to turn our backs to descend upon us.

My telemetry read that the sky above was empty, but it couldn't tell me how many Cray were waiting in the launch tubes or clinging to the outside of the mound.

I kept turning, aware that danger could come from anyplace.

Three members of Romeo Six rushed past us and hurried to the base of the mound. Each of them dropped to a knee and went through the process of activating their devices.

I saw movement high above as several Cray launched into the air. My telemetry tracked them. I sent seven missiles towards them. The slight recoil from their launch pushed my left shoulder down, turning me towards my left, where I saw a dozen drones walking towards us.

My eyes shot wide and on the display my heartbeat skyrocketed to the danger zone. I opened fire and sent my last five missiles point blank into their midst.

Still they came.

I let my minigun fall and swing back out of the way, and grabbed my harmonic blade. We'd practiced with these. We'd cut through wood like it was butter. We'd pretended to be the Three Musketeers. We'd shadow-fenced a battalion of bad guys. But this was the twenty-first century and no one used swords. No one, that is, except Task Force OMBRA. Here I was, in the most technologically-advanced battle mechanism Earth had ever constructed, and I was relegated to defending myself with a length of sharpened metal.

I screamed as my blade sang, coming down on the nearest drone. The metal slid through the alien like it wasn't even there. I had no form. I had no style. I was hacking and slashing with little thought. They were a forest of weeds and I was a bushwhacker. My blade carved a hundred Xs in front of me, until there was nothing left to attack.

Then I heard the screaming.

"Fall back! Fall back!" It was Olivares, one hand grabbing a wing while the other sliced it free from the alien's body.

I spun, looking for a target, and saw the ground around me littered with pieces of drone. My EXO glistened with an oily substance that could only be Cray blood.

Then I noticed the readouts on my HUD. I had red flashing all over the place. I remembered the saying, *Red Is Dead*. I turned to fall back and fell to the ground, my blade impaling the earth. On my knees, I pulled the blade free and resheathed it.

I'd fallen over an EXO. I checked my HUD and saw that it was Thompson. His systems and vitals were green.

"Get up, kid."

I pulled myself to my feet and jerked him up. Through his mask I could see the fear in his eyes. I pointed back towards Boma Ng'ombe.

"That way! Move!"

He stumbled a moment, then took off running.

After looking around to see if there were any more members of my team on the ground, I took off after him. I'd gone about a dozen meters when I passed an EXO that had been ripped in half. The stencil on the breastplate read *SGT Neeld, Sean*. I knew him. He was from Florida and had been assigned to Romeo Six. His entrails lay on the ground amidst body fluids, soaking into the harsh African dirt. There was nothing I could do, so I continued moving as fast as I could.

Somehow I made it to the rendezvous point by the wing of the 727. All members of Romeo Three were present. Four members of Romeo Six were also there. An infantry platoon waited for us, carrying M32 grenade launchers with six revolving barrels. I watched as they fired into the air; my HUD told me they were using HEDP rounds, which exploded against the surface of the mound behind us. The others carried HK416 assault rifles, and fired carefully at their own targets. Although I was happy to see them, I was worried for their safety out in the open without an EXO.

"Everyone gather around," shouted a sergeant, the HUD identifying him as *Donnelly, Russell, USMC (Ret), Gunnery Sergeant*. He was about sixty and had owned a fast food franchise in Sweetwater, Tennessee when the shit had hit the fan. Now he was an infantry platoon sergeant and the leader of our security forces for this mission.

MacKenzie turned to me. "Brother, what happened to you? Looks like you fought a food processor and lost."

I glanced down at my arms and saw the scrapes and scratches from the Cray. Thankfully, I'd never let them get a good hold on me. All they could do was claw desperately at my armor.

I checked my battery level. I was sixty percent shot. Still enough to reach base, but time wasn't on our side. We had less than an hour to return to safety and try to protect the base in case the Cray attacked.

"Okay, you grunts," Gunny shouted through our comms. He wore only an MBITR intersquad commo set beneath his Kevlar helmet. "Double file, bounding overwatch, return to the rear. I don't want no lollygagging and I don't want no bullshit. The sun's against us, so scoot and move. Clear?"

The men and women of the squad responded with *Aye Ayes* and *Yes, sirs*. I was assigned to bring up the rear of Team Two as the squad separated into two teams. Olivares was in Team One, but Aquinas was in my team and my job, other than to kill Cray, was to keep her ass safe, just as hers was to keep mine safe.

As we peeled away from the dead airplane, I set my HUD to split screen, one side displaying my goal ahead, counting down the meters, and the other the mound behind, counting up the distance.

I was still flashing red, but I was hoping that ignoring it would make it go away. I was more than halfway to my objective when my servos screeched and seized. I didn't even have enough time to scream. I tumbled, tearing through the cracked, broken surface of the Serengeti plain. I blacked out. When I came to, I was upside down, my HUD sizzling from short circuits and my breathing labored.

A single thought owned me in that moment. *Why had they left me behind?*

Then, as if anything could possibly be worse, I watched as the HUD snapped to black. That could only mean one thing—the Faraday cage had been breached by the fall. My servos weren't responding. And worst of all, neither was my air supply. Like so many millions before me, the aliens' EMP burst had finally got me.

I tried to bring my arms up to remove my helmet, but without the servos, the suit was impossibly heavy. I kept trying anyway, my arms moving inches as I screamed inside my helmet, using every last breath of air that had been held inside. By the time my hands reached the catch for my helmet, I was seeing stars. I felt my fingers play past the clasp, but I didn't have the strength to do anything with it.

For a brief moment I pictured an old science fiction movie; a man tugging at his neck as he strangled to death in the poisonous atmosphere of a dead planet. I'd seen it back when no one had known about the Cray. Back when politics was a blood sport and people actually took the words of world leaders seriously. Back when there was a Hollywood. Back when someone could fly from New York to Paris and sip White Chocolate Macadamia Nut Lattes, delivered from the manicured hands of a well-endowed flight attendant. Back when humans still ruled the planet.

Fuck it.

I'd had a good run.

It wasn't like I hadn't been ready to die before.

Here's a news flash: No soldier gives his life. That's not the way it works. Most soldiers who make a conscious decision to place themselves in harm's way do it to protect their buddies. They do it because of the bonds of friendship—and it goes so much deeper than friendship.

Eric Massa

CHAPTER TWENTY-EIGHT

SOMEONE RIPPED MY my helmet off and smacked me on the face, and I felt my suit coming free. I reached out for a weapon and grabbed the first thing I could. As I was pulled upright, the harmonic blade slid free.

"Whoa there, Nelly," came a voice, followed by ten tons of weight coming down on my wrist.

I felt the blade being removed. I gasped and blinked, trying to see through the shower of stars that had filled my vision as my brain went snap, crackle and pop. How long had I been without oxygen? As I thought about it, I passed out again...

...and came to as I was being passed down the trench and into the arms of half a dozen grunts. They grabbed me, then ran down the gangway and past our squad bay. I struggled and wanted to tell them they were going the wrong way. But as I opened my mouth to speak, I embraced the darkness...

...and awoke lying on an examination table with an oxygen mask on my face. The world was a blur. My eyes weren't ready for reality. I blinked until I could see. Olivares and Aquinas stood at the foot of my table, still in their suits but with their helmets off, holding them in the crooks of their arms. They both appeared concerned.

Aquinas especially.

I grinned and pulled the mask aside. "Come back for that ride in the back of the car?"

Her eyes widened and she made an exasperated sound. She frowned, turned on her heel and left.

"Smooth move, ExLax." Olivares stepped to the side of the bed.

"What happened?" I rubbed my head. My brain felt like it had been slugged.

"Oxygen deprivation. You were dead for a bit, there."

"Seriously?"

"Not something I'd kid about." Noticing my frown he asked, "Why?"

"It's just that if I was dead, I thought I'd know it." Seeing the look on Olivares's face, I added, "I thought there'd be a big ball of light or at least a million scrawny hands pulling my ass to hell."

"What a grunt you are. Complaining of the quality of the afterlife instead of appreciating being alive."

I smiled weakly. "Grunts aren't happy unless they have something to shoot or complain about."

"I suppose I might have exaggerated that you were really dead. Probably more *deadish*," he said. He turned at the approach of a nurse wearing a combat uniform with Colonel birds on her collar.

She strode in and was immediately in charge. "You disturbing my patient, Staff Sergeant?"

"No, ma'am. Is he going to be ready for duty soon?"

"I can't be sure. We need to run some more tests. Why don't you come back tomorrow?" She moved to my side so she could take my pulse.

Olivares paused for a moment, then brought his left hand to his forehead in a mock salute.

I did the same, except with my right.

When he was out the door, I asked, "What kind of tests do you need to run?"

She smiled, warming to me. She had laugh lines I could get lost in. "No tests. We saw your battle on the screens. You were amazing."

She saw me on the screens? Was our battle televised? I hadn't even thought about it, but with all the video feeds available, why wouldn't they be?

"I was just trying to survive," I said. I wasn't comfortable with the way she was looking at me. I could take a little appreciation, but the glow in her eyes was akin to hero worship, and I was just a damn grunt. "Do I really not need any tests?"

She shook her head. "Can I get you something? This is a good time to relax. You need to rest."

"So there's nothing wrong with me?"

"Nothing at all." She shook her head. Never once had she looked away.

I slid off the bed and stood, a little wobbly, on the other side of the examination table. My boys were flying free, so I slipped the sheet off the table and wrapped it around me several times.

She seemed to realize what I was about to do and made a move towards the door, but I was one step in front of her.

"Thanks so much for all the help, but I'll see you later." Then I was out the door and jogging back to the squad bay.

I turned the wrong way twice. Each time I encountered someone who at first seemed as startled as I was—after all, I was a half-naked guy in a sheet. But then their eyes went wide and a smile broke across their face.

"You're that guy."

"Wait, I know you."

Both times I backed away. What the hell was going on? I didn't want to be famous. I just wanted to get back to my squad.

I finally made it back to our bay. MacKenzie and Thompson were there, playing cards on the bench. When they saw me, they both laughed.

"Look at the hero of the hour," MacKenzie crowed, as big a smile on his face as I'd ever seen.

Thompson stood. His smile was as broad, but there was something else in it. He'd been straddling the bench and brought his leg over. He walked stiff-legged to me, favoring one of his legs a little more than the other, and then to my surprise, he threw his arms around me.

I kept a grip on my blanket with my left hand, but returned his affection with the other, as unmanly and uncomfortable as it was.

"Bro, what's happening? Why all the love?"

He looked at me. "Don't you remember? You saved my life."

I shrugged. "You would have done the same."

He stared at the ground, his smile shining only half as bright and no longer focused on me. "I only wish. I was scared. I'd fallen. I didn't know where to go. And then you came along."

"If you hadn't tripped me, I wouldn't have found you." I disengaged and went to my locker. I let the sheet fall and began throwing on a spare uniform. "What happened, anyway?" I glanced at MacKenzie. "And why does everyone seem to know me?"

Thompson lowered his gaze and went to the end of the bench and sat down.

"You're the guy on the box of cereal," MacKenzie said cryptically.

"What?"

"You're making all this shit taste better, because you're a hero."

"Actually, he just makes people forget about how bad it tastes," Ohirra said, entering the bay. She was coming back from the shower in all her naked glory.

I averted my eyes... mostly. "How bad what tastes? Is it just me or has the whole world gone insane? And what's this about a box of cereal?"

"It is insane." Olivares entered, making it an almost complete squad. We were still missing Aquinas, but she was probably sulking somewhere. "It's insane that they decided to make you the face of the battle. You, Hero of the Mound." He pointed to the wall where a plasma television had been affixed to the wall. I could have sworn it hadn't been there before.

"Where'd that come from?"

"Out of the blue, just like you," Olivares said. "They put televisions up all over the place."

A replay of the battle was on the screen. In the upper right corner was a picture of me, smiling. It was actually a pretty good picture. But on the screen was the video image of me, *Man vs. Alien*, firing my minigun, then releasing it, then swinging madly with my blade. It was a triple feed, from me, from someone in Romeo Six named Errington, and from Thompson's view from the ground. In triptych, Cray claws and hoof spikes scored the outside of my armor as they battled to break through, but they couldn't. It was like a bug scrabbling against the inside of the bottle, only I was the bottle, and I fought back, killing, ripping, slicing, hacking, and stabbing until there was nothing left except myself, exhausted, red lights blinking inside my suit. And then it showed me helping Thompson to his feet. A photo of him went into the upper left, not half as flattering.

"And with every hero comes a heel," MacKenzie said. He went over to Thompson and put his hand on the boy's shoulder. "Never you mind. It could have been me who fell."

"Yeah," Thompson said. "Could have been anyone." But he had yet to meet anyone's eyes and answer the question, *But why didn't you get up?*

"No one will remember you tomorrow," Olivares said flatly.

Thompson nodded. "Thanks."

I exchanged glances with everyone except Thompson. We felt for him, but we weren't the problem. He was his own problem, and unless he figured out how to get past it, things would only get worse.

I finished putting on my uniform and was tying my boots when MacKenzie and Olivares took Thompson away in search of the mythical possibility of a rumored case of beer. That left Ohirra and me.

I untied my boots and slowly began to retie them as I tried to think of how to broach the subject of Aquinas.

I glanced at the door to see if she was anywhere near. "What did Thompson mean about her religion?" I asked. There was no need to identify who *her* was.

"Don't you know?" Ohirra gave me a look to see if I was testing her. "You don't know. Oh, this is way too precious. Didn't you hear her on the feedback in Phase I?"

"I heard a lot back then. I was dealing with my own shit, too."

"Maybe you were in Alabama when she said it."

"You slept through my Alabama trip."

"Are you sure?"

"Not at all. So what's her deal?"

Ohirra stared at me for a long moment, then without preamble she said, "Aquinas used to be a nun... or, I guess, almost a nun."

I actually took a step back. "What do you mean?"

Ohirra shrugged. "I don't know any other way to say it. She was a nun. She isn't anymore. She's here now. That's that."

"Wait a moment. That can't be that. I need to know."

"Why?"

Now it was my turn to shrug.

Her eyes narrowed. "I'm not going to help you get into her pants. She's even more broken than the rest of us."

"I don't want to get into her pants," I began, but stopped once I saw the doubt in Ohirra's eyes. "Okay. So maybe I want to get into her pants, but that's not now. That's way the heck down the road. I want to get to know her better. I want to figure out what makes her tick."

"You want to get to know her?" She put her hands on her hips. "If I had a dollar for every time I heard that line."

"Come on, Ohirra. Help me understand."

"Maybe she doesn't want people to know."

"We're all experienced enough to know what happens when we hold things inside," I countered.

She nodded. "Consider this. If she'd wanted you to know, she would have told you."

"I don't buy it. She told you because you're like a sister. She told Thompson because she thinks of him as a brother. She doesn't think of me the same way."

Ohirra laughed. "Now that's a leap of logic if I ever heard one."

"Not a leap. Fact. Either she sees me one way or the other."

"What if she'd rather have nothing to do with you?"

I shook my head. "I don't get that vibe."

Ohirra stared at me for a long moment. "I don't get that vibe either. You know, one minute you can be the densest man I've ever known, the other you seem to understand things better than all the rest of us."

"Trust me," I said, "it's a curse. So she was really a nun?"

"Yeah. A certified Bride of Christ in training, or whatever they're called. I don't know if she made it to full nunship, but she was on track."

I thought for a moment. "Was it the peace and quiet?"

"I think so. She talks about it like a time where she didn't have to think of anyone else except herself. She spent six months in a nunnery south of Seattle. Saint Joseph's, I think she said."

"Do you know why she left?"

"She hit one of the other nuns."

"Hit... as in struck?"

"Hit as in coldcocked with a right cross."

"What the hell happened?"

"They touched her."

"Touched as in..."

"No, silly. Not like that. In this case, one just put her hand on Aquinas's shoulder. Next thing you know, she was lying flat out on the floor, Michelle standing over her. PTSD." Ohirra's gaze shifted to someone behind me. Her face went white and her mouth fell open.

"Is this what you do with my confidence?" came a voice from behind me.

I spun, but Aquinas's eyes were only for Ohirra.

"I thought we were friends."

Ohirra glanced painfully from me back to Aquinas. "We are. It's just that he wanted to..." She frowned and glared at the ground. She slammed her locker door. "I knew I shouldn't have become involved. Now this is all messed up."

"And you," Aquinas directed her attention at me. "What gives you the right to pry into my life?"

"I want to get to know you better," I said with as much honesty as I could muster.

The Filipina stared at me, emotions playing across her face. It was clear she hadn't expected my response. Finally she said, "Take a number," and she spun on her heel and left the room.

Both Ohirra and I stared after her. Neither one of us said anything for a few moments.

Then Ohirra brushed past me. "You better fix this," she said. "Last thing I need is the only other girl in the squad to not be talking to me. Got it?"

"Got it," I said.

STEP 1. Action on Enemy Contact. The platoon initiates contact. The platoon leader plans when and how his base-of-fire element initiates contact with the enemy to establish a base of fire. This element must be in position and briefed before it initiates contact.

Field Manual 7-8,
U.S. Infantry Rifle Platoon and Squad
Standard Operating Procedures

CHAPTER TWENTY-NINE

I CHECKED MY armor before I left. It was a roadmap of what the aliens had tried to do to me. A tech had applied some sort of liquid metal to the scratches, filling them in as best he could. Even semi-fixed, it was a terrible sight. The Cray's claws, heel and elbow spikes were deadly appendages. Any single scratch could have cut me in half had I not been wearing armor; taken together, they would have left me in dozens of little pieces. I checked my minigun and saw that it had been reloaded and cleaned. My blade was charging as well. The missiles had been replaced in all but one of the tubes, which had been crushed in battle.

It took me a few moments, but I tracked down the tech who'd worked on my suit. He gave me the same silly smile as the rest of them. For a moment I was afraid he'd ask me for an autograph. Thankfully he just let me ask my questions about the integrity of the EXO. I was concerned about the red lights and wanted to make certain that the next time I wore it that the suit would seal.

He said he'd fixed the tears in the Faraday cage and replaced the processors and much of the circuitry. The only thing he was waiting on was a circuit board for my communications gear, but otherwise he promised the EXO was battle ready.

I made my way back towards the common area and realized I was starving. Several times I caught people of all ranks, even some colonels, grinning and approaching me. Most of them just wanted to tell me how great and awesome I was. A few others wanted to touch me for luck, which I found creepy and strange. After all, I was the same dumb grunt I'd been before the battle.

I didn't know how to respond, so I kept my head down and hurried to the line. They had T-rats, good old just-add-water-and-make-it-edible food. In this case it was chilli mac, a concoction of chilli and macaroni that tasted just enough like its predecessors not to be called cardboard. It was a grunt food staple and I actually liked it. I let them heap the food on my plate, and grabbed several pieces of dried fruit and two bottles of water. I found a table, sat down, and calmly and efficiently inhaled my food, aware all the while that everyone was staring at me.

Now I knew what a movie star felt like. I'd always wondered. I'd always wanted to be one. Now I'd rather have been anyone but. All this notice made me feel as if ants were crawling on my skin. I was about to get up when Olivares set his tray down in front of me.

"Is it getting old yet?" he asked.

"It was old after five minutes."

"Was that before or after the nurse chased you down?"

I glanced up at him. "How'd you find out about that?"

"Did she touch you in your special place?"

I rolled my eyes. "Everyone's a comedian."

He smirked. "Seriously. She stopped by. Left a note."

I shook my head.

"I put it on top of all the other notes."

"Other notes?"

"Yeah. Looks like half the women and several of the men in this place want to sleep with you."

"You read them?"

"What? You expecting us to honor the sanctity of your fan letters? Not a chance. We all know what's going on here." He leaned close so that no one could read his lips. "What they did was screw up my team and I'm pretty pissed about that."

"You talking about Thompson. What happened to him?"

"What does it matter about Thompson?" He shook his head. "It could have happened to any of us. Could have been you. Could have been me. That's not what I'm talking about, though. I'm talking about you."

"Me? What'd I do?" I gestured with my hand towards the dozens of people watching us. "I'm a hero, didn't you see the video?"

He stared at me to see if I was being serious. I made sure my expression promised that I wasn't.

"Which is the problem. Do you think the Hero of the Mound is going to get to go out and fight again?"

"Of course I am."

"This army is held together by a single idea: that we can defeat the Cray. Nothing we did, including flying a commercial jetliner into the hive, seemed to have any effect, except for your sorry ass playing Mason the Barbarian with that silly blade they gave us. You are their hopes. You are their dreams. Think they're going to let you fight now that you're a hero?" He shoveled food into his mouth and chased it with water. He swallowed and gave me a hard look. "Haven't you seen the movies? Heroes can't die."

"Do you really think they'll keep me off mission?" The idea was terrifying. I couldn't stay inside; I'd go crazy.

"If they haven't realized it yet, they soon will, which is why we're set to go on mission in another ten hours at 0400."

"Ten hours?" The food was settling and my eyelids were beginning to droop.

"You can sleep when the aliens are gone." He downed the rest of his water, grabbed his tray, and stood. "Come on. We have a brief, then we're getting six hours of your precious sleep before we have our final mission brief."

We dumped our trays and returned to our squad bay. Everyone was there. MacKenzie was standing over my cot with a piece of paper in his hand.

"...and then I'm going to touch you and feel your strong arms and—"

I ripped the paper from his hand.

"...kiss you all over. Love, Bob," he concluded.

I swung the paper at him, but he backpedaled deftly away.

I grabbed the stack of papers on my bed, wadded them up and dropped them in the nearest trashcan.

"Mind if I have a couple?" MacKenzie asked, pulling them from a pocket.

"By all means. Have them all."

"No. I just want the ones from Susan, Mary and Francie." He turned to Thompson. "I like the name Francie. Think she's hot?"

I shook my head and threw myself down on my cot. I lay there, one foot on the floor, one arm over my face, trying to remember who I'd been and what I'd become and if I'd even had a choice. Mr. Pink, wherever he'd gotten himself off to, had designed it so that even if I ignored his invitation, OMBRA would get me. Down to the net they'd hauled me up with instead of letting me drown.

D'Ambrosio danced in the flames and I pressed my arm down harder, letting the image evaporate in a blizzard of black and white spots. The conversation in the room was nothing more than a buzz. I lived in a fireball of white and black. There were no memories, no present, no future, no past. Here I wasn't famous or a jerk or a man, I just was. And I was satisfied for a moment. I was content.

Then something hit me in the face.

I moved my arm and watched as Olivares dripped more water on to me.

"Dude, what the fuck?" I leaped to my feet.

He backed away. "Just seeing if you were alive or not."

I sat back down, grabbed a towel from the foot of my bed, and wiped my face. "Yeah. I'm alive. Let's get this meeting over with."

"Let's."

For the next ten minutes, he went over what had happened at the mound. Of Romeo Three, we knew what happened, each of us, with the exception of Thompson, having told the others. Romeo Six had lost three grunts and the entire Vulcan team when their guns jammed and drones descended upon them. Video feeds showed gunners and scouts being jerked into the air just as one of the cannons cleared, ripping them all to shreds as a thousand bullets took their lives, their attackers, and any chance of escape.

Romeo One was gone.

Of Romeo One, there were three scouts left. Two were in critical condition and the third wasn't talking to anyone. He was catatonic, and from the reports he wasn't coming out of it anytime soon.

"And now for the good news," Olivares said.

"That this is all an intergalactic joke and they're going to bring back television, Guinness, and the game of football?" MacKenzie frowned as he said the words, not even trying to be funny.

"The good news is that eleven of the devices deployed, fired into the earth, and sent their images back to the servers. According to the techs, we have a seventy-per-cent solution and are able to read the underground chambers."

If we'd cared, we all might have stood and applauded. But we didn't. So we sat there.

But Aquinas spoke up. "Wait a moment. You said eleven of the devices deployed, giving us a seventy percent solution? We carried more than forty-eight devices to the mound. Are you saying they only needed eighteen?"

"It's more complicated than that," Olivares said.

"No, it isn't," said Ohirra, giving me a challenging look. "I'm Asian. It's math. Built in redundancy. Either us or them. We were sent in case the others couldn't make it."

Olivares stood. "Let's not go second-guessing command. We're grunts. All of us. We're here for one thing: to save the planet. No one said it was going to be pretty. No one said we weren't going to be tools for command to use as they saw fit." He grimaced and shook his head. "Get used to it."

He glared at the rest of us, then his face softened. "We have another mission."

"What is it this time, karaoke on the Mound?" MacKenzie asked. "We going to line dance to the tune of *It's Raining Men*?"

"The techs designed a new bomb."

We shut up at this. We weren't going out to take radar or sonar images. We were going out to blow shit up.

"It's a thermobaric bomb, and we need to have it in place before sunrise tomorrow."

"Now we're talking," Ohirra said, rubbing her hands together. A smile cracked her face, for the first time in a long time.

Thompson stood. "I want to carry it. I want to carry the bomb and put it in place."

I looked at Olivares and he nodded.

"I think that's a good idea," he said. "Mission brief in six hours. Until then, get some shuteye." He pointed to Ohirra. "And you, no snoring."

She flipped him off and we all chuckled. She was the only one of us who *didn't* snore, poor girl. We were so tired, she'd be lucky to get to sleep before the rest of us started sawing logs.

We're hearing of a group called Ombra. They're rumored to be fighting the Cray. Go Ombra. Kick their asses. Kick them all the way back to wherever they came from. For all of you out there who still believe in God, give a kneel and a prayer for these men and women. They may just be our only hope.

Conspiracy Theory Talk Radio,
Night Stalker Monologue #1008

CHAPTER THIRTY

I WOKE TO the screams of Romeo One, begging me to come save them. Blood and entrails rained from the sky. I shot upright, bleary-eyed, expecting to be covered in their remains, and swiped madly at my face before realizing it had been all a dream. I sat, gasping, trying to calm myself.

I'd only been asleep for a few hours and I desperately needed more. But try as I might, I couldn't find the sweet spot. Every time I closed my eyes, Romeo One's screams kept me from finding sleep. Finally, I surged out of bed and stalked to the bathroom in my shorts. I stared sleepy-eyed into the mirror for a moment, then dashed my face under the ice-cold running water.

"You dreaming of them too?"

I turned to see Aquinas sitting on the end of a bench, back to the wall, knees drawn up in front of her.

"Romeo One?"

She nodded. "They were *gone*. Just like that. I hear them screaming for me, but there's nothing I can do to help them."

"We can't save everyone." I wiped my face. "I just wish they'd go away so I could sleep."

"Do you really hear them too?" she asked.

"Yeah. I guess it's because we're more empathetic than regular people. You know how us PTSDs are." I laughed, but it was empty.

She didn't return my laugh. The sound fell to the cavern floor and lay there, about as unfunny as anything I could have said. I was in the middle of mentally hammering myself for my insensitivity when she began to speak.

"They left me in the turret of the vehicle. I had overwatch. I was supposed to keep them safe."

I held my breath. She'd never been willing to open up before.

"But there was a group of children on the side of the road. They'd been playing soccer when we arrived and were just standing there, watching my squad pass. They were no threat, so I scanned other sectors."

I closed my eyes. I knew what was coming.

"Then one of the kids walked out of the crowd, a little boy. He wore a vest packed with explosives. I knew what was coming next, so I looked for him. I knew there had to be a man, with a detonator or a cell phone. It didn't take long for me to find him. He stood behind the children. There was no way I could take him out without killing a few kids, but if I didn't, my entire squad would die."

"So I fired three bursts. The first missed entirely and ended up going through the wall of the home behind him and killing a woman. The second burst took him out, as well as a little girl standing next to him. I couldn't stop myself from firing the third burst. It took out two boys. I can still see them twisting. I can still see the utter horror in their eyes. I mean, who would do such a thing?"

Opening my eyes, I found her staring at me.

I smiled weakly.

"Right? Nobody. Then I saw everyone staring at me, wondering what had happened. Everyone, that is, except the young man on the bicycle who had stopped beside our vehicle. He glanced up at me and grinned. I can still see his stained teeth in my dreams. Then he pressed a button on the phone he'd been holding. I turned quickly back to my squad just in time to see the boy explode, killing all of my squad and seven more children. They'd packed ballbearings into the jacket. No one stood a chance."

I uncrossed my arms and walked to her. I sat on the bench a mere foot from her. "No one would have. It was a no-win situation."

"Next thing you'll say is that I tried my best. Listen, I've heard it all. I've had some of the best minds in rehabilitation fail to unscrew my brain."

I felt a smile slip into place.

She caught it right away. "You find this funny, Mason?"

"No. I just figured it out."

"Did you now? Please, tell me."

I shrugged. "You want to be guilty. You want to be responsible. I get that. Us PTSDs understand this. Those experts, no matter how many letters they have after their names, will never be able to understand the redefinition of responsibility we live by. After all, it really wasn't our fault. We were in a bad situation at a bad time. It was the *Kobiashi Maru* without Captain Kirk cheating his way to victory. But our definition of responsibility and our idea of guilt won't let us get off that easily. Do you know why?"

"Why?" she asked softly.

"Because there has to be someone to blame."

Her knuckles whitened.

"There has to be someone to blame," I repeated. "So why not blame ourselves?"

"I'm the one who pulled the trigger."

"And you shot the wrong person."

"And I shot the wrong person. I killed people who wouldn't have been killed otherwise. They died because of me. Not because of the bomber."

"But perfection is the problem, isn't it?"

"What do you mean? Do you think I'm trying to say I'm perfect?"

"Not you. Society. The army that recruited and trained you. The Bible. God. Your parents. Our friends. The universe. They all believe in perfection. And for some strange reason, they pull decent young men and women off the streets, train them for a few weeks, give them weapons, and tell them not to make a single mistake... ever. But we *can't* be perfect. We're bound to make mistakes. They knew that when they put us in these positions. They accepted it as risk."

"You don't know that."

"Don't I? Then tell me, what is the SOP for the situation you found yourself in? Did you follow it?"

She nodded.

"So you did what they trained you to do and came back with a different result than expected."

She nodded again.

"Then how is it your fault?" I held up a finger. "Oh, wait. I know this one. I've used it myself. You should have known, like we're some new breed of psychic soldier. If I was, I never would have joined the Army. I would be living on a boat in the middle of some lake, getting fast food delivered by parachute three times a day."

Her knuckles relaxed.

I shut up for awhile. I'd said enough. Instead I looked at her, taking in her delicate features and the slight uptilt of her nose. I got lost in the freckles beneath her left eye and didn't notice when she began staring back at me.

"You don't have to spend your time trying to make me feel better," she said. "I've had the best try and fail."

I spread my hands. "What I do with my spare time is my decision."

She smiled, "You don't have to protect me, you know."

"I think I do." I understood that she was her own woman, and that she was a grunt just like me, but my feelings dictated that I protect her. She was something special to me, something valuable, and no matter how impervious and tough she might appear, I had to ensure her survival because my life was better with her in it than without.

"But you don't own me."

"Don't I?" I said. "Don't I own you? Don't you own me? Don't all of us own a part of each other?" I reached out and took her hand. "This is your hand attached to your body, but it is a human hand, a hand of my species. We are kin, you and I. Outside are aliens who would have us all die and inside, here we are, one species, one tribe, one family, all of us different versions of the same person."

She sighed. "I'm just a dumb grunt at the end of the world, trying to make some aliens pay up for killing off my people."

"Is this your pitch?"

"Is it working?"

"Not yet."

I took that as encouragement. "I feel the connection between us. I can't not look at you when you walk into room. I can't not think about you when you're in pain. I just want something special before I die."

She looked up, and for a moment I was sure she was going to grin. Instead, her shoulders slumped and she rolled her eyes. "You might have had me if it wasn't for that last line."

Damn. "I forced it, didn't I?" I shook my head. "I'm not used to being honest with someone like you. Hell, I'm not used to being honest with myself."

"So are you going to kiss me now?" she asked.

I nodded, and I did. For ten long seconds we weren't in a cavern beneath the Serengeti waiting to be picked off by aliens. We were a boy and a girl, alone, together.

Then we separated.

I went in for another but she pushed her palm into my chest.

"I think that's enough, big boy."

She stepped around me and walked out of the room.

I stood there for a moment or two, savoring the sensation of her lips on mine.

"There you are," Olivares said as he entered the room. "Guess you wanted to get an early start." He washed his face before turning back to me. "And you know? I had the strangest dream."

"Let me guess. You dreamed about Romeo One."

"How do you know?"

"That makes three of us dreamed the same thing."

"That's not right."

"Agreed. Not right at all."

Does the patriotism demonstrated by the main character in Robert Heinlein's novel *Glory Road* fall flat against the character's demonstrated hatred for his own government's social welfare system? Discuss.

TF OMBRA Study Question

CHAPTER THIRTY-ONE

WE DRESSED WITHOUT a word, trying to forget our dreams as best we could. Each of us made our way to the mess chamber for a little breakfast before the operation. Nothing that would make us slow, but enough to keep our metabolism flowing. I sipped an energy drink and lazily ate a bowl of tasteless oatmeal.

Thirty tables were arrayed in lines with a mess table along the far wall. A bored mess sergeant and two KP-duty privates mixed and served powdered eggs, dehydrated meat and potatoes. Everyone else helped themselves to the other odds and ends on offer. There was normally a healthy buzz in the mess hall as people chatted about their day, planning this and that, remembering the times before, arguing over the superiority of sports teams that no longer existed. But today everyone seemed subdued. They barely even noticed as I entered. While most of me was happy that they were distracted by something else, a small part of me wondered what it had taken to make them forget so quickly.

When MacKenzie finally joined us, he all but slammed his tray down on the table. "You're not going to believe this." He grinned from ear to ear.

We chewed on our food and looked at him quizzically.

As it turned out, everyone had dreamed about Romeo One. Not just us, but *everyone*. I don't know why MacKenzie found it so funny, but he thought it was a riot. I was both too tired and too intrigued about what had happened with Michelle to dwell much on our shared dream.

Olivares looked like he was about to say something, when Ohirra stood and pointed out it was time for us to get moving.

Thirty minutes later we were in our suits.

Forty-five minutes later we were checked out.

Sixty minutes later we were poised at the end of Trench One.

The bomb looked like a fuel pod for a jet fighter that had been wired by a platoon of kindergarteners. A Faraday cage had been placed around it. The whole thing was too large to carry, so we had been provided with a sled.

0500. We had thirty minutes to put the bomb in place before the sky began to lighten. Not much time, but the engineers had had to build the sled and finish making the bomb operational, so it was what it was. And that was okay. We'd been bloodied, so to speak. We'd attacked, the Cray had defended, and we'd killed each other. I no longer felt the same butterflies I'd had on our last assault. I'd gone into the alien food processor and come out the other end, only slightly worse for wear. Where before I'd had to swallow pure fear, now I just wanted to get moving. It was the waiting that caused the most agitation. So when we got the go-ahead, I was relieved to finally be in the mission.

Olivares and I pulled the sled first, while MacKenzie and Ohirra ran ahead of us and Thompson and Aquinas brought up the rear. We'd been warned to keep an eye on the heat index as we pushed the suits to their maximum pace. I tried to pay attention to the readouts, but was more concerned with the approaching hive and the imminent threat of the Cray.

As I ran, I wondered again why there weren't more drones out at night. Was it a sleep cycle issue? It couldn't be the cold, because the temperature didn't drop that much at night here in Africa. I would ask those in the know once we returned to base.

We made it to Boma Ng'ombe and switched positions. I loped out in front, enjoying the free and easy movement. As we passed the far edge of the village, I spied a Vulcan sled moving parallel with our position, about fifty yards to our left.

The TOC sent a warning. "Activity above the mound."

I checked my telemetry and saw five Cray. I wondered what they'd make of the giant pill-shaped object we were carrying.

A flash of light was followed by Olivares saying, "EMP. Everyone check their suits."

Systems check. Ninety-one percent power. All green.

We didn't have to reply; he had access to our status. He was just making sure we were maintaining our vigilance. If one of us had a problem, we'd let him know.

"One mile to target."

One mile. Four minutes, at current speed.

"Provide status of device," Olivares commanded.

The TOC returned, "Green and ready."

"Incoming!"

The rounds impacted the mound high up. The mission planners had insisted on the artillery, even if their rounds did little discernible damage. Personally, I felt that the barrage was like knocking on the door to a wasp nest. Once the rounds began to hit, every Cray inside would be on alert.

Another barrage came, scouring the hive low down.

Knock knock.

"Switch," Olivares commanded.

Thompson and Aquinas took up the sled while MacKenzie and Ohirra covered the rear. We were less than half a mile from the target.

"They're getting curious." I tried to keep the worry out of my voice as I noted two drones heading our way.

"Fire when ready," Olivares said.

I targeted both Cray and launched two missiles, and then a third. The first two disintegrated the aliens while the third kept going, falling to earth far from our position. I let go with a fourth missile as I saw another shape come into view. Seconds later, the Cray was dispatched.

This seemed far too easy.

By now the drones should be boiling out of the mound, attacking us in waves, trying to wipe us from the plain. But there were just three Cray lazily circling the mound, as if I hadn't just killed three of their kin and we weren't transporting a bomb.

"Prepare to activate device." The voice over the comms was familiar and I knew if I only had a few more minutes I'd figure it out, but we were running short on time.

Olivares ordered us to slow. I kept my minigun pointed towards the sky, scanning both visually and with telemetry. MacKenzie and Ohirra were doing the same behind me. We stopped a mere fifty meters from the mound. The sonar readouts had indicated this was the best position for the bomb; the depth between the surface and the tunnels beneath was at its thinnest point here.

"Thompson, Ohirra and Aquinas, return to base," Olivares ordered.

Thompson hooted and punched the air. I didn't doubt his theatrics were for the cameras. I didn't begrudge him his moment one bit. Whatever had happened during the last battle, he'd earned this moment; he'd had a hard last twenty hours.

While MacKenzie and I provided cover, Olivares checked the wiring.

"All green. Initiating countdown." Olivares was already running as he said, "Countdown initiated. You guys waiting for an invitation?"

"He did not just get a running head start, did he?" McKenzie cried.

"I think he did."

"Then let's show that Mexican wanker how to really run," and he took off faster than I believed the suit was capable of. Soon he'd passed Olivares, leaving me in the dust.

We had ten seconds and had already traveled five hundred meters. As long as we maintained our speed, we'd be more than safe. Still, when the countdown reached five, Olivares ordered us to the ground. I skidded, then fell, sliding along the dirt headfirst, arms outstretched, waiting for the explosion—

Which never came.

I counted to ten, then twenty, then thirty.

"Base, I read the device as green. How do you have it?"

The voice from the TOC was perplexed. "We have green as well." There was a pause. "We don't suppose you could go back and check the device."

We all turned and glanced at the mound. There were about a hundred Cray circling, soaking in the morning sun that had just crested the horizon.

"You want us to check the device?" Olivares strained to keep his voice steady. "Do I read you clear?"

"Affirmative. If you could... check the connections once more."

I got to my feet. This was stupid. The damn thing could blow any second.

MacKenzie scrambled up from where he'd skidded in front of me and began to jog back towards the hive.

"Where are you going?" I demanded.

"To fix the *focking* piece of shit bomb."

I scanned the sky. "I'm coming with you." There was no way I could let him go alone. As far as I knew, we'd get within ten feet and the thing would explode. But on the off-chance it didn't, someone needed to cover MacKenzie from air attack.

"What are you two doing?" Olivares asked.

Now running side-by-side, MacKenzie and I turned to each other and grinned.

"Can't hear you, sergeant," I said.

"Breaking up." MacKenzie made false 'static' noises with his mouth. "We must be going through a tunnel."

I laughed. This was too much fun. Olivares was going to be so pissed at us, but I didn't care. I couldn't leave a man behind.

We slowed to a walk as we approached the bomb. We didn't want to seem to be in too big of a rush. We were extremely aware of the growing number of Cray above us. One had to wonder what they were thinking.

Suddenly Olivares was jogging to a stop between us.

"A tunnel, huh?" he asked.

"Oh, yes," MacKenzie said straight-faced. "It was a big *focking* tunnel right back there. You couldn't have missed it."

Olivares looked up. "I wonder what they see when they look down at us."

"Cockroaches, probably," MacKenzie said.

"Hope not. Don't want them stomping us out. Break. Break. Base, this is Romeo Three. Prepare Vulcan for ground to air support."

"WILCO."

"So one of three things is going to happen, boys," Olivares said. We only had a football field's length between us and the device. "One, we're going to walk another hundred meters and get blown to smithereens. Two, I'm going to attach whatever wire is messed up and we're going to get back to base in time for a tasty brunch." He paused long enough for us to wonder if he was going to finish. Then he said, "Or three, *really* bad shit happens."

None of us needed any explanation about what that *really bad shit* was. Romeo One had given us plenty of their own memories, just in case we didn't have enough of our own.

"Okay, you grunts," Olivares said, running the last few feet and dropping to a knee in front of the device. "Let's get this shit over with."

Both MacKenzie and I trained our miniguns toward the sky.

Telemetry told me there were now one-hundred and thirty-seven Cray above us. They were all between eleven hundred and thirteen hundred feet over our position, which was exactly where I wanted them.

"Know what I wonder?" MacKenzie asked.

"What?"

"What or who were the Smithereens? I mean no one wants to get blown up like them. Makes you wonder if it wasn't some unlucky family or something, maybe bombed in the Blitz or something."

"Comes from the Irish word, *smidirin*. Means many small pieces," Olivares said. "Had to look it up once. Break. Break. Base, provide schematic overlay."

"*Focking* Irish. Figures it's an Irish word. Probably stole it from *smidgen*."

The Cray had descended to nine hundred feet. I readied my Mini-Hydra and re-checked to make sure my minigun was in the green. "Never heard anyone say they didn't want to get blown to a smidgen, Mac, sorry."

"Of course not. We're not that stupid. I still say it was probably a family named Smithereen. They were probably Irish."

My HUD suddenly lit up.

"Here they come!"

The Vulcans unzipped the morning with a thousand rounds and more, pouring into the phalanx of incoming drones.

I held my aim until I saw who'd survived the Vulcan rounds and unloaded my remaining complement of missiles. Once spent, I fired my minigun in controlled bursts.

"There you are, you little fucker." I glanced down at Olivares as he reattached a wire and snapped a panel back in place.

When he stood, he snapped his minigun into position and yelled, "Get to backs."

We all formed on each other, standing back-to-back as best we could, just as MacKenzie released the last of his missiles. We moved like a six-legged crab towards friendly lines, spinning slightly clockwise as we went. When he was to the rear of our formation, Olivares would release missiles, until he was out, too.

We alternated fire to conserve ammunition. My telemetry counted forty-three Cray still airborne. It was only a matter of time before the rest came out to join the fun.

"We're going to need to run in a moment, gentlemen," Olivares said. "We have fifty seconds to detonation and need to make a lot more distance than we're making now."

It was my turn to fire and I began to take out the Cray in bursts. My bullets smashed through heads, chests and wings.

"When do we need to start running?" I asked. It was beginning to dawn on me that I'd need to draw my blade soon.

"Now!" Olivares shouted and took off.

MacKenzie and I exchanged a frenzied look and bounded after him.

As I ran, I fired blindly into the air behind me, spitting out the last of my ammunition. One five-hundred round magazine emptied, then there was a whine as the barrels spun and the feed mechanism moved to the next magazine. Realizing how little effect I was having, I let the minigun swing back out of the way and pulled free my blade.

"Get those *focking* Vulcans crackin'!" MacKenzie cried.

I glanced over to him, only to see a pair of Cray holding him by the head and arms. I spun and ran back for him, then leaped, catching a hold of his leg, our combined weight pulling him back to earth.

One of the Cray had let go, but the other doggedly hung on. I swung and removed its arm.

MacKenzie turned to grin at me and then he was gone again.

I jerked my gaze upwards and saw him rising straight up, a drone gripping his helmet. I was about to scream his name, when I felt myself jerked into the air. I swung madly with my blade, frantic in my attempts to be free. I hit something and felt myself falling.

I slammed into the ground and all the air left my body. I tried to get up quickly, but could only manage to move my limbs one at a time. My servos were still functioning, but the adrenalin surge had left my body like stone. An alarm went off in my helmet. My telemetry was warning me of an incoming mass.

I managed to stagger to the side just as MacKenzie hit the earth with a sickening sound.

I screamed as the reality of his death hit me. A Cray came at me, wings spread, claws out, and I brought my blade around.

Then the device blew.

The world became a tornado of earth, wind, fire and body parts, with me caught in the centre of the maelstrom. I lost my grip on my blade as I tumbled. I closed my eyes in anticipation of pain, but my suit took most of the force of the explosion. I hit the ground at an angle and began to roll end over end. My servos jerked my arms and legs into my body, making me somersault across the ground. As I slowed, I opened my eyes. My HUD flashed green and red; beyond it, ground and debris tumbled past.

When I finally came to a rest, blood was dripping down my visor. I tried to stand but felt an immense weight on my back. My telemetry was inoperative. Access to the other team members' feeds was down. My suit and servos read green. Unless a building had fallen on me, I should be able to get up.

I placed my hands on the ground and, using my knees as a fulcrum, I pushed my upper body up. The weight on my back shifted and I dropped down and rolled to my right, coming face to face with a Cray. I lashed out and drove my fingers into the clump of eyes at the center of its triangular head. It jerked back and I staggered to my feet, looking around for anything I could use as a weapon. Amidst the debris, I found a piece of Cray claw large enough to wield as a club, picked it up and stalked after the wounded drone.

It stood, slightly hunched over. It was missing an arm, and bleeding from a dozen wounds. Its wings had been ripped away. It made a pathetic sight as it hobbled back towards the mound.

I held the arm out and shook it. "Hey! Are you forgetting something? Is this yours, you motherfucker?"

It turned and seemed to study me, before it charged.

I brought its severed arm around, swinging like I was Babe Ruth channeling Sammy Sosa. The arm broke across the creature's head and it fell sideways. I fell onto the creature and began hammering it over and over with my fists. I remembered the death of MacKenzie, my rage driving me on. Was this the Cray who'd taken him? My breath clouded the inside of my face shield until I couldn't see anything past my own blood-red fog.

I felt my arms being pulled back and turned and swung, but a Romeo caught my fist in his own.

He screamed at me through his mask.

I could barely hear him.

He screamed louder.

"We... Romeo Seven... follow... back... TOC..."

I understood enough and started to move towards friendly lines, but my legs gave way. Another scout from Romeo Seven joined the first, and both of them helped me back. When we finally arrived, I was greeted by the rest of Romeo Three, and was lowered into their arms. I felt a surge of pride. I loved my grunts. I was so happy I almost forgot that MacKenzie was dead.

Almost.

For funerals where there is a separate firing party, once the casket is borne between the firing party members, and taken into the chapel, the NCOIC commands *Order ARMS*. The firing party departs under the control of the firing party commander and travels to the gravesite. Once at the gravesite, the firing party makes preparations for the gravesite ceremony. The bugler, if not already at the gravesite, travels with the firing party.

U.S. Army Training Circular 3-21.5

CHAPTER THIRTY-TWO

MACKENZIE'S DEATH HIT me hard. It wasn't like D'Ambrosio or the others. With them I'd felt a sense of helplessness, unable to change a course of events that began when God woke up and decided we were going to have a bad day. This was different. For one, I hadn't been in charge of the mission. The orders hadn't flown through me. I was a mere grunt, just as MacKenzie had been. In fact, we shouldn't have been there. The mission should have been over. Had we not gone back, we'd have been safe, watching the effects of the explosion in plasma TV clarity.

Being a leader, I was alone in my decisions and removed, to some degree, from the deaths of my soldiers. Where before I'd been someone to blame, now I was someone who wanted to blame someone. Sure, it could have been anyone who'd died. Sure, we could have lost someone sooner. Sure. Sure. Sure. But none of those things mattered. MacKenzie was my friend and

I didn't want him to be dead. The truth of it was that I'd have traded any one of the grunts I didn't know just so the smiling Scotsman could still be alive. I'd even play Poof with him, whatever that was.

We'd brought him in two hours before. His body had ended up a mile from the trenches. The Cray were too busy taking care of their own dead to care about us anyway.

We laid MacKenzie out on the bench in the middle of the squad bay and gently removed the suit, careful of the damage that had been done. Even with the EXO's protection, he'd been dropped from such a great height that his insides had liquefied. The bones in his legs had shattered so completely that his limbs were like rubber.

Even with all of this damage, however, his face remained virtually unscathed. I could almost picture him waking up and calling us a *bunch of focking wankers* for acting all weepy-eyed. I knew he wouldn't have wanted this impromptu wake, but it was more about us than him.

I caught myself staring at Olivares during our vigil. He waited until we'd finished attending to MacKenzie's body and after the surgeon had removed him before saying anything to me about it.

I'd cleaned up and was getting ready to change back into my fatigues when he sat next to me on the bench.

"He was a good grunt," he said.

"That he was." I pulled my socks on, then my pants.

"We've all lost friends."

I pulled on a t-shirt, tucked it in, then buttoned up my top while I thought about what I was going to say. I could get angry, but what would be the point? We were the ones who had fucked up. MacKenzie and I had chosen to go on our own and disobey an order. I grudgingly acknowledged that with a shake of my head and the words, "It was nothing you did, Sarge. It was just stupid-ass bad luck, is all."

I could feel him watching me as I pulled my boots on and laced them up.

"That's what war is." He stood up. "One stupid never-ending piece of bad luck." He headed towards the door, then paused. "We have a meeting in thirty minutes, and then your time is your own for the next eight hours. At tonight's memorial we'll read MacKenzie's honors. You going to be there?"

I nodded, not sure if I could actually speak.

Out of the corner of my eye, I saw him nod back. Then he turned and left.

I slammed my fist into the wall locker and left it there, embedded in the thin metal. Finally, I wiped away the wetness that had somehow appeared on my face and slid on my dog tags. I was about to head out for something to eat when my gaze was drawn by something playing on the television.

They were replaying the mission. The screen showed me beating the Cray to death with its own arm. I sat down and waited for it to end, knowing it would soon start to replay from the beginning. Like old TV shows, you could count on it starting over again. I could see MacKenzie. I could see him smile. Then I could see him die.

Again and again and again.

Ten minutes later I walked out, the bench only slightly worse for wear from where I'd used it to bash in the screen.

I ignored the looks from the others. I was in my own world, my own Hollywood blockbuster, one in which me and Romeo Three existed and everyone else was an extra. Everyone knew extras didn't talk, so I didn't talk to them.

I sat at an empty table with three bottles of water and a cup of coffee. Three people came by to talk to me. I ignored them all. It wasn't until the fourth that I even looked up.

Aquinas dropped a note on the table and kept going. I watched her leave, wondering what that was all about. I opened the paper, feeling a little like I was back in high school, although I reminded myself that back then I never would have gotten close to a girl like her. I turned it several times before I realized that it was a map of the base. On it was an X. The only other directions were the words *After the Meeting!*

I suddenly realized I was late for the briefing. I shoved the note in my pocket, slugged back the now-lukewarm coffee, and took the bottles of water with me. I hurried, but I didn't run. I entered the room with my head down, aware of the eyes that turned towards me. I didn't want any more attention. I really just wanted to get this over with so I could get some rack time.

"Thanks for joining us, Mason," said a voice I knew. "I was wondering if you were feeling up to this."

Mr. Pink was back. His was the voice I'd heard on the comms. Now he stood in front of me, looking more like his namesake every day. His face was haggard and wan, like he hadn't slept in weeks. He wore fatigue pants and boots with a tucked-in black TF OMBRA polo shirt. A red beret with the TF insignia finished the look.

I felt an unusual sense of pleasure at seeing him standing before the row of tables. I could trace many of my worst moments to this man, but we had history, and in the military, this was something akin to brotherhood.

Instead of saying anything, I merely nodded, sharing the briefest eye contact.

The rest of Romeo Three were already present and seated. Behind Mr. Pink were two large maps and a blown-up panoramic photo. The photo was a triptych of the side view of the mound, taken from three different angles. One of the maps was a pre-invasion satellite representation of the area without the hive, but with curious blotches running from white to red. The second map was a wire diagram and could have been anything.

"As I was saying," he resumed, nodding politely in my direction, "You're not the first squad I'm giving this briefing to. We've learned a lot in the last few weeks." He went to the satellite map and began pointing to the mysterious blobs.

"This is a pre-invasion photo. These heat overlays show us pockets of lava beneath Kilimanjaro and this plain. It's what geologists call a stratovolcano. Kilimanjaro consists of three cones. Two of them, Shira and Mawenzi, are extinct, but the third, Kibo, is merely dormant. Fumaroles in its crater still emit volcanic gasses; these are deadly and contain vaporized sulfuric acid, so even getting near it will kill you.

"Add to that the fact that Kilimanjaro is the highest mountain in Africa. It's just shy of six thousand meters above sea level and topped with an ice cap. Thanks to intense study, we not only have maps of the dormant cones, but also of the Kibo caldera, although it's filled with a pile of volcanic ash to an unknown depth."

Olivares raised a hand. "We appreciate the geology lesson, Captain Science, but what does it have to do with us? We're grunts, not geologists."

Mr. Pink nodded and continued, undeterred. He moved to the panoramic photo. "This is a triptych of the outside of the mound. As you can see, we've done little damage to it. We've detected traces of crystallized iridium from the mound's surface, which is probably the reason for its almost impenetrable hardness. Note that our highly-skilled artillerymen have been trying desperately to get a shot into one of these launch tubes, but so far they are 0 and 724 and the chances don't look like it will get any better."

"What are they doing under there?" Thompson asked.

"Million-dollar question. We don't know, and we need to. This is one of the smallest hives on the planet and it's in the middle of nowhere. So why have it here? What makes it so important? Why have the mounds at all?"

"Maybe because we'd beat them in straight combat," Ohirra said, a look of pride on her face.

"You say that now." Mr. Pink smiled. "But that's because of TF OMBRA's suits. BCT OMBRA has them, but hardly anyone else does. Since before the invasion we were in negotiations with most major powers—we even made a presentation before the United Nations—but no one wanted to invest the money or pay the subscription for service."

"Do you mean you charged for them?" Thompson sounded shocked.

"We're a corporation, Private Thompson, not a charity. We spent hundreds of billions preparing for this event. Far more, I might add, than the entirety of the world's governments. It's only right we should be paid." He smiled. "We repeatedly offered payment plans, but now that there is effectively no such thing as an economy we've begun negotiating in land and mineral rights."

Olivares scowled. "Sounds like blackmail to me."

"Is it?" Mr. Pink crossed his arms. "Is it blackmail when you warn the world that something is coming? Is it blackmail when you recommend they should engage in some sort of unified response? We warned them this was coming. We offered them assistance. Now that it's a bald fact that they failed to handle the situation, we offer again, but from a more solid negotiating position. This isn't blackmail. This isn't even an *I told you so*. This is business. If we spend money, we have to recoup somehow."

I had to speak up. "If our situation is so dire, then why not do it for free? I'm sure you'll be rewarded."

"Corporal Mason... Always the romantic. When we finally push the Cray off our planet, this isn't going to be like the final scene in *Return of the Jedi*. There will be no parades. There won't be anyone left to give out awards. The governments have fucked it all up and won't be in charge anymore. OMBRA, and dozens of other corporations which have formed since first detection of the pending attack, will become the world's governments."

"It just doesn't seem right," I mumbled.

"No, it doesn't. Blame your congress for not being able to get out of their own way long enough to save the planet. It's not like they haven't been doing this sort of thing for decades. Blame the world leaders. Blame anyone. But don't blame the people who *told* everyone there was going to be an invasion. When this is all over, and I have no doubt that we will win the day, we're going to have two choices as a species. Start from scratch and huddle around our fires, or have leaders ready to stand up and lead. You can't count on your governments, but you can count on OMBRA. We have underground bunkers, like the one you all were in during training, filled with scientists and academicians ready to confront the problem and get our planet back on track. Should we be rewarded for that? For being ready to help?" He paused. "I think so. Daring plans and sacrifice should always be rewarded."

"Okay. I got it, Mr. Pink," Olivares said. "Thanks for your views on the economy and the state of planetary ignorance which preceded the coming of the Cray. But we've *been* invaded. We've had our asses kicked. Most of our great array of weapons don't work anymore and here you are talking smack about how OMBRA is going to rule the world one day, but you can't even seem to break into the smallest alien termite mound on the planet. I'm hoping you have a plan."

Mr. Pink stared at Olivares for a moment. All of us wondered if he was going to get mad, but then he broke into a smile. "Very eloquently said, Sergeant Olivares. Very eloquent, indeed. We do have a plan. We have several, as a matter of fact." He began pacing. "Back to the question Private Thompson asked. What *are* they doing under there? Why the mounds?"

We all waited.

Mr. Pink pressed a button and a projector blossomed light from the ceiling. He pulled down a screen and a view of Earth began to rotate on the blank white surface.

"We understood why the aliens would set down in the cities. This is a battle for conquest. They had to be where the people were." Red spots began to appear on Earth. "These are all of the population areas which have been attacked."

There were hundreds; I never knew it was so many.

"Now let's look at the less-populated areas."

Seven white spots appeared, all within twenty degrees of the equator. The Gobi Desert. The Australian Outback. Kilimanjaro. Mount Ararat in Turkey. Texas. Hilo Island. Venezuela.

"In five months Earth is going to be in aphelion." He pressed a button and the view changed to a wire diagram of the galaxy. A pulsating blue spot appeared. "This is the destination of the pre-invasion communications. It's presumably either the Cray's home planet or a world which they had already taken over and used as a staging post. In five months, the plains of Kilimanjaro will be in a prime spot to communicate with this location, as far as possible from the sun's radiation, at the perfect angle of declination. We believe it's been placed here as some sort of communication node."

"What about the other six locations?" Aquinas asked.

"The angle won't be right for accurate and effective communication from these sites."

"But doesn't the Earth turn on its axis every day? What about the... er... wobble?" I remembered something about the Earth not rotating exactly perfectly each time.

"If you're speaking of the Chandler Wobble, then that was taken into account, yes." Seeing our concern, he said, "This is classified above your pay grades, but know that we have other forces in place to deal with the others."

"Other BCTs?" Ohirra asked.

"Above your pay grade."

She shook her head. "Jesus."

"So we have a possible—correction—*probable* communications array we need to remove." He turned the projector off and raised the screen. "The problem is that we can't effectively attack it from the outside." He pointed at a diagram on the screen. "This is what we were able to construct based on the ground penetrating radar and sonar."

Lines emanating from the volcano ran beneath the plain and intersected other lines, many of them near our location.

Then it became clear. "Am I reading this right? Is there a way for the Cray to travel underground to our location?" I said.

Mr. Pink nodded. "We've identified several tunnels which have breach potential. But there's still several hundred meters of rock between us and them."

"Have you started working on that?" Olivares asked. When Mr. Pink hesitated, Olivares cursed under his breath and stood. "Hey, sir, you're the one who decided to brief a bunch of lowly grunts. And you've clearly done it for a reason. Don't start getting touchy if we ask questions you weren't expecting. Most of us are a lot older than the average baby soldier, and in the end, pay grade or no pay grade, we're going to have the need to know if our lives are going to be at stake."

I've had my issues with Olivares, but just then I wanted to slap him on the back.

Mr. Pink waved for Olivares to sit again. Once Olivares was seated, the company man offered us an apologetic smile. "No, I get it. And I'm not briefing everyone, just a few select units with the understanding that this information is closely held and sensitive. And yes, we have an element working on that now, but we're trying to work quickly and quietly, more so because we don't know exactly what we'll find when and if we break through."

"Is that what you want us to do?" Aquinas asked. "Do you want us to go in first?"

"Not here," Mr. Pink said, pointing at our location. He moved across the wire diagram and pointed to the top of the volcano. "Here."

"You want us to scale the mountain and climb inside a volcano?" Thompson said. "That's cool."

We all turned to stare at him.

He shrugged. "What? You never wanted to go inside a volcano before?"

"Uh... no," Ohirra said.

I agreed. I didn't mind fighting, but the idea of going into an enclosed space where the rock could melt your skin somehow failed to excite me the way it did Thompson.

"I need two persons to volunteer."

We all looked at each other. We'd been in the military long enough to know that you never volunteered for anything.

"I'll go," Aquinas said.

"I'll go, too," Olivares added.

Olivares saw me gaping at him and shrugged.

Thompson looked back and forth with a stunned look on his face. "Shit. Put me on standby then," he mumbled.

"Okay. We have one more mission to lay more ground penetrators, then we'll begin preparing for the mission to breach Kilimanjaro." Mr. Pink gave me a look as if he was disappointed that I hadn't volunteered.

I frowned and crossed my arms. I might have volunteered, but I'd thought we knew better than to do something so stupid.

"We'll reconvene after the memorial this evening," Olivares said, getting up. "Until then, your time is your own."

"Can I ask one more question?" Thompson asked.

Olivares fixed him with an exasperated look, but sat back down.

Mr. Pink had been heading for the door. He stopped, glanced around the room, and directed his attention at Thompson. "Go ahead."

The young blond drummer boy looked around self-consciously. When he finally spoke, it was with a quiet voice. "What about our dreams?"

I watched as Mr. Pink's gaze flicked over us, then settled back on Thompson. "What about them?"

He cleared his throat. "Romeo One. We hear them."

"What do they say?"

"They're not saying anything. They're screaming."

"We know about the dreams." He shook his head. "We're working on it. That's all I can say at present." Then he left.

Olivares stood. "I guess that answers our question, huh? If you got something to do, don't do it here."

Thompson and Ohirra came up to me on my way out.

"Can you believe those two?" she asked.

"They volunteered," I said, still a little numb.

"Do you know what MacKenzie would have said?" Thompson asked. We both looked at him. "*Focking* stupid to volunteer."

Still, we laughed. If nothing more than to see Thompson trying so hard.

On my way back to our quarters, I remembered the note. I took it from my pocket and tried to navigate by the rough map. After three false turns, I found the spot, behind a generator in one of the farthest caverns. I turned the corner behind the immense, growling machine, and saw Aquinas, sitting on a cot in her underwear, reading the sort of magazine one used to buy at the checkout line back when there was a Hollywood and we cared about who was cheating on whom. The savagery she'd done to herself was etched on the insides of her arms, from elbow to wrist.

She caught me staring at them. But instead of covering herself, she simply regarded me calmly, and what seemed like a hundred years of fighting disappeared in a moment. The ghosts of Frakess and MacKenzie and D'Ambrosio and everyone I'd ever known were torn apart by a hurricane of need. I forgot everything but me and her, a boy and a girl in a cave at the end of the world. My hands reached out to her and she moved into them like a freight train, catching me off balance.

Our lips met, and I felt her need meet mine. She ripped at my clothes as I reveled in the feel of her hot skin beneath my rough fingers. We forgot ourselves, falling onto the cot in a desperate embrace. We loved each other for almost an hour until we finally fell into a restless sleep, our sweat slick and cooling between us.

For once I didn't dream.

If you know the enemy and know yourself you need not fear the results of a hundred battles.

Sun Tzu

CHAPTER THIRTY-THREE

I AWOKE TO the sound of a banshee screaming. At first I thought it might be of remnant of a dream, but I shot bolt upright when I realized that the sound was real. I was alone and naked on the cot; the blanket that had covered us had fallen to the floor. I looked around, but saw no sign of Michelle.

The banshee call came again.

Bagpipes.

Oh, shit! MacKenzie's wake!

I struggled into my uniform and boots and rushed around the corner to find a young woman attending to the generator. She gave me a look and I offered her an embarrassed smile and broke into a run. I followed the sound of the pipes until I skidded to a stop in the back of the mess hall. All the tables and chairs had been folded and stacked against one wall, leaving the center free for the ceremony. Several dozen body bags lay in a row in front of the gathering.

I looked for Romeo Three and, spotting them near the front, made my way towards them. Thompson saw me coming and moved aside to make room for me. Ohirra was on his other side. Beside her was Michelle, and then Olivares.

As the lamenting wail of the bagpipes died, a chaplain stepped forward. He began to speak of service and sacrifice. Military chaplains weren't much on God's wrath and fury, because of the vast differences in beliefs amongst the soldiers, but they were fond of delivering speeches about duty, and this one was no different. And as he spoke of our duty to our fellow man, I thought back to the day I first entered the military. Fresh out of high school and not a care in the world, except that I didn't want to work fast food, I was pumped up on the red, white, and blue and wanted to fight for my country. Only back then I didn't know what that meant. To me it was little more than an idea fueled by TV and movies.

The idea of serving and the reality of it were two different things. I remember talking about it with MacKenzie. He'd joined because of the situation in the former Northern Ireland. He'd hated what both sides had done, but felt a duty to England to help her defend against what he'd perceived as a campaign of terror. When I asked him what it was like working against the terrorists, he said, "It's okay to know me, Benjamin, but you don't want to be my friend. Terrible things happen to my friends, and there's nothing to be done about it."

"But we're friends, aren't we, Jimmy?"

"No, Benjamin. We're not friends. We're mates. That's a whole different thing."

I still didn't understand what the difference was, but as I stood and stared at his body bag, I felt a special connection to him, more so than most of the others. The way he'd turned back to fix the device was the definition of duty. He did it knowing he'd die. He did it for us. And when I'd turned to join him, I did so as his mate.

The chaplain ended the service and the gathering began to disperse. I bid farewell to my mate, and hoped he was in whatever heaven or libidinous hell he'd desired.

I turned to go, and bumped into Olivares. I smiled and moved to push past, but his eyes flashed angrily. I saw Michelle over his shoulder chatting with Ohirra. Did he know?

"You were late," he said, stilling me with a hand on my shoulder.

"Sorry," I said, and moved to get around him, but he held me fast. "What gives?"

"I've worked hard to get this unit working together."

I nodded, not knowing where this was going.

"I've been trying to make sure someone doesn't ruin it."

"I got it, Sarge. I won't ruin it. I'm with the program." I didn't want to make any trouble.

He shook his head. "You ain't got shit." He dropped his hand. "We have a mission brief in an hour. Be there and wait outside the room for me and don't bother suiting up."

Then he stalked out.

Don't bother suiting up? What the hell was he talking about? Without me that would leave only four. Sure, I'd proven to be hell on the EXO, but I'd demonstrated my worth and they knew they needed me. Was he joking?

Thompson came up to me. "What was that about?"

"I don't know, but he was pissed. He said I shouldn't bother to suit up. I can't imagine he was serious."

Thompson shook his head. "You better think again, Mason."

"What makes you so sure?"

"Your shirt," he said. "It doesn't belong to you."

I looked down and saw Aquinas's name badge. I glanced up and saw her staring at her own chest, Ohirra laughing and pointing. We made eye contact. I tried to smile, but she wasn't in the smiling mood. Her face was a mask of anguish as she stomped out of the room.

"What happened?" Thompson asked.

"Just a mix up, is all."

Back in the squad bay, I found my shirt hanging on my locker. I removed hers and put on my own. As I did, I noticed her lingering smell. I couldn't help but smile.

"Now I know why we're called Romeo... Romeo." Ohirra laughed behind me.

I turned away from her as I pulled on my shirt.

"Don't be mad about it, Romeo. It was only a matter of time anyway."

"Oh, yeah? Says who?"

She smiled secretively. "You know. Girl talk." As Ohirra passed, she patted me on the shoulder. "Take it easy, big boy. It's probably only a wartime crush."

Wartime crush.

I let the idea percolate for a while, before realizing that I'd be late for the briefing if I didn't hurry. I needed to talk to Olivares and get him to change his mind. He was just pissed at me. I seriously doubted that he would put the mission in jeopardy because of some juvenile jealousy.

But at the mission brief I discovered I was completely wrong. Whether he took our tryst personally because he'd had his own intentions was unknown. He was keeping his feelings for her close to his chest. Whatever the reason, he was sticking to his directive that I sit out the next mission.

From what I was able to gather, this mission would be a lot like the previous mission to emplace ground penetrating sonar and radar. This was also the last mission for Romeo Three as a cohesive unit. Upon completion, Olivares and Aquinas were falling under Mr. Pink's command for tactical control for the Kilimanjaro Mission. The rest of us were on standby, relegated to professional thumb-twiddling while everyone else fought.

Even now as I paced back and forth outside the mission room, I could barely restrain myself. How could Olivares let his personal feelings influence the mission? It was one of the most unprofessional decisions I'd encountered and I was prepared to have it out with him, if necessary. I wouldn't be denied the mission. Not only did I need to be there to help my friends, but they needed me. Not that I was taking the *Hero of the Mound* bullshit to heart, but there was no doubting the value of my contribution.

The door opened and Thompson, Michelle and Ohirra passed by me. They didn't look at me, but I could tell by the looks on their faces they were embarrassed for me.

And I hated that.

Mr. Pink came out next. He seemed about to say something to me, then thought better of it and moved on.

Olivares finally came out of the room, head down, deep in thought.

I stepped in front of him. "We need to talk."

He stopped and regarded me. "I've already had a conversation with you."

"I don't accept it."

"You don't..." He put his left hand in his pocket and pointed at my chest with his right. "You're a corporal and I'm a staff sergeant. Last time I checked, you don't have to accept what I tell you. You just have to do it."

"I was a staff sergeant."

"That was a different army and a different war." Olivares laughed and I wanted to smack the grin from his face. "Do you think you can be the leader? Do you want to be the staff sergeant, Mason? Do you think you have what it takes?"

"I was a damned good leader."

"That was then. This is now. Like I said, different war, different time. You want to be a leader, then you can't sleep with your subordinates. What the hell were you thinking?"

"So that's it. You wanted her for yourself."

When he next spoke his words were slow and firm. "What I want and don't want has no place in a military unit, Mason. Were you as good a leader as you think, you'd know that. Listen, I know your story. I know about the men you lost—keep losing— and the sad fucking fact is that you just don't get it."

I tried to interrupt, but he motioned me to silence with his hand.

"There are three types of grunts in this world: leaders, followers, and killers. You don't want to mix them up. I know you've been a leader before, but that was a mistake. Not as if the military had a way to fix it. They like to pretend there's no such thing as a pure killer. When they find them, they try and get them into special operations. Green Berets. SEALs. Rangers. It gets them away from the others.

"Know how you can always tell a leader who's really a killer? He always gets his men killed. It's not like it's their fault, either. Killers can't help it. We've had them in every war since Gilgamesh was King of Babylon. We *need* killers. They become our heroes.

"But when killers are put in charge, they can't stop doing what they're good at. They keep killing, and their grunts follow them. Only the followers aren't killers; they don't have the knack or the instinct. So they die."

I hated Olivares right now, but even as I listened I saw the spark of truth.

"You ever had any of your people die before, Mason?"

"You know the answer."

"The reason I'm in charge and you're not is because you are a killer and I'm a leader. The others, they're followers. OMBRA once thought that maybe Thompson was a killer. I know; the drummer boy as a straight-ass assassin. But they changed their mind. He registered in the gray area."

"Thompson? A killer? What brainiac had that idea?"

"The same brainiacs who put me in charge of you. The same ones who devised all of those questions we answered during Phase I. It's the way you answered all of those dumb-as-shit study questions at the end of every book. It's the way you responded to the surveys after every movie. They have some algorithm where they sucked in your answers and punch out *killer*."

"But aren't we all killers?"

"Some of us are better at it than others." He took a step back and crossed his arms. "Only one of us is the Hero of the Mound. How many people did you bring back with you on those missions, Mason?"

"You better watch it."

"Where's MacKenzie? I thought you had his back, Mason."

"Where were you, Olivares?"

"I left you alone with him. Why'd you let him die, Mason?"

I lashed out without even thinking about it, catching him on the side of his face. He went down and it took everything I had for me not to fall on him and pound the shit out of him. Instead, I stood there, fists balled, fuming.

He sat up and put a hand to the side of his face. "Do you want to know why you're a corporal and I'm a staff sergeant? Because when I lead everyone into battle, I'm not going to get them killed." He stood. "I might not be as effective a killer as you. I might not be the Hero of the Mound. But I'm also not going to get people killed."

As he walked past me, he said, "No hard feelings. No drama. It's just the way you are. Don't bother suiting up. You're going to watch this one from the trenches."

You come home from school one day to discover that your parents have left a gift for you on the kitchen table. It's a large box with holes poked into the top. You hear a scratching coming from within. After investigating, you discover a Golden Retriever puppy, all fur and paws and wet mouth. You play with it for awhile. It licks you. You can't help but love it. Then you see the note. You read it. It says, 'Mason, dear, if you really love us you're going to kill the puppy.' So the question is, how are you going to kill it? Strangle it with your bare hands, or put it back in the box and put the box in the middle of the street and walk away? You decide.

TF OMBRA Personalized
Screening Question
for Staff Sergeant Benjamin Carter Mason

CHAPTER THIRTY-FOUR

MR. PINK TRIED to calm me down by distracting me with science, but it didn't help. Still, as my team prepared to conduct the mission without me, perhaps the last mission Romeo Three would ever do, he persisted. I knew what he was doing, but I couldn't stop him.

"Have you ever wondered why the Cray don't like to travel at night? No, that's not the right question... why they are reluctant to do *anything* at night, in the dark, without light, other than a little moon and starlight?"

I shrugged as I stood staring at the wall of plasma monitors in the Tactical Operations Center. Each one was set to a split screen, front and rear display, of the members of the recon teams out in the field—Romeo Nine, Romeo Two and Romeo Three.

Around us, soldiers ranking from private to captain sat monitoring laptops. By their patches, they were headquarters and signal sections. An African-American master sergeant ran in with a piece of paper and began reading coordinates into a head set.

Mr. Pink continued watching the screens. "Phototrophic organisms align themselves to the light to better achieve photosynthesis."

Two men fussed with a keyboard, connecting and reconnecting the cord to the back of an old hard drive tower. "Are you saying the Cray are like plants?"

Why hadn't Mr. Pink overruled Olivares? Why wasn't I outside? I sought Romeo Three's feeds so I could get a view of Michelle. It took a few moments to get a handle on the shaky images.

"We have no proof of any photosynethetic qualities in the Cray. We believe what we're seeing is phototaxis, an automatic movement toward light, much like moths. Their response to light is euphoric, akin to drug-induced stimulus. They are hypnotized by light.

"Actually emotional stimulus probably isn't the right term. The problem is that there's been very little study regarding phototactic response. Take the fiddler crab, for instance. Are you aware that it aligns itself sideways to light?"

Michelle—I had to stop thinking of her that way—*Aquinas* and Thompson were partnered, while Olivares was partnered with Ohirra. They stood in our usual positions near the trenches, waiting for Romeo Nine to move first.

"One University of Wisconsin study showed that light can be employed to direct the movement of fiddler crabs. They follow a light source anywhere, even if the angle changes sharply."

It was an infuriatingly one-sided conversation and I was unable to resist an easy smart-assed remark. "Maybe if we had a giant flashlight we could defeat them."

"We'd need a giant hand for a giant flashlight. Problem is we're fresh out of giants." Mr Pink moved to one of the techs and directed her to bring up images of the mound in infrared.

"I'm more inclined to stick with the moth theory, however," Mr. Pink continued. "Imagine if moths were at the top of the food chain. What sort of offensive and defensive capabilities might they have evolved to get there? Are the Cray affected by starlight? Can they navigate by it?"

"You talk as if they're not very smart."

"Do I? Force of habit, I guess. Have you ever wondered why they don't use more complex tactics when attacking? Maybe they *aren't* very smart."

"If they're not very smart, then how did they get here?"

"Good question, Corporal Mason, but for now"—he pointed towards the screens—"we're moving."

Romeo Three was on the move and the Tactical Operations Center became a madhouse as orders were called and returned. I asked for a headset so that I could listen in on the intersquad communications.

Olivares and Ohirra went out first, carrying the sonar between them in a large gator box. Thompson and Aquinas stayed to the left with their own boxes. The idea was for them to remain staggered, keeping at least thirty meters between each group.

To their right, Romeo Two moved in three teams of two.

On the far left, Romeo Nine had already been moving for fifteen minutes. They were to place their units near the rear of the hive and had two Vulcan sleds in support.

Two infantry platoons stood ready to assist, but remained within a hundred meters of our lines. They'd moved into position at the low crawl, their camouflage blending into the Serengeti.

Romeo Three avoided the village. Telemetry had previously detected Cray at that location and Romeo Three decided to give it a wide berth until an infantry company could sweep it clean. They also had to steer clear of the hole created by the previous day's blast. The extent of damage hadn't been calculated, but by the bits and pieces of alien littering the plain, it had to have been tremendous. Mr. Pink had mentioned that the special weapons section was working on three more thermobaric bombs, which would be ready in a matter of days.

The Vulcans began to fire and activity in the TOC increased as several officers began yelling. Romeo Two was hit hard by two waves of Cray. Both Vulcan cannons roared, slinging metal-jacketed lead into the air. An entire column of Cray evaporated into mist as they plunged headfirst into the fusillade, but the second column made it through. Romeo Two held their own, using their miniguns to create interlocking fields of fire. More Cray began attacking from above and the Vulcans opened up again.

The ground opened beneath both of the cannons. One minute the gun crews were firing, the next there was a cloud of dust and no more cannons, and Romeo Two suddenly found themselves terribly outnumbered. Two of the six soldiers broke and ran, and were soon hauled into the air by pairs of Cray and dropped from hundreds of feet. I was transfixed by one of the feeds as the ground rushed up to meet the camera. I jumped and a wave of nausea washed over me as the soldier struck earth.

The remaining four members of Romeo Two were fighting back-to-back. They might have made it, had they not run out of ammunition before the Cray ran out of aliens. When the drones descended, it was a maelstrom of hand-to-hand combat; a deadly whirlwind.

A sudden note of concern in Ohirra's voice caused me to turn and focus on her.

"Look at the ground ahead. Does it look soft?" she said.

Everyone in Romeo Three stopped.

I watched as Olivares zoomed in and ran through the available spectrums, but this revealed little other than a barely discernible change in the color and texture of the ground.

Ten seconds ticked by as he contemplated their next move. Finally he said, "Fall in behind. Minefield rules. One path. Stay in each other's steps. I'll go first."

Thompson and Aquinas did as ordered, carrying the box between then. They concentrated on maintaining their distance, while keeping to the footprints of those in front of them.

I turned back to Romeo Two. Five of their feeds were dead and, as I watched, the sixth went offline.

I checked on Romeo Nine, who were as free and easy as a couple taking a Sunday walk through a city park.

Mr. Pink grabbed a headset. "Romeo Nine, be aware of changes in the sand. There might be spider traps ahead."

Romeo Nine acknowledged and kept moving. After a moment, they saw them. It looked like the Cray had been busy.

"Freeze," Olivares commanded.

My gaze swung to his feed. I saw sand, stippled and off-color. I could clearly see regular sand between the suspect areas, becoming narrower further out. What was it?

Then I saw it: a V-shaped ambush straight out of the manual. Wide at the entrance, intended to funnel an opposing force into the kill zone. Once inside the ambush site, it would be impossible to get out unscathed.

"Listen closely," Olivares ordered. "Target your Hydras and face your quadrant. Aquinas vector left. Ohirra vector right. Thompson vector rear. I'll take the forward vector. Comply."

The team all complied, and I saw their weapon statuses change on Olivares's command screen.

"Listen to me." Olivares's voice was slow and steady. If I didn't know any better, he might have been demonstrating the correct way to break down an M9 pistol instead of preparing everyone for attack. "Carefully lower your cases, then straighten."

"Mr. Pink, you watching this?" I said.

"We're on it, son."

"Listen to me, Romeo Three," Olivares said. "We're about to be attacked. No, don't look around. Remain still. They're going to come from the ground. I've set each of your Hydras on automatic. They will fire when movement is detected. Let them fire. Do not move until all the Hydras are fired."

"Jesus," Thompson murmured.

Olivares chuckled. "Jesus was a corpsman, son. He didn't know shit about being a grunt."

Damn, but it was true. Olivares was a good leader. I couldn't help but admire his coolness under stress.

"And Satan was a grunt," Ohirra said, finishing the old line. "So let's give them hell, Romeo Three."

All four gave subdued *huahs*. I gave them one myself.

The TOC's battle captain shook his head. "They need to move. It's nothing but sand out there."

"Nope," I said. "There's enemy there. This is an ambush."

He turned and glared at me for disagreeing with him, but I wasn't about to take my eyes of the screen.

"And I say it's nothing, corporal," he said angrily. "And you will address me as *Captain*."

Oh, he was one of those. I wonder if he made his mother call him *Captain*, too.

He turned to Mr. Pink. "We need to get them moving."

Mr. Pink remained silent. He was chewing on his thumb.

The battle captain grabbed a headset. "This is Captain Gianforte. Get your asses in gear and move out!"

"Get off my net," Olivares snarled.

"Staff Sergeant Olivares, get moving. We can't wait on you

for long. This is an order." The captain covered the mike with his hand. "What's the status on the Howitzer rounds?"

"Waiting for Romeo Three to make Point Bravo."

The battle captain cursed something in Italian and let go of the mike. "Romeo Three, this is Battle Captain Gianforte, you will do as—"

He never finished. Sand and rock and Cray exploded from the spider holes surrounding the four recon scouts. The Hydras fired, detonating their targets on all sides. The concussion from the explosions buffeted them in their suits, causing the feeds to skip with static. I watched each of the team members' statuses on Olivares's feed.

A second wave of drones leapt free. These weren't so quick to attack, but balanced on the edges of their ambush holes, long wings fluttering in the night. Then they exploded as the remaining missiles found them.

"Romeo Three, reverse! Move!"

Now out of missiles, they turned, swinging their miniguns forward. Last was now first, with Thompson, followed by Aquinas, Ohirra, and Olivares, each keeping to their sectors. My gaze was pulled from one feed to the other as the Cray began closing the trap.

Into the Valley of Death Rode the Six Hundred.

The words came unbidden. I blinked them away as I watched my mates fire in controlled bursts, taking out target after target. Had they not gone so far into the trap, professionalism might have gotten them out of it. But there were just too many Cray.

Thompson's minigun jammed. He fought with it for a moment before returning it to a travel position. He reached back for his blade, which he held before him two-fisted, like it was a holy cross.

"Jesus Christ," muttered the battle captain. "He looks terrified."

I impaled the man with my gaze. I'd met officers like him before. All he cared about was being right, even if it was at someone else's expense.

Mr. Pink noticed my displeasure. "Rolf, sit down." To the room, he ordered, "Get an infantry platoon moving in their direction now."

The battle captain sat, his smirk now replaced by a wounded look. The only thing that kept me from kicking the shit out of the smug asshole was my concern for my team.

Thompson had gone down and Aquinas and Ohirra were standing over him. Aquinas still had ammunition and was firing tight bursts into the heads of every Cray that came within arm's length.

Ohirra and Olivares did the same, only the sergeant was besieged from the rear. Several times he had to kick out, once as his minigun paused to switch from one 500-round magazine to the other. Cray claws slipped and scratched against his suit, desperate to get at him.

"Sir, we've identified three possible escape routes," one of the technicians said. "I've plotted them on the overlay of Romeo Three's position."

One was back the way Romeo Three had come, back into the apex of the V where they'd originally been headed. Sure, once they reached there the presence of Cray would be lessened, but it looked as if there were a hundred creatures between them and the exit.

The other two routes were perpendicular to the trap.

Suddenly all attention was diverted to Romeo Nine, who were coming under attack while laying their devices.

"Is anyone going to be able to complete this mission?" Mr. Pink asked.

"Check for pings on devices 9-1, 9-2 and 9-3," a tech called.

"I have ping confirmation," the tech beside me answered. "And here comes the readout."

"And there goes the machines," said the first tech. "They were on for six seconds before the EMP killed them."

"It's enough, though," answered the other tech.

Romeo Nine had other things to worry about besides the success or failure of their mission. Cray were surging towards them from the mound. Romeo Nine was already moving, bounding overwatch in dead sprints of a hundred meters. As each stopped in turn, they turned and fired both missiles and minigun.

As I turned back to my team, my heart flipped as I saw Aquinas's feed drop to static. I stopped breathing before I saw her running in Thompson's feed.

"What's wrong with Aquinas's feed?" I failed to keep the panic from my voice.

Mr. Pink glanced at me.

"I'm reading all systems go," the tech beside me said. "She might have taken a blow. Could be a loose wire."

I rolled my eyes. What a time for a loose wire! The thought that she'd been dead had terrified me. A hole had opened where my heart had been. Ohirra and Olivares were running in the other direction, splitting their enemy.

A gutsy move, and it appeared as if it was going to pay off.

Romeo Nine lost a man as he stumbled and fell. Three Cray were on him, lifting him from the ground. His mates took them down with a hail of gunfire, the Kevlar-titanium armour shielding the soldier from stray rounds, but the suit didn't help when they dropped him. The EXO hit neck first, the body buckling behind it. Blood covered the screen before the feed went to static.

Back to Romeo Three, and Thompson and Aquinas were fighting back-to-back, wielding their blades. They were surrounded. I balled my fists, believing beyond reason that if I'd been there, none of this would have happened.

"Alpha-Two-One ready to engage. Two-hundred-and-fifty-meter offset," the battle captain said. "Alpha, prepare to engage."

Mr. Pink nodded. "Do they have a Vulcan ready for support?"

"Thirty seconds."

Mr. Pink waited.

I turned to the digital overlay on the right wall and saw an infantry platoon ready to engage the Cray assaulting Romeo Three. The platoon was two hundred and fifty meters away, but their weapons would be just as accurate as if their targets were at fifty meters. The distance allowed the unarmored soldiers to support operations, and still be able to escape if necessary. The key to their support were the Vulcan cannons, without which they were sitting ducks. As much as I wanted them to engage the Cray and come to the aid of Romeo Three, I knew the infantry needed their cover support.

Back to the action, and Thompson was down on the ground again.

"What's wrong with Thompson?" I asked.

"Leg servos are inop," a tech replied.

Aquinas was standing over Thompson, protecting him. I couldn't see a thing through her feed, but I saw her through his, facing upwards. She held both their blades, her torso twisting as her arms windmilled like a Kali Escrimadora from the old Philippines. Between her twists and thrusts, I saw flashes of her face, eyes determined, mouth set, jaw firm, beautiful.

A Cray barreled into her, sending her sprawling onto Thompson. He grabbed one of the blades she'd been wielding and stabbed the drone in its flank.

The Cray fell, but as Aquinas straightened, another replaced it.

"Vulcan cannon in place," came the call.

"Order Alpha-Two-One to open fire," Mr. Pink commanded.

"Romeo Three, this is Tactical Control. Hit the dirt."

I'd long ago memorized Field Manual 7-8: Infantry Platoon and Squad Operations. We'd had to recite entire passages from it. Our ability to remember it dictated whether or not we received extra duty or were allowed off compound, and was the golden ticket to alcohol, sex and freedom. The field manual had been my bible for years and I knew exactly what was happening.

A Deliberate Attack: *Firepower is the capacity of a unit to deliver effective fires on a target. Firepower kills or suppresses the enemy in his positions, deceives the enemy, and supports maneuver. Without effective supporting fires the infantry cannot maneuver. Before attempting to maneuver, units must establish a base of fire. A base of fire is placed on an enemy force or position to reduce or eliminate the enemy's ability to interfere with friendly maneuver elements. Leaders must know how to control, mass, and combine fire with maneuver. They must identify the most critical targets quickly, direct fires onto them, and ensure that the volume of fire is sufficient to keep the enemy from returning fire effectively, and the unit from expending ammunition needlessly.*

Thirty-nine rifles began spitting 5.56mm rounds at the Cray. Members of the headquarters section and three rifle squads fired HK416s, selecting their targets through night vision devices with aiming points, concentrating on sectors of fire, each soldier responsible for his own area. Weapons squad added their own sustained rattle with M240B and SAW machine guns, conducting grazing fire as they swept their barrels back and forth.

Thompson's feed showed Aquinas, and the Cray dancing above her as the rounds ate through their carapaces. Alien body parts rained down upon them. The fire sustained for ten more seconds, then silence.

"Reloading and standing by."

"Romeo Three, what's your status?"

"Still in the wire," Olivares said.

A-2-1 opened fire again, and this time explosions could be heard off feed, punctuated by a significant lightening of the sky by white phosphorus grenades from a battery of M32 six-shot multiple grenade launchers. The chemical would stick to any flesh—alien or human—it came in contact with and burn until there was nothing left. It was deadly, terrible stuff.

"Romeo Three, prepare to return to base," a tech ordered.

I became aware that I hadn't breathed in at least a minute. I released my fists, feeling the indentations my nails had made in my palms. I wasn't the praying kind, but I prayed for my team.

"Romeo Nine is available to assist," a tech called.

I turned to Mr. Pink. He chewed on his thumb for a moment— it had to be half-eaten by now—then shook his head. "Negative. RTB."

Return to base? I thought about arguing, but he was right. Romeo Nine had done their jobs and needed to get back. Romeo Three had been the ones to enter the ambush. Throwing more EXO-wearing recon soldiers at the problem would only put more of them in the shit. Plus, Romeo Three was already receiving assistance from the infantry. I got it, I understood it. But I didn't like it. If it had been up to me, I'd have sent the entire Brigade Combat Team to help. But then again, that's why they don't let some grunt corporal like me make the important decisions.

"Alpha-Two-One reports all targets down."

"Get Romeo Three out of there," Mr. Pink commanded.

"Romeo Three, converge with Alpha-Two-One."

"Roger, control."

Olivares stood and pulled Ohirra up beside him. They headed towards Thompson and Aquinas. They tossed bodies aside as they came upon the pair. Aquinas got to her feet, but Thompson was unmoving.

I checked his stats and he was doing fine.

"Legs won't move," Thompson said. "Something wrong with the servos."

Back in the Tactical Operations Center a tech shook his head. "They're offline, and I still can't get them back up. I'll try and reset one more time, but I think they're shot."

"Alpha-Two-One, fire at will," the battle captain ordered.

The infantry platoon began to fire as targets became available.

Olivares reached down and hauled Thompson to his feet. He ordered Aquinas to take the other side and Ohirra to lead the way.

"Okay, Romeo Three. We're going to move. We're not stopping for anything. You see something, kill it."

I felt a surge of pleasure that the team was back together. Together they stood a chance. They had five kilometers. Just 5K. Back before the aliens had decided to take the world away from us, a 5K was something people did for fun. And, of course, because I was in the military, I had had my own share of mandatory fun, being forced to run in the Fourth of July 5K or the Christmas 5K or the Thanksgiving 5K.

Of course there were no more holidays. The very idea of Thanksgiving had been irrevocably stolen by the invasion. If we were to ever win our planet back, I didn't think the holiday would survive.

Back in the day I could run a 5K in twenty-three minutes. With the EXOs, it should be much quicker, perhaps fifteen minutes. Fifteen minutes of trying not to be jerked into the sky by the Cray and bounced from a thousand feet.

Romeo Three began to jog towards friendly lines. There wasn't any contact at first. Had A-2-1 done such a terrific job? Then I saw something on one of the feeds which mystified me: dozens of Cray, standing around a glowing mound on the ground. Overhead, I could see the flitting shapes of many more. They were gathering around a clump of burning white phosphorus, like moths to a flame.

My team didn't spare a moment to investigate. They continued moving.

"Alpha-Two-One is holding fire," a tech said.

"Telemetry?" Mr. Pink asked.

"We count sixty-five Ks in a single mass above the mound. They have yet to engage."

Aquinas's feed, both front and back, was still fuzzed by static. I only knew she was alive because Olivares would sometimes glance at her, and it was her keeping Thompson upright.

"Thompson, you have bogies inbound to your location."

"I... I see them," he said, switching to night vision. The switch made the lower left hand corner glow so bright from the residue of a white phosphorus grenade that it washed out detail. But the rest of the view was the greens and blacks everyone knew.

Seven Cray had taken flight from somewhere on the ground and were chasing after them.

"You got to take them out," Olivares said.

"Go, got it handled."

Thompson brought his minigun up, but it jammed again. He fought to clear the jam even as the Cray drew near. The weapon finally cleared and the gun accessed the second magazine; the barrel spun a few times before rounds began to pour from the end. Three of the Cray faltered, then tumbled, but the remaining four kept coming.

"Easy on the ammo, son." Olivares sounded calm, but I could hear his concern.

Thompson slowed his rate of fire, but had trouble aiming because of the way he was being carried. For every ten rounds, only one found a home.

The Cray were now only a dozen feet away.

Thompson forgot about aiming and really opened up.

The lead Cray, only five feet away, took the rounds in the head. The others ate more rounds.

Ohirra opened up from the front.

Her feed showed a huge pit in front of them. Cray soared from it, angling directly toward them.

"We count an additional thirty-five Cray from the new location," telemetry said.

New location? What new location?

"Romeo Three, veer left and keep left. There's been a cave-in. Probably the result of yesterday's explosion."

"You couldn't have told us this yesterday!" Olivares shouted.

"Sorry, Romeo Three."

"Mason, are you there?" Olivares asked.

I looked at Mr. Pink and shrugged. How was I to reply?

"He's here and monitoring," Mr. Pink said for me.

"Hey, slacker." Olivares fired his minigun at a cluster of Cray, then continued. "Do me a favor. If any of those REMFs says they're sorry again, feel free to kick the holy hell out of their asses, please."

I chuckled and nodded.

"Corporal Mason says affirmative," Mr. Pink said, straight-faced.

God bless him.

"What is a REMF?" the battle captain asked.

I smiled as I replied, "Rear Echelon Mother Fucker. It's for those who'd rather watch than fight."

Aquinas screamed.

Everyone turned towards her; three feeds showing her terrified face as she was pulled into the air. Thompson had a grip on her leg. The added weight of him and his suit was like an anchor, holding her to the earth.

I balled my fists. "Don't let go, Thompson. Don't you fucking let go."

Olivares grabbed Thompson's leg and heaved backwards.

Suddenly Ohirra was staring at Aquinas... no... *past* her as she opened fire on the Cray trying to haul her higher into the air.

Aquinas fell to the ground. For a moment, her feed worked and I watched as she stumbled to her feet. But then as she turned to the others her feed disappeared again.

Then we lost the others. Thompson's feed went to static. So did Olivares's. All I had was Ohirra's feed and she was running away from the others.

"We've lost all but one feed," a tech said.

"Where'd they go?" asked another tech.

"Was there an EMP?" I asked.

"We didn't record one," someone answered.

Then what the hell was going on?

"I have eighty-four Cray heading towards Ohirra," telemetry said.

"Have Alpha-Two-One provide cover support," Mr. Pink ordered.

Within moments, I saw telemetric markings on the map wink out, one after the other.

"Where's she going?" I asked, but no one answered my question.

All I could see was Ohirra's feed, jittery and moving as each servo-powered leg pushed her forward.

"Sir, we have an issue. Looks like the Cray are targeting the infantry."

"How many?" Mr. Pink asked.

"Over three hundred."

"Pull them back now," he said. Mr Pink glanced from one screen to the other, taking in all the information. "That's too many. There's something wrong here." His eyes narrowed. "Get me a report from the tunnels, now!"

I watched as one tech ran from the room while another began to speak rapidly into his mike. I remembered the tunnels we had, several hundred meters from those belonging to the Cray. *Not your pay grade.* Had they been wrong about the distance? Had the Cray broken through? Was the attack on Romeo Three intended to be a distraction?

"Seismic sensors reporting no significant disturbance," a tech said.

Mr. Pink shook his head. "I want eyes down there right now."

"We have two platoons on site, sir," the battle captain said. "They're reporting nothing."

Mr. Pink stared at the battle captain as if he wasn't going to believe him, then nodded and returned to the feeds.

I wondered what all that was about. Were we really that close to the enemy? With our firepower and the tunnels limiting the Cray's ability to fly, wouldn't that be to our advantage? Or were there things he was keeping from us? I wondered what Olivares and Aquinas were going to discover when they snuck into the volcano and traced the tunnels to the hive.

If they made it.

I turned back in time to see Ohirra spinning and catching a Cray in the head with her blade, slicing through mandible and skull. She got another fifty meters before the ground fell away in front of her. She slowed for a millisecond, then poured on the speed and leaped.

I could read the calculations on the right of her HUD and knew she'd make it. I was about to turn my head to check the others when Ohirra suddenly plummeted.

One of the Cray must have grabbed her. I could see the lip of the hole as she passed it, then chaotic darkness.

Mr. Pink called orders and a tech began flipping through the usable spectrums, but nothing was coming clear.

Ohirra's screams were punctuated by grunts as she punched and kicked. Everywhere there was movement, but it was too dark and too fast to see.

"Get her strobe on." Mr. Pink grabbed one of the technicians. "Come on, son. Faster!"

The screen was suddenly assaulted by light as a hundred thousand candlewatt bulb began to pulse on the front of Ohirra's helmet.

I stepped forward to get a better view and walked right into the back of someone's chair. I apologized, then joined Mr. Pink at the front of the room. We stared at the scene as our eyes adjusted to the combat rave in the alien hole.

Each time I saw a Cray head, it was frozen in the light. Was the light stunning them, perhaps hypnotizing them?

With each flash, I watched Ohirra's hands and feet move in stop-motion violence, eviscerating and hacking her way out of the hole as she eventually found her grip and pulled her way free.

"Turn off the strobe," Mr. Pink said.

Ohirra ran back towards the village, and as she came close, Cray began to pour out of the buildings. Another ambush. But when they saw her strobe, the Cray slowed and moved towards her at a pace less intent on murder and more akin to need.

"Turn off the fucking strobe," I shouted.

"I can't," a tech shouted. "It's not responding."

I checked Ohirra's power. She was down to thirteen percent. I wasn't sure if she could make the distance..

She tripped and fell but managed to get back to her feet in time to see a wave of Cray descending on her. But these were different. It took me a moment for me to notice that they lacked wings; in their place was an extra set of arms. Ohirra hacked at them with her blade. She was no longer as fluid with her movements as before. She was exhausted and terrified.

I grabbed a headset from a technician. "Connect me to her."

She looked at Mr. Pink for confirmation. He nodded.

"Ohirra... *Ohirra!* Relax and listen to me. They can't pierce your armor. They can't get through. Can you hear me?"

"Mason?"

"Just relax. You're going to make it."

"Where are the others?"

I glanced at the blank feeds of Aquinas, Thompson and Olivares and lied. "They're okay. But don't worry about them. Worry about yourself. Look at your power."

It was down to seven percent. It had to be the strobe.

She fought desperately, but precisely, her martial arts training kicking in.

I covered the mike with one hand and leaned over. "Will that strobe keep working if she takes off her suit?"

"As long as there's no EMP," the tech said.

I moved my hand away from the mike. "Listen closely. I want you to run to our lines as fast as you can. Watch your numbers. When your suit reaches two percent, remove it and come the rest of the way without it."

"But I can't... they'll kill me."

"No they won't. You're faster than them. These have no wings. Come on, Ohirra. You have to run. *Now!*"

She looked back towards our lines, then turned to engage the Cray again.

"Ohirra! I said move! *Now!*"

She flung her blade into the chest of the nearest Cray, then turned and ran. She was soon at full speed. Her power level was dropping one percent every five seconds.

"When you get out of your suit, run for us. I'll meet you there."

I tossed the headset back at the technician and bolted from the room. I peeled around one corner, almost knocking over several soldiers. I didn't have the time to get a suit on. I'd have to go out as I was.

When I made it to the trench, she was out of her suit and running. I just prayed that she'd put enough distance between herself and the Cray. I didn't know how fast the ones without wings could run; I knew they couldn't keep up with a suit, but they could very well be faster than a human.

I snatched an HK from one of the sentries and leaped out of the trench.

I ran twenty feet, then went down on one knee, resting my elbow on the other knee as I took aim. I sighted through the EOTECH and put the red dot on the figures directly behind Ohirra. Poor Ohirra wasn't running all-out. She'd let fear get to her. She kept turning her head to look behind her, and each time she did, she'd slow, and sometimes stumble. She hadn't gone down yet, but it seemed only a matter of time.

I squeezed off a round and missed. I tried another and caught the nearest Cray in the head.

Red dot dead.

Ohirra dodged like she thought I was shooting at her. Her movement opened up my sight picture and I was able to fire faster, taking four more out and giving her more time.

I stood and yelled. "Come on, girl—get your ass in gear!"

I was suddenly joined by a squad of infantry. They must have come from A-2-1. They fired surgically, removing her pursuers within moments. I stood to run, but felt a hand on my shoulder.

I turned and saw a sergeant major I didn't recognize. The name *Marshall* was printed on his chest. He pointed off to the right.

An EXO was cruising towards Ohirra. It covered the ground at amazing speed. I'd never seen it from the ground like this before. I felt like a human watching a god. As I watched, it ran at Ohirra, picked her up and sprinted towards our lines without breaking stride. As it got closer, I recognized it as belonging to Olivares.

I searched behind him. Where were the others? What had he done with Thompson and Michelle?

When he reached our lines, he placed Ohirra on the ground. She struggled to regain her balance. I helped her for a moment, then turned to Olivares, slapping the back of his suit to get his attention.

He turned and stared through his faceplate. His eyes were glassy, and he couldn't meet my gaze.

"Where are the others?"

He shook his head.

I grabbed him, but he shrugged me off and walked towards the trench. I ran after him, anger blossoming inside me, but he was in and gone by the time I was there. I descended and handed the rifle over.

I ran back to the Tactical Operations Center.

"Where are they?" I shouted. "Where are the others?" I grabbed a monitor and threw it across the room, then grabbed another as I screamed, "*Where are the others?*"

I felt a hand on my shoulder and spun around to face the battle captain. I punched him before he could open his mouth, and when he was down, I fell on top of him and began to hammer at him over and over until they pulled me off.

In that moment of silence, I heard through the static a repetitive sound. It was a pattern, something I almost recognized. Just as I was about to get it, a hand came and slammed into my face.

Then I had it. Drumming.

Our little drummer boy.

Could it be? Was he alive?

Then the hand came again and it all went black.

Thank the gods of capitalistic excess for all of our electronics. Our televisions, movie disc players, computers, cars, airplanes, movie theaters, hospitals, schools, vibrators, microwave ovens, and *Sunday Night Football*. They are what makes life worth living, and they're also our ultimate downfall. We don't even read real books anymore. Instead we read using electronic devices. But there's a single threat lurking out there, one which could kill us as easily as a global pandemic. It's called EMP: electro magnetic pulse. A perfectly placed EMP could shut everything down. We've seen this on television and on movies. But let me ask you, what would you do if everything in your life suddenly ceased to function? Could you live? Could you find a way to continue? Answer the questions if you dare.

Conspiracy Theory Talk Radio,
Night Stalker Monologue #702

PART THREE

Why did Harry feel like he'd wasted a good portion of his life?

TF OMBRA Study Question from
The Snows of Kilimanjaro
by Ernest Hemingway

CHAPTER THIRTY-FIVE

A BLACK SILHOUETTE rose into the sky. We hunkered down, convinced we'd been spotted. We'd been so careful, even going so far as to turn off our telemetry to reduce our radio profile, yet still it came. It descended towards us, and as it did so, we were able to discern its shape. No, not a Cray: a vulture. Its wingspan must have been more than seven feet. I'd spent most of my life ignoring them or trying to keep away from them on battlefields. I didn't find them as beautiful or as graceful as some.

But that was before the Earth was taken from us.

Seeing it circle overhead, the wind ruffling its broad wings, sun glistening off its feathers, I learned a new appreciation for the Jackdaw of the Air. Then it struck me. I couldn't remember the last time I'd seen an animal or bird of any type. Was it all the way back in Wyoming when I'd seen the prairie dogs in the grass next to the underground complex? I was reminded that we weren't only trying to save Earth for ourselves, but for everything else that lived upon it... vultures included.

I watched it soar for a time, thinking back to Hemingway's *The Snows of Kilimanjaro*. You had to know that when a story began with vultures circling, it couldn't end well. His main character spent the entire narrative reminiscing about what he'd done or not done, rethinking things. I didn't have that leisure. With Aquinas and Thompson missing, I had to remain focused. We hadn't found them on the battlefield, so it was believed that they'd been taken by the Cray. I knew it was a long shot, but that idea was at least more palatable than the probable truth they'd been scattered across the plain in such small pieces that we couldn't find them.

Harry. That was the character's name. Such an old man's name, even though he'd never lived to become old. I remember one of the questions we'd had in Phase I about what we'd want to remember most when we became old. Harry had been so lonely towards the very end of his life. I remembered reading that shortly before I'd tried to kill myself for the last time, thinking to myself about how terrible an existence would be when you had no one to be there with you.

I'd always been a loner. I'd lived inside my own head most of the time. But that story made me understand. It made me want to reach out. It had given me the courage to let my feelings be known to Michelle.

I laughed softly to myself at the irony. Here I was, sitting on top of a mountain I'd read about ten thousand miles ago, before the Earth was invaded. Such an improbable string of coincidences. Then again, knowing Mr. Pink, it probably wasn't coincidence. His team of psychologists probably knew and understood my psyche and psychosis better than I ever would, and had planned on this moment since the beginning.

I rolled over and stared across the plain. Not for the first time, I relished looking down on the mound rather than up at it. In the distance I saw drones coming and going, while sentries soared in lazy circles above the hive, much like the vulture above us.

I closed my eyes and prayed to the universe to protect Thompson and Aquinas. The bowels of the mound were probably the most alien place on the planet and they would almost certainly feel alone.

I pushed myself up and turned to my hated comrade.

"Come on, Olivares. Let's go."

"Chill out. We still have an hour."

He lay next to me in his EXO. Like mine, it had been painted black. CBT OMBRA base techs had used tar sealant to cover the metal, which also gave it a texture to which dirt and dust could adhere. The last thing we wanted while climbing up the side of a six-thousand-meter-high mountain was for the Cray to see a reflection and investigate.

Still, I was eager to get moving. Waiting meant thinking, and I didn't want to live inside my head right now. I had a lot of bad thoughts, especially against Olivares. Leaving the others to die was an unforgivable sin, outstripping anything I'd ever done. For all the terrible decisions I'd made and all of the soldiers who'd died under my command, I never once left them on the battlefield.

But this was a two-man mission.

"Ease up on your anger, Mason," he said. "Your breathing... when you're angry it increases. You're already through seventy-eight percent of your oxygen mix, while I'm only sixty-six percent down."

"You have a smaller heart," I said. "It doesn't need as much."

"Jesus, Mason. Give it the fuck up. You always have to have a reason for someone dying and it always has to be someone's fault. Sometimes there isn't a reason. Sometimes it's no one's fault. It's a war, man. Shit happens. People die. Life goes on."

His words meant nothing. These were excuses.

"Do you have a comment for that too?" he asked.

I ignored him and concentrated on slowing my breathing.

He said nothing more for a time, which was exactly the way I wanted it.

We were getting used to the altitude. The trip up the side of Kilimanjaro would normally take six to seven days. It was steep, and climbers needed to acclimatize themselves. Without the time or oxygen mix, high altitude pulmonary or cerebral edema was a dangerous and very real possibility. In fact, it was believed that more people died climbing Kilimanjaro than Everest for this very reason.

But our EXOs had been equipped to be self-sealing. We were no longer breathing the outside air. Instead, we were breathing an oxygen-rich mix that mimicked the atmosphere at the base of the African mountain. It allowed us to make the trip in a single day. We didn't *have* seven days, or enough battery power for the trip. A little way after entering the mouth of the volcano, we'd be forced to ditch the suits, opting for multicams and body armor until we'd descended far enough inside the volcanic tunnels to return to normal atmosphere.

We each carried rigid battle packs, holding water, rations, med kits, rope, an MP5 and a 9mm pistol each with armor-piercing ammunition, multicams to change to once we were inside the volcano, batteries, lights, a tablet, Semtex, thermite grenades, and spare odds and ends.

The very idea of climbing down the inside of a volcano was amazing. Reading *Journey to the Center of the Earth* in Phase I, I'd never thought we'd be repeating the same sort of trek. I doubted there'd be an entire new world below, complete with fauna and fowl, although we were obviously expecting to encounter Cray.

What type of Cray was the question. Would it be the sort with wings? Or those without, like the ones that had attacked Ohirra? Or a new kind all together? What about the Sirens?

Mr. Pink had alluded to the possibility that the Cray were not the real threat, but an alien invasion force sent to weaken us. Were they 'uplifted,' like in the David Brin books; aliens genetically manipulated to achieve a sentience they wouldn't have normally had? Or were they merely a marauding species, similar to David Gerrold's?

I remembered reading the Gerrold books. Hadn't the aliens tried to warm the planet and establish their own fauna? I tried to imagine new plants and a change of seasons. Something like that would truly change the nature of Earth. In fact, it would become our planet in name only.

Whatever their nature, I didn't have the curiosity of a xenobiologist. Once I encountered them, I wasn't going to be too concerned about what they ate or what language they spoke. I wasn't worried about communicating with them; I wasn't even planning on learning much about them. I was here to kill them, and that's what I planned on doing. Olivares had already established that I was a killer. It was time to live up to the title.

Hero of the Mound.

I was thinking I might try on a new title. Maybe the Butcher of Kilimanjaro. That had a nice ring to it. I imagined a marquee playing across my mind and began to breathe a little easier as I mentally rehearsed all the ways I was going to kill the aliens once I got inside the tunnels.

I seriously couldn't wait.

Why is it important that the characters didn't have any idea about the nature of the creatures that they'd find inside of the earth?

TF OMBRA Study Question from
Journey to the Center of the Earth
by Jules Verne

CHAPTER THIRTY-SIX

MR. PINK'S PLAN was as inelegant as it was necessary. We were getting nowhere attacking from the surface; the iridium-reinforced shell of the mound had defeated us entirely. Although we had combat superiority over the Cray drones, we knew neither how many remained nor whether they were capable of reinforcing in mass quantities. For all we knew, they had a giant Cray queen squeezing out larvae that matured into combat drones in a matter of hours. If that were the case, we'd run out of humanity before they ran out of drones.

They needed someone on the inside. Our mission was two-fold. First, we were to make our way inside, killing where we had to kill and bypassing where we could, and get in as far as possible. CBT OMBRA needed recon. We desperately needed to know what we were up against. Did they have more Sirens in the mound, or were they a pre-invasion species only? Were there other species we hadn't seen before? What about the Cray's EMP projectors? Were they self-generating, or did they require charging? These and a hundred other questions needed to be answered.

Original plans had called for a two-person reconnaissance team to infiltrate using EXOs, but the geologists and volcanologists had argued against it, pointing out that the EXOS were far too bulky to make it through the questionable labyrinth mapped by the sonar and radar results we'd given lives to provide. Hence the Kevlar body armor. Still, in order to provide enough data for the attack to be successful, we required some way to record the necessary data. CBT techs created a mesh to enclose the helmets when removed from the suit, a portable EMP shield. Powered by batteries, the helmets would be able to provide full-spectrum recording, complete with intermittent radar, sonar, and power generation detection, enabling planners to look at the inside of the mound.

Assuming we survived.

Assuming we were able to either transmit the data, or ensure that the data chip was transported to friendly lines. If we had to chip it, we were lucky to have the height of technology available for our use—a flare gun with a parachute flare, which was probably the pinnacle of advancement during World War II.

The second part was a little trickier. CBT OMBRA had a three-pronged attack planned, which would occur with or without our input.

Part one encompassed the use of M712 Copperhead laser-guided projectiles, originally designed for the 155mm self-propelled Howitzer. CBT OMBRA Techs had been working to design a way to retrofit the eight-inch Howitzers with tube sleeves that would enable the projectiles to fire. Romeo Two's EXOs were retrofitted for speed and camouflage and assigned as Forward Observers, equipped to paint the mound with laser designators to direct the Copperheads into the launch tubes, where they'd then deliver their packages. This marked an evolutionary leap in the gun bunny's ability to provide cover support, and used lessons learned from previous battlefield interaction with the Cray.

The projectiles themselves were a mixture of high explosive and endothermic payloads. While more than half of the Copperheads had been fitted with high explosive, the rest—and the first to be fired—had a payload of binary gas mixture; impact would create an endothermic reaction resulting in sub-freezing temperatures for anything within the effective range of the explosion.

While the Copperheads stirred the hornet's nest like it had never been stirred before, part two encompassed an assault on the mound by EXOs. All remaining recon elements would attack along prescribed lines, culminating in climbing into the lower Cray launch ramps. Armed with additional endothermic grenades, they'd add to the sub-zero temperature, hopefully creating an environment which would dull the aliens' senses. Once inside the mound, the EXOs would fire strobes in an attempt to further immobilize the Cray.

With the EXOs' success in part two, part three would continue with an attack by the remaining battalions. One infantry battalion and special-troops battalion would be poised in the bunker and prepared to battle once they pushed through the underground wall into the mound chamber. The other infantry battalion, as well as the fires battalion, would infiltrate using the three holes the Cray had created in the earth, as well as the unfilled maw where the thermobaric bomb had detonated.

Then, of course, there was Mr. Pink's new weapon. He'd had it built in secret and had rolled it into the mess hall right before we left. The Black Box: roughly the size of a van, it rested on wheels and needed its own generators. Whatever was inside remained hidden. Mr. Pink had said, through an executioner's smile, that its true purpose would be eventually revealed.

All in all, we had a plan that might even work.

But first we had to get into the volcano.

We were a hundred meters from the top when we heard the noise. There was something up there. Was it waiting, or did it live there? We moved slowly and carefully, ready to defend ourselves.

Kilimanjaro had seven man-made routes to the top: Lemosho, Machame, Marangu, Mweka, Rongai, Shira, and Umbwe. Umbwe was the steepest and quickest, taking us in a direct line to Uhuru Peak where the Kibo caldera remained. Past the scrub, the heathers, the forest, then the tree line, the last hundred meters were almost vertical... almost. We were still able to find places for our feet and hands, but just barely.

The cold didn't help much. The suits were designed for function and not for comfort. Although sealing the suit necessitated air conditioning and heating, we were forced to keep almost all of these off to conserve battery power. My fingers had begun to shake as we entered the ice field.

Olivares was moving first, and I was backing him up. We had no plan or choice other than to rush the top by pure brute force. We wanted to stay as far away from the fumaroles and vaporized sulfuric acid of Kibo as possible, but we might have to skirt it. Frankly, the idea was mind-bogglingly terrifying. It was going to be hard enough descending into a volcano without imagining lava bubbling through the same tunnels.

But there was time enough to be scared for that. We had to get to the top first, and then we had to survive what we encountered. As this was a covert mission, we didn't have our usual suite of weapons. Gone was our Hydra missile system, and we no longer carried our miniguns. Instead we carried MP5 submachine guns and 9mm pistols; both were silenced to keep any killing we had to do as discreet as possible. We'd have loved the firepower, but the last thing we needed was for the Cray to come for us alone on top of this damn mountain. That is, if they could fly this high; CBT OMBRA's xenobiologists weren't certain about the Cray's altitude restrictions.

Olivares crept steadily towards the summit. I moved right behind him, copying his ascent as best I could.

I checked my grip on the rock to make certain I wasn't on ice.

"Move on three," Olivares said.

I followed him to the summit, jerking free my pistol from where it was strapped to my thigh and grabbing my harmonic blade with my other hand. A flurry of black and brown greeted us. I was temporarily blinded as whatever was there attacked my face. I swung at it with my blade and stepped to the side.

A moment later the fight was over.

Olivares and I had killed three vultures. They'd been feeding on a desiccated body that looked like it had been up here for months. Glancing around to make sure the area was secured, I saw more bodies. The ground was about a football field long and covered with rock, leading up a ridge that hid the caldera. Dirty snow and ice dotted the field. Strewn across the length and breadth were bones, pieces of clothing, and cooking tools. I found a pot that showed little rust, suggesting it had been here for a relatively short time. We'd been wondering what had happened to the villagers. I think we'd just found some of them.

How they'd died was another matter. I knelt beside a pile of bones. Each one had marks on it, like from a knife. But were they from the vultures, or had the villagers been attacked as they lay sleeping?

Breathing with the assistance of the suit and an oxygen-rich mixture, I couldn't help wonder how they'd lived up here. I didn't see much that could have been used for fires. Nor did I see much of anything to eat. This sky-high killing field reminded me of all the people we'd lost. Not just my fellow grunts, but the *people* people. We were soldiers; we'd signed up knowing that there was a possibility we'd die. We accepted that and even joked about it. But our mothers and our fathers and our families, our neighbors, the people at our favorite stores and restaurants—there was a good chance that all of them were dead, murdered by an alien force intent on removing us from our own planet. These bones accentuated that.

"Are you seeing this?" I finally said.

Olivares looked out over the landscape. "A little overwhelming, isn't it?"

I walked towards a heap of bones much smaller than all of the others. These were their children. They'd probably piled them in the middle, not knowing what to do with them and unable to bury them. I tried to imagine sitting and staring at my dead child in a pile of other dead children and felt my throat tighten.

Easy, I reminded myself. I had to stay on mission.

I blinked away the moisture forming at the corners of my eyes. "What now?" I said.

Olivares cleared his throat. "Now we look for the way in." He called up several maps on the HUD. They were little more than squiggles on paper, transferred from expedition maps to overlays of the different craters. Unlike the moving maps we were used to, they were merely flat pictures that we had to try and superimpose on reality.

"I think it's over there." Olivares began moving. "Cover me."

I held my MP5 at the ready as I picked my way through the bones to the rocky outcropping.

"This is it," Olivares said, pushing against the rocks. "Only these rocks aren't shown on the map. Someone's concealed the entrance; but could the villagers really have moved them?"

"They could have used saplings as levers." We'd passed through an entire forest on the way to the summit. "Then burned the wood to keep warm. Makes you wonder why they felt the need to cover the hole, doesn't it?" I said, knowing the answer even as I asked.

Olivares knelt and reached into a space between two rocks. He pulled on something; he had to bend it back and forth, until with a *crack* it came free. He held up a Cray claw.

"My guess is that this was the reason."

"As I suspected. Damn."

"Let's fan out and see if there are any other entrances," he said.

I headed to the far edge of the area, careful where I stepped, avoiding treading into the caldera altogether. I didn't see any way to get inside. I climbed the slope until I could look down onto the caldera. The hole in the center was easily large enough to swallow a Cineplex. The ground around it was strangely smooth and covered with light gray rock.

"Get down," Olivares said.

I ducked and turned to see Olivares plastered against a mound of rocks, and two Cray busily climbing above him. I slid my feet over the edge, towards the caldera, and gripped the ledge in front of me. I made myself as low as possible, activated the magnification tool on my HUD and focused on the aliens. No wings, and the extra set of appendages; the OMBRA techs had called them worker drones, but by the way they turned to each other and began communicating, they seemed more sophisticated than that.

One of the Cray had something tucked in a belt that looked suspiciously like a weapon. They'd never had weapons before. The very idea of a Cray with weapons terrified me. It was almost funny. I'd been thinking of them as giant insects for so long, the idea that they were from another planet, possessed of technology hundreds of years beyond ours, had completely escaped me.

"Olivares, they have weapons."

"What the hell are you talking about?"

"Weapons. And they're coming towards you."

I tried to make out the shape of the weapon in their hands, but the magnification just wasn't enough.

"Are you sure?"

"Yes, I'm sure." Was I? "Almost. I mean they have to be."

"Jesus. You got to be sure."

"I can't make them out properly. Listen. Do you want to just run at them and see what their weapons do, or do you want to play it safe and just assume they might fuck you up?"

The Cray moved in short bursts, their legs moving almost faster than I could see. Olivares had his pistol in one hand and his blade in the other.

The Cray moved from one pile of bones to the next, peering, examining, searching. But the bones didn't seem to hold their attention. Where we'd taken great pains to step around them, the aliens trod on them without regard for their provenance.

In sudden bursts the aliens covered the ground from the edge of the plateau to the other side of the rock formation. When they discovered the alien claw that Olivares had tossed aside, their demeanor seemed to change from curious to predatory.

"Careful. They found the claw," I whispered.

"What are they doing?"

"Getting pissed."

Their movements became increasingly jerky as they separated and came around the mound formation from either side. The one on the left was carrying a device which looked similar to a 1970s remote control. Maybe it wasn't a weapon at all. Maybe it was a communications device.

"Be ready. They're almost there."

What the hell was that strange device?

Both aliens rounded their respective corners at the same time, and Olivares did nothing.

"Kill them!" I urged.

But he wasn't moving. His body had gone rigid. The alien on the right burst forward and stripped him of his blade and pistol, tossing them away.

Olivares fell to his side and began to convulse.

"Olivares. Staff Sergeant. What's wrong?" I fought the urge to shoot. At this distance my weapon was virtually worthless. I had as great a chance of hitting Olivares as I did the Cray.

I began to hear a whine in my commset. At first I thought it was some sort of interference, but I soon realized it was coming from Olivares.

"Daddy," came a little boy's voice, cracked and broken. "Please don't go, daddy. I love you daddy. I love you so—" His voice broke as he began to cry.

I was transported back to the basement of the house in Dothan, Alabama. I remembered the shared nightmare, the death dreams of Romeo One.

They had weaponized psychological warfare. They were turning our own memories against us.

The Cray hovered over Olivares. The one that carried the device reached down and touched the faceplate of Olivares's mask.

The movement made me check my own oxygen: twenty-one percent remaining. I rolled over and pulled my blade and pistol free. I looked at them and imagined leaping over the edge of the ridge and running down the incline and across the field. I'd never make it. I put both weapons away and grabbed the MP5 again. The submachine gun had a maximum effective range of two hundred meters.

"Olivares." I whispered. "You there, man?"

I heard a whimpering. I had to take the Cray with the device out first. I couldn't afford to have it pointed at me. We'd be as good as dead with both of us disabled.

I turned my sight towards them only to find them gone.

Gone?

What the hell had happened to them?

I saw movement on the other side of the rock formation. It looked as if they were trying to move the rocks themselves, perhaps trying to get to their dead companion.

I had to move now.

I pushed myself to my feet and ran. I had the MP5 in a two-handed grip, struggling to keep the silencer-tipped barrel on target, knowing that I'd only have one chance. As I came round the corner, pulling the trigger, the Cray turned the device on me. I felt a wave of memories as I sent twenty-seven bullets into both aliens.

I remembered the first time I had sex, with Monica Albright in South Carolina. The rush of ecstatic pleasure jolted me like a live wire. I felt my eyes begin to close as I remembered skin the texture of new paper, eyes the shade of the sky on the first spring day, and breath coated with the taste of grape soda and grain alcohol.

And the Cray fell, its weapons pointing at the sky. It was like a switch had been turned off. Gone were the sensations of that long-ago time, replaced instead by the need to save Olivares.

I fought back to my feet, slipping once as her lips brushed the back of my neck. I slapped a fresh magazine into the MP5. I jerked back the bolt carrier.

The Cray on the right moved a claw towards me. I gave it ten rounds. Then I gave it six more in the face.

The other one stared at the sky. I raised my weapon and prepared to shoot, but it was dead already. I knelt carefully, keeping my aim on the creature as I leaned forward and removed the device. There wasn't much to it: a composite-metal rectangle a little too large to fit into one hand and filled with unknown alien electronics. I couldn't see anywhere to activate it, but I was careful nonetheless, especially since I wasn't sure which end was live.

Olivares groaned. I put the device down and leaned over him. "You okay, man?"

The inside of his faceplate was coated in vomit. I was afraid he was going to choke on it, so I hurriedly unlatched his suit. There was a hiss of compressed air as I pulled the faceplate free and checked his mouth, hooking a finger into it.

Olivares batted at my hands and moved his head away. A good sign. His mouth and throat were clear. He wasn't going to choke.

But now he had another problem. I'd removed his helmet, which meant he'd just depressurized at almost twenty thousand feet. Hypoxia was an immediate concern. He had maybe twenty to thirty minutes before his organs would start shutting down.

"Take it easy, man."

I wiped his faceplate clear, then snapped his helmet shut before resealing his suit. He was moving slowly, but he wasn't fighting me. Another good sign. The procedure took seven percent of his oxygen mix, which meant that if we got in trouble, he'd be hurting before me. I just hoped that wasn't something we'd have to worry about. I checked his breathing and oxygen levels and watched them climb back to normal. I kept an eye on the dead Cray, but my main concern was for Olivares. It's a funny thing being angry at someone in the military. You could hate them to their very core, but once the shit hit the fan, they were closer to you than your own family.

I stood and scanned the perimeter, securing the Cray device in an ammo pouch. I checked Olivares one more time, then jogged towards the other side of the plateau.

My ammo was good. My head was clear. This was something I could do, without question. I almost hoped to find Cray. Olivares was right. I was a killer. It's something I've always been good at.

When I reached the edge, I dropped and low-crawled the rest of the way. I was almost disappointed to see nothing there; just scrub and rock and the tree line far below. I rolled over and stared at the sky.

The mound seemed so far away. And to think we had to find a way underground and travel back there. I chuckled. It was the definition of a wild goose chase. And what happened if we couldn't do it? Not much. It was only the entire human race depending on us.

I'm not sure how long I lay there, but I started to relax, staring at the bright white clouds floating in the upside-down sea of the sky. I blocked out all the bad that had happened and began to remember things I'd forgotten. Like the first time I'd stormed up Victory Tower in basic training at Fort Jackson, or the feeling of accomplishment after my first twenty-one mile ruck march. Winning Soldier of the Month competitions and my promotion to sergeant, which had seemed so long in coming, but had really only taken three years. Thinking about those times was bittersweet, however, because as I remembered each thing, another part of me reminded myself that each of those people and places no longer existed. I fought the idea; they might not exist in the real world, but as long as I remembered them they existed in my mind.

The sky was blocked suddenly by the head and torso of a figure.

"You sleeping?" Olivares asked.

"Just resting."

"Come on, you can—"

"I know, rest when I'm dead."

He helped me to my feet.

"You okay?" I asked.

He nodded. "Smells like a prom date in here, though."

"Need better prom dates then."

He laughed. "No kidding. At least ones who can hold their liquor."

"I should point out that eighteen-year-old girls shouldn't be able to hold their liquor."

"We knew different sorts of eighteen-year-olds," He looked down the side of the mountain for a moment, then back to me. "What'd you do with them?"

"What do you mean?"

"The Cray. What'd you do with their bodies?"

"Their what?" I sat up and stared back towards the rock formation. "I didn't do anything."

"Then where are they?"

They'd been dead. I knew they had. But then I remembered I hadn't checked the other one. In fact, I'd held my fire. It must have been playing possum.

Damn!

We're surrounded. That simplifies the problem.

General Chesty Puller, USMC

CHAPTER THIRTY-SEVEN

WE TOOK OFF running. Olivares went left and I went right. We met on the other side. Sure enough, the dead Cray were gone.

Olivares was turning in circles, scanning the terrain.

We saw it at the same time: drag marks.

Again, we took off running, following the trail across the plateau to the rim of the caldera. When we got to the ridge, we searched but didn't see anything.

There was no way it had moved that fast.

"Are you sure you shot it?

"At least ten rounds."

"I'll cover you from here."

I jogged across the ground, jinking from side to side. It took a moment, but I picked up the trail again and began to follow. It led me in a meandering but unmistakable route to the caldera. I got within ten meters, then slowed. We'd been told that the volcano was dormant, but what did that really mean? I was pretty certain there was still lava down there somewhere. We'd already been warned about the gasses and ash, something neither of us was eager to encounter.

I stared across the width of the giant hole and watched the air shimmer with heat.

"So what now?" I said.

"We go in after it."

"Into that?"

"Right now I'm not seeing any other way into the volcano—"

The hole was one hundred meters down a sharp incline of broken and smooth basalt. The black rock was scored with sulfurous white in several places, evidence of a previous violent episode. Vents emitted deadly gasses in six separate locations, but the entrance itself, thankfully, appeared to be clear.

"So do we just walk on down and peek over the edge?" I said.

"Either that or I throw you in and you can tell me what you see."

"Ah. Can I take what's behind door number three?"

"That would be going back down the hill to the mound."

I hated it when there was little or no choice. In this case, no choice. We didn't have enough power or oxygen to go back, so we had to go forward. In fact, if we didn't find a way down, in less than an hour Olivares would be dead and I'd be joining him shortly thereafter.

I took a few steps forward, then stopped and looked back. "Want me to hold your hand?"

On our way down the slope, we saw no more evidence of the Cray or its passage. When we got within ten metres of the hole, Olivares stopped.

"Okay, Corporal. Here's where you earn your money. Why don't you get on your belly and scoot down and let me see through your feed."

I knew better than to argue. Lowest grunt did the most dangerous things. Lowest grunt held the least value. I remember in Infantry School we'd had an immense Portuguese sergeant named Silva. He was a bombastic instructor who never missed a chance to tell us a story, most of which we believed were true. He told us one tale about the Cold War and what grunts were supposed to have done if America and the Soviet Union ever decided to actually fire missiles at each other.

"The lowest ranking grunt, and I mean the bottom-of-the-barrel, wet-behind-the-ears, gotta-wipe-his-nose, can't-put-his-underwear-on-without-his-mama grunt, is the first to go. When the balloon goes up and radiation is all around and we got no communications, it's these grunts gonna get us to safety. The human body can take fifty rads. So we send the lowest grunt out and tell him to go in a direction until he reaches twenty-five rads. Then he marks it on the map and comes back. That's another twenty-five rads. He's a goner, so we get the next grunt. And the next and the next, until we know which way we can go without killing ourselves. Wanna know why there are so many grunts in an infantry company? So the rest of us can come out alive."

The funny thing about it was that every time Sergeant Silva told that story he was laughing so hard he could barely contain himself. "Ever see a guy who has so much radiation inside of him his blood is boiling?" he'd asked a stunned group of wannabe grunts. "Me neither," he'd roar. "Because I'm a sergeant." Then he'd get serious. "But if the balloon goes up and you find yourself at the bottom, you better be a professional and do your duty for the rest of us. Sure, you're going to die a horrible and unpleasant death, but you'll be doing it as a grunt and you'll be proud."

As I slid across the volcanic rock to stare into the mouth of hell, I channeled Sergeant Silva. I was the lowest grunt. It was my duty to put myself in danger to save the others, even if that was Olivares.

As I got closer to the edge, I was worried it might give way. I pulled out my blade and jabbed at it, but the rock seemed sturdy. I was almost at a forty-five degree angle. Any steeper and it would be more like a slide. When I was close enough to grip the edge, I used it to pull myself the rest of the way, inch by inch until I could see right over the edge.

"Gotcha," I said.

One of the Cray was lying in a heap at the bottom of the shaft about twenty meters away. Check that. As I switched spectrums, then returned to the visible spectrum and turned on my headlamp, I saw that the alien had merely fallen on a large ledge. The shaft descended past the light's ability to reach. Was this the alien I'd shot first, or was it the one who'd held the device?

"Seeing this?" I whispered.

"Got it." Olivares began flipping through my spectrums.

"Can't see a thing without the light," I said.

"That's the point. Other than moderate heat from the walls, I'm not getting any heat signatures. It might actually mean it's safe down there."

I stared into the darkness beyond the reach of the light. Of course we were going down there. We had to. As I waited here on the edge, it just seemed so improbable. Then again, so did getting invaded by aliens.

I licked my lips. "What next?"

"We need to get down there. I'm at less than five percent oxygen. We can't climb without these suits, so we need to start moving."

I observed the walls; they were far from sheer. There were ledges everywhere, ranging from inches to feet wide. It was definitely doable, but it was going to be slow going. We each had a hundred feet of rope in our packs, but the tensile strength of the line wasn't made to hold the suits. They were to be used once we got rid of the EXOs.

"I'm going in." I swung my legs around until they were dangling over the edge. I'd seen several outcroppings I could use for hand- and footholds. I reached blindly with my foot for the first, found it, and tentatively put my weight on it. I still held onto the lip as I eased most of my weight onto my foot, ready to pull up if it gave way.

It held. Now was when I put myself in the hands of the universe.

I smiled weakly, then reached out for a handhold. I gripped it and released the lip, lowering myself into the mouth of the volcano.

My hand closed on a ledge and I let the rest of my weight go down. I glanced down and found the other hand grip, grabbed it, then let my free leg dangle down to the next perch.

"How's it going?" Olivares asked.

"Like climbing down the outside of the Empire State Building. I'm just happy I can't see the bottom."

"I heard the Cray tore it down."

"Aren't you the motivational speaker?"

"I try," he said.

I switched to his view of me from the top down. It was dizzying at first, but then I reconciled the image and used it to find my next three holds. But then I ran out. It still looked to be about five meters to the ledge where the Cray rested, which was down and to my left. The alien took up most of the ledge and I had to plan it so I wouldn't land on the body.

I counted to three then pushed off with my right foot. But as I did, the rock gave way beneath it and I felt myself beginning to slip. I pushed off hard with my left foot, working against the awkward angle to make sure my trajectory was towards the ledge. For a brief moment, I was in space, then I was falling. For all of my planning and attempts to land softly, I landed on my side, falling on the dead alien. I felt it give beneath me.

"You okay?"

"Sure." I picked my way to my feet, wary of the edge. What had seemed so wide from above now seemed tiny, my own perch precarious. There was no more space on the ledge, certainly none for Olivares. I stared down at the Cray. It was a little flatter, but otherwise, knowing only what we'd learned about alien physiology from the model we'd had, this one appeared to be pretty dead.

"What now?"

"Search it."

"What am I looking for?" I squatted and appraised the body. It appeared a little different from what we'd seen before, wearing armored, form-fitting shorts that probably covered reproductive organs and served to hold a belt. That had an empty slot as well as two containers, which I hadn't seen behind the Cray's back. Gauging from the empty slot, this was the alien that'd had the device. So what happened to the other one? I peered into the darkness and relayed what I'd found.

"Open them, but be careful."

I jiggled with nerves. How careful did I need to be? It wasn't like I was on the inside edge of a volcano with a dead alien. Whatever would jump out at me from the small containers was probably the least of my worries.

The first one contained what appeared to be seeds. Were they rations of some sort? The next contained a spongy type of cloth. Unfolded, it was about a foot square. I had no idea what it was, but it had to be important if they'd brought it along on the mission. I had my doubts that it was merely a face cloth.

"Some sort of seeds, maybe rations, and a mystery cloth. What next?"

"Secure the items. And remove your rope."

"What's the rope for?" I asked.

"We're going to hang the alien over the edge so there's enough room for me to descend."

"Are you sure that's a good idea? Why not just toss it over?"

"We might need the body in one piece. I can't be sure. For now let's hang onto it as long as possible."

"Think the other one is down below?" I asked.

"I'd bet on it."

"But why?"

He paused for a moment. I saw his feed go to the darkness, then back to me. "Haven't you wondered why the Cray want to hide their bodies?"

"I thought maybe they were trying to get home through the back door."

"Either way, they didn't want us to have their bodies. I think they have something we could use. Something they don't want us to have."

"Like what?"

"It could be anything. Right now we don't have the luxury of playing Mr. Science. We'll have to wait until we get to the bottom."

I stood and tried to turn around, but my foot was wedged between the body and the wall. I tried to pull it free as gently as I could, but it wouldn't budge. I tried a little harder and my foot moved an inch or two, so I jerked it out and turned. The Cray's body rolled over again, its legs and two of its arms dangling over the abyss. I saw it too late to stop and could only watch as it continued to roll, then plunged into the darkness.

"Oh, hell," I said.

"What's that?"

"We don't need the rope anymore."

I saw his feed looking at me as I looked at him. All I could do was shrug inside my suit.

I miss Twinkies and Pepsi and Ranch-flavored Doritos. I have a box of the latter and am considering treating it like fine wine, because when I run out, there's going to be nothing left. When we win back this planet, I seriously doubt one of the first orders of business will be to rebuild the corn chip factory. I'll be lucky if I have them again in my lifetime, once I eat these. Funny thing is that you really never know how important something is to you until it's gone.

Conspiracy Theory Talk Radio,
Night Stalker Monologue #1113

CHAPTER THIRTY-EIGHT

ON THE BRIGHT side, without the Cray to worry about, we could move faster, which was imperative with Olivares's oxygen mix so low. We had to travel at least a thousand feet to make it to the demarcation from extreme high altitude to very high altitude. Without our EXOs we'd be subject to marked hypoxemia, hypnocapnia and alkalosis. This was why there were no permanent human habitations above six thousand meters. It would also mean our deaths unless we hurried. Even after one thousand feet we were still in significant danger.

The CBT techs had provided us with a carbonic anhydrase inhibitor, which would reduce the risk of edema. And make us feel as though we'd been hit by a truck. All of our muscles and organs would begin firing adrenaline as they sought to defray the effects of lack of oxygen and pressure. Narcosis would set in and get progressively worse until we could barely function. Nothing like mountain climbing on drugs.

"Take your shot?" I asked.

"Already done," Olivares responded. "But I still feel like hell from when you evac'ed my suit."

"Sorry, man. I thought you were going to choke." I sought for a foothold beneath the ledge and found one, then another, then another. "What was it they made you remember?"

Olivares grunted several times as he moved down the face of the vent, finally landing on the ledge I'd just vacated. "Bullshit I thought I'd forgotten."

He needn't say more. We all had secrets. Having done bad things in our life didn't make us bad. But not trying to hide them or deal with them most certainly did. I'd known more than a handful of fellow soldiers who relished their memories of death and murder. Most of them were broken. A few were truly evil.

We kept our conversation to a minimum as we descended; exertion was already doing a number on our oxygen levels. Every dozen feet or so, I'd glance down to see if my suit light revealed anything, but the shaft was relatively straight. Eventually I noticed that the distance between myself and Olivares was increasing. I checked my HUD and saw that he was at one percent; almost out of air.

Damn.

I glanced down and still couldn't see the bottom.

"Hey, man. Give me your rope. We'll rig a harness and let you dangle from my suit. It can hold you."

I waited for a response, but received none.

"Olivares? Can you hear me?"

"I can hear you just fine," he said. He was shucking his pack to get at the rope.

"Drop one end of the rope to me and let me tie it off before you unseal your suit, okay?"

"I don't think we're going to do that," he said with a strange calmness.

I halted. "What do you mean, we're not going to do that? You have to let me help you with this."

He laughed hollowly. "There you go again, Mason. Always trying to be the hero."

He wasn't making any sense. I wondered if the narcosis was already affecting him. "I thought you said I was a killer," I said.

"Killer. Hero. In the end aren't they the same?" He unslung his pack. "Hold out your arm and catch this. Just don't be a dumbass and let go of the wall."

I held out an arm and looked up at him. I saw his grim, determined smile through his faceplate. "Catch." He tossed the pack down to me as his level hit zero.

The pack bounced off the wall and into my chest. I scrambled for it and managed to hook it with my fingers at the last moment. "Dude, what are you doing?"

"Going to be a leader," he said, coughing. "Don't want to kill you, too."

I suddenly realized what he was going to do. "Don't you do that!" I yelled.

"Can't help it." He coughed.

"Sounds like you want to be a hero instead," I argued, but time was up. He was completely out of air. He had to open the suit or he'd die.

"Don't you get it? In the end—"

And then he jumped. He didn't scream. He didn't cry out. He was just gone.

I finished his sentence for him. *In the end they're the same.* Leaders are heroes are killers. All along they were the same. Only Olivares would be able to teach me a lesson by doing something I would have done, and it pissed me off.

I clipped his pack onto mine using a spare carabiner, then continued my descent. Although I concentrated on the climb, I couldn't help seeing my own meter creep into single digits. I fought the creeping feeling that Ohirra and I were the only ones we positively knew were alive. Although I held out hope for Michelle and Thompson, it was only hope at this point. My whole career had been like this. From Bosnia to the Middle East to the fields of Africa, I'd always watched as others had died around me. I used to curse my luck and wished I could share it among my fellow grunts.

And I still felt that way. If I could change any moment in the last two weeks it would be to change places with any of my dead friends. MacKenzie, with his ever-present smile and profane humor. Little Thompson, forever trying to overcome his time in the band. Olivares, asshole leader extraordinaire, who I'd hated since the beginning but respected more than anyone else. And, of course, Michelle. I held out little hope that there was any real love between us.

We all had stories.

We'd all seen our friends and fellow grunts die.

We'd all tried to kill ourselves, only to discover we were needed to save the planet.

And we'd all die doing it.

During the Vietnam War the average life expectancy of a grunt had been twenty-eight days. During the Korean War it had been twenty-one days. During WWII, forty-eight. And now, during the War Against the Cray, it was five days—just five. It was a sad state of events, I couldn't help but think. After all, if we all died, who was going to save our planet?

My oxygen mix was down to two percent. I had less than ten minutes. I moved fast, but not in desperation. I knew now I was going to join Olivares. He'd tried to save me, I'll give him that. We just hadn't known how deep the tube was.

I was down to one percent. I glanced down. My light speared the darkness and nothing more.

Fuck that. If I was going to die it was on my own terms.

When my meter snapped to zero, I pushed off the wall. As I began to fall, I splayed out my arms and legs. I was facing down, the light guiding my way to death.

Starship Troopers and *The Forever War* are both widely seen as anti-military books. What techniques do the authors use to disguise this, or do they? Does the sentiment of the authors change your opinion about the books? How might our opinions of other cultures change in a post-alien invasion world?

TF OMBRA Study Question

CHAPTER THIRTY-NINE

THERE WAS A ghostly image in the darkness. At first it was a speck, but it soon grew to fill my view. Then I knew who it was, and I was pleased to join Olivares in death. He reached out to me as we plummeted towards another life.

I struck bottom and the ground gave and gave and gave, sucking me in, drawing me into its bosom. Then there was nothing. No movement. No sound. Just a white light, enveloping me.

My hands scraped against the side of my helmet, searching for the release. I couldn't find it. I felt my fingers go numb. My chest burned.

Then I was being moved, pulled backwards. I came up and up, a light spearing from my face into a blizzard of white. My helmet was jerked free and I gasped, inhaling as much ash as air. I coughed and wheezed. The ash began to fill the inside of my suit; it stuck to my face and lips. It tasted of rock and sulfur. But I didn't care about any of that.

I was alive.

And as I turned, I spied Olivares, frowning with concentration as he fought to keep me from sinking deeper.

Olivares punched me twice in the face and I knew it was hell. Only in hell would the man I hated and loved get to punch me when I was dead.

He wrapped a rope around me. At first he tried for my throat, but it missed and he ended up hooking my arm. He pulled and I came towards him. I laughed. What had he said about heroes and killers and leaders? How special was he now, unable to even kill me? Instead of hanging me by the neck, he was hanging me by the arm.

"You can't hang my arm!" I yelled, only it came out as *yougant hangamarm* as I spewed spittle and ash.

He screamed something at me that sounded like *stpiting!*

I laughed at him, daring him to try and hang my other arm.

But he ignored my laughter and hauled me up until I was no longer in the blizzard of ash, and found myself on a hard surface.

I suddenly felt sick. I coughed, bringing up ash and bile.

Olivares unlatched my suit and I felt a sting in my arm.

Then I felt nothing for a while. I know my eyes closed. I know I dreamed of a place where Olivares and I skied down a mountain of EXOs. I know I felt the earth tremble beneath me.

Then nothing.

Then light.

I opened my eyes. I felt like I'd been pummeled from head to tail by brass knuckles. A light came from somewhere to my left, and my mouth tasted like three miles of road. My breath was ragged. My stomach twitched like it was ready to spasm at any moment. If I'd been home, I'd have rolled over and gone back to sleep. But I wasn't home. I had no home. I was in the bottom of a volcano in the middle of Africa, and somehow I was still alive.

"Hold on. There," Olivares said, cradling my head. "Breathe easy. Talk about prom dates. You reminded me of Cindy. She puked all over the back of my El Camino."

"I didn't puke," I managed to say after several failed attempts.

He patted me on my cheek. "That's right. You didn't puke. You just keep thinking that."

Oh, yeah. I did puke.

But why was I alive?

He saw the question in my eyes. "Myo-inositol trisphyosphate," he said. "Increases the amount of oxygen released by your hemoglobin." He held out his hand. "And take these, too."

I glanced down and saw two eight-hundred-milligram ibuprofens. "Seriously? Ranger candy?"

"It'll reduce the nausea and inflammation."

I sat up to take the pills. He handed me a water flask and I drank deeply.

"Easy now." He sat back as I swallowed and got my bearings. "Feeling better?"

"I told you I didn't puke," I said, both of us knowing better.

"Then watch where you step so you don't put your feet in the places you didn't puke." He stood and I realized for the first time he was in his fatigues and boots.

"How..." I asked, but I couldn't finish. I had too many questions.

I pushed to my feet and it seemed like a hundred miles. As I looked around, it was like I was noticing the world for the first time. I felt like I'd been reborn. Never before had I reached the moment where I'd been so sure I was dead... so sure that I'd given up.

Then I saw the rope.

The incredible pile of ash.

Two dead aliens.

Our smashed suits stacked against a wall and our helmets angled to light the cavern we were in.

"There's a pile of ash in the other room at least sixty feet high. I think the aliens were dead when they hit. I'm afraid I landed on one."

One of the Cray looked like a bug that had been stepped on by a giant foot.

"If it wasn't for the ash and the suits, we'd definitely be dead."

I put a hand to my head. "We're not dead. I feel too much like shit to be dead."

"That's pretty much how I feel, too."

It was then I saw the right side of his head. It was red and purple and swollen in several places. His right eye was black and blue. His right arm hung strangely.

He saw me looking at it and raised it halfway. "This is as high as I can get it."

"What about the side of your face?"

"Not sure. It might be because of decompression. It doesn't hurt."

I laughed. I was probably still a little drunk from the narcosis, but I remembered an old joke. *Does your face hurt? Well it hurts me.* But as I laughed, I felt pain in my own face, too. I felt around my eyes and they felt different.

"You got a pair of shiners and your nose is broken. You hit the inside of your faceplate so hard you cracked it."

"Always was headstrong."

"Very funny."

"And the rope?"

"I was already out of my suit and couldn't move your heavy ass. I had to rig ropes to pull you out, or you'd have suffocated."

"I remember choking. I couldn't breathe."

"Part of that was because of your face," he said with a grin. "It was a close thing. The rope kept stretching and I was afraid it would snap."

I looked down and realized I was in my skivvies and toe shoes, but I wasn't cold. In fact, I was pretty warm.

"We must be close to magma," I said.

He nodded. "It's somewhere near for sure, but we're safe for now. If it was closer, we wouldn't be able to breathe. Acid vapor."

"Thank God for small miracles," I said, going over to my pack. But the moment I began to move, all of my muscles clenched and reminded me of what my body had just done. I'd taken two ibuprofens. I wanted about fifty more. I limped on both legs and began to pick my way through my things. Everything else had been emptied from the pack except my clothes. As I pulled on my multicam uniform and boots, I asked, "Did you do an inventory?"

He moved to where he'd laid everything out and began to catalogue them. "We have nine liters of water, two first aid kits with more medicine for altitude sickness, three hundred rounds of 9mm ammunition, four kilos of Semtex with mechanical detonators, four thermite grenades, our blades, our pistols, one submachine gun, and enough rations for thirty-six hours." He pointed to another stack. "We also have a full set of Kevlar each, including shin and forearm guards and ballistic masks."

"Only one MP5?"

"Yours got bent to shit on impact."

"What about the tablets?"

"They didn't make it either," he said.

"Shit. How are we going to navigate?"

"We'll figure something out."

I looked at him standing there, beaten up, one arm dangling. I know I looked even worse than he did. And we were the cavalry. We were supposed to save the day. I couldn't help but feel that the human race had the short straw.

"So what's the plan?" I asked, tying my boots and shoving the loose ends into the top, Ranger style.

He regarded me for a moment, then turned to look at the dead aliens. He put his hands on his hips. "So I've been wondering about them, and why they came to the volcano."

That again? "Maybe it was one dragging the other and dumping him in," I said.

"Even better. There was no way down. They had to have known that. They weren't from inside the volcano, or else they would have climbed up from here instead of on the outside rim."

"What are you getting at?"

"What were they trying to hide?" He gently felt the swollen side of his face. "I can't help thinking it's something important."

"Well," I began, standing and buttoning my fatigue top, "there's one way to find out."

"And what's that?"

I reached down and pulled my blade free of my suit. "We operate."

"Yeah," he said, scratching his chin. "I was thinking the exact same thing."

I miss cheeseburgers. I miss the melted cheese and the fat popping in my mouth. I miss everything about them, even the stupid commercials back on television, when we had television. Stupid thing to get emotional about, but it's what I think about when I'm scrabbling for rations.

Conspiracy Theory Talk Radio,
Night Stalker Monologue #1113

CHAPTER FORTY

FOR THE RECORD, the inside of a Cray smelled like nothing else I'd ever encountered. We had both of them laid out along one wall. I wore gloves mainly because it was too gross to root around inside the thing's body barehanded. I didn't mind killing something, but I'd never been the type to want to play in their entrails after. The entire idea made me a little ill. Still, Olivares had a theory and we had to check it out.

We started with the one that had been carrying the device. I didn't know jack about autopsies, but I'd seen enough television to know you had to slice them from stem to stern.

"Does anything look strange?" he asked.

I turned to him, as I held my bloodied hands up like a surgeon. "Seriously? Did you just ask if anything is strange?"

"You know what I mean."

We searched through the body cavities and then the brains. It was in the second brain that we found something interesting. Something seemed to be attached to the rear interior wall of the skull with several wires, then implanted into the Cray's brain. From the outside I couldn't even tell it was there, but from the inside it was readily apparent.

"I think this might be what we're looking for!"

He knelt and we both examined the wires. A flap of skin on the back of the head hid a triangular interface. Not having studied their anatomy other than during firefights, I wouldn't have been able to see the flap if I hadn't seen the wires from the inside.

I glanced at the other skull and didn't see anything even remotely similar. My guess was that the two drones had different functions. I'd always thought of all the Cray as being the same except for the wings, but it made sense that they'd have specialties. So if this one had a brain implant, then what was its specialty?

"Think it's for tracking?" I asked.

Olivares seemed to consider for a moment, then shook his head. "I'm guessing it's a transmitter."

"A communication device?"

"I think so. Let's get it out of there. It might come in handy."

"What are we going to do with it?" I began to pull the wires free.

He shrugged. "Better to have it and not need it than to need it and not have it."

It was an old Army saying, but it had merit. It took a few minutes, but I was able to extract the device without damaging it. I rinsed it with water and once I was satisfied, Olivares took it and placed it in a small plastic bag inside his pack.

We covered the alien corpses with ash. We didn't want them to be found, especially how we left them. I could only imagine how an American squad might feel, coming upon evidence of their own dead cut up and examined. I wouldn't want to be on the receiving end of that kind of anger.

I slid on the Kevlar vest, the forearm guards and the shin guards. I slipped the ballistic mask into a pocket of the vest, not really willing to wear it right now. During our tactical briefing, we'd been warned that trying to go up against a Cray without some sort of armor would be our deaths. We'd become used to the protection of the suits and had ignored defense for the most part. I know I was exceptionally guilty of that. In fact, counting the present mission, I'd never gone out on a mission and returned with a functioning EXO. The designers would hate me if they knew.

I checked our timer. We had twenty-three hours to make it to the rendezvous.

Volcanologists had planned probable paths from the central cone to the mound. They hadn't been certain of the exact route, but they'd been able to preprogram our tablets to provide directions based on probabilities. Traveling the warren of tunnels carved into the earth by a millennium of lava would have been a whole lot easier had our tablets not been ruined in our falls.

Olivares was unwilling to give up on them, so he decided to stay behind and try and get them to work while I conducted reconnaissance. I had two choices: wait and twiddle my thumbs, or scout ahead a little. I went in black-out; for all I knew, we had Cray stacking up around the corner, waiting to attack, so the last thing I wanted was to draw them with light.

I wore an AN/PVS-7D Generation III Night Vision Device with a single monocular lens. Strapped tightly to my head, it felt top heavy, but experience told me that I'd soon stop noticing it. The MP5 had a HK grip-mounted IR illuminator which would provide a thin spotlight of readable light. But I also had an OMBRA-created illuminator that fit like a collar beneath my chin. Both the NVD and the illuminators used AA batteries and we had seventy of them. The weight was significant, but as we ran through the batteries, the load would become lighter. The illuminators required the most juice. The collar took the most power, so my plan was to use it sparingly.

The last thing I grabbed was a can of Nightmarker-brand infrared marking paint. In the event we had to backtrack, I wanted to make certain we knew where we were going. There was the potential for getting completely lost in the caverns and tunnels beneath the volcano. If we did lose our way, no one would find us except, maybe, the Cray a thousand years after they'd successfully conquered our planet. Our bones would go into a museum along with our equipment, just as we'd enshrined losing populations before us.

I began my trek and left Olivares sitting amidst wires and batteries. I moved down the tunnel until there was no longer any visible spectrum bleed, then powered on my NVD. Without any light, it was as blind as I was, until I toggled on the spot illuminator. I turned and let the light play across the wall, catching the cracks and grooves and creases of the rock. Outside the half-meter-wide circle of light was an abyss of darkness and shadow.

I partially depressed the trigger of my MP5 and watched another IR illuminator spear the darkness. Like a surgeon's laser, it sliced through the shadow, but it did little to show my way. It was meant for targeting.

Finally I depressed a button on the back of my left hand. A band of sixteen IR LEDs on my collar fired, creating a supernova that temporarily blinded me as my NVD whited out. After it adjusted, it was as though I'd brought the sun itself into the depths of Kilimanjaro. Everything was washed out. There wasn't anything I couldn't see. Had there been a beetle with a mite on its ass, I would have been able to count the whiskers on the mite's cheeks.

I remember being afraid of darkness when I was young. Every kid had the same issues, whether it be the mystery of the shadows in the closet, or those under the bed. There was darkness here beneath the earth, but it was a different sort. The idea of darkness taking over the light was what was so scary. Beneath the earth there had never been any light to take over. It had always been dark. If anything, I felt uplifted, bringing light to a place which had never seen it, even if it was IR light.

I counted my steps. When I reached twenty-five, I brought out the spray can and put an X on the wall. In visible light it would have been a dull black mark, but in IR it blazed.

I moved another twenty-five feet and did the same. Then another twenty-five. Then after moving thirteen steps, the tunnel branched. I pierced the darkness with my weapon's spot, but it didn't show me anything. I turned on my IC, allowed my NVD to adjust, then beheld the two paths before me. One went to the right and appeared to be relatively easy going. The other way ran straight ahead, the darkness littered with rocks the size of automobiles. Further in, my spot lit a gallery of glittering crystals along the ceiling and walls. I could just make out the ground far below, maybe fifty feet down. It was a huge room, no telling how large. It had once held magma, or perhaps water.

I went down on one knee and turned off the illuminator collar. I turned off the NVD as well. I leaned my head against the cold hard rock and listened. Complete silence.

While doing night maneuvers at Fort Bragg, I distinctly remembered the way the tall pines scraping against the moon-hung sky felt like the earth itself reaching up. I'd felt absolutely insignificant at that very moment; the creak of the trees as the wind teased them; the feel of the wind against my cheek; the sounds of insects commiserating about my presence in their night place.

Here I felt the same sense of insignificance. I could die and it would mean nothing. I could fall and break a leg and no one would ever know where I was. Suddenly the immensity of my situation hit me. The invasion. Billions dead. My teammates dead. Thompson dead. Michelle... dead or missing. The ferocity of the Cray attack. The mound. That fucking mound.

A sob surprised me, escaping into darkness. It flew through the stygian blackness and became part of the barrow.

The earth sobbed back at me, echoes of my anguish, pain and loss.

I wiped my eyes and relaxed my breathing. I sat there for a time, clearing my head, just being. The coming hours would be the most important of my existence. My success, my failure, the ability or inability to find a way through the maze of tunnels to the lair of the Cray, might mean life or death for the human race. It would have seemed impossible if it hadn't been cold hard fact.

I breathed again and sought to find a place of peace, however temporary it might be.

A scraping noise came from somewhere below.

It came again, and I knew I wasn't alone.

> Look at how a single candle can both defy and
> define the darkness.
>
> Anne Frank

CHAPTER FORTY-ONE

I DARED NOT breathe.

Waiting for the sound to come again was interminable; when it finally did, it was from way down, somewhere in the darkness of the vast chamber below.

I had two choices. I could return to Olivares and inform him of the situation, and both of us could return in force, creating interlocking fields of fire that could maximize our position and firepower. Or I could go it alone.

I marked the edge of the opening with the IR paint and carefully began to descend. I wasn't playing around. The descent was difficult. In the NVD, I lacked depth perception. I felt the way with my feet as I went, facing forward, ready to bring my MP5 to bear if needed.

When I finally reached the ground, the floor of the vast chamber was relatively flat and smooth, covered in a thick layer of disturbed dust. I sprayed a mark on a rock near the ground that would be visible from the opening.

I began to try and decipher the marks in the dust. A mess of human footprints were jumbled in a large area. They moved off in every direction, most likely trying to find a way forward. Villagers who'd found their way into the volcano? Or another team?

My opinion of Mr. Pink had never changed. However competent he may be, there was always more to every mission than he let on. The tracks made me wonder if we hadn't been the first group to try this mission. Of course, I reminded myself that there was no wind and there was no weather, so these footprints might have been here since the time of Jules Verne.

My gut said otherwise.

I followed the prints, until I found the first of hundreds of 5.56 and 9mm shell casings littering the floor. More recent than Jules Verne, then.

We were not the first.

So who or what had that noise been?

The cavern was larger than I'd originally suspected. As I moved forward, the IR began to reveal more and more of the scene. The footprints had become smeared in several places. A smell intruded into my awareness.

I saw a boot. Vibram soles, military issue, and attached to a dead soldier wearing the same fatigues I was wearing, right up to the CBT OMBRA patch on his shoulder.

Huh?

The scraping came again.

I ran in small, controlled steps towards the sound, past several more bodies. A Cray, its leg trembling. I stabbed it with the laser targeting indicator from my weapon. Its body had been riddled with bullets. Its eyes were glazed, and green fluid trickled from the corner of its tiny, insectile mouth. This one lacked wings, just as the other two had. Its clawed hands had closed like the legs of a dying spider. Its back was arched. One knee was up, the other leg slung out.

I let my MP5 hang by its sling and pulled my harmonic blade free. I removed the alien's head and felt a little better.

I scouted the rest of the chamber and found six more Cray; possibly more, if I were to piece together all of the parts. Several grenade pins littered the floor. They'd been lucky there hadn't been a cave in.

A thought struck me. Maybe there *had* been. Maybe there wasn't any way out. I forced myself to remain calm. No use working myself up until I could see for myself. I decided to wait to check further until I had Olivares with me. If there had recently been grenade explosions in here, there was no telling how unstable the cavern might have become.

In total, I found ten Cray and six dead soldiers.

I knelt beside one soldier and checked the nametag: Robinson. I checked another: Fredricks. And another, Cozzens. This name I remembered. He'd had a conversation in the mess hall with MacKenzie once, something about Wales. Then it all snapped into place. Romeo Five. This was Romeo Five! I hadn't seen them performing any actions on the mound. They'd been sent here instead.

Why hadn't Mr. Pink told us? He had to have known we'd come in contact with their remains. But then I answered my own question. Why would he state the obvious? Telling us in advance would have just created more questions and more doubt.

Of course, he'd sent a full team before and only two soldiers this time. He could have at least sent Ohirra, but no. For some reason he was unwilling to risk more grunts, which meant that he probably didn't expect us to succeed.

I scowled.

It was always daunting on some level to realize one's own expendability. One moment you believe you're a critical element to mission success, and the next you realize you hardly matter. Not for the first time, I wondered what else Mr. Pink had kept from us. I decided then and there that I'd find a way to prove to him that we could make a difference.

I went to work separating the bodies. I laid all of the members of Romeo Five in a row and stacked their equipment in a separate pile, grabbing an MP5 to bring back for Olivares to use. I left the Cray where they lay, but checked to see if any of them had that strange device on the backs of their heads. Four of them did. I separated these from the rest, just in case Olivares could think of a good reason to remove the devices.

Then I did one last sweep around the area and found the boundary walls. There were six ways out of the cavern, but it was obvious from marks on the floor which way the Cray had come. I didn't immediately check it; for all I knew, there were a hundred Cray waiting for some poor fool to stick his head in. Instead, I made another final check of the chamber floor and returned to Olivares.

Climbing back out of the chamber tired me more than I expected. By the time I made it back to where Olivares had everything laid out like a science project, I was exhausted. I briefly told him what I'd seen, then threw myself down, leaned against the wall and gave myself an hour of well-deserved shuteye.

As it turned out, Olivares gave me four.

And took two himself.

I dreamed of Michelle. She was whispering to me. I kept laughing and trying to figure out what she was saying, but she never became clear.

When Olivares woke me, he had a grin on his face.

"Want to hear something funny?"

"Sure. What is it?"

He held out his hand, revealing the thing we'd removed from the Cray. He'd attached the wires coming from it to a battery.

I grinned. "I still don't get it."

Then he raised his other hand, holding the helmet from his EXO. Sounds were coming from it.

I stood and bent my head towards it. We were far too deep to get any reception. It was impossible that there was anything coming from it, yet I knew I wasn't dreaming. Then I realized that it wasn't just sounds. There were what seemed like words coming from the earpieces in the helmet, unintelligible. And as impossible as it seemed, in the familiar tones of a human voice. And not just any human voice either.

Michelle's.

Hell, there are no rules here—we're trying to accomplish something.

Thomas A. Edison

CHAPTER FORTY-TWO

I COULDN'T HELP the expression sliding onto my face. "What kind of sick trick is that?"

He backed up a step. "Not sure myself. I had an idea that this might have been some sort of receiver. I saw two wires and decided to attach them to a battery."

"How'd you tune it in?"

"I didn't. The helmet did. Once I turned it on, it searched for the nearest active frequency and this is what I got."

I listened for a moment. "You know who this sounds like, don't you?"

He nodded. "It can't really be her, though."

I gave him a curious look. "Why not? Do you know where she is? We never did find a body."

We listened for a few more minutes, and I knew with every ounce of my being that what I was listening to was Michelle's voice. Even though it was coming from some sort of alien brain receiver, it gave me hope. She was still alive, captured by the Cray. Which meant that our mission had just gone from infiltration to rescue.

"I can tell what you're thinking." Olivares watched me as he unhooked the power to the device. He put it into the helmet, set it on the floor, wrapped the Faraday netting around it, then began strapping on his Kevlar and weapons.

"So what? It's not like we're *not* going to rescue her if we get the chance."

He leveled a finger at me. "Listen. I'm still not sold on the idea what we're hearing is her. That we're getting reception down here at all is incredible. The only way I can figure it is that each of these transmitters acts as a relay, signal-boosting the others."

I remembered the other Cray I'd found with devices in their heads. How many more Cray were down below? More importantly, why didn't he believe that the voice was Michelle's? I asked him.

He shrugged. "Occam's razor. In the battle of competing hypothesis, the simplest answer is most often correct. Until otherwise proven, I'm going to go with coincidence."

"Yeah? Ever hear of Mason's Razor?"

Olivares couldn't help but smile.

"Mason's Razor: If the alien brain receiver sounds like your fucking girlfriend then it probably is your fucking girlfriend."

"Does Mason's Razor explain why an alien would need to use her voice?" Olivares looked up as he slapped in his pistol mag and shoved the weapon into his chest holster.

"Ever hear an alien speak?" I countered. "Maybe they don't. Maybe they have to use something else to communicate. Maybe it's aliens like us who have the capacity to translate thought into something audible. Or in the case of the device, maybe something that speaks directly to the brain."

Olivares was staring at me with a curious look on his face.

"What?"

"For a second there you sounded intelligent. I could almost believe your idea."

"Oh, yeah?"

"Yeah. But I still go with Occam's razor. You prove otherwise, then we'll talk."

We finished packing up the gear and slid on our packs. I briefed him in more detail about what I'd found as we checked each other's packs, ensuring the Faraday netting was secure. Within minutes, we were moving back the way I'd come.

We used our NVDs and IR illuminators to guide our way and we made good time through the path and down the rock fall into the gallery. I showed him the exits, then the bodies.

He spent several minutes studying the corpses. He checked their wounds, rolling each of them over. When he was done, he pulled out a pad of paper and recorded their names by red light.

Then he checked the Cray. He was as thorough with them as he had been with the members of Romeo Five.

When he was done, he stood. "You separated the weapons?"

I showed him. One pile consisted of the same weapons and equipment we carried, with the addition of the M4s. The other held three small boxes, identical to the one I'd confiscated back on the surface.

"Same things that got you." I handed him the one I had taken from aboveground. "I got this from the one on the surface."

Olivares took it, all the while staring at the others with a gaze made glassy by the IR. "I saw them one minute, next thing I knew I was on the ground. I knew I was in Africa, but my brain was back in Minnesota. Memories I'd tried to block. Terrible things. It was that Siren that made me feel that way. And to think now they've weaponized it." He looked down at the box in his hand. "Did you try it?"

I shook my head. "I wouldn't wish that on my worst enemy."

He eyed the boxes warily. "I don't know what to do with them." He looked from the one in his hand to the ones in the pile.

"We're grunts, not scientists," I said. "If I can use it to kill Cray, then give it to me. If not, give it to a scientist."

He pulled free a Gerber knife and worked at prying one open. I moved closer to get a good look.

Inside was a bundle of wires running towards a small, pulsating oval. Correction; not wires. I looked more closely and could see these were biological, not mechanical, filaments. Oily green and orange liquid glistened in the red light, giving off a rank aroma as it dripped and clung to the strands. The threads ran to a gently pulsing organ held in place by a metal surround. This mix of the biological and the electronic conjured up a whole new slew of questions concerning the Cray.

The first was about their EMP pulses. Why had their bodies evolved such a capability? Were the EMPs used purely as a weapon, or were they essential to some other purpose?

I shared my thought with Olivares.

He had another point of view. "So let's look at it the other way. Let's say we can only think of ways to use EMPs defensively. How can we do that?"

I stared at him blankly, waiting for him to continue.

"Electromagnetic pulses are radiation. Radiation has many uses. We cook with it. We grow things with it. We use radiation for power."

Ever think how alike the Cray are to bees in a hive? Thompson had once asked. I'd agreed, but hadn't really given the concept the attention it deserved, probably because I'd been too busy trying to keep my ass from getting handed to me. But now it seemed relevant. How would a bee use an EMP? What did the bee have that was missing in a Cray?

"A stinger!"

"That's not a defensive use for EMP."

"No, listen. Thompson once said that Cray are like bees. We've all seen the similarities. Bees leave their hives, gather pollen and return. If you mess with them you get stung, right?"

"Right."

"Maybe the EMP pulses are their stingers," I said, feeling like I'd hit on something.

"I'm hearing you, but could be anything. Maybe they help gather *pollen*," Olivares countered. I blinked with uncertainty.

"You could be right, Mason, but you're so focused on offensive capabilities that it's the only thing you can think of. What if the EMPs are necessary wherever they come from, much like ultraviolet light or fluorescent light can be used to stimulate growth in plants?"

I couldn't believe it would be that complicated, and I said as much. "I think you're reaching. What do you think happens? Does a Cray swoop down, beam its EMP on a plant, then watch as the plant opens up?"

"Maybe. Could be." Olivares shrugged. "Just don't be so sure of your own ideas. We're not going to know. What was it you said? *We're grunts, not scientists.*"

I nodded, then added, "I realize this all seems like worthless supposition, but have you ever wondered why we had to read all of those books and watch all of those movies and answer all of those questions? It had to be for moments like this. They wanted us to think about this, to talk about it and, probably in the end, figure it out. It was far easier to train a bunch of snake-eating soldiers to think critically than it was for them to create ground-pounding soldiers out of scientists. If you think about it, Western culture has been training for this for years. Every science fiction movie, miniseries, television show, comic book, novel, short story and cartoon became source material for our end of the world dissertation on planetary survival."

Olivares grinned. "The training sure made us smarter. I never would have understood a word you just said had it not been for those hellish months inside the cage."

"But it's true, isn't it?" I pressed.

"If a grunt makes a scientific discovery in the bottom of a volcano and never gets out alive to tell anyone, did he really make the discovery?"

"You're right, of course."

"What was that?" Olivares leaned close and fingered his lapel. "Can you speak into the microphone?"

"Fuck you very much," I said. "Maybe we should get going."

"You think?"

"Which way?"

"Hold on and let me see." He'd managed to download some data from the least damaged tablet. He set everything down, then found a clear space. He took the helmet, removed the Faraday netting, then put on the helmet and keyed on the internal mapping system. All we had to do was figure out where we were and plot our way to the mound. That I'd found a large gallery with multiple exits was terrific. It didn't take him long to figure out where on the map we were, and to project where we'd have to travel and when we'd have to turn.

The mission had finally given us a break.

In Lucius Shepard's *Life During Wartime*, the fate of the world and the fate of the main character's soul are intrinsically linked. Discuss how you felt about this before you knew about the possibility of an alien invasion, then juxtapose your response with how you would feel about it afterwards.

TF OMBRA Study Question

CHAPTER FORTY-THREE

EVEN WITH THE aid of IR, the going was grueling. We began trekking through the tunnels. We were aware of the rock walls, outcroppings, and precarious footing, but without depth perception the dangers were still very present. We were forced to move slowly as every bone-bashing, flesh-gashing, ankle-twisting meter passed behind us.

I'd scraped and rubbed against the walls so many times that without the Kevlar to protect me, I would have bled out a long ways back. Likewise the ballistic mask had protected me from several outcroppings that had reached out to tap me, leaving gashes in the bonded Kevlar.

Olivares had fared little better.

The IR illuminators ate our batteries, as did the occasional map check on the HUD. Six hours had passed and we'd changed batteries three times. At least our packs became lighter with each change.

After the third change of batteries, we stopped for food and water. We ate silently in the darkness, conserving what energy we could.

As we moved through the subterranean maze, my mind replayed battles with the Cray: the way they fought, their tactics, their insectile savagery. I'd been through so many close calls it almost seemed impossible that I was still alive. Had the Cray shown any real skill at combat I'd have been dead a dozen times over. Their tactics were simple; once they had a target, they attacked until either they or their target was dead. It was a tactic you used when you had overwhelming odds, like the Chinese at the Battle of the Chosen Reservoir in the Korean War. Or when you didn't care about the loss of life needed to attain a goal.

If the Cray were human, I would have called them savages. Perhaps *other* aliens saw the same way, and whatever was masterminding the attack on Earth had gathered to them the Cray as a sort of barbarian horde and sent them to us, like Mongols, or locusts, to soften us up before the main assault.

What then were the true enemy like? As tough and deadly as the Cray had proven themselves, how much worse did the other aliens have to be if they had the Cray working for them? And the Sirens?

But then I recalled the Romans and how they'd used the conquered over and over again to conquer others. It wasn't that the Romans were the best fighters, or had the most fighters. By all accounts, the number of pure Romans in the Empire had been terribly small. No, their superiority was derived from their discipline and tactics.

The Cray. The Sirens. Humanity. If we didn't find some way to fight our way free, we'd be on our own planets, enslaved by some unknown alien empire, doing their bidding, human barbarians on the edge of the world, giving our lives so we could take another's home from them for an unknown and unnamed mutual enemy. We'd become the Cray.

The very idea of it made me furious.

We now had less than nine hours to make it to the mound before the attack. We figured we had three miles before we'd encounter the closest breach made by the thermobaric bomb. We could run a mile in six minutes. We could walk a mile in fourteen minutes. If we'd been on the surface and in our EXOs, we could have made it in ten.

In front of me, Olivares motioned me to a halt.

We'd been traveling through a twisting labyrinth of broken rock and had come to a mercifully level area. I was reminded of the arid flatness of the dry lake beds at Fort Irwin in Death Valley.

Olivares pointed and I could just make out a Cray, standing on the very edge of our light.

Then Olivares backed away.

I fought to control my breathing. My body screamed to attack, but my mind wanted more information. Like, why hadn't it attacked us? Couldn't it hear us? Couldn't it smell us? Could it not see in the dark?

Olivares pointed again and I saw another Cray, and another.

He turned to look at me.

I realized then that there was a line of them standing before us. I'd never seen them before like this before. A defensive formation, as if they had something to protect, something they didn't want us getting to.

A thrill went through me as I realized that they didn't yet know we were there. How could that be? It wasn't as if we'd been silent. I could smell the rankness of my uniform. We'd made so many assumptions about their abilities—what if they didn't have senses like we'd assumed?

The one thing I knew was that they reacted to light. I were to fire, the muzzle flare would act as a beacon. But if I attacked silently with my blade, there'd be no light, no warning.

I slowly released my grip on my rifle and let the sling take its weight. I pulled out my harmonic blade and swung it in an arc at the nearest alien.

The blade bit into the center of a Cray's head, then slid through, shearing neck and chest, exiting somewhere near the creature's hip. As its torso fell, its cavity emptied. I leaped back, awaiting a reprisal, but nothing happened.

I saw movement and backed away as a pair of Cray moved towards their downed brother. These were the wingless variety.

The one on the left touched the dead Cray with its lower set of claws.

"What's going on over there?" Olivares asked.

"I killed one and the others found it." Even though they seemed unable to detect us, they somehow knew their brother was down. Was it the smell? Or could it be some form of communication we couldn't track?

"What'd you do that for?"

"To see what would happen."

I heard him cursing, but didn't have time to worry about it. The Cray were coming for me.

"They're all moving forward."

Damn. Killing one had alerted them all. I fell back for a moment, until I realised they were filling in the space where their fallen comrade had been. Still, there was enough room to pass between them. I did that, slipping carefully between their outstretched arms.

"Go between them. Don't fight. I repeat, don't fight them."

I moved towards where I thought Olivares would appear. It took longer than I expected, but suddenly he was in my green nimbus of light. I grabbed him and pulled him farther along.

"They can't see in the dark," I said. "They can't hear. For all I know, they can't smell, either."

"How can you know?"

"They don't react. Look at them." The Cray stood in a picket, unmoving, waiting, but for what? Then it came to me. "Light. They need light. It's the same phototactic response Mr.

Pink told us about. But it's more than a response. It's their universe."

"But how did they get here?" Olivares mused.

"My guess is they were guided here by another Cray or another species using light. These damn things are probably stuck here."

I watched as he turned towards the Cray. "So as long as we operate in blackout, we can beat them." He turned back to me. "Could it be that easy?"

"It could, and it is. Come on, let's go. They're not going to be hurting anything. As far as I'm concerned they can stand guard there forever."

Confront them with annihilation, and they will then survive; plunge them into a deadly situation, and they will then live. When people fall into danger, they are then able to strive for victory.

Sun Tzu

CHAPTER FORTY-FOUR

ARMED WITH THIS new information, we were still hyper-attuned to the possibility we'd encounter more Cray. Every rock and shadow gave us pause.

We were also terribly aware of the time inescapably counting down. We had less than two hours to make it to the rendezvous. When I asked Olivares how far away we were, he held up his hand and put his thumb and forefinger an inch apart. "This far on the map," he said. No matter the distance, our path was like walking through a maniac kitten's ball of yarn, twisting and turning to the point I was sure we'd double back and see ourselves.

Twice we encountered lone Cray and twice we took them down with our harmonic blades. They didn't seem to have any communications gear like the others. So when we found them, we were quick, silent, deadly.

That is until we saw the light. It grew bright very quickly, followed by the scuffle of dirt, the clack of claws, the scrape of rock—all coming from the direction we were heading. With no other choice, we backtracked and looked for somewhere to hide. We found a narrow passage that rose sharply from the tunnel, and I knelt and helped Olivares climb up before securing myself above the floor.

No sooner were we in place than the first Cray came into view. It carried a light, which blazed the darkness before it.

I felt my heart pound in my throat, and tightened my grip on the blade. If any of them looked up, I'd be forced to dive in among them. Thankfully they passed beneath, unaware of our presence.

I made a move to lower myself back down when Olivares grabbed my arm.

"Not yet," he said. "Wait for them."

"Who?"

"You'll see."

Ten minutes later the return crew filed past beneath us, carrying the three Cray we'd taken down.

"Some sort of patrol," Olivares said. "Or maybe a guard duty shift change."

We'd decided to follow them, keeping as close as we could without being detected. They moved fast, causing us to jog to keep up. Without the ability to see, I had to wonder how they were doing it. Was it muscle memory? Or was it something more akin to a bee returning to its hive? I made a mental note to bring that up with Mr. Pink when I returned from mission.

One thing they didn't do was smoke and joke like the soldiers I was familiar with—no camaraderie at all, at least none that I could discern. It didn't matter where you were from; it was human response to break up the monotony with stories, either real or invented. It had killed American soldiers, back in the day.

But not the Cray. And it was unnerving, especially since I realized that they might just be talking shit about how easy it had been to kill us, but using some form of unspoken communication.

We'd been traveling exactly thirty-seven minutes when they stopped. Then as one, they turned. The pair who'd been carrying the dead Cray dropped their load and advanced on us. They almost caught us unawares. I was slightly out of breath and had been wiping sweat from my brow when they approached.

I only just had time to bring down my blade, splitting the head of one of the creatures.

"Back up!" I screamed at Olivares.

But he was already ahead of me. "Come on."

As the rest advanced, I turned and ran back several meters. I felt claws score my Kevlar, slicing through the material. I tripped as the armor plate on my back slipped free of the rent in the fabric. While the Kevlar seemed capable of withstanding the strikes, the cloth holding it in place was no match for alien claws. I fell to one knee, then felt myself jerked into the opening of a passage.

Olivares stepped over me, taking a strike against his Kevlar armguard as he grabbed the blade he'd dropped against the wall to rescue me. The strike sliced the Kevlar pad halfway through. He managed to snatch up the blade and slice through one of the Cray's four hands.

The alien jerked back, then attacked with the other three claws.

I remained on the floor, Olivares standing over me. I managed to turn so I was facing up, and bore witness to the aliens' savagery from a new perspective. I now knew how Thompson had felt that first time.

Olivares managed to slice through the torso of another Cray, and as it fell, I pulled myself through his legs and climbed to a standing position. I pulled my MP5 around and fired over his head, slamming thirty 9mm rounds into the alien horde. I didn't pause to see the result, but ejected my mag, grabbed a fresh one, slammed it in and rode the bolt forward. I fired several more bursts into the aliens and saw them fall back.

We now had room to maneuver. I counted seven Cray still standing. Each of them bore evidence of my MP5, green blood pouring, seeping, gushing and weeping from multiple wounds. They crouched, wary in my enhanced night vision, unwilling or unable to attack. I raised my weapon to fire again and my vision winked out.

Blinded, I wondered if we hadn't just been hit with an EMP. I loathed the idea of being stuck blindly beneath the earth. What would we do if we were turned around? We'd miss our deadline. We'd end up wandering around down below until we died of thirst or were killed by Cray, our bones hidden forever.

Then somewhere on the far edge of my hearing came the rattle of a snare drum. It seemed so real I had to remind myself it was all in my mind. Still, it served as the soundtrack for my determination to survive.

I felt with my left hand and pressed Olivares against the wall. "Stay back. NVDs out." I stepped into his place and fired from the hip in controlled bursts, sweeping carefully across the room. Three. Three. Three. Three. Reload. Drop. Grab. Slap. Bolt. Three. Three. Three. All the while, I heard the drums, as if Thompson himself was there to inspire me.

"Cease fire, grunt." Now it was my turn to feel a hand on my arm. "You got them."

"All of them?" I kept my weapon level and brought my left hand up to smack the side of my NVD. Nothing.

"All of them. A couple are squirming, but I'll take care of them. Take a moment and replace your batteries." Then he let go of me and pushed past.

I knelt, keeping the weapon out of the dirt as I loaded a fresh magazine. Then I opened my pack, grabbed fresh batteries, and replaced the dead ones in my AN/PVS-7s. I was immediately rewarded with a return to the black-and-green universe. Thank God.

I appraised the small battlefield. Olivares must still have life in his batteries. I watched as he easily dispatched the last of the Cray. When he was done, I handed him fresh batteries, which he used to quickly replace the ones in his NVD. After a quick inventory, we decided to get rid of one of the packs. His arm had been hurt before, but now it was completely disabled. With one arm, he wasn't as capable as I was, so he decided that he'd carry the other, leaving me to move point.

We had forty minutes left.

Olivares checked the map in the helmet again. We were on the right track. In fact, we were already well beneath the plain. It was just a matter of time.

> A hero is no braver than an ordinary man, but he is brave five minutes longer.
>
> Ralph Waldo Emerson

CHAPTER FORTY-FIVE

WE SAW THE light before we saw any aliens. It was so bright that it washed out the NVDs; we pulled them down and let them hang around our necks. One moment there was a mere glow and the next we were in almost full daylight, even far underground. We were forced to stop and backtrack.

We knelt and made our plan. We had less than twenty minutes until the attack and we still had to recon the interior and try and get the information out. Our chances of mission success were extremely low. Our objective was a crapshoot at this point, and we were playing with dice loaded with snake-eyes on five sides.

Still, we had to Charlie Mike.

Olivares decided to try to contact friendly forces. We were close enough that we believed a radio message might get through. But without the suit, to ground the radio and create the ELF antenna, we couldn't reach anyone. We took a moment, unraveling an antenna wire and rolling it out a hundred feet behind us. We'd leave it here when we were done. As far as I was concerned, it was good riddance. That much less weight in the pack.

Olivares removed his ballistic mask. Standing with the helmet on his head without the suit, he looked sort of comical, but when we'd practiced it in the cantonment area, it had worked, albeit poorly. I was reminded of the sound we'd gotten when we'd created crystal radios in school, pulling in crackling broadcasts of a baseball game, the voice like something from the past, rather than out of Wrigley Park in Chicago.

I couldn't hear Olivares, but I watched his eyes as he spoke into the helmet's internal mic. He tried several times. Once it looked as if he might have gotten contact, then he just shook his head. Finally, after trying for several moments, he removed the helmet.

"Nothing but static." He frowned as he put the Faraday netting back on. "We must not be as close as we thought we were."

"Or there's interference," I said. I had another thought I didn't share. *What if there was no one left to answer?* We'd been incommunicado for more than thirty hours now. There was no telling what could have happened in the interim.

As I mulled over the possibilities, I once again became aware of the sound of a drum from far away. Each time I'd heard them before, we'd been in the presence of Cray. I suddenly felt a surge of worry. I grabbed Olivares and shoved him against the wall.

Just in time.

A winged Cray surged around the corner.

Still kneeling, I swung with my blade and separated its feet from its legs.

It fell hard, smashing the front of its head into the ground. Its wings began to beat, lifting it into the air, but Olivares grabbed it, using his weight to pull it back down. It reared up and thrust two claws into Olivares's chest, but they were deflected by his armor.

Olivares grabbed the alien and pulled himself into its embrace.

The Cray tried to push itself upwards so it could gain purchase, but Olivares wasn't letting go. He had his hands locked together behind the creature's back. Good thing. Knowing how badly his right arm was hurt, if he was to break the lock, he'd be as good as dead.

I was about to come to his aid when another Cray surged around the corner. This one wasn't messing around and took flight, rising to the ceiling. One claw reached down and raked against my ballistic mask and the other tore it free, gouging the side of my face in the process.

I ducked and jibed, blood flowing down my neck. The alien came towards me again, forcing me to roll. I brought up my blade, but it knocked it out of my hand.

I rolled again, this time receiving a slash to my unprotected back. I wanted to roll away and keep on rolling. I wished I had my EXO. But it was just me and Olivares down here, with nothing but a little old fashioned Kevlar to protect us.

I glanced towards him and saw his eyes pleading with me. My gaze shot to his hands. He was losing his grip.

I felt blindly for my MP5, but it kept slipping out of my grip as I pushed myself backwards, using the heels of my boots to propel me along as I strived to keep out of the damned creature's reach. I finally got my hands around the gun and brought it up. I started firing before I was ready and raked the ceiling before I found the alien above me.

I kept firing until the magazine was empty, then rolled hard to my right.

The Cray fell, its limbs splayed.

I scrambled to my feet, began to run, put a foot on the body to propel myself into the air, and jumped just as Olivares lost his grip on his attacker.

The Cray reared back, prepared to strike, and I hit it from the side like a Kevlar-armored linebacker. I sent it slamming into the wall.

Both of us were stunned for a moment.

I turned onto my back and shoved my right hand into my cargo pants pocket, looking for another magazine, but I couldn't even find my pocket. I swatted the side of my pants, but my head was too fuzzy to complete the search.

Olivares fell on top of me with his MP5 outstretched and fired twin bursts, sending the Cray into alien oblivion. Then he turned his head toward me without moving from my chest. "You're bleeding like a stuck pig."

I groaned. "I'd probably stop bleeding if you got your fat ass off me."

He backed off and checked our perimeter. Satisfied we didn't have any live aliens in our midst, he moved back to the corner they'd come around.

As he checked, I managed to sit up, then found my left cargo pants pocket and pulled out some bandages. My head had pretty much stopped bleeding, but my back was burning. Probably had a pound of dirt in the wound. At least it might stop the bleeding. It's not like I could actually bandage it.

I struggled to my feet. My NVD knocked against my chin from where it hung; I ripped the useless device free and tossed it across the room, then found a full magazine and slapped it home.

I moved to where Olivares was standing above the helmet, frowning at it.

"What's going on?" I stared down at the Faraday netting that now hung free.

"One of them must have pulsed. I didn't get a chance to cover it."

Now we had no way to get information to the attacking force. Our mission, after all we'd gone through, couldn't be completed. The attacking forces were going in without our aid.

Damn it!

I felt my face turning red. I recognized what was going on. I'd never been able to put it into words before, not until Olivares had gotten in my face and laid me low.

Yeah, our mission was a failure, but it didn't mean we couldn't make a new mission. And where the previous mission required a leader, this one required a hero.

I licked my lips and said the words most men never live to regret. "I have an idea."

Luck is a matter of preparation meeting opportunity.

Lucius Annaeus Seneca

CHAPTER FORTY-SIX

OLIVARES LAUGHED HUSKILY. "Let me guess."

I nodded. "Hero time."

"I thought we talked about that."

"Was that before or after you took a swan dive into the volcano?"

He thought for a moment. "Before."

"And then you jumped to certain death trying to save my life."

"But it didn't work out that way." A thought struck him. "And anyway, didn't you try and kill yourself right after my"—he made air quotes with his good hand—"'heroic gesture'?"

I sneered. "We both messed that up, didn't we? I guess we weren't meant to die."

I grabbed the pack and opened it, passing him two thermite grenades and sliding the other two into pouches on my vest.

I removed the four kilos of Semtex, inserted blasting caps, and attached them to the homemade kitchen timers the techs had created. They'd thought it was a joke, until we told them what we'd wanted it for. Going old-school was the only way to keep the devices on the working side of the Cray EMPs.

When I was done, I handed two to Olivares and shoved the other two in my pockets.

"What am I going to do with these?"

I shrugged. "Blow shit up. How's your weapon holding up?"

He nodded. "Good. Why?"

"Mine's shit. I got too much dirt inside it. It's going to seize up and I don't want to be depending on it." I tossed all but three of the magazines to him and shucked out of my MP5, letting it fall to the ground. "Take these." I shoved the remaining three mags in my pockets.

"If you aren't going to carry a weapon, then why are you..." Then he got it.

"If you go down, I don't want to be rifling through your pants to get spare ammo." I cleared his weapon, slapped in a full magazine, and handed it back to him. "Just don't go down."

He smiled. "I don't even know what we're going to do."

I grinned like the maniac I felt. "Me neither. Are you ready?"

He checked himself, then reached for the pack.

I stopped him. "We're not going to need that. We're going to move fast."

"But I'm still not sure where we're going to move *to*."

I grabbed him by his shoulders. "Listen to me, Olivares. You're a damn good sergeant. Don't ever tell anyone I said this or I'll deny it, but you're a better one than I ever was. But you are a terrible killer and you're not much of a hero either. You don't like for me to tell you how to be a leader and I really don't appreciate you telling me how to be a killer. Just follow my lead, keep your head down, and keep up." I let him go. "Think you can do that?"

When I finished, he stared at me a moment, then said, "For a second there I actually thought you had a plan."

I grinned. "That's one of the secrets to being a hero."

"What is?"

"Plans are for people who worry too much."

I picked up one of the blades and stuck the other in the empty scabbard in my belt. "I'm not scared of dying at all. Hell, I tried to off myself enough times and failed. If the damn Cray want to try and do what I've failed to do, more power to them and I wish them luck. But I think I can't be killed." I glanced at him. "And you better think the same. Being worried about dying is what gets other people killed."

He rolled his eyes. "Now you tell me."

"Ready, steady... go!"

I took off at a jog, my eyes turned to slits against the sudden assault of light. I couldn't figure out where it was coming from—everywhere and nowhere at all.

Several non-winged Cray stood to the sides of the path, their arms hanging limply, their heads raised towards the ceiling.

I passed them by, not bothering to attack. We kept moving deeper into the light. When we went past the first alcove, I found myself stopping and staring. I fought to find the right word, but the only thing I could think of was *larvae*. There were hundreds of the things, man-sized caterpillars, squirming and undulating in a pile that filled the alcove. Were they food? Or immature Cray?

Olivares was standing agog beside me. I grabbed him and we took off again. The reproductive cycle of the Cray had little to do with the efforts of the moment. That they were creating even more soldiers was more of a reason to hurry.

The light became so bright it was a constant stabbing pain. I blinked as we jogged past several other alcoves. I began to feel something brush the top of my head. I saw lines of darkness above us, like curtains hanging from the high ceiling.

Olivares opened up behind me.

I spun in time to see one of the curtains fall to the ground, only to resolve itself into a standing Cray. It fell back under Olivares's assault.

I brought my blade up and began to cleave the dark lines above me. Dead and dying Cray fell from the ceiling. They came down headfirst, their wings hanging down to brush our heads.

"Follow me!" I shouted to Olivares as we moved deeper into the lair.

I pulled out a thermite grenade, removed the pin and tossed it into the next alcove. It fell atop a mound of Cray larvae and ignited, its flame suddenly brighter than the light we were drowning in. The violent heat made the grenade melt through the larvae. They sizzled as they burned.

The air was suddenly split with screams as Cray ran towards me. I brought my blade up but they went past me. One. Two. Six. Ten. All furiously trying to rescue their offspring, making sounds I'd never heard them make before. The first reached in and grabbed the grenade, only to have its appendages melt off. The one behind tried to do the same with the same result.

I backed away as more and more piled into the alcove to try and stop the damage I'd caused. For a moment I felt a little sick, then I spied Oliveras down on one knee. Dead Cray lay around him. His face had been opened by a terrible gash. Blood dripped to the ground.

I pulled out my other thermite, pulled the pin and tossed it in the alcove we'd just passed. Then I ran to him, got his thermites and tossed them into two more chambers. I had just enough time to press him to the wall as hundreds of Cray ran to save their brood.

We edged deeper into the light until the corridor finally opened into an immense chamber. In the center was the source of the brightness. It was like a miniature sun. As we stared, it pulsed, firing intense light out in all directions, then resumed its normal blinding state. What we'd thought had been round was actually an oblong shape roughly the size of a tractor trailer. I realized it was organic as it began to brighten again to its impossible brilliance. Like an incandescent bulb slowly turning up to supernova. I tried to peer through the painful light. At one end, larvae appeared. At the other were Cray, hovering over a pile of human bodies.

I remember wondering if there wasn't some alien queen creating more Cray. I'd been right—and they were feeding it our dead. At least I *prayed* they were dead.

The light soon became too painful to look at again.

I turned towards the wall and prepared my explosives.

Olivares did the same.

When the light pulsed once more, we readied the timers, setting them for one minute.

I looked at Olivares and he nodded. I took his Semtex bundles in my arms and ran towards the creature. I became aware of the cavernous space above me, filled with Cray. They hung on the walls and flew in the air. Directly above the creature, the mound rose higher and higher, thousands upon thousands of the Cray hanging onto the walls.

Their sheer numbers staggered me. How could we defeat so many? It seemed impossible. And this was the smallest of the mounds.

Non-winged Cray began to run towards me from the alien queen. Looking up, I could see that I had the attention of the winged Cray as well.

I reared back and threw the first bundle as hard as I could. It landed on the ground beside the queen. The timer shattered and I cursed. Too far—I'd have to get closer.

I grabbed the second explosive and brought my hand back. As I did, a Cray grabbed it from me and soared into the air.

I only had two left and they were coming for me from in all directions. I made a desperate choice and ran towards those running towards me. They reached out as we closed on each other, me with my hands filled with explosives and them with their hands tipped with talons. There were more than twenty of them; I couldn't get around them, I couldn't go over them, I doubted if I could go through them. So I tried a desperate tactic, perfected one summer in seventh grade when my baseball couch had made me practice stealing base over and over until my legs were covered in purple bruises. I started the slide at full speed and felt the hard ground eating away the fabric of my uniform.

My skin caught fire and I screamed. But my muscle memory was true and I slid beneath their outstretched arms, one leg extended, the other bent, to enable me to push up to a standing position right before I came to a stop. Which I did, now past them, and began to limp rapidly towards the queen.

It pulsed again, throwing light in every direction. It was almost physical in its intensity, and I flinched. In some way, the EMP was connected to the creation of new Cray. This was the mother of these creatures, and I was about to commit matricide. And I was about to get ripped to shreds. The knowledge left me strangely calm.

I'd halved the distance to my target and eaten up some of the delay. Thirty seconds left.

I threw one of the explosives along the ground and let it slide until it struck the side of the immense, pulsating beast. Then I did the same with the other one. But as I stood, I felt myself surge into the air, gripped around the shoulders by a Cray.

I twisted around and grabbed one of the claws holding me, and with my other hand, I pulled my harmonic blade free and swung, severing one of its wings.

I fell immediately, but before I struck the ground, I was plucked out of the air, this time by a Cray clutching the back of my vest. I flailed with my blade, but couldn't get to it. We flew higher and higher; I looked up and saw it was taking me to the very top of the mound. I began to curse it at the top of my lungs. I knew exactly what it was going to do, but I was powerless to stop it. I'd share the fate of MacKenzie and so many others, smashed to a pulp as I fell from a terrific height.

I still had the choice to end it first. I had the blade. It would take nothing for me to slice across my neck, or stab myself in the chest.

I started to laugh at the irony of it all. This had all started with me trying to off myself, and now it was going to end the same way. I turned the blade on myself, holding it with two hands. I was preparing to thrust it into my chest when the first explosion rocked the mound.

Not from below; from above.

I strained to look up as pieces of Cray rained down around me. It must have been the one that stole the explosive. The creature carrying me flew to the side of the hive as the inner wall of the mound began to crumble. It latched onto the wall, but was hit by a truck-sized fragment of the mound tumbling into the darkness and was crushed. As it let go of its perch, I swung my blade into the interior wall of the mound. It sank two feet deep and I held on with both hands. The dead Cray swung below me, claws still entangled in my vest, and jerked suddenly on my arms, nearly ripping me loose. My vest rode up and pressed against my throat. I shrugged my shoulders and tried to dislodge the creature, but to no avail. I felt my fingers begin to slip. Just a few seconds ago I'd been ready to die, but the thought was gone. I wanted to live. I glared at my weakening fingers and tried to will strength into them. But inevitably they slipped, and my grip came free. I was falling.

The light flashed once more from below, and then all hell broke loose as the remaining two Semtex explosives detonated, setting off the one with the broken timer in turn, blowing the mother-creature in all directions. Every Cray capable took flight, but there were too many to fly. They fought and tore at each other in the explosive light. I felt one slash at the creature attached to my back, releasing its dead-hold on me. Then everything went dark.

I bounced off several more Cray, then hit the wall. I blindly grabbed at it, scrabbling to stop my fall, and my hand struck an outcropping and somehow I held on. I dangled by one arm for a moment, then reached up with the other and pulled myself up. I believed I was on the inside of what we'd thought of as a launch tube. I scrambled as far back into it as I could and prayed the Copperhead rounds wouldn't find me here.

The air inside the mound was a frenzy of panic. I heard more explosions, then the sounds of Hydra missiles going off. Suddenly the entire universe was filled with the rattling whine of Vulcans firing from somewhere below, the sound like the universe being unzipped and rezipped. I heard Cray falling like ducks in winter as the rounds scythed through them.

The cavalry had arrived.

The rest of the Romeos had made it inside.

I allowed myself a smile as I leaned back, put my arms behind my head, and watched the Cray die by the hundreds. In the back of my mind I was aware that a Copperhead might take me out at any moment, but I found myself unconcerned. I'd been so willing to die for nothing, that to die for something now meant everything.

I believe our future depends powerfully on how well we understand this Cosmos in which we float like a mote of dust in the morning sky.

Carl Sagan

CHAPTER FORTY-SEVEN

WE'D DONE IT. The massacre was complete. There wasn't an alien left alive that hadn't already been taken by Mr. Pink and the surviving members of his team for further study. After the battle, I'd managed to climb down the outside of the mound and cross the plain to our compound. Now I stood inside what had once been the mess hall, staring across the floor and thinking of the movie *Zulu*. Was this what the old sergeant major had felt, in the aftermath of the Battle of Rorke's Drift, his hundred and fifty men having survived a battle against five thousand Zulu warriors? Dead Cray lay whole and in pieces on every possible surface.

For every ten Cray corpses, there was one human. The tired grunts who'd served me rations lay in a cluster, as if they'd fought back-to-back, their food-serving apparel no match for the claws of the aliens. The colonel who'd hero worshipped me and had been the first officer I'd ever known to undress me with her eyes stared towards the ceiling, perhaps gone to a place where God waited to explain to her why her life had been meant to end at this moment, her torso and stomach skewered by Cray claws. The generator mechanic who'd probably seen me naked had survived and now lay on a gurney with her left arm ripped free, trauma surgeons working feverishly to save her.

Damn, but I was tired.

Was this what the Army of the North had felt at the Battle of Gettysburg? Even after winning the day, were they stunned at the immensity of the mission? D-Day? Pusan? Did we have the will to continue?

One thing we finally did have was knowledge. The Cray had had a terrific advantage with our ignorance. They'd leveraged their weaknesses by keeping them unknown. That they couldn't see below our visible spectrum, making them effectively night-blind, would have been an incredible boon for our early battles, had we known. We would have attacked in blackout, covering all light sources, including the operational lights on the outside of our EXOs, keeping the Cray off balance and on the defensive.

I picked my way through the mess hall and into the TOC. The carefully constructed operations center was completely destroyed. Pieces of desk merged with pieces of flesh and plasma televisions. A fire had raged inside and melted the whole mass together. I couldn't tell where a computer monitor stopped and a Cray began. I remembered wanting to kill the Italian battle captain, but even he hadn't deserved this.

As it turned out, Olivares and I might have saved the day. I learned that the Cray had attacked thirty minutes before our scheduled assault. They'd destroyed the Howitzers first, as if they'd known the capability of the Copperheads and had feared them. Then they'd surged through the underground, engaging in hand-to-hand melee like the Earth had never before seen.

I moved on, bumping into another grunt.

We exchanged bone-tired glances, then staggered off in different directions.

I was heading towards our squad bay when I saw Olivares. His face had been bandaged, but it would leave a terrible scar.

"You made it."

I nodded. "You as well." But I noted the look on his face. Something was wrong.

"What is it?"

He stared at me with sorrow in his eyes, then made a decision. "You have to see this."

I trudged towards him, careful not to step on the remains of a human, but gleeful in the way the Cray crunched beneath my booted feet. When I got to him, he put out a hand to stop me.

"You need to be ready."

"Brother, I don't need no drama. I just need some sleep."

He shook his head, his eyes flint hard. "Remember the device the aliens tried to hide from us?"

"Device? What are you talking about?"

"You need to be ready," he said again. He paused, then said, "You were right. We found Michelle."

My breath left me. "Show me," I somehow managed to say.

"They weren't sure she'd survive. Mr. Pink said she'd be perfect for the mission. He said her mind was attuned..."

I pushed past him, rounded the corner and saw the black box. Two recon scouts in EXOs cleared dead Cray from where they'd piled up all around the outside. The once black surface of the box was etched with the marks of a thousand claws. Whatever was in there, the Cray had wanted it badly. How Michelle was involved, I couldn't fathom.

I hurried up to the black box and looked inside.

And my mind howled.

Michelle.

Or what had once been Michelle.

"What have they done?" I wailed.

She hung from a pod affixed to the ceiling of the box, connected by cords through which moved fluids, presumably keeping her alive. She faced me. Naked, the rivers of pain on her arms stark white reminders of who she'd once been. If only that girl was still around. But she'd been turned into a horrific marionette. A hundred multicolored wires and cables ran from her shaved head to a computer terminal. I could only imagine her horror, were she aware what had happened to her. What was it she had said? *Can you imagine? Being taken over by another entity and not being able to control your own body?*

Her body shook and trembled. She took a great breath and raised her head. Her gaze met my own. For one brief moment, we were those same two people, reclining behind the generators, interlocked, the end of the world not even mattering, living only in each other's eyes as we made each other laugh, cry and sing with pleasure. Then her face changed. She became sad, then angry.

Killmekillmekillmekillmekillmekillme

The thought slammed into my head, making me back away. As I fought for balance, two people I hadn't realized were there rushed to her from the other side of the black box.

"You get her stabilized. I have a helicopter en route. We need to get her to safety." Mr. Pink turned towards me. He regarded me, then he shook his head. "Olivares, get him the hell out of here."

Killmekillmekillmekillmekillmekillme

A technician was at Mr. Pink's side, hurriedly unhooking Michelle from the box.

"What—what is this?"

Killmekillmekillmekillmekillmekillme

Mr. Pink looked for a moment as if he'd answer, then he turned back to his task. "I don't have time for this."

Killmekillmekillmekillmekillmekillme

I stared into her eyes and knew what had to be done. They'd turned her into some kind of communications mechanism. OMBRA had figured it out, and then used Michelle as their tool. She was a person—she was *my* person. She was nobody's tool.

I found a rifle on the ground and brought it up in a single move. I sighted in on her forehead.

Her message switched to a single feeling of goodwill as she repeated *lovemelovemelovemelovemelovemekillme killmelovemekillmelovemekillme*.

Through my tears, the sighting device placed a red dot gently between her eyes. My forefinger squeezed the trigger slowly. At the last moment, I closed my eyes, unable to watch.

As I fired, I felt my weapon lurch upward.

Olivares's hand was on my weapon, but I ignored him, all eyes for her.

She glared at me, her gaze as furious as the medusa's. I had let her down. She'd needed me to do one thing for her and I'd failed.

Ihateyouihateyouihateyouihateyouihateyou

Then her head sagged as Mr. Pink ripped wires free. Once she was disabled, he turned to us.

"I thought I told you to get him out of here."

Olivares jerked my weapon so it spun me around.

I was still unable to parse what had happened, her words still echoing through my mind, over and over and over, *I hate you*. He led me down the mound of the dead, stumbling, blank, staring. He'd taken my weapon away from me sometime during the process. So when he led me into our squad bay and I sat down, I found my empty hands were a perfect place for my head. I held it, tears falling, my chest empty, my brain caught in a loop where the girl I loved had been transformed into a cybernetic machine that hated me.

I don't know what I'd been thinking. It wasn't as if this was life as it had been. Still, the more I imagined her, the more I thought about what *could* have been. But the world I imagined couldn't be. All that was gone.

I pounded the side of my head.

Why couldn't she have told me? Why couldn't she have included me in her secret? She must have talked to Mr. Pink for days before this. All the while I'd been trying to get to know her, she'd already decided to end her life, or at least her life as she'd known it. Oh, but I wanted to scream.

I put my head between my knees. All of my injuries pulsed for attention, but I pushed the pain away. The agony in my heart was far greater. Why did this girl I barely knew make me feel this way? How had she worked her way so deeply into my soul? But even as I asked the question, I knew the answer. Michelle had been more to me than just a strong, beautiful, olive-skinned girl. She'd been more than the faraway look in her eyes. She'd been so much more than the geography of her scars. She was *America*. She was the smell of cotton candy at a fair. She was the warm summer breeze cooling the sweat on my brow. She was the red hot heat of the love men and women felt everywhere for each other. What we'd felt for each other.

She was everything we'd lost.

I heard a noise from the other side of an overturned locker, and turned. Cheap metal cabinet moved; Someone was beneath it, and might still be alive. I got to my feet and stumbled across the body of a tech and the remains of the bench we'd all once sat upon. I pulled the locker aside, but beneath it wasn't a person. It was a Cray, trapped and prone. Perhaps its back had been broken, or maybe its legs. It reached towards me with four arms, its entire body shaking.

I stared at it for a long minute.

Then I straddled the creature and began to hit it. I hit it and hit it and hit it. Its proboscis cracked and bled green ichor.

I hit it with the anger of an entire planet.

I hit it with the anger of a single man who'd lost everything... fucking everything, including his girl, and his trust in those who were supposed to know better.

I glared into its cluster of eyes as it stared back at me.

"I might have tried to kill myself, my whole *planet* might have been trying to kill itself, for generations, but that doesn't give you the right to come and do it for us."

My arms tired as the alien's cracked, broken face became a mosaic of what it once was. One more strike and all the pain of the world would flow through my hands. I brought them down like the hammer of God, but the Cray reached up and stopped them at the last moment. It was as if it had been saving its energy until this very last moment, knowing that it would have but once chance to save itself, and this was it.

I struggled to follow through with my swing.

Its arms began to shake as it held me, claws gripping my wrists. I pressed forward with my shoulders, and it pressed back against me. And then I saw it for what it was. I released my fists and sat back, resting my weight on its abdomen.

It kept its hands ready to block, but seemed to regard me differently from before.

"You're just a fucking grunt, aren't you?"

It blinked back at me through the eyes I hadn't bludgeoned.

"You're just a dumb fucking grunt just like me, doing what you're told." The sudden sympathy hit me square in my patriotism. Somewhere along the line I'd ceased to care about America, or the Army, as much as I cared about the men and women I fought with. MacKenzie, Ohirra, Thompson, Aquinas, Olivares and even Frakess were what I fought for. I bet the Cray were the same way. I saw how they fought. I shoved the image of Michelle way, way down.

No. The Cray weren't our enemy. They were just grunts following orders. They'd come here and fought us at someone else's bidding. Some master species had come along and discovered their EMP capability and found a way to harness that power to their advantage, much like OMBRA had come along and used us, maximizing our power, counting on our need to redeem ourselves, giving us a chance to make amends by playing combat guinea pigs so their company would be in a position to sell itself to the highest bidder.

Just as the Cray had come and proved their worth by knocking us back into the Stone Age, we'd returned the favor by discovering how to best kill them. And in the end it wasn't such a hard thing. But the damage was done. The cities were destroyed. Hundreds of millions of people were dead. Soon we'd give as good as we got and do the same to the Cray.

But they weren't the *real* enemy. Who was? That was the real question, because now that we'd been softened up, they'd be coming in force... if they weren't already here.

I got up from the alien and staggered away. I ended up in the trench we'd first stood in as we'd watched the heretofore-indestructible mound and the planes that hadn't even hurt it. I raised my hands to pull myself out and fell twice. On the third time, I climbed out onto an overcast day on the African plain.

I heard the sound of drums. Not like the distant sounds that had been inside my head whenever the aliens arrived—those I still attributed somehow to Thompson—but a close sound, pounding from the roots of the world, thumping through the soil of the land. It wasn't the martial insistence of the snare, but a syncopated rhythm of the soul, conjuring a resolve and a need to gather together as one.

I saw them near the ruins of the mound. People. Humans. The natives of this land that we'd fought and died upon. I'd thought them gone, but that was me in my ignorance. The last I'd seen of the population were the dead atop Kilimanjaro. But these thousands were far from dead. They'd been waiting, hiding, planning.

I watched as they marched towards us, chins high, drums beating, weapons brandished. This was their victory, too, though they hadn't fought. We'd fought for them; we'd died for them. The idea that I'd had an impact other than to feed OMBRA's greed filled the emptiness inside of me.

The drums sang to my spirit as the men, women and children

of Tanzania strode towards me. Their faces were a mixture of rage and exultation, moods I'd shared myself too many times to count over the last few weeks.

An ancient woman dressed in an orange and purple dress stopped next to me and put her hand on my shoulder. I glanced at the hand and saw how gnarled it was, as if it had been split from the roots of a tree, something that had staked its place in the earth long ago. Then she moved her hand to my head, said a few words I couldn't understand, and moved on with the rest of them.

They took up my Cray and bore him above them as they left. They found more and took them too. This was a time of grieving, and to begin with in grief there's a whole lot of rage.

I could understand that.

I still felt it for what had been done to Michelle.

To Thompson, wherever he was.

To the rest of Romeo Three.

I stood for a time on the plain and watched the helicopters come. All shapes and sizes, all makes and models, civilian and military, with the only unifying marks on them the OMBRA logo. Without the EMP, they could once again roar through the sky. Not everywhere, but at least in this little piece of reclaimed earth.

A group of men pushed out of the trench from behind me, carrying what looked like a metal coffin. Mr. Pink walked with them, supervising the transport.

"Hey!" I yelled.

He ignored me.

I yelled again.

He turned and regarded me with tired eyes. "What is it, Corporal Mason?"

"Is this it? Is this what we've been fighting for?"

"This is only the beginning. You should know that."

"No. I mean is this the last time you use us to achieve your own goals?"

He started to leave, then seemed to think better of it. "Grow up, Corporal. This is your planet. You were going to kill yourself and I convinced you not to, so you could fight for something other than yourself. I see that in your case I failed." When I was about to respond, he added, "What is it about you grunts nowadays, I wonder? You used to fight for things because they needed fighting for. Now you need reasons. Now you need explanations. Sometimes there isn't a good explanation. Sometimes we don't know the reasons. And sometimes companies prosper because of their forward thinking and service to the greater good. None of these things take anything away from the victory, nor does it do anything to sully the lives men and women gave for the cause."

This time he did turn away. He waved his hand and called, "Until next time, Corporal Mason."

The last man trailing the group was Olivares. His right arm was bandaged in place to keep it from moving. His other wounds, unlike mine, had been dressed.

He stared at me, as if waiting for me to ask what I'd been dying to know.

I said one word. "Michelle."

He nodded as if he'd known what I was going to ask and spoke slowly. "She volunteered, Mason. They knew all along about her. They'd compared her brain scans to those in Minnesota and Alabama and all those other places. She was a match and they had a plan for her. Don't you get it? She'd rather do that to herself instead of being with anyone. This isn't about you, Mason. This is about her. Her choice."

"But she was begging me to kill her?"

"That's not your choice."

A memory of our last moments together crashed into me: the passion, the way she'd taken charge. "Why her?"

"Mr. Pink found out about the Cray's communications system. He discovered a way to tap into it, to disrupt it."

"So you knew all along?" I was too tired to be angry.

"No. Just about her. We faked her suit malfunction so everyone would assume she was dead. As far as what they were going to do with her..." He stared morosely at the ground. "I didn't know that until a few moments ago."

I regarded him for a moment as helicopters came and went. "When did she make the decision?"

"The night before the final mission. The night before they took her and made her into..."

I was with her that night. It must have been before, which meant...

Which meant she'd chosen her last moments to be with me. I turned and stared into the distance. If only we'd met some other place. But life wasn't like a movie or a book. There were no happy endings.

"What about Thompson?" I asked.

"What about him?"

"Did he make a choice, too? Was he going to be in some other special project?"

Olivares shook his head. "No. I saw him die. I've told you that."

"But you have to be wrong."

Olivares shook his head sadly. "If only I was."

"Then what was that sound? I hear it in my dreams. I hear it in the wind. I hear it all the time. His drums."

Olivares shrugged.

"Listen," I insisted. "I heard it at the end of that last mission. I heard his drumming. Olivares, seriously. It was *him*."

He looked at me with more than a little pity.

I shook my head savagely. "Don't do that. Don't act like I'm crazy."

"What am I supposed to do? He's dead. I saw it happen. He couldn't move his legs anymore and we couldn't move him so he opened his suit. He took two steps—two goddamned steps—and a Cray skewered him."

"Then what did you do?"

"I did what you would have. I killed the Cray that killed him."

"And then what?"

"Then I killed some more." Olivares grabbed my shirt with his uninjured arm. "You have got to get over this, man."

I latched onto his wrist and held him still. My face was an inch from his. "Did you see him die?" I asked, looking him in the eye, searching for even a hint of a lie.

"He couldn't have survived it, Mason."

We stared at each other for almost a full minute, then he shook my grip off.

"No one could have survived that."

He turned and headed for the helicopter.

Then why did I hear the drumming? How had the kid saved my life? That little drummer boy with the infectious smile. He'd been the puppy among us, eager to please, forever trying to make up for his shortfalls, however real or imagined they were. But then, weren't we all like him? Weren't we all trying to make up for the things we'd done poorly or not done at all, hoping, praying, working to build a better future?

Olivares turned around one last time.

"Come on, you grunt. Let's go. This shit was just the beginning."

Then he turned and climbed into the waiting helicopter.

I closed my eyes and remembered Michelle the way she'd been on the mattress behind the generators.

Then I opened them and ran to the helicopter.

ACKNOWLEDGEMENTS

SPECIAL THANKS TO Jon Oliver for giving me the opportunity to sit in the middle of the intergalactic science fiction sandbox and toss sand gleefully into the air. This has been a dream ever since a nine-year-old boy first cracked open *Have Spacesuit Will Travel*, and wondered, not only what it would be like to be a soldier, but what it would be like be a writer. Both of those dreams seemed so unreachable when I was nine. Thanks also to David Moore for his brilliant editing. Thanks to my agent Robert Fleck for doing all of his spectacular agency things. Much appreciation for the use of Brian Gross's brain. I think I learned more from Brian about science than I did in high school, college and graduate school combined. Thanks to all the folks at the CJIOC-A and ISAF J2x in Afghanistan who had to deal with me talking about this book as I was writing it during my six-month-all-expenses-paid vacation to the suck. Thanks to my wife Yvonne, who not only supported me, but made this a better book. Thanks to Joe Haldeman for being my inspiration both as a writer and as a citizen soldier. And last, but certainly not least, thanks to every man or woman who ever put on a uniform to fight for a cause greater than themselves. Each and every one of you are grunts and I'd follow you to the end of this earth and the next.

Weston Ochse is the author of twenty books, most recently two *SEAL Team 666* books, which the *New York Post* called 'required reading' and *USA Today* placed on their 'New and Notable' lists.

His first novel, *Scarecrow Gods*, won the Bram Stoker Award for Superior Achievement in First Novel and his short fiction has been nominated for the Pushcart Prize. His work has appeared in comic books, and in magazines such as *Cemetery Dance* and *Soldier of Fortune*.

He lives in the Arizona desert, within rock throwing distance of Mexico. He is a military veteran with 29 years of military service and recently returned from a tour in Afghanistan.

THE SEQUEL TO THE INTERNATIONAL BESTSELLER

HELIX
WARS

ERIC BROWN

The Helix: a vast spiral of ten thousand worlds turning around its sun. Aeons ago, the enigmatic Builders constructed the Helix as a refuge for alien races on the verge of extinction.

Two hundred years ago, humankind came to the Helix aboard a great colony ship, and the builders conferred on them the mantle of peacekeepers. For that long, peace has reigned on the Helix. But when shuttle pilot Jeff Ellis crash-lands on the world of Phandra, he interrupts a barbarous invasion from the neighbouring Sporelli, who are now racing to catch and exterminate Ellis before he can return to New Earth and inform the peacekeepers.

Eric Brown returns to the rich worlds he created in the best-selling *Helix* with a vast science-fiction adventure populated with strange characters and fascinating creatures.

 WWW.SOLARISBOOKS.COM